HUNT THE DAWN

ABBIE ROADS

sourcebooks
casablanca

*To those whom life has given thorns and
storm clouds...*

Never stop searching for roses and sunshine.

Published by Sourcebooks Casablanca, an imprint of Sourcebooks, Inc.
P.O. Box 4410, Naperville, Illinois 60567-4410
(630) 961-3900
Fax: (630) 961-2168
www.sourcebooks.com

Printed and bound in Canada.
MBP 10 9 8 7 6 5 4 3 2 1

Scent is the most pervasive of our senses. In an average twenty-four-hour period, a person will breathe approximately 20,000 breaths. For every inhale, the human brain automatically catalogs the scent in the air with the activity happening at the time of the breath, creating a scent memory.

—Dr. A. K. Isler, *Journal of Olfactory Sense*

Chapter 1

MINDS OF MADNESS AND MURDER. THE GLOSSY POSTER advertising today's seminar was taped to the closed auditorium door. Someone had drawn tears of blood dripping from each of the M's.

Lathaniel Montgomery's gut gnawed at his backbone, but not because of the poster or the bloody tears.

Holy Jesus. How was he going to manage being in an audience surrounded by hundreds of people, with all their smells, all their memories?

Gill touched his arm like he always did to get Lathan's attention. "Going in?"

"Yeah." But Lathan's feet had grown roots into the floor. He hated how nothing in his life was normal. He hated the fucked-up sequence of genetic code that had enlarged the olfactory regions of his brain. He hated that he smelled everything. And he especially hated the ability to smell the energy imprints of people's memories. Scent memories. Memories that could overwhelm him and annihilate *his* reality.

Gill stepped up close and examined Lathan's left eye—the eye the SMs always invaded first, the eye that would roll around independently of the other one, making him appear in need of an exorcism.

"Quit with the eye exam. I'm all right." For now. Concentration kept the SMs out of his mind. Vigilance kept them under control.

"Your seat is directly in front of the podium. You won't have any trouble reading Dr. Jonah's lips. After the presentation, introduce yourself. He'll recognize your name." Gill gave him the don't-screw-this-up look. "Convince him about the Strategist."

The Strategist.

Lathan's freakish ability had generated leads for nearly every cold case he worked. Except for the Strategist's.

"Explain how each person has a scent signature. Explain that you smell the same signature on thirty-eight unsolved murders. Explain that the FBI won't do anything unless *he* confirms there is a connection among the kills."

"Save the lecture. This whole fucking thing was my dumbass idea." Could he maintain control of the SMs long enough to make it to the end of the presentation? "If I—"

"There is no 'if.' You're not going to lose control." Gill had read his worries as easily as Lathan read his friend's lips. "Maybe I should go in with you."

"I don't need you holding my hand." Lathan showed him a raised middle finger—a salute they always used in jest, forced a smile of bravado across his lips, and then pushed through the doors before he made like a chickenshit and bolted from the building. Barely inside, the SMs hit. Millions of memories warred for his attention, tugged at the vision in his left eye. He sucked air through his mouth to diminish the intensity, to maintain control.

Never in his life had he been around so many people at once and been coherent. Maybe he should leave.

No.

He clenched his fists. Knuckles popped, grounding him, giving him an edge over the SMs.

He strode down the steps toward the front of the room. Thank whoever-was-in-charge the presentation hadn't started yet.

An empty seat in the front row had a pink piece of paper taped to it: RESERVED. Lathan would've preferred the anonymity of the back row, but he couldn't see Dr. Jonah's face from that far away. He ripped off the sheet and sat in the cramped space.

His shoulders were wider than the damned chair. His arms overflowed the boundary of his seat. The woman on his left angled away from him, the cinnamon scent of her irritation infusing the air. Typical reaction to his size. And with the tattoo on his cheek, she probably assumed he'd served a sentence in the slammer.

The woman on his right reeked. But it wasn't her fault. The rot of her body dying was a stench he recognized, along with the sharp chemical tang of the drugs that were killing her so she could live. Cancer and chemo. Her emaciated features evidenced the battle she fought. And yet, she was here. At this presentation. She was a warrior. And he was a fucking pussy for bellyaching about the SMs.

His ears picked up a faint snapping noise. Clapping. Everyone applauded enthusiastically.

Dr. Jonah walked to the podium. His clothes were baggy and ill fitting, his face wrinkled, his head topped with a mass of fluttery gray hair. Even though he looked like he'd just awakened from sleeping under an overpass, he possessed the look of frazzled genius. The look of someone whose work mattered more than living life. The look of the nation's most respected profiler.

A door on Lathan's right opened. A young woman lugged a folding chair across the room. Toward him.

He held his breath.

No. She couldn't be there for him. No one here knew him. Knew about him. Except Gill. And Gill wouldn't—

She opened her chair and sat facing him. With an overly enthusiastic smile that showed the silver in her back molars, she started to sign.

He looked away. A long bitter whoosh of air escaped his lips.

He didn't need an interpreter.

The combination of what little hearing he still possessed, speech reading, and his nose worked just fucking fine. Most of the time.

Anger burned a gaping hole through his concentration. The interpreter's memories invaded the vision of his left eye.

She swiped a quick stroke of mascara across her lashes and examined the effect up close in the bathroom mirror. Good enough. Getting the day over with, getting back to Cara mattered more than her makeup.

"I should go." Her voice lacked as much conviction as her will.

"Baby, come on back to bed, just for a little while." Cara threw back the covers. She'd strapped Big Johnnie around her waist. He pointed proudly perpendicular.

She glanced at the bedside clock. She was going to be late. It'd be worth it.

The SM continued to play in front of his left eye. His right eye focused on Dr. Jonah. Lathan pressed his left eye closed with his fingers to block out the images, but they projected on the back of his eyelid. Hard to focus on reality. Disorienting as hell. *Don't lose control.*

His right-eyed vision of reality wavered. Almost like a double exposure, he was able to see the stage, see Dr. Jonah, but superimposed over it was the interpreter and her sex bunny having a girls-only party.

Lathan's heart punched against his chest wall, pumping so hard he felt the echo of it in his damaged ears. Fuck. The SMs were about to stage a coup.

"I'm out of here." Did he shout the words, whisper them, or even speak them at all? Didn't know. Didn't care.

He sprinted out of his seat and up the auditorium stairs, feeling the weight of hundreds of eyes watching him.

Gulping giant fish-out-of-water breaths through his mouth, he slammed through the door, burst into the hallway, and then barreled out the exterior door.

Away from the people, away from the damned interpreter, the SMs vanished. His sight returned to normal. He'd figure out some other way to talk to Dr. Jonah. No way was he taking that kind of risk again.

The stark fall afternoon held a hint of winter chill, but he didn't mind. He was always hot, and the temperature suited his mood. He hurried across the lawn to his motorcycle.

A wisp of scent tickled his nostrils. The fleeting aroma possessed a sickening familiarity that felt out of place for his surroundings. He plugged his nose against the smell, refusing to allow one bit of air to enter his nose until he was on the road.

Someone grabbed his arm from behind.

His heart stopped. Adrenaline shot from his brain straight to his fist.

He swung at the same time he turned. Punch first, ask questions later—his body's default reaction ever since the attack that cost him his hearing.

He barely stopped himself from impacting with the guy's face. Lathan lunged forward a few steps, feigning aggression, expecting the guy to retreat, and he did, tripping over his own feet, almost falling on his ass. Good. That was one way to get someone to realize he took his personal space seriously.

"Don't fucking touch me." From the force of the vibrations in his throat, he had yelled the words. He didn't care. He forced himself to breathe from his mouth. Didn't want to look like more of freak than he already did by standing there plugging his nose.

The guy swallowed and nodded, then swallowed again. "I'm Dr. Jonah's partner." The guy's mouth formed the words in perfect precision. "Dr. Jonah wants…return…presentation."

The words *you, to, do, new* all looked identical when spoken. Conversation with a stranger was a recipe. Mix the bits of sound he heard with the speech he read. Sprinkle in the context of the sentence. And bake with the emotions he smelled.

Why would Dr. Jonah want him to return to the lecture? Why would Dr. Jonah stop the presentation to tell his partner to come after him? He wouldn't. Lathan must've read the guy's words wrong. He sure as hell wasn't going to ask the guy to repeat himself. Every time he did, people spoke in such an exaggerated manner even God wouldn't be able to divine the words leaving their mouths.

The guy opened his mouth to say more, but scratched at a spot on the side of his nostril, blocking every word from Lathan's view. His ears only picked up random sounds, nothing that added up to a word. The best way to handle not understanding speech: silence. Anything else ended with people looking at him like he was stupid.

He sat on his bike and flicked the ignition switch. Underneath him, the engine pulsed; the vibrations traveled through his body. His heart, his breath, the engine all moved in one synergistic rhythm. The closest he ever got to music.

The guy stood in front of the bike, waving his hands like an amateur cheerleader to get Lathan's attention.

He backed the motorcycle from the space.

The persistent little pecker jogged next to him.

Lathan kicked his Fat Bob into gear and shot out of the parking lot. He needed to be alone. Alone meant no SMs. He needed to be home. Home meant sanctuary. But every sanctuary was part prison.

—⁓—

"What time you off work, Evan?" Carnivorous anticipation spread across the trucker's face.

At some point during every shift at Sweet Buns and Eats truck stop, Evanee Brown was grateful the label maker had run out of ink halfway through her name. The patrons spoke the name on her tag with a familiarity that made her stifle her gag reflex. If they had used her complete name… Well, full-blown barfing would've been bad for business.

She pasted a super-huge smile across her mouth and lied. "Oh, I'm, uh, working a ten so, hmm, whatever time ten hours from now is." Hopefully, her voice carried the right amount of empty-headed dingbat. Acting stupid earned better tips than being smart.

"Evan, one of these times I'm passing through I'll have to show you the inside of my truck. It's real nice." He stretched the words *real nice* into one long taffy-like string.

She smothered an eye roll.

The trucker was old enough to have known the original Casanova, yet still made the same X-rated offer every time he came in. She glanced at the clock hanging above the door. Any minute, Shirl—her replacement—should be arriving. Couldn't happen quick enough.

"How about an Ernie Burger, rare, everything, side of onion rings?" She worked to maintain her light tone. She wanted the twenty-dollar bill he always left for her tip.

"You remembered my usual." He smiled, his teeth a post-apocalyptic city—abandoned, jagged, decayed. "You know I can't resist an Ernie Burger."

She scrawled his order on the slip and then left the table, feeling the slime of more than one man's gaze on her body. That was to be expected when the uniform requirements were four-inch heels, shorts that barely covered her ass, and cleavage. Lots of cleavage.

Ernie liked his girls barely decent, said it was the best business decision he'd ever made. He was right. Sweet Buns was packed twenty-four seven, three sixty-five. Most days, the tips were great. Hell, there wasn't anywhere within forty-five minutes where she could earn as much as she made at Sweet Buns.

Ernie met her at the kitchen window with a pair of tongs in his hand and anger on his face. His sharply slashed brows met over his eyes, a scowl constantly gripped his lips, and the strange vibe of restrained violence intimidated most everyone and kept the patrons from being too grabby-feely. He looked like a homicidal hashslinger, but he didn't have any bodies stashed in the freezer. At least none she'd found.

Bald head glistening from working over the grill, he scanned the new order, then turned to flip a burger while he spoke. "Shirl's in back. Today she's green."

"Kermit or neon?" Shirl changed her hair color as often as most people changed their socks.

"Kermit." Ernie flashed one of his rare smiles in her direction and then hid it behind a frown. "You keeping up the maintenance on that little car of yours?"

Her Miata. The only thing that remained from her old life. Keeping it was impractical, stupid even, but she refused to lose everything. It was her beacon of hope that one day she'd have enough cash to drive it right out of Sundew, Ohio, and never look back. "I haven't been driving much." Code for *paying my bills and trying to save money is my priority.*

Ernie smacked two quarter-pound burgers on the grill. Flames hissed and sizzled over the meat. He didn't look up. "After shift tomorrow I'll change your oil and check it over for you. And I don't want nothing for it."

His offer percolated in a slow drip through her ears and finally into her brain.

He gave her a sideways glance. "You hear me?"

She'd forgotten how to flap her lips and make sound to form words so she rocked her head up and down on her shoulders. His unexpected kindness left her muddle-minded. When was the last time someone had been kind without expecting something in return?

When was the last time she hadn't felt absolutely alone?

Ernie removed a burger from the grill and slapped it on the bun. He motioned with his head toward the back room. "Get out of here. Soak your feet in Epsom salts and stay off them for the rest of the night."

His words, spoken at the end of every shift to every one of his girls, knocked her out of her stupor.

"Okay." She started around back.

"Shirl! Order up!" Ernie yelled, his voice loud enough to be heard throughout the diner.

Shirl dashed down the hall, her heels clattering as loud as a shoed horse. Evanee handed her open checks to the green-haired girl like a member of the Olympic relay team passing a baton, then walked out the back door.

The first thing she noticed was the rumble, roar, and release of pressure from the eighteen-wheelers parked behind the diner. The noise was as constant as a heartbeat.

A brisk autumn breeze raised goose bumps on her skin. Sunshine melted them away. Tilting her face to the sun to soak up some vitamin D, she leaned against the building and pried her pumps from her swollen feet. Each shoe came off with an indecent sucking sound and left a deep red cleft around her foot.

Ahhh. The cold pavement was a delight against her hot soles.

She walked across the parking lot, her legs moving in an awkward flamingo step as they recalibrated to being flat-footed.

The hardest part of the day wasn't the eight hours in the heels. It was this moment, when she had time to remember her belly flop off the cliff of comfort into the cesspool of white trash. From a safe, easy life to this truck-stop waitress existence. From her trendy apartment to living behind Sweet Buns at Morty's Motor Lodge. From privacy to sharing a room with Brittany, the town whore. From profound ignorance to the realization that everything good she *used* to have came from being a whore too.

But she wasn't going to think about that. Nope. Not going to.

Halfway across the parking lot, she spotted Brittany's special signal.

The ribbon tied to their doorknob used to be pretty-girl pink, but had long since faded to a shade of old and used.

"Damn it, Brittany."

The steady stream of truckers kept Brittany bumping around the clock. At least she always made her guys rent another room for the hour. Unless she had a loaded one. Someone with thousands to burn. Being customer service–oriented, Brittany gave those guys a discount by letting them use *her* room—the one she shared with Evanee. They'd be in there all night, possibly even days.

Now Evanee stood eyeball to eyeball with being homeless for the night.

A weight bore down on her shoulders, threatened to buckle her knees, crush her into the pavement.

She shook her head, flinging the bad thoughts out of her mind like a dog shaking off water. There had to be a bright side. If she looked hard enough, long enough, she could find something good hiding behind every bad thing. Or maybe the search for good was just a distraction from the bad. She'd have to think about that one later.

She wasn't homeless. Homeless meant no roof over her head, nowhere to go. She had her car and could drive herself anywhere.

She fished through the wads of cash and change in her tiny apron pocket, finding her key ring. Once inside the Miata, she locked the doors and then counted through the day's tips. Some ones, but mostly fives, tens, even a few twenties from the most desperate of truckers who thought if they tipped high, they'd eventually earn some alone time with her.

With her tips from yesterday, she had enough cash for her car payment with twenty-three dollars left over. Not enough for another motel room. She shoved the money back into her apron pocket and set it on the floor.

The bow on the door fluttered on the breeze, its movement more effective than a neon sign flashing Sex In Progress. Heat scorched her cheeks. She felt like a slow-witted Peeping Tom staring at the ribbon, knowing all manner of sexual acrobatics were occurring inside the room.

Evanee started her car. The motor turned over with a quiet hum that instantly lifted her mood. No matter how impractical or how flashy, she loved her Miata.

With no particular destination in mind, she pulled out of Morty's and headed toward the country, away from semis and people. She took one winding, hilly road after another until she found an isolated spot.

The road passed through a serpentine valley encircled by low, undulating hills. A barbed-wire fence ran parallel with the pavement. Cows probably grazed there in the summer, but this late in the fall, the grass had shriveled to spikes of straw. The lonesome beauty of the land, the way the hills folded around her, soothed something inside her she hadn't realized needed comfort until that moment.

See, there was always a bright side. She would never have found this place if Brittany hadn't confiscated their room for a conjugal visit with a horny trucker.

She pulled over and cut the ignition.

She could spend the night here. It'd be like camping out. Sort of.

Leaning back against the headrest, she let her eyes slide shut. Sometimes she forgot a world existed beyond Sweet Buns, Morty's, and the constant rumble of semis.

Silence. Pure and perfect. The best thing she'd heard in weeks. The quiet lulled her into relaxation, into sleep.

———————

Evanee startled awake with a full-body lurch. Her heart ping-ponged off the walls of her chest. Breath choked in and out of her lungs.

She'd had a nightmare.

Another nightmare in the infinite string of bad dreams she could never remember. But this time fear walked up her spine while she was awake, like the nightmare was just beginning.

"I thought you might be in trouble." The words, muffled and muted through the closed driver's window, didn't disguise the voice's sinister chocolaty smoothness.

Junior Malone.

Fight or flight or freeze? She froze, solid as an ice sculpture.

She glanced in the rearview mirror. Junior's tow truck was parked behind her car. Confirmation. It really was him. She couldn't remain paralyzed. Fight and flight stood on either side of her, better friends to her than frozen ever would be. She turned her head toward the window to face her stepbrother.

Her molester.

Her rapist.

Junior's straight nose, his plump lips, his sharp, handsome features captured the best of Zac Efron, Tom Cruise, and a young Robert Redford in a body that everyone in Sundew was irresistibly drawn to. Women fought for his attention, men wanted to be him, and everyone adored him for his wholesome nice-guy personality.

No one saw the real him, except for her. Junior Malone was nothing more than a beautifully wrapped package. Gorgeous on the outside, but inside he was something more vile than maggots squirming and writhing on rotting roadkill.

"Fuck off." Anger and a childhood full of pain—caused by him—dictated her volume.

"Darlin', I was worried about you. You've been out here awhile." Sincerity, kindness, concern all sounded in his voice—all bullshit. His voice might be the sweetest siren's song to everyone else, but she knew the *real* him. He didn't have any feelings, except for the sadistic kind.

"How do you know how long I've been out here?"

He raised his palms in the air. "I'm sorry. It wasn't my idea. I swear. Tiffany at Sundew National wanted me to make sure you didn't skip town with their car."

Their car? What kind of bank freaked if the payment was only a few days late? The kind in Sundew where the loan officer knew every mistake Evanee had ever made and expected her to dive headfirst into the shallow end of stupid. Again.

But what if Junior's words were chock-full of lies and designed to manipulate her behavior?

Had he been tracking her? Had Tiffany told him to? Tomorrow, she'd get answers when she went to make her payment.

Evanee started the car, shifted into gear, and then slammed her foot down on the gas pedal. Her hip punched off the seat from the force. The Miata's tires spun, she heard gravel flying, imagined the stones hitting Junior's perfect face. Ha!

The engine sputtered. Died. The car coasted forward only a few feet.

Her heart sank down, down, down, until it rested on the pavement beneath the Miata.

Damn her and her genius idea to save money by canceling her cell phone service.

Hands in his coverall pockets as if he were out on a nature jaunt, Junior strolled the ten feet—all the further her Miata had gotten—to her. Each step closer squeezed the air from her lungs until the only sound was her wheezing.

"You got a leak in your fuel tank."

"You did it." She knew that as well as she knew his name.

"I'll patch it for you. But I need you to get out of the car so I can jack it up."

"I'm not getting out of this car." She wasn't going to give him what he wanted. Her.

"Aw…now don't be that way. Come on out here. We can chat—you know, catch up on things—while I fix your car." He paused, waiting for her to capitulate to his wishes.

She had never given in passively or politely, and she wasn't going to start now.

"I saw Matt in town the other day." His tone was innocent gossipy, but the words were a barbed whip, lashing her, raising painful welts of memory—of her choosing to stay in town for Matt, of her deluding herself into believing sex and money equaled affection, of him randomly casting her off like a used napkin.

"Dad's watching Matt. Looking for that special moment when Matt sticks a toe out of line, and then he'll arrest him. He's not going to be passive like Sheriff Bailey was." Junior and his dad hated Matt solely because being with Matt had made her untouchable. Matt was rich, prominent, and good friends with both the old sheriff and the mayor.

"Leave Matt out of this." She didn't want Junior's dad, the shiny new sheriff, to cause Matt any problems.

"You shouldn't be defending him." Junior lashed the barbed whip again.

She heard the quiver of anticipation in his words—a warning. He pulled a tool from his coveralls pocket and held it in the middle of the driver's window. The glass shattered. Shards sprinkled over her legs like glittering confetti. The glass hadn't even stopped falling, and she was already scrambling across the console to the passenger side. Grabbing for her shoes, she jumped out the door.

Her heels were her only weapon. Fight her only friend.

Chapter 2

WHO WOULD'VE THOUGHT DEATH COULD SMELL SO GOOD? Lathan maneuvered the Fat Bob down the curvy country road. The aroma of autumn streamed over his face. Decaying leaves, emaciated grass, burning wood. The best-smelling time of the year was full of the scent of death.

Death. He should've stayed at the presentation, waited outside to talk to Dr. Jonah when it was over. Why hadn't that twenty-four-karat thought occurred to him an hour ago? Thirty-eight kills by the Strategist, and Lathan had fucking walked away from his chance to prevent number thirty-nine. The real kick in the ass—he only worked cold cases. How many active cases were the work of the Strategist?

His insides turned into a cavernous tomb. Guilt echoed off the walls.

He opened the throttle on his Fat Bob and surged forward at a reckless speed, full concentration locked on navigating the twisting roads. Countryside blurred by him. Bad thoughts got left behind, replaced by the thrill.

A tow truck parked in the middle of the narrow pavement forced him to slow.

Vehicles rarely traveled this far out into the country. Probably horny teenagers, frantic for a place to screw, had broken down and needed a tow. He skirted the edge of the pavement and started to pass.

The lollipop-red Miata on the other side of the tow truck grabbed his attention for only a second, but the woman standing in front of the car, waving her shoes at him, completely captured him.

Her skyscraper legs ended in a pair of miniscule black shorts. The neckline of her shirt plunged to the valley between her breasts. And those shiny black shoes she gestured with were hooker-sexy in her hands—he didn't dare imagine what they'd look like on her feet.

Pressure built inside his torso like a dangerous case of indigestion. The air flowing over his face stung like a charge of electric current. His grip on the handlebars faltered. The bike wobbled. He felt unsteady as a kid without training wheels.

When he drove by her, the pungent scent of garlic permeated the air. Fear. Fear always stunk.

Was she frightened of his appearance? Typical reaction. One he counted on to keep people away. He steadied the bike, and continued forward without increasing his speed.

Something was peculiar about her. Something felt peculiar within him.

No SMs.

No SMs tugged at his concentration or battled for his attention.

It was like they never existed, like he was…normal. *Normal.* Almost. He could still smell her fear—her emotions; he just didn't get any memories from her.

He had to meet her, discover what made her different from every other human being.

He gripped the brake. Hard. His Fat Bob fishtailed around on the pavement. He turned the bike in a tight

U-ey in the middle of the road and saw what scared her. A guy crouched in the ditch, nearly hidden by her car, creeping toward her as stealthy as a hawk stalking a rabbit.

"Behind you!" As he shouted the words—words he wasn't certain she could hear over the roar of his bike— the guy sprang. Grabbed her arm. She whirled around, awkward in her movements, her limbs loose like a ragdoll ballerina. She pushed at the guy, tried to pull away from him, but the asshole shook her, shoved her. She fell to the pavement, landed on her ass and elbows, shoes bucking from her hands. Pain hacked across her face.

Every muscle, every tendon, every cell inside Lathan clenched. Fury zipped along his neural pathways, then outward to his extremities. He shot forward on his Fat Bob, closing the distance between them in mere seconds. He didn't even stop the bike, just dropped it and launched himself at the asshole, tackling him, driving him back until the car stopped their momentum.

Underneath him, the asshole's muscles strained like a slingshot pulled back, ready to snap. Lathan tensed, bracing for the blow, the swing toward his ribs the only move open. "Go ahead. Fucking try it."

The guy punched. Lathan blocked, then mashed *his* fist into the guy's ribs. Lathan stepped back, watched the guy fold over, clutching his side. A plug to the ribs hurt, but it wasn't on the scale of a knockout. Someone who buckled from a simple rib shot probably only picked on women and the weak. When confronted with someone he couldn't easily dominate, this guy pussied out.

Lathan turned to the woman sprawled on the road. She didn't quite wear the holy-shit expression he expected, but she gaped at him with wide doe eyes the color of the sky on a full-moon night. Flecks of gray twinkled in the irises. Her eyes drew him in, engulfing him in their depths. He swore he glimpsed a shard of heaven.

His heartbeat shifted to a lackadaisical rhythm. His breathing relaxed until the metallic mineral tang of blood mixed with the garlic of her fear. She was injured and still scared.

"Are you okay?" His gaze locked on her lips to read her words, but she didn't speak. He'd read that telling a person your name put them at ease. "My name is Lathan." He knelt next to her, careful to keep the guy in his peripheral vision, and held his gloved hand out to her.

She grabbed his hand with greedy strength. She sat up but didn't release him. "I'm a funny."

His eyes read her words, but his ears heard nonsense. *I'm a funny?* Did she hit her head? Or was he not reading the words right? *V*'s and *f*'s looked exactly same. Vunny? Avunny? Didn't make sense.

The guy lurched to his feet, reached into his shirt pocket, and removed a yellow paper. Stitched across that pocket was the name Junior. Great. Somewhere out there was a *Senior*, who was probably just as big an asshole as his son.

"She's none of…business." Junior's volume was loud enough Lathan heard the essentials. He rose to his full height. He had at least four inches and fifty pounds on Junior.

Still clutching his hand, the woman scrambled to her feet and hid behind him. He had a solid hunch that if she could, she'd open a door on his spine, crawl inside, and hide until Junior left.

"She's standing with *me*, holding *my* hand. I'd say she's *my* business."

Junior started yelling, the histrionic lip movements making it impossible to read any of the words. He jabbed the yellow paper toward her car.

Answers. Lathan needed honest answers, and SMs never lied.

The SMs. His heart skittered. He hadn't paid any attention to controlling them. Hadn't needed to. For the first time ever, they waited, patient as a shelf of DVDs for his attention. *Whoa*. What was going on? He'd figure it out later.

Watching an SM of Junior's would take only a few seconds. He inhaled through his nose and let Junior's memory play in front of his left eye.

He chased her down the hall.

Her glossy, black ponytail swung across her shoulders, its movement almost as sexy as the sway of her running hips.

She ran into her bedroom, slammed the door.

"Open it!" He put a pound of menace in his voice to disguise his satisfaction. He admired how she always ran, and when cornered, how she always fought.

"Leave me the fuck alone!" She screamed the words loud enough for everyone in the house to hear.

A smile pulled at his mouth, but he forced his face into a stern expression to convey his tone. "Don't cuss."

"Fuck you."

He felt the wide smile slash across his mouth. Why

did his father insist that he tame her? Her spunk, her spark, her spirit continually amused him.

With a well-aimed kick, he busted the knob and charged into the room. She held her softball bat in a batter's stance, prepared to slug his head off his shoulders and score a home run.

One hundred percent warrior to the end. God, he loved that about her.

He rushed into the room, arm raised to deflect the blow. The bat cracked against his bone. Pain spiraled up and down his arm. She would have to completely incapacitate him before he stopped. He rammed forward, knocked her to the floor, and threw his body over hers. His weight was his greatest advantage in subduing her without really hurting her. He pinned her arms above her head.

She thrashed and bucked underneath him. Twisted, gnarled anguish played across her face. She grunted and strained against his hold.

Those perfect little sounds of pain, those facial expressions belonged only to him. She belonged only to him. How could his father not understand how special she was, how amazing it felt to earn his time with her? Because his father was used to her mother's complete submission.

She opened her mouth wide, so wide he could see the back of her throat, so wide he wanted to shove his dick in the pink hole. But his naughty darlin' would bite it off the first chance she got.

The scream burst out of her mouth in a rush of peppermint from her toothpaste. "Mom! Mom! Help me."

By now, she should know—her mom wanted them together.

Lathan opened his mouth, diffusing the amount of air going to his nose, and then pulled his attention away from Junior's memory before he saw something he'd regret forever. With hardly any effort, the SM retreated to his preconscious. Complete vision returned to his left eye faster than ever before. But the urge—oh God, *Junior's* urge—to ram his dick into her was overwhelming.

Nausea gyrated in Lathan's gut.

Not *his* urge. *Junior's* urge. Not *his* urge. *Junior's* urge.

No amount of telling himself it was someone else's memory eliminated the feeling that *he'd* done that to her. Why couldn't the SMs be like watching a TV show? Something he could walk away from. Easily forget.

"What're you—" Junior's expression froze halfway between a snarl and a sneer. The scent of burning cinnamon choked the air around him—rage at not getting what he wanted. Her. That amount of anger led down a road named Violence and ended in town called Body Dump.

"Take the car and leave." Lathan nodded toward the Miata. The car would have to placate the asshole. If it didn't—he flexed his free hand—Junior would be leaving with a fractured face and his 'nads shoved so far up his chest cavity he'd need open-heart surgery to extract them.

He heard odd sounds. No, female sounds. The woman was talking, but he couldn't link a meaning to the noises his ears picked up.

She tugged his hand but didn't let go. Probably protesting *him* giving *her* car away.

Lathan spoke over his shoulder, but never let his gaze stray from Junior. "Give him your car. I'll help you figure things out after he leaves."

She leaned full-body against him, letting him take her weight, support her like a crutch. Her head rested on the wing of his shoulder, and she nodded her agreement against his back.

Soothing coolness spiraled through his insides. It was just a silly nod, but the gesture symbolized more. Trust. Her trust in him to make this decision for her and to keep her safe from Junior.

And he would keep her safe. It made him gut-sick that the same girl who was such a fighter in the SM was now a frightened woman. And why shouldn't she be? Get knocked down enough times, it becomes harder and harder to get up swinging.

Junior smiled, a malicious upturn of the lips, the kind of smile a bully has right before he wallops on someone weaker. "Darlin', I'll see you soon."

"No." Lathan said. "You won't call her. You won't look at her. You won't touch her. You fucking try it, and I'll hand you your balls on plate. Then I'll stuff them down your throat and enjoy every second of watching you choke to death." He meant every goddamned word.

It was only after Junior hooked up her car and drove out of sight that she stepped out from behind Lathan, her gaze locked on the narrow place where the road disappeared from sight. And *still* she didn't let go of his hand. Not that he minded. Not one bit.

Dusk had begun to settle around them, sucking away the light. In a few minutes, it'd be too dark to read her speech. He should tell her he had trouble hearing. But he wasn't going to. For this one moment in his life, he was going to be normal. Just an ordinary man.

He shifted to face her, to see her mouth. "There's no

place for him to double back, so you don't need to worry about round two. Do you want me to call the police?"

She closed her eyes and shook her head with an anguished expression. The scent of her fear had begun to dissipate, but he still smelled her blood.

Where was she hurt?

Her ebony hair was pulled up in one of those artfully messy hairstyles that showed off the contour of her neck and an expanse of pale skin leading all the way down to the hollow between her breasts. He forced his gaze away, searching for blood. Along the side of her left arm, streaks of red meandered to her wrist.

"You're gonna need a Band-Aid at minimum, stitches at max."

She looked down at her arm. Even in the dim light, he could see the color rinse out of her face. She'd better not pass out, not here, with only his bike for transportation.

"You don't do well with blood, do you? Look at me." He waited until her gaze shifted away from her arm. "Don't look at it anymore. It'll only make you feel bad."

She didn't look away from him. Pass-out crisis averted.

"Is there someplace you want me to take you?" Why was he all of a sudden a Chatty Chucky? Because she was being too quiet. He clamped his lips closed, forcing himself to wait for her response.

She didn't move, didn't look away from his eyes. Most people never met his gaze during a conversation; they ogled the tattoo on his cheek. The black feather started on his cheekbone and angled downward toward his chin, the spine of it torn apart with jagged edges that dripped blood down his jaw and neck. How could she not stare at it?

After a full thirty seconds where her lips didn't so much as twitch, he concluded she was in shock—in no condition to make decisions. After the sick shit he'd seen in Junior's SM, she had a right to take a mental time-out.

"I live a few miles from here. I'll take you to my house and help you figure out what you want to do next."

"Okay."

She'd finally spoken. Maybe she wasn't as far gone as he'd assumed.

He started toward his bike lying in the ditch. Whoa. He didn't remember dropping his Fat Bob so carelessly.

She trailed behind him, *still* attached to his gloved hand. Not once in his life had he ever held a woman's hand. He'd never known how intimate cradling a smaller palm against his could be, or how protective it'd make him feel, or how strongly he'd desire to rip off the glove and touch her, skin to skin. *Not going to happen. Ever.*

He tried to release her, but *she* remained fastened to *him*. A selfish corner of his mind reveled in her desire to cling to him. He raised their hands between them to catch her eye. "I need to get the bike out of the ditch."

Her brows rose an infinitesimal degree. Embarrassment flashed in her eyes at the same time the spoiled dairy scent of it hit his nose. She dropped his hand and stepped back.

"Hey, no worries." *You have no idea how much I'd sacrifice to keep hold of you.* He clenched his empty fist a few times to eliminate his hand's memory of what it felt like to hold hers.

While he hauled his machine onto the road, he didn't look away from her. She stood bereft in the middle of the pavement, staring out over the pasture. Emotions

infused the air around her. Shame. Hate. Embarrassment.
Sadness. Fear. Desperation.

He recognized that tangled combination of scents.
Knew them intimately. Knew the feeling of being hurt
and vulnerable and powerless to stop the pain. Knew
how memories, like the one he witnessed, had left
wounds on her soul and Junior had just ripped off all
the scabs.

She was raw, bleeding emotionally in front of him,
and yet holding it together by a spider's thread. He could
see the effort in the way she stood straight and stiff.

Fury simmered low in his gut. After he got her
squared away, maybe he'd pay a visit to Junior. Show
the asshole what it felt like to be the victim.

He walked the bike to her. After he straddled the
seat, he held out his hand to her. She grabbed him, her
grip hungry.

"Climb on up."

She tossed her leg over the seat, using his hand to
balance her weight.

He sat at the same time she did, her body settling
against his back.

Holy Jesus. He couldn't activate the ability to think.
His brain short-circuited from her nearness. Everything
disappeared but the feeling of her open thighs wrapped
around his ass with nothing but a tiny pair of black
shorts and his jeans between them.

Her sweet, musky scent, almost like honey, but
better—way better—folded around him like a celestial
pair of wings. The scent of her entered his nose and
flowed into his lungs, then out to his extremities, spreading a cooling wave of solace that he wanted to savor but

couldn't. Not with her perched behind him, waiting for him to drive down the road.

He placed her hand against his stomach, pressed it tightly to him. His abdominal muscles twitched under her touch.

"Hold on." He let go of her hand, and she slid her other arm around his waist. She pressed her front to his back, holding as tightly to his body as she'd held his hand. She was a clingy little thing. Not that he minded. Her touch felt like—what was the word he wanted to use—kismet. Exactly as he'd always imagined a lover's touch. Two pieces fitting together perfectly.

He kicked the machine into gear, trying to ease it forward instead of moving with his normal burst of speed. She rested her head on his spine, nestling her cheek across the fabric of his shirt before settling.

His heart grew, straining against his chest wall, threatening to come up his throat in a shout of absolute ecstasy.

Lathan eased the Fat Bob next to his back porch steps and cut the engine. The woman's tenacious grip around his waist had never faltered. He felt another bout of shivers roll over her. Those sinful shorts of hers pushed the boundaries of decency and definitely weren't seasonal for November in Ohio, especially not for riding on the back of a motorcycle.

He waited for her to loosen her hold. She didn't. "Honey." He didn't know her name, but the endearment belonged to her better than any name he could imagine. "You can get off now."

Immediately, she released him and climbed off the

bike. That was good, but a woolly mammoth–sized problem remained—how to snap her out of her emotional free fall. He set the kickstand and got off the bike. She hovered close like she expected Junior to materialize at any moment.

Anger at Junior—at what he'd done to her, at what he had wanted to do to her again—heated Lathan's blood, singeing his veins and arteries. He clenched his fists tight, popped each of his knuckles, and wished his hands were wrapped around Junior's throat. "You don't have to worry about Junior. You're safe with me."

She latched onto his hand again, squirming her fingers between his gloved ones.

He squeezed her hand to reinforce his words.

She squeezed back, and some of the anxiety in her eyes eased.

Damn. He liked her touching him.

"So…" Jesus, what was he supposed to say? His mind tornadoed around in his skull, looking for words. He walked up the steps and turned to see her. The back-porch light cast a warm glow across her skin, giving her a heartier color than she naturally possessed. The mass of her hair, so perfect before the ride, now sagged precariously close to her ear. Wispy tendrils had escaped, shooting out at awkward angles around her head. She didn't look one millimeter less beautiful. "I built the place myself. It's not fancy, but it's mine."

She didn't say anything, but her gaze darted around, taking in the wide porch spanning the entire length of his house and the small yard that ended abruptly in a thick screen of trees and underbrush.

He led her into his home. With no hesitation, she

followed him across the threshold. She had to be way the fuck out of it to have no anxiety about this situation. Not only was he a stranger to her, but he was a big man. His size alone intimated most people. Add on his face tattoo, and most everyone avoided him. He guided her through the wide-open kitchen to the living room.

"I don't normally have company." He sniffed the air, making certain Little Man hadn't found a dead animal in the woods and dragged it through the dog door. Again. "You sit and rest. I'll get a bandage for your elbow, and then we'll figure things out."

She let go of him and sat on his sofa. Stared at her lap.

He immediately missed her touch. Her mouth moved, but the angle was wrong for him to see her lips. He picked up the erratic sounds of speech.

She looked up. Desperation lit her eyes. "…I sleep."

What could she have possibly said that ended in *I sleep*? Her emotional scents were all over the universe—no help at all. Without the context of the entire sentence, he couldn't even be sure he'd read *I sleep* correctly. He knelt at eye level with her and covered her hands with his.

"Honey."

She stared into his eyes—his eyes, not the image on his cheek. Heat flared up his neck and onto his face. She looked at *him*—saw *him*, the real *him*. How did she do it?

"I've got a favor to ask. When you talk to me, look me in the face." He should explain, but he wasn't going to. "Please."

"I'll be better after I sleep. I always am."

The sounds and sight of her speech matched perfectly,

but he still wasn't certain what she meant. "You want to take a nap?"

"I have to."

The seriousness of her gaze worried him. "You have to?"

"I'll be better after… I promise."

Huh? Maybe she knocked her head when she fell. No, she had landed on her ass and elbows. "Ohh-kaay…" He drew the word out, showing his confusion.

She shifted her legs up onto the couch, laid her head on the arm, and heaved a deep breath. Her eyelids fluttered shut. He waited for them to open again, but they didn't. The tangled scent of her emotions faded, and her honeyed scent signature intensified, enveloping him in a vaporous caress. Only one thing magnified a person's scent signature. Sleep. She'd been trying to tell him she felt the adrenaline crash coming on. Damn. It had hit her hard.

He should go into the kitchen, make himself a peanut butter sandwich, a steaming pot of coffee, a large helping of rational behavior. Instead, he ass-planted on the opposite end of the couch, submitting to the urge to watch over her, to make sure nothing bad happened to her.

She frowned in her sleep. Shifted. Straightened out her legs until her feet ran into his thigh. She inhaled a slow breath, her expression settling, as if touching him soothed her. It sure as hell felt good to him.

He memorized the length and width of the lines across her Achilles tendon and the rise and hollow of her anklebones. Shiny new skin, raw patches, and dry scabs covered her toes, the back of her heel. Her feet were a map of misery.

Stop staring at her feet like Little Man drooling over a bone. Touch her—skin to skin.

Fear plunged into his heart, sharp as a scalpel. No. He couldn't allow his bare skin to make contact with another human's flesh. He refused to regress to his childhood—lost in a blur of other people's memories, not being able to find his reality. Touch amplified his ability. Touch incapacitated him. When he'd started wearing the gloves, he'd gained a critical piece of control.

And yet, he yanked off his gloves. His heart rate, his breath rate jacked up to an almost unbearable level.

What the fuck was he doing?

Not listening to logic. He pressed one finger to her ankle. A wave of calm crested over him, quieting his racing heart, dowsing his ragged breathing, and abating the fear of losing control. No SMs. Millimeter by millimeter he settled his entire hand over her, circling her ankle, thumb meeting middle finger. Her skin was cold over the sharp bones.

No SMs. None. How was that possible?

He didn't believe in God, but maybe, just maybe, she was created for him. An Eve to his Adam.

What was he thinking? Crazy, crazy, crazy thoughts.

She probably had a brain defect that prevented scents from linking to memories. His olfactory region was overdeveloped. Maybe hers was underdeveloped.

He pulled his hand off her ankle.

Distance. He needed distance between them. He grabbed his gloves and headed for the back door. He glanced at her only once, to make certain she still slept, then left the house.

An endless plateau of white surrounded Evanee. No sky, no walls. Just white trailing off to infinity.

The White Place. Such a childish name, but she'd named it when she was a child.

She opened her arms wide, tilted her face skyward, letting the tranquility of the space cradle her body. The silence settled her mind. The color calmed her soul. The aloneness healed her heart.

Over the past few months, she'd longed for this escape. But the White Place chose when to admit her. It was a gift granted only in the worst of times.

Growing up, she came here every time she slept. This place rejuvenated her fragmented emotions, granted her the strength to fight, and gave her the will to live when the easier option was suicide.

It'd been a decade since her last visit. Too long.

A sound. She caged the breath in her lungs to listen. Sound had never existed in the White Place.

Fear whispered over the back of her neck, the backs of her arms, the backs of her legs. She was in the presence of a predator. She could sense its malicious energy, its malevolent intent.

The sound—clearer this time.

Humming. The sweet, dulcet tones clashed with the suffocating terror coursing through her.

She lowered her arms to her sides, cinched her hands into fists, and turned.

A child, a little girl, her body in profile. Her pink shirt, her hands, her baby-doll blond tresses matted with reddish mud. The glare of color against the pristine white was repulsive. Wrong.

Adrenaline squirted into Evanee's system. Every muscle mobilized, ready to fight. Or run.

Why was she afraid of a dirty kid?

She could only see the side of the girl's face, but that was enough to see her beauty. She was the kind of child women were jealous of because they knew how stunning she'd be when she matured. The kind of child every father feared having because the boys wouldn't leave her alone. The kind of child parents couldn't help spoiling.

The girl extended her arm, hiding something in her fist. "Take this." The girl's petulant tone raised goose bumps over Evanee's skin.

"What do you have?" Evanee's voice quivered.

One by one, the little fingers opened to reveal the child's treasure.

Round. Puckered. Ashen white. Misty blue circle in the middle.

An eye.

Evanee's legs wobbled. She stumbled back, opened her mouth to cry out, maybe to scream, but something invisible, immovable, immense grabbed her throat, choked off the sound, and stopped her. She was locked inside the husk of herself, unable to move or breathe or fight.

The girl turned. One side of her face was sweet child perfection, the other an abomination. Blood and flesh congealed in her empty eye socket. Rusty brown smears mixed with scarlet trailed down her cheek, some slithering into her mouth.

Gray spots speckled Evanee's vision. She was going to pass out; maybe she was going to die. She'd never feared death, used to wish Junior would just kill her instead of playing with her. And disappearing right now from the mess she'd made of her life would be easier than working her way out.

But she didn't want to die. She wanted to live.

She had an absurd desire to hold Lathan's hand again. Even though the tattoo on his face made him look more intimidating than anyone she'd ever met, he'd protected her from Junior, and that vaulted him way past stranger-danger status to good-guy-hero level.

"You." The girl's voice was a command. "Take this."

The gray spots spread, turned blinding yellow, then black, blotting out the girl. Unable to struggle, unable to breathe, unable to utter a sound, Evanee mouthed the word she wanted to say. *No.*

"Don't say no to me." The girl's tone deepened beyond its natural level, dipping into the range of the demonic.

The Thing holding Evanee released her. Her knees folded neat as a shirt on the display table at Gap, bringing her down to eye level with the girl. Air sucked into her oxygen-starved lungs. The girl opened her mouth, hurling blood over Evanee in a vindictive arc. The warm slickness of it touched her tongue. Before she could spit it out, its heat snuck down her throat and burned in her belly.

Her arm rose to take the eye. She screamed—*she* didn't raise her arm. The Thing did.

The girl dropped the still-warm eye in Evanee's palm. Across the girl's face spread the smirky smile of a spoiled child who'd just gotten her way.

—⁂—

Lathan strode down the lonely road. Shimmering stars pierced the charcoal sky, casting silver light on the pavement meandering among the low hills. A chill breeze carried the feral scents of coyote and possum. Predator and prey.

He stepped into his driveway and headed for his back door. The brisk walk to find the shoes she'd lost out on the road had been exactly what he'd needed to unscramble his thoughts and figure some things out. Some things he couldn't allow himself to forget.

Not getting any SMs from her was intriguing, but it had to be just a random, happenstance occurrence. She was nothing more than a woman he was helping for the night, and he couldn't let himself forget that. No matter how miraculous it felt to touch her.

He trudged up the porch steps and through the door. The stench hit him before he made it across the threshold. Garlic. And something rotting, decomposing, dead.

Damn that dog and his fetish for decaying carcasses.

Honey lay on the couch, her gaze locked on Little Man—his two-hundred-pound mastiff. An unfortunate underbite left Little Man's bottom teeth protruding and made him look like Satan's best beast rather than man's best friend.

"That's Little Man. He's harmless." He set her shoes in the middle of the kitchen table so Little Man wouldn't turn them into chew toys and looked around for the dead animal. "He won't hurt you. He's really just an overgrown puppy."

She sprang off the couch and hurdled the coffee table, crashing into him with full-body impact. He caught her tightly to him, smelling her fear, feeling it in the butterfly tremors shaking her body.

"I should've warned you that he might come in." He

inhaled the scent of her hair—cooking oil, nectarines, and sunshine. "He comes and goes through a dog door in the laundry room."

Her arms slid around him, holding him so tight she could've been his second skin.

His heart crashed against his sternum. His breath tangled up in his lungs. His gut stung with warmth. She settled her head over his heart. Could she feel it pounding? He squeezed his eyes shut, letting the pleasure of holding her entwine with the regret of knowing this was the first time, the last time, the only time he'd ever be able to hold another human being.

Her lips moved against his chest. He heard the stammering sounds of her speaking.

"…dream…"

Dream. He'd caught only one word of what she'd said. Did she think Little Man was a bad dream?

He half dragged, half carried her to the couch and sat. She didn't let go of him and ended up across his lap, her buttocks pressing into his dick. Blood drained downward and swelled into his groin. Lava-hot sweat erupted from his pores. Shame formed a molten lump in his gut—knowing what she'd been through, he shouldn't be reacting to her this way. He shifted, moved her down his legs so she couldn't feel his arousal, and then started blabbing to distract her.

"The worst thing Little Man would ever do is lick you. His tongue is six inches wide, seems two feet long, and he slobbers. A lot." Lathan bent his head to see her mouth, hoping for a smile, but she stared at her hand, her lips pulled back over her teeth in repulsed horror.

She lifted her hand, her slender bicep straining and

bulging as if whatever she clutched in her fist weighed too much to raise.

Her fingers fanned opened.

Lathan stared at the object she held. His heart stalled and his brain shuddered to a stop, leaving him thoughtless for a few picoseconds, before everything turned back on and shifted gears in a direction he sure as hell didn't want to go.

Chapter 3

AN EYE. A HUMAN EYE. IN HER HAND.

Lathan blinked, not quite believing the message his eyes were sending his brain.

"What the... Where'd you get that?" He scented the air and visually scanned his home—only himself, Little Man, and her. No one else had been inside. Nothing was missing or out of place. "Did you leave the house?"

She didn't answer. She looked and smelled befuddled, dazed, stunned.

"Did you find it outside?"

No answer.

Why did she have it in her hand? What would possess her to touch it, pick it up? His innards lurched and sank down into his gut. Was the owner of the eye still alive? He suspected they weren't, and that meant there was a body outside. Nearby.

But he would've smelled a body. He was just out there.

Her hand fell, the enucleated orb went with it, bouncing once, then rolling, iris over white, to a stop in the crevice between the cushions. Her body wilted; her head thunked against his shoulder.

He grabbed her chin, shaking her face. "Honey. Wake up. I need some answers here." But she was twelve-rounds-with-the-champ out. Fuck.

He cradled her limp form against him and reached into his pants pocket to get his cell phone. He took a

picture of the eye, sent it to Gill, and followed up with
a text.

Human eye on my couch.

Gill was gonna hit an eleven on the freak-o-meter.
Either that or think Lathan was trying to punk him. A
moment later, Gill responded.

A little late for Halloween.

Seriously.

You fucking with me?

No.

What happened?

IDK, but I'm pretty sure where there's an
eye, there's a body.

*Don't move. Don't touch anything. I'll contact
Eric on my way.*

For the first time since he'd been hired as a special
skills consultant, he was going to demand a favor from
the FBI, and they would grant it—without question—for
the man who had closed more cold cases than everyone else combined. The most important condition of
his contract was that his privacy, his total seclusion, be
maintained at all times.

He shoved his arm under Honey's legs, lifted her tight against his chest, and stood.

"Little Man. Come."

The dog didn't move. Didn't blink. His attention was focused on the eye.

Lathan nudged the dog's thick haunch with his boot until Little Man gave him *the look*. The I-swear-I'll-never-chew-on-the-table-legs-ever-again-if-you-just-let-me-have-it, please, please, please look.

"No. Leave it." He put the you're-not-allowed-to-play-with-it-or-eat-it tone in his voice. "Little Man. Come."

Little Man heaved a giant sigh that fanned his massive jowls outward, but stood and headed upstairs. Lathan followed, carrying Honey. By the time he got into the bedroom, Little Man was settled on his mastiff-sized dog bed in the corner.

"Stay."

Lathan laid Honey in his bed. Her body was dead-weight and awkward, so he adjusted her arms, her legs, her head until she looked comfortable.

He tore off his gloves, pressed his fingers to her neck, and concentrated on finding her pulse. The steady pressure of her heartbeat tapped against his fingertips with a Morse code rhythm all its own. He laid his other hand on her chest, just below her clavicle, to ensure the rise and fall of her breathing. He tried not to notice how close his hand was to her breasts. Failed.

If he fanned out his pinkie finger—no. He pulled his hand away.

She must've just passed out.

He went into the bathroom, soaped up half the stack

of clean washcloths, and washed the lingering scent of decay from her hand.

Her skin was rough and red, her fingers knobby and strong, her nails ragged and short. She had the body and clothing of a stripper, but he expected something more faux sexy than torn-up fingernails and blistered feet. What kind of job abused her hands and her feet? Nothing seemed to fit.

He had questions and not one answer. What was her name? Why didn't he get SMs from her? Why was he able to touch her? Where the fuck did she get a human eyeball?

He stared at her face as if the answers were written in the delicate arch of her brows or in the gentle curve of her lashes. Or in the small sickle-shaped scar at the corner of her mouth that curved upward, giving her the curious appearance of smiling on one side of her mouth, while the other side frowned.

Her eyelids fluttered. Opened.

"How are you feeling?" That question was more appropriate than interrogating her on how she came into possession of a human eyeball. He'd wait until she was fully conscious before tripping down that trail.

"Cold. So cold." Goose bumps pimpled over her bare skin. She scooted toward where he sat on the edge of the bed, wrapping herself around his hips, seeking his body's warmth.

He *should* get the heavy sleeping bag from the closet. He *should* cover her with it and leave the room. *He should, he should, he should.* He didn't. He pulled off his boots and eased into the bed. She latched onto him before he fully reclined.

She molded herself to him. His shoulder her pillow, her arm around his middle, one of her legs draped over his thighs, her knee just a few miniscule inches from his groin. Everything vanished except the vivid sensation of her feminine curves burrowing into him, seeking his safety, his comfort, his warmth. She was cool where he was on fire. She was soft where he couldn't bend. She was sweet where he felt bitter.

She fit into his arms, against his body, and into his soul like she was designed especially for him. He wanted to believe he could have a happy ending with her, but his reality was a cruel, hard place where good things just didn't happen. Or if they did, they never lasted.

Bzzzz.

Evanee's muscles clenched, and she startled from the sudden sound of a phone vibrating.

Bzzzz. Bzzzz.

"Shhh… Honey, it's just my cell," Lathan whispered against her hair, his breath warm against her skin.

Her tension evaporated. What exactly was it about his voice that calmed her? Was it the timbre, the accent… It wasn't quite an accent, more like a lisp, but not? Maybe it wasn't his voice. Maybe it was him calling her *Honey*. Maybe it was him taking care of her—not advantage of her—when she had been as rational and coherent as a zombie. His size and his tattoo were a warning and a threat, but he'd bought her complete trust the moment he saved her from Junior. Something not one person in her life had ever earned.

"It's just Gill letting me know he's arrived. He'll be handling things, or at least seeing that they get handled privately." He slid away from her, just far enough to look down at her.

His pale-gray eyes stood out against his tan. No, it wasn't a tan. He was thickly freckled. Seriously freckled. Boyishly freckled. She should've realized that from the rich reddish-brown of his hair. A smile tugged at her soul. How could she think his tattoo frightening when paired with a face full of friendly freckles?

"You're feeling better."

It wasn't a question, but she nodded anyway.

"I've got to let Gill in. He's gonna have some questions for you."

"Questions for me? About Junior?" She hated the tremor in her voice and cleared her throat. "I don't want to press charges or anything. That'd just piss everyone off." Not only would Junior be mad, Sheriff Rob would be angry, and Mom would be furious—at her—for causing Junior trouble.

While she spoke, Lathan's gaze focused on her mouth. The way he looked at her reminded her of how a man concentrated on a woman's lips before coming in for a kiss—like he was calculating angle, pressure, distance to the target.

"Not about Junior—"

Bzzzz. Bzzzz. Bzzzz.

"Take a few minutes—however long you need—then come downstairs." He got out of bed and headed for the doorway. A colossal black dog rose from the corner and followed Lathan. A shudder ripped through her.

That she'd had a nightmare wasn't new; that she remembered it was astounding. The dream had *felt* so real, and the part about waking up with the eye in her hand was a total mind fuck. Only when she woke up in his bed with him staring down at her did she realize the entire thing had been one long, gruesome dream.

Evanee heard Lathan open the door downstairs, heard him talking, but his words were a low murmur of indistinguishable sound.

"Where're your gloves?" The guy—must've been Gill—didn't quite shout the words, but his tone of disbelief carried up the stairs. "What the fuck does it matter how loud I talk? The louder the better, right?"

Lathan said something, his voice hushed and quiet.

"She? You've got a woman up there? In your bed?" Astonishment laced with consternation dominated Gill's voice.

Time to go downstairs before Gill got the exact wrong idea, which wouldn't be hard—until a few moments ago, she had been contentedly snuggling with Lathan. He was the bright side to the whole Junior situation. A situation she was gonna have to deal with.

Her stomach suddenly felt wrong. Sweat exploded from her pores, dripped down her face, soaked her clothes. Her skin flamed and itched like she'd rolled in a poison ivy patch. Her insides grew hotter than asphalt on a one-hundred-degree day.

It couldn't be the stomach flu. Not now. A groan of impending calamity escaped her mouth.

"What's wrong?" Lathan stood in the doorway.

"I'm going to be sick." Somehow, she got out of bed, got into the bathroom, and got draped over the porcelain bowl. Thank God and all his fat little angels, the toilet was hygienically clean.

Her stomach contracted. Her throat opened. She wretched a cruel sound halfway between a cough and a sob, but nothing came out. Stomach contracted. Throat opened. Again and again, her innards tried to turn themselves inside out.

A cold cloth pressed against her neck.

She wanted to thank Lathan for that small kindness, but something inside her was wrong. Really wrong. Not just I've-got-the-flu wrong, but I'm-going-to-die wrong. Part of her felt light, untethered from her body, like she was a helium balloon floating into the sky. The other part felt her muscles, her organs tensing, fighting, rallying to save her. Save her from what?

"I need to go to the hos—" Her stomach clenched, choking off the rest of her words. The force of it lifted her body off the ground. Fire scorched up her throat. A scream erupted as black, curdled foulness spewed from her mouth in a giant wash.

She fell forward, unable to hold herself upright. Her eyebrow cracked against the porcelain bowl. Stars winked in front of her eyes.

Lathan snagged her arms, yanked her away from the bowl, and held her back against his chest.

His hands warmed her bare skin. Heat spread up her arms to her shoulders, across her chest to her heart, then pumped outward to her extremities. His hands were twin IVs of feel-good plugged directly into her veins. The pain in her stomach, the throb in her head diminished and then vanished completely. She felt surprisingly all right compared to how she'd felt only seconds ago. Weird.

Lathan shifted her around so she faced his chest and gathered her closer to him. His touch was so gentle, so caring, so intimate it almost brought tears to her eyes. She nuzzled her cheek against his shirt, concentrated on the fabric scratching against her face. Anything to distract herself enough to keep actual tears from forming.

"Gill. Take us to the hospital." The command in his voice harbored no room for question.

She turned her head to see Gill standing only a few feet away from them. He stared at the toilet, his expression as impassive as plastic. He looked exactly like a full-size, real-life version of the Ken doll Rob had bought her as a butter-up-the-kid present before he'd married Mom. Gill had wavy blond hair and surfer boy looks—or maybe the actual Ken doll had been a Malibu Ken and that's why Gill reminded her of a surfer.

It wasn't fair, wasn't his fault he reminded her of that Ken doll, but she instantly disliked him.

"No hospital. I'm fine now."

Lathan drew back from her enough to see her face. "What did you say?"

"I don't need to go to the hospital. I'm okay. Really. I'll end up racking up a five-thousand-dollar bill just to be told I ate something bad." She needed cash to get out of Sundew before she ran into Junior again. If she saved every penny, she might have enough money to start over somewhere new in two or three months.

Lathan stared at her, his eyes intense, penetrating, like he saw beyond her skin and muscle and bone to the person buried beneath a lifetime full of shit.

"You want to borrow a toothbrush?"

Heat blazed across her face. She slapped her hand

over her mouth and nodded. *Dear Holy Mother of Mercy, please don't let him have smelled my breath.*

He unwrapped his arms from around her. She suddenly felt exposed, naked, like he'd taken her clothes with him. She didn't look at Ken Doll while Lathan got her a toothbrush, but she felt his gaze roaming over her, judging her clothes, her body, her motives.

Call her childish—she couldn't help herself—but she looked at Ken Doll, crossed her eyes, and stuck out her tongue.

He tilted his head, a look of confusion on his face. "I think she should go to the hospital. That"—Ken Doll pointed at the toilet—"isn't normal." His voice was as deep as a seventies radio announcer's. And just as sexist—speaking about her as if she weren't standing four feet away from him.

"No. I'm fine." She snapped the words a little too quickly, a little too loudly to pretend she'd been trying to be polite. Which she hadn't. She should be nicer. The guy really hadn't done anything other than remind her of the past.

Ken Doll looked beyond her to Lathan. "I'm pretty sure she's withdrawing from something. Heroin maybe."

"Heroin?" She was only two decibels away from shouting the word.

"Cocaine?" Ken Doll asked her directly.

"Cocaine?" One decibel.

"Pain pills. Ritalin. Doesn't matter. You should still go to the hospital." Ken Doll snagged her arm, just like Junior had earlier. "Then after our interview, you can choose to enter detox. Or you can always choose jail time instead."

"Get your hands off me." She yanked on her arm, struggled to get out of his grasp, but each of his fingers was firm as a handcuff.

A roar of animalistic rage filled the bathroom, the sound so primal, so startling that both she and Ken Doll froze.

"Let her go!" Protectiveness surged beneath Lathan's skin, tapping into some dormant animal instinct to defend his own. *No one touches her*. The words were a subliminal message floating to the surface of his awareness.

He charged forward and slammed his fist down on Gill's forearm.

Gill released her arm and clutched the muscle and tendon Lathan had just bruised. "What—?"

Lathan bulldozed him in the chest, propelling him away from her. Only when Gill's ass met the wall did Lathan's momentum stop.

No one touches her.

Burnt cinnamon exploded in the air. "You want a fight?" Gill shoved himself off the wall and raised his fists—never one to back down from a challenge.

"No one touches her." Lathan heard his own words. Must've yelled them. Didn't care. His anger throttle was wide open, speeding fury though his system, charging his muscles, centering his mind on one thing—the irresistible compulsion to punish Gill for touching her.

Honey seemed to materialize in front of him. "Lathan. No." She put her hands on his chest and pushed him back. Without question, his body yielded to her. Through his T-shirt, the coolness of her palms seeped into him, dousing the anger burning inside him more effectively than if she'd just removed the key from his ignition.

"Honey, I know you're feeling better, but you shouldn't get in the way of two grown-ass men getting ready to throw down." A little pride might've leaked into his words. He might've even smiled. She was feisty and fearless, and he was determined to keep that alive in her. He never wanted to see her as lost and wounded as she had been out on the road.

Gill slashed his hand through the air, beckoning for Lathan's attention. "What the fuck is wrong with you?" He glanced at Honey, silent accusation on his face.

No one touches her.

"She doesn't do drugs." Lathan tapped the side of his nose but used his middle finger in a subtle fuck-you gesture. It was a game they'd played since they were kids— how to tell the other one to fuck off without words and without anyone noticing.

The side of Gill's mouth twitched once in acknowledgment. Some of the anger released, but the tension remained in his shoulders and arms. "I could've sworn she was using."

"She's not." If drug abusers could actually smell their own brains rotting the way Lathan could, it'd probably scare at least half of them into treatment. The other half probably didn't have enough cerebral cells left to make a cognizant decision.

"Something is going on." Gill stepped up to the toilet, put the lid down, but didn't flush. His instincts had always been bull's-eye. Something was going on, something only Lathan could smell.

"She vomited blood. But not her own." None of her

innate honeyed essence was in it. He'd bet his Fat Bob that the eye and the blood came from the same source, but he'd need a side-by-side comparison to be certain.

"Blood?" Honey stood in front of him, her hands still on his chest, her gaze still on his face.

Damn, he loved how she constantly sought to touch him.

"Why would you think I threw up blood?"

Any normal person wouldn't be able to smell the blood, wouldn't be able to tell it wasn't hers, wouldn't have opened his mouth and said something so profoundly revolting.

He stepped away from her, crossing his arms in front of his chest. He didn't want to look at her, was tempted to turn away and end the conversation, but she spoke before he acted on his thoughts.

"Why would you say that?" Her teeth drew back over her lips and he recognized the expression. Revulsion. "Tell me."

"When a person vomits blood, it always looks like that." At least no one else could smell the itchy pepper scent of his lie.

Her eyes narrowed. "But why would you say the blood wasn't mine?"

How was he going to get out of that one without either owning up to the truth or pleading the insanity defense? Neither was an attractive option.

Gill moved forward, getting too close, getting into her space, forcing her attention to him. "Well, that's an interesting addition to the problem downstairs. How about you start handing me some answers." Gill met Lathan's gaze with a you-can-thank-me-later smirk.

She tilted her chin up, her eyes turning into twin sapphires of challenge. "I am *not* pressing charges. And I'm *not* going to talk about it anymore."

Lathan heard both her *nots* clearly.

"You'll talk. I've cracked harder gutter roaches than you. So let's start with a kindergarten question. Where did you get the eye?"

Lathan didn't like how Gill treated her, but he recognized the method. Intimidation to get capitulation.

"What eye?" Confusion furrowed deep rows across her forehead. A tremor started in her shoulders, rippled outward down her arms and her legs.

"Save the I-have-no-idea-what-are-you-talking-about greeting card for someone who celebrates that holiday." Gill paused, waited for Honey to answer, but she met him stare for stare, finding no threat in his silence.

"What eye?" She directed the question to Lathan.

"The eye you had in your hand." How could she have forgotten? Holding a human eye in your hand wasn't the sort of memory that got misplaced.

She scanned his face like she was trying to decipher the truth of his words.

"That wasn't real." She shook her head in short, quick movements. "It was part of my nightmare. How do you know about it? Did I talk in my sleep?"

Gill shoved his cell phone in front of her face, no doubt showing her the picture Lathan had taken of the eye.

Her mouth and nose took on a greenish hue. Her cheeks and forehead blazed with red, mottling her face into shades of Christmas colors. She looked ready to call Ralph on the porcelain phone. Again. She inspected both of her hands. "But there's no blood. There's no blood. There would have been blood."

"I washed your hand." He doused the flame of hope brightening her face. Guilt kicked him in the ribs.

She froze, motionless as a baby deer in a semi's headlights. Garlic choked the air, stinging Lathan's nostrils. She was terrified. Nearly as frightened as she'd been of Junior.

"You're going to have to do better than"—Gill pushed his lips out in a mocking female pout—"*I had a nightmare.*"

Lathan clenched his teeth to keep from calling Gill out. *Intimidation to get capitulation*, he reminded himself.

"But I-I did. Have a nightmare. I'll tell you everything I know, but it doesn't make sense. Dreams aren't real. Right?" She glanced back and forth between the two of them, the question wrinkling her forehead. "I didn't think so. It's finally happened. I've gone nuttier than trail mix." Her eyes took on the slightly unfocused look of someone replaying a memory. She began telling them everything.

Lathan had no problem hearing and reading her words. The story she told was something he'd expect to read in a Stephen King horror novel. And completely implausible. Maybe she hadn't just been in shock out on the road; maybe insane was her baseline. Even as the thought crossed his mind, he X'ed it out, fully aware he was choosing to ignore all the evidence to the contrary.

She began shivering again, her arms, her legs, her chest covered in pimply goose bumps.

"When I woke up with...with it in my hand, I thought it was just part of the dream."

She believed every word she spoke. If she lied, he would have smelled it as easily as he smelled his own lie.

"Wow." Gill reached into his pocket. "I apologize. I didn't introduce myself." He flipped open his wallet to his FBI badge and credential. "I'm Special Agent Gill Garrison. Do you seriously want to fuck with me?"

"Here's what's going to happen." Lathan gave Gill a look full of unspoken words. *Let it go. For now. I'll explain later.* "She's going to brush her teeth, then get back in bed and take a nap. She's tired, she's sick, and she's had a shitty evening."

The sharp jump of muscle across Gill's jawline showed his anger, but they had twenty years of trust built between them that Gill wouldn't ignore.

"This isn't done."

"I know." Lathan handed her the toothbrush that he'd been gripping in his hand the entire time. She spoke to Gill, but her words were too muffled for Lathan to decipher.

Gill smiled at her as warmly as an abominable snowman and sat on the closed toilet lid. "Babe, I'm not moving. I'm guarding evidence."

"Don't call her *babe*." He might not know her name, but he knew it wasn't Babe. "He won't bother you. He's just going to sit there guarding his throne like the king of assholes."

Gill scratched his knee with his middle finger.

She ignored Gill and began brushing her teeth. Gill ignored her and played with his cell phone. Lathan couldn't ignore the reek of hot tar coming from both of them. Mutual dislike.

Lathan waited until she finished before he spoke to her. "Is there someone you want to call?"

"What…ime is it?"

Time and *dime* looked the same. *Dime* just didn't make sense in the sentence.

He yanked his cell from his pocket. "Eight thirty. Why?"

A pretty blush added color to her pale features. "Can I stay until morning?"

"You can stay as long as you like." He meant it. More than he wanted to admit.

"I have to be at work at eight. Could you take me? I'll pay you for the gas." Her mouth fell open. "Oh my God. My money. My apron. My keys. I left everything in the car. I should've—"

"Listen." He waited a full ten seconds for one hundred percent of her attention to land on him. "I don't want your money, and I'll help you get your stuff from Junior." He motioned for her to go into the bedroom, but followed her only as far as the doorway. He pointed toward his dresser. "Pick something of mine to wear. You've got vomit on your clothes."

She started to look down at her shirt, but he caught her chin. "Don't. It'll only make you sick again." He released her. "Toss your clothes out the door, and I'll wash them for you." He closed the door behind him and waited in the hallway, but his imagination remained in the bedroom with her. He pictured her grasping the hem of her shirt with both hands and pulling it up over her head in a long, languorous movement. Her bending, the fragile bones of her back jutting as she shimmied out of her shorts. Her walking across the room to his dresser, her limbs as graceful as a dancer's. Leaning over the dresser to pull open a drawer.

The door opened. She wore one of his sweatshirts.

The sleeves were a crinkled-up mess where she'd pushed them up so her hands could poke out. The shirt was three times wider than her and snugged the tops of her knees. Somehow, on her, it made one fuck of a sexy dress.

He bit his tongue just to make sure it wasn't hanging out the side of his mouth.

"Thanks for offering to wash them."

He took the bundle of clothes from her. "Get some sleep." He turned to walk away, but she grabbed his hand. Her skin was cool and rough.

"Thank you. For—"

He could see her mind replaying what happened out on the road with Junior.

"—everything."

He couldn't think of any words to say. He raised her hand to his lips and kissed her knuckles. Heat exploded across his face when he realized just how intimate the gesture was. He dropped her hand and turned away.

Gill was coming up the stairs carrying his evidence kit. He must've left the bathroom when they walked across the hall to the bedroom. Surprise widened his eyes, then judgment narrowed them.

While Gill recorded and cataloged the eye and the vomit, Lathan threw her clothes in the washer and then spent the next three hours walking the perimeter of his property with Little Man, searching for the scent of a corpse or blood, or anything that might indicate someone hurt nearby. Nothing. He returned to the house and found Gill waiting for him at the kitchen table, a steaming mug of coffee in his hand.

Lathan sat across from him. "She really believed she dreamed about the eye. She wasn't lying. I would've smelled it." How much should he tell Gill about tonight? Enough to give an explanation. Not enough to embarrass her. "She was attacked tonight. The asshole was going to rape her. She was in shock. I brought her here. I figure she'll have a more rational explanation after she gets some sleep."

Gill dipped his head once, acknowledging Lathan's words. "She's still a suspect."

"You don't even know if a crime's been committed." Even as he said the words, he knew how weak they sounded. Human eyes weren't something you'd accidentally run across on a nature walk.

"I called Eric to update him on your situation. The team's caught a case in West Virginia." Gill's eyes were colder than a glacier. "It's more than an odd coincidence that they're working the murder of an eight-year-old girl. Blond hair. Wearing pink. Left eye missing."

Chapter 4

LATHAN SHOVED AWAY FROM THE TABLE, TURNED HIS BACK on Gill, delaying the rest of the conversation until he figured out how to assimilate what he just learned with what his soul told him about Honey. He got a mug from the cupboard and sloshed coffee into it. The liquid seared his tongue and scalded a trail of fire down his throat to his belly. He gulped two more mouthfuls. The burn centered him, cleared his thoughts, and calmed his spirit.

He finally faced Gill. "The team is at the scene of a child's murder. The girl sounds like the one from Honey's *dream*. Logic points toward her involvement. But I don't believe it."

"This isn't about belief or faith or you being horny. It's about solving a murder. Following the evidence no matter where it leads. And right now a big, fat fucking arrow is pointing directly at her."

Lathan ignored the horny remark. Didn't want to acknowledge it. Couldn't argue effectively against it. "When she first saw the eye, I smelled her terror, saw it on her face. Killers—child killers—don't react that way to their own work." He wasn't a profiler, but he was reasonably certain of his assertion.

"What do you really know about her?"

What he didn't know could've filled an entire database, so he told Gill everything he did know. He left out the details of Junior's SM.

"If she wasn't involved in the murder of the girl in West Virginia, we need to consider a range of possibilities. She might be an accomplice. Trying to taint evidence. Trying to influence your work."

"Impossible." Anyone trying to find Lathaniel Montgomery would find nothing. Lathaniel Montgomery owned no property, had no credit, no address. Nothing existed out there in the world that could ever lead to the actual man. That had been the biggest condition of his accepting employment with the FBI—that his total and absolute privacy would be enforced.

"At this point we can't rule anything out." Gill raised his hands in a don't-shoot-me-for-telling-you-the-truth gesture. "My job is to watch out for you and keep the Bureau's interests safe. More importantly, I'm telling you as your friend that you need to watch your back. All of this could be a setup. The damsel-in-distress is one of the oldest tricks in the book."

"I left the presentation early. No one would've known what time I'd come down the road. Meeting her was chance."

"You left?" Disappointment scented the air.

"If you wanted me to stay, you shouldn't have hired an interpreter."

"I didn't." Gill leaned forward in his seat, the scent of his lie absent from the air.

"One was there. For me."

"Who the fuck hired one? I didn't. You didn't. No one but Eric and I know about your hearing problems." Gill's eyes shifted toward the ceiling—blaming her. "She's involved. Her prints aren't in the system so I don't have anything to go on yet."

"How do you know?"

"I scanned her fingerprint while she was sleeping."

Lathan's blood churned and doubled in volume, filling every organ with excruciating pressure. Gill had touched her while she lay helpless and vulnerable. "You touched her? While she was asleep?" The words clawed through him, burning his throat with a rush of acid rage.

Gill shoved back his chair, toppling it over as he stood. "What's wrong with you? Why are you acting like a jealous asshole? You just met her."

"No one touches her." *No one touches her. No one touches her.* The words vibrated through him, thrumming a deep tempo with each thump of his heart.

"I was taking a goddamned fingerprint, not molesting her. If she says otherwise, she's a liar." Gill was face-to-face with him. A hurricane of burning cinnamon-scented rage swirled around them.

From across the living room, Lathan saw her standing at the bottom of the stairs, sleepy confusion and concern marring the soft planes of her face. They must've been loud. Woken her up.

The fury he'd felt no more than two seconds ago vanished. Gone. What *was* wrong with him? He'd been on the verge of giving Gill a fist of five. Gill—his best and longest and only friend.

He'd changed. Turned homicidally protective of her right not to be touched by anyone. Seeing Junior's SM, witnessing her trying to save herself, watching her pain, and knowing how the SM probably ended. He would never let another person harm her. She deserved a life of sunshine, rainbows, and happiness.

"Everything's all right." Lathan tried to sound reassuring.

She glanced at Gill, then at him, her eyes wary, full of the knowledge that they'd almost gotten into a fistfight. Over her.

He started toward her. Gill shifted, blocking his way. "I'm only looking out for you."

Lathan rammed into Gill's shoulder, practically plowing through him. Gill was probably contemplating jumping him from behind, but knew better. That would've qualified as an unforgiveable sin in their friendship.

"I'm sorry we woke you. Go back to bed. You've got lots of sleeping to do before you need to wake up."

A pretty pink color spotted her cheeks. "Come up with me."

Her words painted a masterpiece in his mind. He imagined lying in bed with her again, holding her, stroking her bare skin, kissing her. God. Kissing her. His gut trembled. His fucking dick twitched and started to get hard.

She grabbed his hand and tried to tow him toward the stairs. He followed her for a few steps, then finally remembered how to cogitate. The eye. The murder in West Virginia. The square mile of tension between him and Gill that needed to be resolved.

"I'll be up soon. Gill and I need to talk."

She stopped tugging his hand, but she smelled faintly of garlic. She was worried about him. Him. No one *worried* about him. Except Gill.

"Then I'll stay down here with you."

Should he feel flattered or offended? Flattered she wanted to be near him. Offended she didn't think he could handle himself against Gill.

"Do what you want, but if you stay, Gill's going to question you." He leaned in close and tried to whisper, "Don't worry about me. I can paint the shutters with his face if I need to."

She smiled, the scar on the side of her mouth hitching up higher than the other side, giving her a slightly goofy grin that was utterly adorable. "I know. But he's your friend, and you shouldn't be fighting about me. I'll answer his questions, but he ain't gonna like the answers." Her midnight-blue eyes twinkled with amusement. "I don't really like the answers either, but they're the only set of truth I've got." She dropped his hand and walked to the kitchen. At the kitchen table, she sat with her back straight, her head held high.

Damn. He liked her.

By the time he followed her, Gill had her name written across the top of his legal pad. Evanee Brown.

Evanee. No wonder he couldn't lip-read her name. Those damned *f*'s and *v*'s.

Evanee emerged from the land of dreamless sleep and knew exactly where she was. Alone. In Lathan's bed. When she woke at Morty's there was always a moment of confusion when her brain struggled to remember where she was and how she'd gotten there.

Outside, the sky was an indeterminable shade between white and gloomy that perfectly matched her mood. She didn't need to look at a clock to know it was well past time for her to be at work.

She'd made a stupid decision. One that just might've incinerated her source of income. Without so much as a phone call, she'd missed work. Ernie usually looked at such an offense as inexcusable. Many a waitress at Sweet Buns had been booted out the back door for less.

She needed to call Ernie and explain. She'd say she was sick—she *had* vomited. Then she'd apologize. Then grovel. And if that failed, she'd beg and plead and humiliate herself to get her job back. She needed that job. Needed the money. Because she needed to get out of Sundew before Junior caught up with her again.

Ken Doll had kept her up most of the night asking, then re-asking the same questions over and over. He'd tried to trip her up, tried putting words in her mouth, tried to get her to confess to something, anything other than the story she'd told him. The upside: It wasn't hard to piss him off. She'd just told him the truth, and truth was always stronger than a lie. It wasn't her fault the truth didn't make any sense.

She got out of bed and went in search of Lathan. She found him in the kitchen. His broad shoulders stretched the material of his T-shirt, highlighting each ripple of muscle as he moved. Damn, he was a big guy.

He quietly worked over something on the counter. A golden-brown loaf of homemade bread was neatly sliced and waiting next to him. Her stomach whined a high-pitched sound that dropped to a low, ominous gurgle. She giggled, but the sound died when his dog—easily the scariest animal she'd ever seen—sat up from lounging on a dog bed the size of a twin mattress. She hurried to Lathan. If the beast was going to attack, the safest place was right next to its master, the one person she knew would protect her.

"Should I be scared of him?"

Lathan didn't answer. He just kept working over the counter.

"What's wrong?" She placed her hand on his arm.

He startled. A violent jerking of muscle that threw her hand off his skin. He whirled, arm raised. Fist tight. Elbow pulled back, ready to release in a direct line toward her face. His eyes, nearly the same color as the sad winter sky, didn't see *her*, but looked through time to some terrifying event in his past.

She froze. He wouldn't hurt her. Not after everything he'd done to keep her safe from Junior. Even from his friend.

Recognition brightened in his expression. He stumbled back from her, running into the fridge with his shoulder and hip. Terror poisoned his eyes for only the briefest of moments. He spun, fist driving through the air, its momentum stopped by the refrigerator. Metal crunched, plastic snapped, and something inside fell, clanging against the door on its descent.

Back heaving up and down, hands shaking at his sides, head bowed, he spoke. "Don't ever sneak up on me." The strange accent in his voice was more pronounced.

She knew—she didn't know how she knew, but she knew—something had happened to him. Something bad. Something he still feared. "I'm so sorry. I didn't mean to startle you." She felt like she'd stepped on a puppy's tail.

Low in his throat, he groaned a disconsolate sound filled with pain.

Witnessing his misery gouged at her heart.

"Don't." The word was loud, abrupt as a gunshot.

"Don't you dare fucking pity me." He sounded like he was talking through clenched teeth.

"I—" She started to deny it.

"Don't bother to lie. I can fucking *smell* your pity." His voice shook with emotion—anger or anguish. She couldn't be sure which. "Fear me. Hate me. But don't pity me. Never pity." He sidestepped her without facing her and went into a small room off the kitchen.

Almost instantly he returned.

"I'll take you home." His gaze focused on the floor, he avoided looking at her and held out her clean clothes.

"I don't want to go home." Heat burst across her face. She shouldn't have said that out loud.

He set her clothes on the table and headed for the door. "I'll get the bike." The door slammed behind him.

In less than three minutes, she was on his motorcycle, wind slicing across her legs, burning and freezing her skin at the same time. He'd given her a heavy jacket to wear before she'd climbed on, but she had no protection for her legs. She squeezed her eyes closed and spent the ride wishing she'd stayed upstairs—hidden from the world, from horny truckers, and especially from Junior.

The bike slowed, then stopped. Lathan cut the engine. She clung to him without opening her eyes—her last ode to denial. The soft whoosh of a single car passing alerted her that she wasn't at Morty's.

Her eyes popped open. Gray-painted garage. Two oversized bays protected by giant metal-and-glass doors. Tow truck parked next to the building. In neat letters across the front, Robert Malone, Junior. Mechanic and Towing Service.

She read the sign again, certain something inside her

brain had malfunctioned. But the words said the same thing. Lathan had brought her to Junior. Her heart squeezed into a tightly packed snowball full of shards of ice.

Lathan was probably friends with Junior. How could she have forgotten for one moment that everyone in Sundew loved Junior? Everything that had happened was probably a scripted and choreographed play produced by Junior's sick imagination. Maybe they'd drugged her, made her think she was crazy, then made her think she was safe—fucking her mind worse than Junior ever could her body.

An invisible icicle pierced her soul. She wanted to fall down on the ground, scream, and cry, but that would have to come later.

Fight, flight, or freeze? Flight—escape. From both of them. She shoved hard at Lathan's back and leaped off the bike.

"Honey. It's okay. I won't let him hurt you. I promise." The sincerity in his voice stopped her from reaching for her shoes to pry them off her feet—to run.

She half expected to see Junior's evil in his expression, but his face was all innocent freckles overlaid with a scary, beautiful tattoo.

"Why'd you bring me here?" Her voice trembled with hope.

"I told you I'd help you get your things back."

He had. Last night. In their quick departure, she'd forgotten.

"I always keep my word." He climbed off the bike and reached a gloved hand out to her. "I should've told you. Reminded you."

Junior emerged from the shop, wiping his hands on

a towel dangling from the pocket of his coveralls. Why didn't anyone in Sundew, Ohio, ever wonder why Junior hadn't followed in his daddy's footsteps? Everyone would be surprised to learn that he couldn't pass the psychological exam to get into the police academy.

Lathan stepped in front of her, but reached behind with one hand. She grabbed on to him, lacing her fingers with his, and knew he'd keep his word. He wouldn't let Junior hurt her.

Part of her felt ashamed and weak for not standing up to Junior herself. Another part worried she wasn't strong enough to handle him—mentally or physically. And another part was relieved she didn't have to face him alone.

"Get her keys, her money, her apron." Lathan's voice was a command.

"Darlin'" Junior's voice sung out in a way that hit her right in the stomach. "I told you I'd be seeing you. And I just spoke to your momma. She's *dying* to talk to you." His words were a dirty finger jamming into an open wound.

Everyone in Sundew knew Rosemary Malone cared more about her stepson than her own children.

"You talk to me now. Get her stuff." Lathan's tone was in the homicidal range.

"There wasn't anything in the car." Without seeing the smirk on his face, she could hear it in his inflection.

Lathan spoke over his shoulder. "Stay here." He dropped her hand and started toward Junior. Maybe she should be worried about him. Junior could be unpredictable, but he was no stronger than a pencil-necked geek compared to Lathan.

Junior retreated a step and then withdrew a large wrench from his coveralls.

"Your toy doesn't scare me." Lathan didn't falter, didn't stop.

Junior swung the weapon, aiming for Lathan's left cheek. Lathan caught Junior's wrist and then drove him back against the wall of the shop. Junior's body whonked against the concrete. Lathan angled himself, using his far-superior weight and height to pin Junior against the wall. He braced his forearm underneath Junior's throat.

A small smile tasting of revenge tugged at her lips. How many times had she been trapped like that under Junior? Too many to count. And seeing Lathan pin him so easily was satis-fucking-fying... If she had some pom-poms, she'd shout a cheer. *Go Lathan. Go. Go. Go. Lathan.*

"You're dead. You have no idea how dead you are. You're going to jail. Prison."

Revenge started to taste bitter. Junior wasn't a threat to Lathan, but his dad was even more demented than Junior. Like father. Like son.

"Lathan, maybe you should—"

"Where's her stuff?" Lathan shouted the words, his voice so loud she cringed.

"I don't have it." Junior choked out, his face turning a magenta shade of anger and oxygen deprivation. "What are you doing?"

Everything was silent for a beat.

"Evanee." Lathan spoke her name without glancing away from Junior. "Your stuff is in the red toolbox next to the workbench. Top drawer."

"How did you—?" Junior's voice grunted to a stop when Lathan shoved his arm tighter against Junior's throat.

"Evanee. Go get it. Now."

She sprinted inside Junior's shop, her four-inch heels barely slowing her down. She found the toolbox. Ripped open the top drawer.

Inside there were no tools, no greasy rags, nothing to indicate it was a mechanic's toolbox. Instead, she found her apron folded into a neat square of cloth. Money missing—of course. Next to her apron was her key ring, minus her car key, and next to that a photo of the last happy day of her life. Mom and Rob's wedding.

It was Junior's photo, not hers. She would never own something that represented the beginning of so much pain.

The twenty-year-old picture had a sepia tinge to it, but the memory in her head wasn't dulled in the least. Evanee remembered every detail of that day.

She had felt like a fairy princess in her frilly pink dress. She remembered twirling around and around and around, loving the way the long skirt billowed in the air. She had loved how her new big brother, Junior, had always been there to catch her before she fell to the ground and dirtied her dress.

Rob in his dress uniform had looked dashing as a king. And Mom was a queen in her flowing ivory wedding dress. On that day, Evanee had loved Rob and loved Junior. They were going to give her something she'd never had before. A family. Rob was going to be her and Thomas's dad, and Junior was going to be their big brother.

In the picture, Mom and Rob stood, radiant smiles on both of their faces, Rob's arm resting protectively over

Mom's shoulders. In front of Rob and Mom, nine-year-old Junior stood with his arm around the five-year-old version of Evanee. She'd grown up with a larger print of that photo hanging on the living room wall. She'd always wondered why this particular picture mattered so much, especially since Thomas—her baby brother—wasn't even in it. It wasn't until this moment that she noticed how Junior had his arm around her in the same way Rob had his arm around Mom. She and Junior looked like a miniature version of Rob and Mom.

There was something about that picture. Something about Junior and her. A thought hovered around the edges of Evanee's mind, pushing, pulsating, prodding against the resistance of her consciousness.

"Evanee?" Lathan's voice brought her back to the current situation.

She grabbed her apron, her key ring, shoved them in the jacket pocket, and ran outside.

When Lathan saw her, he let go of Junior. Sagging to his knees, Junior sucked air and coughed.

"What happened?" Lathan was next to her, his gaze darting between her and Junior.

She shook her head, but he waited. "Nothing." *An old picture spooked me* didn't seem like a logical explanation.

Lathan watched Junior until they were on the bike and driving out of the parking lot.

At first, the angry growl of the engine soothed her, but then the realization she didn't want to face exploded in her mind like a firecracker on a quiet night.

A coldness that had nothing to do with the temperature settled over her. That night, the night of the wedding, was the first time Junior messed with her.

Lathan knew something was wrong the moment she emerged from Junior's shop. She looked like she was running across the high wire of sanity and a windstorm had just kicked up.

She hugged him tight as a drowning man would a life ring.

Only one more block and he'd pull into RaeBeck's Grocery. Lots of lights to see her words. Lots of people to witness if Junior followed them.

He pulled in, cut the engine, and twisted in his seat, trying to see her face. "What's wrong?"

She shook her head in short, little Parkinsonian movements and angled off the bike.

Lathan set the kickstand and stood. She continued to shake her head. A sulfur-like scent oozed from her pores. Disbelief. Shock.

He wanted to say something to ease her, but nothing came to mind. He wanted to hold her—knew that would help—but she didn't seek him out like she normally did, so he just stood there like a big dumbo and stared at her.

"You must think I'm a total... God, I don't even have a word for how pathetic I must seem."

"You're not pathetic. You've been through shit with Junior two days in a row. You're dealing."

"This is dealing?"

He couldn't hear the sarcasm in her words, but he witnessed its journey across her face.

"You want to talk about it?" He wasn't sure he wanted her to. The leash he kept on his impulse to kill Junior might snap.

"Ever have one of those moments—you know, the *ding-ding-ding*, we-have-a-winner moments—when you see something that has been right in front of you your whole life, but you were too naive, blind, or stupid to see it? And it changes everything. And nothing. All at once."

"Yeah." She'd just described the moment when he'd gotten the results back from his DNA test, when he'd been told the olfactory region of his brain was enlarged, when he'd been informed that his sense of smell was more sensitive than the equipment they used to measure olfaction. "I know exactly what you mean."

Her brows bounced up a little. "Really?"

He nodded. He could see her curiosity taking over whatever had pained her a moment ago. Part of him was relieved, part scared. He didn't want her to ask about his *ding-ding-ding* moment. He didn't want to tell her, and he didn't want to lie. Time for a distraction. "So where do you want me to take you?" *Say you want to come back home with me*.

A pretty rose of color bloomed on each of her cheeks. "You know Morty's Motor Lodge off 70, near Sweet Buns and Eats?"

"Yeah."

"Take me there."

"Why do you want to go there? Only druggies and whores live there." *Whores*.

No.

She couldn't be a whore.

His gut plummeted into his boots. He shook his head to dislodge the idea that she'd take money for sex, but the evidence stood in front of him partially covered by his jacket. Those tiny shorts, the hooker sexy shoes she wore on her feet. *Hooker* sexy. Fuck.

"You're a..." He couldn't force the word *whore* from his lips. "You use your body for money?"

The roses on her cheeks turned cherry-bomb red and spread to her entire face. Burning cinnamon rolled off her.

She glanced down at herself. "It's none of your damned business how I earn my money."

"You don't have to live like that. There are other options."

She lifted her chin high in the air. "I'm not ashamed of what I do. I work hard for my money. Never mind the ride. I'll walk." She stomped away from him.

She was a whore. He let her go. Watched her walk away.

An ugly urge bubbled up from deep inside him. He wanted to hunt down, eviscerate, and then kill every man she'd ever fucked.

The rage died a sudden violent death. He shouldn't be acting jealous. He should be embarrassed. She hadn't offered her services to him. Obviously, she couldn't tell by the way he lived that he had money. Lots of it. He could probably afford to pay her for a decade of her time. The FBI compensated him very well for his unique ability. Money just meant very little to him. Privacy mattered more than currency.

He watched her as she walked across the parking lot toward the road. Her skyscraper legs and those hooker sexy shoes sent a clear message to every dick.

He ran to catch up with her. "Let me give you a ride."

She acted like she didn't hear him and kept walking.

"Honey, you've got two choices here. Either you're

riding with me to Morty's, or I'm walking with you." Morty's wasn't far, maybe a half mile, but a lot could happen to her in a half mile.

She reached down, barely breaking her stride, and pulled off her heels—going barefoot. Barefoot. In November.

He stayed with her until they reached the flickering Morty's Motor Lodge sign.

Low slung and L-shaped, the motel looked like something from a cheap horror flick. The paint on the concrete walls was so drab it had lost its ability to even be considered a color. Each room had a different style of door, like the owner shopped flea markets and garage sales. In the middle of each door, someone with an obvious case of dyslexia had painted a drippy number. The three, five, and seven were backward.

She stopped. The scent of her anger had burned out her during their walk. "It meant a lot to me that you helped me deal with Junior, but you've got to grow eyes in the back of your head. Junior's dad is the new sheriff, and he's as big an asshole as his son."

"If Junior gives you any more trouble, let me know." He wanted her to ask him for his number, but she didn't. He was thinking like a pizza-faced teenager. "Gill will probably have more questions for you. Will you be here?" He gestured toward the motel.

"For a few weeks." She twisted her lips up in a smile that was so obviously fake it looked like a grimace. "See you around, Lathan."

Before he found words to say in response, she walked down the row of dilapidated rooms to the short arm of the L, unlocked number nine, entered the room, and exited his life.

Chapter 5

EACH STEP CLOSER TO THE MOTEL ROOM FELT LIKE SHE WAS walking against a strong current. Her brain screamed its resistance to returning to the life of working at Sweet Buns and living at Morty's.

She entered the motel room. The door swung inward and crashed against the wall like it always did. On the bright side: the room was empty and its double beds were made with fresh sheets and comforters from Morty's stock of overused, out-of-style, and under-washed linens. Brittany had even plugged in one of those glow-in-the-dark air fresheners. Evanee suspected Brittany was afraid of the dark, but she never mentioned it.

The room looked like it always had, but today Evanee couldn't tolerate its ugliness. She wanted the light, airy, open atmosphere of Lathan's home. The sense of safety and security she felt there with him. She'd even take Gill interrogating her over one more moment in this decrepit space.

She left the room, locked the door behind her, and went over to Sweet Buns.

The moment she walked through the back door, Ernie looked up from the grill. The angry planes of his face softened for a moment, but then were replaced with an expression that rivaled Freddy Krueger's for scare value.

"Where the hell have you been?" He shouted the words. The entire diner went silent. He threw his spatula at the grill with the force of a baseball pitcher. The *clang, bang* of it rang out like a death knell.

Oh, shit. She was so fired. She might even end up being the dead body he stashed in his freezer.

"Ivy! Get back here and watch the grill!" Ernie tore off his apron, threw it on the floor, and stalked toward Evanee.

This was bad. Beyond bad. Ernie never left the grill. Never. She backed into the door, pushed it open, managed to get one step, just as he reached her.

Should she run? Yell for help?

Slowly, as if giving her time to react, he reached up and tipped her chin to the side. His fingers were gentle, light against her skin. "Who hurt you?" His voice was soft kindness floating over her. She didn't know his vocal cords had that kind of range.

Absurdly, she wanted to tell him everything about Junior. Miserable memories lined up, each one attached to one name—Junior. She opened her mouth, not sure where to begin, but then noticed Ernie's gaze was locked on her eyebrow. He only saw her eyebrow—that was it. Had no idea about all the hurt hidden underneath her skin.

She stuffed the lid back down on the garbage can of her life. Waited a second to make certain the lid would hold, and then spoke. "I hit my face." At his look of disbelief, she elaborated. "On a toilet. I was sick. Vomiting. And kinda passed out for a moment."

He stepped closer, examined her brow, tilting her chin at odd angles under the light of the back door.

She hadn't even thought to look in the mirror. "It probably looks worse than it is."

"What happened? Where were you? Your car was gone, but when I talked to Brittany, she said your wallet was still in the room."

"You talked to Brittany?"

"Shirl and Ivy were worried about you."

She knew *he'd* been worried about her and didn't want to admit it.

She didn't tell him everything. She left out the part about Junior attacking her, and the part about her dreaming up an eyeball, and the part where Ken Doll interrogated her.

Ernie's face hardened more with each of her words. The softer, sweeter Ernie disappeared. Freddy Krueger Ernie returned.

"What the fuck are you thinking? Going home with a guy you just met."

Technically, Ernie had a point. But Lathan had never *felt* like a stranger. "He was nice. Kind. Took care of me when I was sick." She missed Lathan. She pictured him—his freckles, his tattoo, looking at her in that way only he did.

"He don't own a phone?" Ernie's volume had risen back to normal.

"I was sick. I forgot. I'm sorry. Really sorry. It will never happen again. I swear."

He stared at her face, and she could tell he was ascertaining whether she was telling the truth. "You still want your job?"

"I do."

"You're on second shift from now on." In the world of Sweet Buns, that was a demotion. Second shift was not only a sucky time of day to work, but the supper truckers were the creepiest of the creepers. "Get in there and relieve Ivy. She's been on her feet ten hours. You find a way to make that up to her."

"Thanks, Ernie."

"Evan." The anger in his voice was gone. He turned and walked inside. Over his shoulder he said, "If you're in trouble, call me. Don't go with a stranger."

"I don't own a phone," she whispered to his retreating back.

Evanee walked out the back door of Sweet Buns. Even though it was midnight, the rumbling semis continued to beat a cadence that picked at her nerves. Another annoyance among the multitude of things she couldn't control, couldn't act on, or couldn't let herself think about—yet.

She did her owl impression, craning her neck in all directions to make sure no one was lurking around, and then jogged across the parking lot to Morty's. No way was she going to allow Junior to ambush her. Being back on his radar put him back on hers.

She unlocked and opened their room door. Like normal, it slammed against the wall.

Apricot light from the parking lot illuminated Brit asleep in her bed.

"Sorry, Brit," Evanee whispered and shut the door. Blackness closed around her. Their room was never dark. "Brit? Are you okay?" Her heart twitched like a rabbit's nose searching for the scent of a predator, finding it just as the hawk's talons pierced its flesh.

"She won't bother us." Junior's voice came from right next to her.

Evanee's breath hitched in her throat. An odd hic-
cupping noise squeaked from her mouth. She careened
forward into the room, away from Junior.

"Whajadoter." The words fell out of her mouth too
fast to make sense. "What. Did. You. Do. To. Her?"

No answer.

She spoke around her gritted teeth. "What did you
do to her?"

No sound, except for the semis outside.

"Answer me!" she shouted. But he didn't answer. His
silence an answer all its own. "Did you kill her?" She
gagged on the question, already knowing the answer.

He'd killed Brittany.

Poor Brittany. All she ever wanted was the same
thing Evanee did. To get ahead enough to leave Sundew,
to move somewhere new where she didn't have to live
like a roach, where she didn't have a past, where she'd
be anonymous. "Why? She never did anything to you."

"She was your friend." His tone was flat, emotionless.

He had killed Brittany because they were friends.
Maybe Evanee should feel guilty about that, but the only
emotion she had was anger. He wouldn't get away with
it. She wouldn't let him.

Step One: Draw him away from the door.

Step Two: Escape.

Step Three: Talk to the police, but they'd just sweep
everything under the rug. Maybe the media would be
the better option. No matter what, she'd get justice for
Brit. Only after justice had been handed to Junior would
she allow herself to break down and feel guilty for causing Junior to take Brit's life—because in the end, it *was*
her fault.

"I'm calling the police." She hoped her threat would draw him away from the door. She lunged across the dark room, her arms in front of her, blindly searching for the phone that always sat on the nightstand between their beds.

Her knee cracked into the stand. She pitched forward, smacked the lamp. It clattered to the side, then fell to the floor. She swept her fingers over the nightstand.

Nothing was there.

Nothing.

Ice slid down her spine. He'd taken it. Of course, he had.

Sch. Sch. Sch. Fabric rustling. Right behind her. Junior's breath chuffed moist and hot against the back of her neck. It reminded her of a lion licking the gazelle before ripping its throat out.

At least he wasn't guarding the door anymore. Time for Step Two.

His arms closed around her, fastening her hands to her sides. She startled, but didn't fight him. A better opportunity would present itself. She just had to find it. And not let herself get scared.

Concentrate. Think. Don't let fear dictate your fate. Shut down your emotions—for now. There'd be plenty of time to freak *after* she got away from him.

He shifted so his mouth was at her ear. "I owe you an explanation." He spoke softly, almost whispering. "For everything."

For everything. Uh-huh. Like an explanation could magically take away all the years of pain and hurt and perversion. She curled her lips inward and bit down to keep from smart-assing back at him.

"You saw the picture in my box. But I don't think you understand."

"It was Mom and Rob's wedding photo. What more is there to understand?" Her tone was too high.

"Darlin', you should talk to your mom before it's too late. She can explain better than I can. All I know is she owed a debt, not of money, but of life to my dad. She paid that debt by marrying him and giving you to me."

"What's that mean—she owed a debt of life?" Part of her was trying to assimilate all the information into something that wasn't malicious and sick.

"That's between your mom and my dad. Dad's primary rule was that you were never to know, but Mom says we're adults now and can make our own rules."

He'd actually talked to Mom about *them*? Like they were a couple or something? *Sick. Fucking sick.*

He delicately kissed her ear. "That photo is more than their wedding photo. It's *our* wedding photo too." Junior's words hung in the air.

Bile sloshed the sides of her stomach, and her mind ripped wide open. Memories, terrible ones she'd never wanted to remember, flashed into existence again. Memories of begging, crying, screaming for Mom when Junior was hurting her. And Mom never once intervened. Never once admitted anything was wrong. Never allowed Evanee to talk about it.

Her insides spasmed. Her bladder burned with the need to release.

"You are mine. No one else's. And I'm done waiting for you."

Stop! She silently screamed to the memories. Later

they could take over and ravage her as badly as Junior had in the past, but not now.

Focus. Concentrate. Escape. She had to escape.

He nuzzled her neck. "We can start over. I can be tender. I can be loving. Mom says that's what you want."

Mom said to be tender? What the fuck planet was her mother living on? Did either of them really think that simply offering to be nice would melt her into a warm, pliant puddle?

No. No. No. Junior be kind? To her? Impossible.

Another of his mind games. But deep down in the darkest corner of her soul, she knew he'd at least told one truth. She had been sacrificed to him.

His mouth moved over her neck, then began sucking her skin. Maybe if she could uncoil some of the tension in her muscles, he might think she was into it and maybe he'd let his guard down. And maybe that would give her an opportunity to escape.

He kept one arm around her, still pinning both her arms at her sides, but moved his hand up to cup her breast.

Tension gripped all of her muscles. She waited, expecting the pinching, grabbing, pulling, but his touch was tender, almost reverent.

"Relax," he whispered against her skin.

"I'm trying," she snapped, then changed her tone. "This is new to me."

"This time will be different."

No, it wouldn't. It was going to end like it always did. Either she'd fight him off until she escaped. Or he'd hurt her.

She endured his touch. Kept her mind away from the sensation of it and instead became vigilant about her surroundings. The rumble of semis outside—one had just pulled out of the lot. She closed her eyes and visualized her room and their position in it—standing between the beds. Sweat filmed her skin.

His hand moved away from her breast, trailed down her stomach, pushed into her shorts.

An idea bolted into her awareness. If she timed this just right, she'd be out the door in less than ten seconds. Her heart convulsed like it was being repeatedly electrocuted.

She raised one leg, rested her foot on the edge of the nightstand, and opened her thigh for him.

"Ahh…see. This is nice." His hand moved lower and lower. She shut off the sensation of him touching her and counted. One one-thousand. Two one-thousand. Three one-thousand. Four one-thousand. Five one-thousand.

She groaned, trying to create a sound of pleasure, rather than one of repulsion, and arched back into him. He braced, just like she wanted, giving her the leverage to lift her other leg to the nightstand.

She pushed off it into him with every bit of strength she possessed.

He stumbled back in the space between the beds, taking her with him.

Let me go, she wanted to shout, but shouting would take extra energy and she needed every bit she had to get out the door and away from him.

She felt the moment when he lost his battle with balance. It meant freedom. Her moment of escape.

In midair, she twisted to the side, out of his grip, and landed on her hip beside him. Pain detonated, and every bone clattered from the impact. The agony was too great to move. Could she even walk?

She'd fucking crawl if she had to.

She was a jumble of knees and hands and feet, propelling herself toward the hopeful crack of light that framed the ill-fitting door. The initial burst of pain had already faded. If she could just get her feet underneath her. Knee, hand, knee, foot, hand—

A weight landed on her back. She went down on all fours again. Her arms gave out. She slammed cheek first into the floor. The blow sloshed her brain. She couldn't move.

Junior turned her over. Pinned her hands above her head.

"I wanted this time to be different." He spoke softly. A drop of spittle landed on her cheek. "You chose this. Not me. Remember that."

"Lathan!" His name burst from her lips in a scream that split the pain in her head, then doubled it.

Junior's grip on her wrists tightened. "Don't ever say his name."

"Lath—"

Junior clamped his hand over her mouth, grinding his palm against her lips. Skin tore; blood rushed across her tongue, dripped down her throat.

A warm, moist circle settled over her nose. What was that?

His mouth. He covered her nose with his mouth.

Fear slammed into her so hard she bucked from its impact.

He blew into her nose.

The moisture choked her, burning like she'd gotten

water in her sinuses. She thrashed against his hold, but his mouth was suctioned to her face. Her lungs expanded larger and larger. Pressure threatened to rip her wide open.

—∿∿—

Lathan knocked on her room door.

It was late. Too late. Past midnight. And yet, here he was.

The air was heavy with diesel and fried food from the restaurant across the parking lot. Morty's itself smelled foul. A combination of mildew and rot. How could she stand living here? How could anyone stand living here?

"Honey. Uh, Evanee." Her name felt weird in his mouth. "It's me, Lathan. We need to talk."

From the moment she'd left him and walked into her room, something had felt wrong, but he'd ignored the feeling. Or tried to. Now he was acting all OCD over her. Obsessed about her safety. Compelled to make sure she was all right. Disordered enough to do it at midnight.

He banged a little harder on the door, feeling the hollow echo underneath his gloved knuckles. "I know it's late. I just need a minute. Then I'll leave."

He waited. She might be sleeping. She might be telling him through the door to come back tomorrow, and he couldn't hear her. He leaned in, sticking his damaged ears to the crack, trying to make them listen.

Her sweet honey scent floated to him. God, he loved her smell. He inhaled deeply and found garlic and motor oil and gasoline mixed with her.

Garlic? Motor oil? Gasoline?

Junior's name slammed into his mind harder than

a baseball bat upside the head. Adrenaline, or maybe it was fury, gripped every muscle to the point of pain. Only one thing was going to take care of that particular pain. Killing Junior.

Lathan went through the door. He didn't remember how he got through it; he just went from outside to inside.

It took him less than a picosecond to catalog the scene. What he saw nearly slayed him.

Junior lay over Honey, holding her arms above her head, even though she wasn't fighting, wasn't moving. His hand over her mouth. His mouth over her nose. *Her nose?* What the fuck was he doing to her? Junior raised his head and looked directly at Lathan.

A smile stretched across Junior's lips. The smile of someone who savored his dominance. The smile of someone who got jacked off by it.

"You don't touch her." The words ripped from his throat like a snarling cornered coon.

He was on top of Junior before his brain even sent the message to his body, grabbing him by his shirt, dragging him off her, away from her. Junior tried to hit him, but the blows were less than effectual. Lathan tossed him onto the floor in a dark corner of the room. He kicked into the dark, packing all the force of his fury into the movement. He connected. One. Two. Three. Four. That should keep Junior down for a while.

He turned to Evanee.

She lay in the patch of orangish light spilling in from outside. Her chest bellowed up and down in giant movements. He knelt next to her.

"What did he do to you?"

Her eyes were wild, and fear rolled off her.

"I'm here now. He won't hurt you anymore." To keep that promise, he needed to get her out of there. No telling when Junior might get a second wind.

He scooped her up in his arms. She felt so good he buried his face in her hair, inhaling deeply as he stood. She turned into his neck and fisted his shirt in her hand. He ran from the room, heading for the restaurant across the parking lot.

He wanted to punch himself in the head for not listening to the warning in his gut. He'd known. He'd fucking known something bad was going to happen. And what did he do? Spent hours driving around until he stopped—a-*fucking*-gain—at the carving. The giant, snarling bear sculpted from one big-assed hunk of wood that stood atop a hill outside town. He'd wasted an hour staring at that carving and asking himself why he felt compelled to visit the thing so damned often. Just like every other time, he got no answers.

He shouldn't have squandered his time on such a useless activity. He should've been watching out for her. Protecting her. He'd fucking known Junior would make a play for her. He just hadn't thought it would be so soon.

"I'm sorry. I'm so sorry. I should've been here sooner. It's my fault. My fucking fault." The words leaped from his mouth before he could contain them.

At least she was alive. Everything else they could deal with. They. Because he was going to act like a tattoo and permanently attach to her. There wouldn't be a *next time* when it came to Junior. Or if there was, there wouldn't be a *Junior* after next time.

"Call 911," he yelled the moment he pushed through

the door of Sweet Buns and Eats. A trucker three booths in had just stood. Lathan shoved the table full of dishes back with his leg and sat in the empty booth with Evanee.

"Honey?" He tilted her face up to him.

She was purple. Fucking purple. Gasping for air like it was in low supply.

"Shh… Honey. Breathe. Just breathe."

Her eyes were ravaged, consumed by an agony that went deeper than any physical pain ever could. Her mouth was a horrifying smear of crimson that wasn't lip gloss.

Fury burned through him. He shook from the power of it.

Cold steel pressed against his temple. *A gun. Shit. Fucking damn.*

Lathan cut his gaze to the side, expecting to see Junior, but a Mr. Clean impersonator held the shotgun to his head. Mr. Clean backed off a few inches and Lathan faced him.

"…her down real easy and I'll… arrested without putting any holes in…head."

Lathan didn't catch all the words, but he got the gist. He didn't blink away from the threat. "I'm not letting her go."

Burning cinnamon flowed off the guy.

Honey straightened, her backbone going rigid one vertebra at a time. She spoke, but Lathan didn't attempt to hear the words. He was locked on Mr. Clean and the gun aimed at him, which was too close to being aimed at her.

Anger snarled Mr. Clean's lips and clenched his jaw,

but his eyes were full of soft tenderness for Honey. The guy had a fucking thing for her.

Lathan pulled her in closer, and she responded by looping her arm around his neck.

Mr. Clean lowered the shotgun barrel to the floor. Only then did Lathan's attention go to her words.

"...killed her."

Killed her? Did he hear that right?

"Stay in here." Mr. Clean pointed at the floor and ran out the door toward the motel.

A waitress—dressed in shorts so skimpy they might've actually been underwear—approached the table. "Evan...okay? Is there anything I can do?"

Evan. The waitress called her Evan. Was that a nickname? Lathan craned his neck in an unnatural position to see Honey's response.

"I'm okay now, Amy."

Amy tucked a stray strand of hair behind Honey's ear. "Is it true? What you said about Junior?"

A cop car slid into the parking lot. Its red-and-blue lights danced around the diner. Honey twisted in Lathan's arms to look out the window at the officers exiting the vehicle and heading toward the restaurant. Fear scented the air around her in a garlic cloud.

Mr. Clean emerged from the motel room and waved the cops toward him.

"Why are you afraid of the police?" Lathan asked.

"Junior's dad is the sheriff. I'm in trouble. You're probably in trouble."

Yeah. She'd told him that earlier, but he'd filed that under not-important information. Great. He'd probably have a chance to meet Senior, who had to be just as bad as Junior. Except Senior was in a position of power. That made him lethal.

"Everything will be fine." He shifted to get his cell from his pocket and quickly texted Gill.

Lathan: Probably going to be arrested. Things might get ugly.

He shoved his phone back in his pocket without waiting for a response. "Gill's on his way. He'll take care of everything."

Amy leaned against the booth across from them. "I can't believe it…just handed over your checks ten minutes ago."

Lathan watched every word Amy spoke. And then it clicked.

Honey was a waitress. Not a whore. Relief and guilt waged a small battle for supremacy. Relief won.

"You work here?" he asked.

"Yeah." She glanced away from him, and a small puff of spoiled dairy hit his nose. She was ashamed of her job. And he hadn't helped matters with how he'd acted earlier.

"Evan, you've got…" Amy motioned toward her mouth.

Honey wiped her hand over her lips. Blood smeared her fingers. All the color that had built back up in her face drained away.

Lathan covered her hand with his. "Don't look at it. You keep those twin sapphires on my face. Is there someplace we can get you cleaned up?"

She nodded.

"Show me." He helped her stand, putting his arm around her to ensure she was steady on her feet. It was only then that he noticed the diner full of men. All of them staring at either Amy or Honey, lust in their eyes. He shifted to shield her with his body.

She led him down a hallway that ran alongside the kitchen to a tiny bathroom.

"Close your eyes." Without hesitation she obeyed, but reached out and gripped his shirt like she was afraid he'd try to sneak off. "I'm right here. Not going anywhere."

He wet a towel and began cleaning her face. Her lips were puffy and painful looking on the outside—probably mangled meat on the inside. Her right cheekbone had a lump the size of an egg on it.

He tried to be gentle, but she still winced and flinched—and it tore at his heart.

When he'd wiped away the last of the blood, he tossed the wad of towels in the bathroom trash and gathered her in his arms. She fit like she'd been chiseled especially for him.

Holding her took the edge off the rage simmering inside him. If she was in his arms, he couldn't find a knife from the kitchen and cut Junior into little pieces. That's exactly what he wanted to do.

He knew that was how it would end. He *would* kill Junior.

He smelled a man approaching and turned. A cop. With his hand hovering over his weapon.

"Step back from her and raise your hands in the air."

Chapter 6

JAMES ADJUSTED THE FOCUS ON THE VIDEO CAMERA, THEN stepped back to view the entire scene. The orange bulb in the porch light cast an intimate glow akin to candle-light. Color and shadow contrasted sharply with each other as they fought for dominance on Subject 85's trembling body.

She was bound, staked to the ground, spread-eagled on the hard-packed earth just outside her back door.

He walked over to her, careful not to block the cam-era's view. This was how he trained, how he developed his skill, how he learned to catch killers—by being a killer. By watching and re-watching the recordings. Cataloging his reactions, his thoughts, his frame of mind. And those of all of his subjects too.

"I *want* you to escape." He spoke slowly so Subject 85 could understand his every word. He checked the time on the clock he'd placed next to her face. Six p.m. "I'll give you thirty minutes. If you escape by six thirty, you are free to go. If not—" He bent down and lightly grasped the pinkie toe on her left foot with his gloved fingers. "I will begin here, breaking every bone in your foot, then your ankle, then your leg until I reach your hip. Then I will switch to your right foot."

Her pupils were fully dilated from terror. Sweat soaked her face, mingling with tears and yellow ropes of snot. Duct tape covered her mouth. Her cheeks puffed as she pushed air out her nose. Her hips thrust off the ground. She raised her head, searched around her for help.

"Popping a hip out of its socket isn't difficult if you know the right angle to apply pressure. I will then remove your intestines. You will be alive during this entire process—"

Subject 85 wailed. A buzzing noise sounded from a loosened section of duct tape. It reminded him of the *ti-ti-ti-ti* sound his ten-speed bike made when he was a kid. No matter how much noise she made, it didn't matter. The nearest neighbor was seven miles away.

He waited until she finished. "Do not worry. I will leave your heart and lungs untouched. Then I will begin breaking the bones in your left hand. Then your right."

She strained against the bonds, hips thrusting. A vein in the middle of her forehead bulged with blood. She might pop a vessel before he had a chance to get that far.

"I know this is terribly distressing, but if the pain becomes too great, all you have to do is ask, and I will put you down in a humane manner."

She froze as that last little bit of information worked its way through her adrenaline-soaked brain.

"Before we begin, I will remove the tape over your mouth. I would never forget that. You may start."

Subject 85 redoubled her struggle for freedom.

James sat on the wicker settee, facing the camera's viewfinder to wait. A clean-room suit covered his body and hair. His fingerprints were hidden inside the latex gloves he wore. Thick boot covers guaranteed he would not leave a viable footprint. There would be no trace of him when he left this home.

For a few moments, he watched Subject 85, but her struggle was the same struggle he'd witnessed from eighty-four other subjects. The struggle to survive. But tonight he just wasn't engaged.

"I am feeling very disinterested in this entire process." He spoke directly to the camera, then turned his attention skyward. The sky was different here in West Texas. No bright city lights muted its brilliance; no sounds distracted him from its dark beauty. Pastel-colored stars flickered like sequins on a dancer's dress. The night's version of color was more astounding for its understated glory than the gaudy blue of day.

Subject 85 screamed and screamed and screamed. Until she choked on the blood of her raw vocal cords. A fine mist of red blew from her nostrils.

A coyote answered her, howling from no more than a quarter mile away. Might have smelled blood in the air and come to investigate.

James turned his attention back to the camera. "I don't need this anymore. I already know enough."

Until he spoke the words aloud, he hadn't realized how done he really was. He was bored with killing. But as illogical as it sounded, he was almost afraid to stop. From the moment of his first kill, it was as if he and Death had formed an alliance. He fed Death, and Death fed him. Would his profiler skills still be as sharp without Death?

The only obstacle was Lathaniel Montgomery. Somehow, the special skills consultant had managed to link thirty-eight of James's experiments and claimed an active serial killer was on the loose. Impossible. Lathaniel couldn't know. Each experiment was carefully choreographed so nothing would link it to any of the previous ones. There were variations in race, sex, age, body type, hair color, religion, socioeconomic status, sexual orientation, geographic location, mode of death, and method of discovery—he'd made sure of that. There was no signature, no modus operandi.

But Lathaniel wouldn't drop it. He had tried to get to Dr. Jonah to convince him of the presence of a new serial killer. That's when James started doing his own research. The layers of secrecy surrounding Lathaniel made it difficult to find answers. Why the secrecy? It had taken months of surveillance just to find Lathaniel's home.

From where he sat, he could smell the warm tang of blood and sweat. A smell he was familiar with, but one he wasn't particularly fond of. Subject 85's wrists and ankles were shredded. Blood dripped from her wounds. The thirsty ground soaked up each drop.

The wireless receiver in his ear pinged. Work most likely. They were the only ones who ever called him.

He walked over to Subject 85. "I apologize for the interruption. I'm getting a phone call that I need to take." He stepped on her throat, cutting off her air and the last of her voice. He tapped the button in his ear. "Hello."

"Eric here. We caught an interesting one."

"Yeah?" James held his tone at the mildly interested level.

"I'll need you and your father at Quantico in the morning to generate the profile."

"Dad's not available until early afternoon." Actually,

James wouldn't be back in the area until late morning, and since father and son were a package deal, always working cases together, Dad was the perfect excuse. Nobody questioned the great Dr. Jonah.

James's skill was overshadowed by his father's fame. But he was his father's equal in every measure and more, so much more. With the way he trained, his knowledge ran deeper, to a more visceral level than any other profiler's. Someday, when his father chose to retire, James would be the best the world had ever known.

"Want a teaser?" Eric's tone carried a hint of humor.

"Sure."

"You familiar with the Janie Carson case?"

Intimately. "Yes."

"Janie Carson's eye was found in—"

Tension grabbed James's neck and squeezed all the muscles in a painful embrace.

Found. They couldn't have found it. It was hidden in—

"—in Ohio."

You fool. You have the wrong eye. "Ohio?" He kept his tone at the mildly confused level.

"Yeah. Lathan Montgomery called it in. It's a bizarre story."

Lathaniel Montgomery. The name just kept coming up. It couldn't be simple coincidence that the special skills consultant *claimed* to have found Janie Carson's eye. Why would he make such a claim anyway when DNA was going to prove it wasn't? What did Lathaniel have to gain by such a bizarre assertion?

"Can't wait to hear the full story," James said instead of asking for the details. Self-control was his god.

"Later." Click. Eric was gone.

James tapped the receiver to disconnect from the call.

He stepped back from Subject 85. Shades of purple mottled her face. She snorted in nostrils full of air.

"Six thirty-two." He bent down and pulled the duct tape from her mouth. "Time to get to work."

Subject 85 screamed—at least tried to. The best her shredded vocal cords could do was a harsh whisper.

He removed two pairs of snub nose pliers from his gear—one to hold the toe bones, one to snap them—and began.

Chapter 7

THE GLARE FROM THE FLUORESCENT LIGHTS IN THE interrogation room burned Evanee's eyes. She rubbed them for the millionth time, but didn't find any relief. It wasn't the lights. It was the waiting and the worrying. Waiting for Sheriff Rob—a.k.a. the stepdad from hell—to make an appearance. Worrying about what was happening to Lathan.

She probed the cuts on the insides of her lips with her tongue, welcoming the sting of pain.

"Why don't you tell me what really happened in that room?" Hal asked for what seemed like the millionth time.

"Seriously, Hal?" She couldn't contain the frustration in her voice or the way her eyes rolled.

"It's Detective Haskins."

"It was Hal's Your Pal when you were running for student body president."

"We're not kids anymore."

"Yeah, but you're still best buds with Junior, aren't you? Does he have to call you Detective Haskins?" She set both her arms on the table, showing him the murky bruises cuffing her wrists.

He averted his gaze.

"Why won't you document *my* injuries? You want to charge Lathan for assaulting Junior, but what about charging Junior for assaulting me?" God, it felt strange to say those words aloud. Sacrilegious almost. Which was stupid. "What about Brittany? Have you talked to her? Junior did something to her." She'd found out Brittany was alive after they'd gotten to the station. "And what about my car? He stole it from me. He claimed to be repo-ing it, but the bank never issued the order. I bet if you drove behind his shop, you'd find it."

"Sheriff Malone isn't going to put up with you spreading rumors about Junior." Hal's voice softened a bit. "How could you do this to your mother? This is going to kill her. For what? A tattooed freak you just met. Are you really going to choose him over your suffering mother?"

Chose him over my suffering mother?

Hell yeah.

What had Mom done for her? Given her to Junior. That was unforgiveable.

Lathan cared for her. Believed her. Protected her.

"No one is going to buy this." Hal gestured to the statement she'd written out hours ago. "When we find evidence that proves you're lying, you'll be looking at jail time. You know what jail is like? Ever had lice?"

She tuned him out as he went on about the epidemic of lice the female inmates spread among one another.

Nothing he could say was going to change her story. She *would not* let Lathan be punished for helping her. Deep down, in the gut of her guts, she knew something very bad would happen to him if he stayed here.

Hal's phone chirped. He read the screen, scowled, and then flipped the report closed. "You can go."

"Where's Lathan?"

"Go. Before I change my mind." He jerked his thumb over his shoulder, indicating the closed door.

"I'm not leaving without him. Where is he?"

"Where is she?" Lathan's voice boomed somewhere outside the door. "I'm not leaving without her."

Her soul smiled. She was as important to him as he was to her. She practically ran for the door.

Lathan barreled down the hallway toward her. His gaze ranged over her, cataloging her from tippy top to toes. He reached for her, an invitation for her to bury her face against him and let him be strong for her. Evanee stared at his chest, at the spot over his heart where she would rest her head, and couldn't resist. She was inside his arms and never wanted to leave.

That was the only place the world made sense, where she made sense.

"You're coming home with me." Even though he'd made a statement, she heard the tiniest hint of question.

She nodded, rubbing her cheek against his shirt. "I am." She wouldn't have been able to go back to Morty's. Not only was the door destroyed, but bad memories lived in that room and they'd attack her the moment she walked in.

Twenty minutes later, Gill parked them in Lathan's driveway. The defend-Lathan adrenaline that she'd been galloping on had bucked her off five minutes ago, but there was one thing she needed to do before she could allow herself the oblivion of sleep. Wash Junior's touch off her skin.

Inside, she went straight to the bathroom.

Alone. For the first time in hours. But she wasn't really alone. Junior was in her head. His words a recording stuck on repeat, playing over and over and over. Had been since the moment he'd spoken them. The only difference was their volume. At the police station, their volume had been low, but now that she was alone, his words thundered through her mind.

Your mom owed a debt, not of money, but of life, to my dad. She repaid him by marrying him and giving you to me. You were a wedding present. A wedding present.

"A wedding present." Speaking the vile words, tasting the rot of them in her mouth, suddenly made them real. "Stop. Just stop. Stop thinking. Just stop. Stop. Stop."

The thoughts wouldn't go away, wouldn't retreat, and wouldn't relent.

She stripped off her clothes, turned the hot water knob as far it would go, and moved under the spray. Molten lava poured over her, cauterizing Junior off her skin, but nothing could boil his words from her brain.

She repaid him by marrying him and giving you to me.

Mom *gave* her to Junior. Gave. Willingly. Voluntarily. As if Evanee had been no more than a stick of chewing gum. Her mom had known. Had condoned.

Everyone had known. Mom, Rob, Junior. What about Thomas? Did he know? Had her baby brother known and done nothing?

She shoved that thought deep down into a cold, dark place—the compost bin where she stored all the bad memories, keeping them dark and cool and waiting for them to break down into essential elements. Elements that would eventually fertilize and heal her.

A sound escaped from that place, rumbling up and out through her body. Hiding behind the sound was a lifetime of pain. Her knees buckled, and she folded to the slate floor. Beneath the scalding shower spray, she hugged herself and rocked. She wanted to cry, but couldn't. She wanted to be angry, but couldn't. She wanted to die, but couldn't—wouldn't—do that either. She wanted to feel something—anything—other than the obliterating agony that threatened to eviscerate her, to rip her wide open, dumping parts of her all over the floor.

"Honey?" Gentleness and concern were braided into Lathan's voice.

The steady thrum of water was interrupted. Lathan moved under the spray—clothes and all. He wrapped a towel around her, covering her nakedness, her vulnerability.

She looked up at him. Water washed over her face, stung her eyes, and dribbled into her mouth. "Mom gave me to him." The tears she couldn't cry soaked every word. "I was a wedding present. A present."

He didn't offer vacant words of comfort. His face said everything. His freckles recognized her vulnerability. His tattoo offered her protection. His eyes were a promise of devotion and affection.

He settled on the slate floor next to her—a silent offer to share her pain. She scooted the few inches to him and leaned against him, letting him cocoon her in his strength.

———

Austere, infinite whiteness surrounded Evanee.

The White Place.

After her last visit, no relaxation existed in the space. Intuitive fear bubbled up inside her. And then she felt it, felt the presence of evil. Fear wrapped its cold, dirty fingers around her. The skin on the back of her body tightened, flinching as if waiting for a blow. Her heart double-kicked against her sternum. *Duh-dum. Duh-dum.*

She snapped her eyes shut. "Wake up. Wake up. Wake up." Her voice boomed around her as if she were in an amphitheater hooked up to a thousand mikes. Knives of pain pierced her ears from the megaton volume.

The sound vanished. Gone. Not even an echo. Like it never existed.

Silence. Heavy and expectant.

The evil thing was still there. Behind her. Waiting.

Should she turn and face it? Or should she play the if-I-ignore-it, maybe-it-will-go-away game?

She'd never been fond of games.

She flung herself around before she could talk herself out of it.

A woman that wasn't a woman anymore—a monster—stood behind her.

The woman's head was cocked unnaturally to the side, ear touching shoulder. Brown stringy hair hung in her face, obscuring all but her mouth and one filmy eye that was locked on Evanee.

Dirt caked every crevice of the woman's naked body. Her enormous breasts sagged to her waist, like socks filled with pennies. Her left foot faced the wrong direction, heel toward Evanee, toes pointing backward.

Backward. Her foot was backward.

Abhorrence rolled through Evanee's stomach. Her throat opened. "Bbwwaa." The gagging sound crashed through the space. She clamped her lips closed. Every sound she made was a punishment. She forced her gaze away from the foot before she actually vomited. Her hearing wouldn't survive that particular cacophony of noise.

No movie monster could compare to the hideousness

of the woman standing in front of Evanee. She tried to back away, but hit something solid, something immense, and she knew the Thing that immobilized her last time had her again.

She tried to run, her muscles twitched, mimicking the action of running, but she remained motionless. Invisible fingers pried her eyelids wider open.

Not again. Please, not again.

Adrenaline shot through her system, burning a tail fire of energy, but she couldn't move. Her muscles, her innards, her eyeballs shook from the unexpressed pressure building. It hurt. Tears drizzled down her cheeks. That only made her mad. She wasn't a crier. Never had been. Crying solved nothing. And yet her body wept.

The woman's torso tilted to the side, head still stuck on her shoulder, her arms swimming through the air. She swung her backward foot forward, plunked it down. Then a relatively normal step. Then the mutated step.

The woman stopped in front of Evanee and opened her mouth, like she wanted to say something, but one of her front teeth fell out.

Duh-dum, duh-dum, duh-dum. Evanee's heart pounded a panicked rhythm. Maybe she'd have a heart attack and it would all be over.

No. She wanted—needed—to be with Lathan. A tiny bit of the pain and panic eased as she pictured his face. His tattoo. His freckles.

The woman bent, her breasts swinging wildly from her torso, and retrieved the tooth.

She reached into her dirty hair, fishing around under the locks, and pulled out a tangled mass.

Evanee's arm rose. But she wasn't in control of the

movement. The Thing that had her on lockdown moved her arm.

No. No. No. She screamed the words inside her head, fearful of making a sound. The woman carefully placed the hair in Evanee's palm, curling it into a nest, and then set the tooth in the center like a precious egg.

Evanee couldn't breathe.

"Montañas. Guadalupe. Parque. Nacional. Montañas. Guadalupe. Parque. Nacional." The woman pointed to herself as if that was her name.

The Thing released Evanee and she fell.

And fell. And fell.

Evanee slammed against the bed. She fought to sit up in the jumble of limbs—hers and Lathan's. Her body convulsed as if it were being electrocuted repeatedly. An absurd need to scream and release some of the suppressed energy came over her, but enough of her sanity remained to know that wouldn't be a good idea.

"What's wrong?" Lathan's voice in the dark. His arms around her. "Holy Jesus. You're shaking."

She clutched at him and sagged in the safety of his embrace.

"A nightmare. Another nightmare. It can't be like the last one. It can't. That can't happen again. It can't." The words rushed from her mouth.

"Honey, I can't hear you. I don't understand. Let me turn on the lamp."

She gripped him as tight as she could, knowing she'd twist off into crazed oblivion if he let her go. "It was only a nightmare," she yelled against his chest.

He winced, but his arms tightened around her.

Someone pounded up the stairs.

"What's going on?" Gill ran into the room, flicked the light switch.

More than light filled the room. Certainty filled her mind. She pulled back from Lathan and looked down at her fist.

She flung her fingers open. Hair. Tooth.

She screamed then. Couldn't contain it any longer.

"How the fuck…" Gill said, but his voice began to fade—or maybe she was fading. She felt an odd sizzling sensation inside her head. The world burst into blinding X-ray color, then went black.

—⁂—

Soft afternoon light filtered through the bedroom window. Evanee lingered in the delicious place between waking and sleeping, where dreams of anything were possible.

Reality finally drifted in, bringing unwanted memories with it.

Yesterday had been one long, slow swirl down the toilet bowl of life. Almost losing her job. Thinking Brittany was dead. Everything attached to Junior. Fighting for Lathan's freedom. And the cherry on the shit sundae—the nightmare.

Today was going to be a better day. Last night, when she'd felt the most broken, Lathan had pieced her back together, shifting the parts around in a combination that made her better than before.

She raised her arms above her head and squirmed around, lengthening every muscle in a long, luxurious stretch. A million different aches and pains should be screaming from her fight with Junior, but she felt surprisingly good. Stable in mind and body.

She got out of bed, used the bathroom, then headed downstairs to find Lathan. Like a smoker needs his cancer sticks, she needed Lathan. The world felt right when she was near him. The dude had healing properties or something.

At the bottom of the stairs, Evanee looked through the living room to the kitchen. Gill stood at the counter, typing into his phone. Part of her was grateful he'd shown up last night. Lathan's release probably had more to do with Gill's FBI status than her stubborn fight for him, but that still didn't make her want to socialize with him.

She turned to tiptoe back up the stairs.

"You're awake." Amusement sounded in his tone. He knew she'd been trying to sneak away and had called her on it.

She turned and stuck her tongue out at him. God, she couldn't stand how he looked. Too perfect. Too pretty. He reminded her of Junior. But he was Lathan's friend. And she should at least try to be cordial to him. "Where's Lathan?"

"Coffee's on." He indicated the half-full pot. "And we need to talk."

Great. Another *talk* with Gill. She didn't know him well, but she knew *talk* was his code word for interrogation. Three interrogations in three days. Gill, Hal, now Gill again. Had to be some sort of record.

"Where's Lathan?"

Gill poured her a cup of coffee, set it on the table. "Have a seat." He straddled a chair.

"I'm not moving until you tell me where Lathan is."
She crossed her arms spoiled-brat style.

"Working."

She hadn't thought about him having a job. Of
course he had a job. How much time had he taken off
just to help her? Maybe she should feel guilty about
that, but she just wanted to kiss him. "When will he
be back?"

"I don't know." The way Gill said the words made
her believe he really didn't know.

"Cream?" she asked and walked to the chair across
from him.

"He doesn't do dairy."

"Doesn't do dairy?"

When Gill didn't elaborate, she sipped the coffee and
tried not to grimace at its bitterness.

"Who gave you Janie Carson's eye?"

The cup slipped from her fingers, crashed to the table,
spilled. She jumped up to get a towel, but Gill put a hand
on her arm.

"Sit." His tone was warm. He began cleaning up the
coffee with a wad of paper towels.

She sat, not because she trusted him, but because at
this point she needed some answers for herself. "Janie
Carson. She was a *real* little girl?"

"DNA preliminaries point to the eye being hers,"
he said and tossed the wad of wet towels into the trash
bin. "We're running some other tests—checking out a
few other things—but that's the one thing we are fairly
certain about."

She met and held his gaze. "I already told you everything I know about the eye."

He seemed to calculate her words before he spoke. "What about last night? What was that?"

"Another one of *those* dreams." Another one. She'd had two of them. What if she kept having them? What if she had one every time she slept? Good-bye, sanity.

"Tell me everything."

Just like the first time, he picked apart every sentence and tried to trip her up. But the truth was easy to remember. Finally, he asked her write the dream down. After she finished, he read over her words.

"Lathan says you aren't involved in the Janie Carson case or whatever case the hair and tooth belong to."

"Lathan says? Does he work for the FBI too?"

"What Lathan does is nobody's business but his own." A bit of the asshole tone crept back into Gill's voice, and the way he glared at her warned her never to ask again.

What was going on? Was Lathan some top-secret spy or something? Her own personal James Bond. A smile ticked up her lips. No wonder she felt so safe with him.

"Junior drugged Brit—your roommate. Slipped her a roofie." Gill's voice was calm again.

The smile faded. Poor Brittany. "Is she all right?"

"She's not physically harmed."

"You know nothing's going to happen to Junior. Nothing ever does." The dull sound of resignation took over her vocal cords. Time for a subject change. "What time is it?"

"Two forty-five."

She had just enough time to arrange a new room, take a shower, and get over to Sweet Buns. "You really don't know when Lathan's going to be back?"

"I don't." Gill sounded sincere.

"I hate to ask this of you, but can you take me to work?"

"Call off today," he said, as if her job were no more important than a grain of sand on a beach.

"No."

His head snapped up at her abrupt answer.

"If I'm not at work tonight, I'm fired. If I'm fired, I'm homeless in two days." She wished she was exaggerating, but she wasn't.

"How do I know you're not going to skip town?"

"I don't have a car. Junior took it, and the police won't ask him about it. I don't have any money. And if I wanted to skip town, I would've hopped in one of the long-haul semis and been gone by now."

"Lathan wanted you to wait for him." Distaste crossed Gill's features as he spoke.

Right there was part of his problem with her. He didn't want Lathan to want her. Why? Gill didn't look like the type to have a boy crush on Lathan. So that wasn't it. She wasn't exactly a pillar of Sundew society. But she wasn't the lowest *gutter roach* either—to use Gill's term. She worked. Supported herself. No longer relied on anyone for anything. That was respectable. Right?

Or did Gill somehow know about her past with Matt? No, he couldn't. Everyone speculated, but no one knew for a fact, except her and Matt. And neither of them was likely to tell anyone.

"Trust me. I'd rather stay here than wait tables, but I need the money."

"If Lathan's pissed, I'm blaming it on you."

"Fine. I just need to get my stuff." She ran upstairs to

get her clothes. Lathan had washed and dried them again. She wiggled into her shorts and the Ernie-approved shirt, but when she caught sight of her reflection in the mirror—breasts spilling from her cleavage—she put Lathan's T-shirt back on over everything.

She followed Gill out to his car. Neither of them spoke as he pulled out of the driveway and drove them through the isolated countryside toward town. The silence wasn't awkward, but it wasn't exactly friendly either.

"How much do you know about Lathan?" he asked when they reached the outskirts of Sundew.

"What do you mean?"

"I mean, do you know his birthday, his favorite color, his favorite food, what kind of childhood he had..." He rattled off an extensive list, all of which she didn't know. But somehow, none of it mattered.

She kept quiet.

"Listen, I don't mean be a dick, but my top priority is protecting Lathan."

Yeah, she knew how to read between the lines. "Protecting him from me?"

Gill gave one solid nod of confirmation. "Why are you messing with him?" he asked as he waited to make the left-hand turn into Sweet Buns parking lot.

She felt his gaze on her, studying her as if he expected the way she looked to give away some vital answer. "What do you mean?"

"He's a big, scary-looking dude, but he has the heart of a puppy. I don't want you messing with him."

"I'm not messing with him."

He turned to her, gave her a full-body scan—eyes

lingering on her bare legs. "Sleeping with him qualifies as messing with him."

Suddenly, the giant T-shirt dress and the clothes underneath felt invisible. "I'm not *sleeping* with him. I slept with him—the snooze, snore, snore kind of sleep."

Gill cocked an eyebrow at her. It was the same as calling her a liar. He parked in front of the diner. She opened her door.

"I don't know what your motives are, but if they are less than lily-white angel-babies, I'm going to find out. And the full force of the FBI will come down on you."

She got out of the car but left the door open, trying to formulate a response that didn't sound defensive, but she couldn't come up with anything.

Gill leaned over the passenger seat to see her. "There's a lot you don't know about him. Ask him about himself. Ask him about his hearing. Ask about his childhood."

She slammed the door and walked toward Morty's.

Gill might be a big and mighty FBI guy, but he wasn't subtle. She recognized his last words for what they were. A setup. He thought something about Lathan's past would scare her off. Nothing about him could scare her off. The only thing she really feared was her own past.

Lathan left his office, shutting the door behind him, then stepped up to the retinal scanner, and waited for the internal light to switch from green to red—locked. He stepped off the porch and started down the short trail back to his house.

His office looked like a hunter's cabin in the middle of the woods. Except that it had security rivaling a bank and an underground air-filtration system so there would be no scent contamination among the evidence.

He massaged his chest. It had ached all day. Well, not really all day, but from the moment he'd left the house, it'd felt like he had a bad case of indigestion and it hadn't eased one bit. In fact, it had only gotten worse. He saw a roll of Tums in his future. He hated to eat things like that, but sometimes they were all that helped.

When he walked through the back door, he saw Gill at the table, typing on his laptop.

Lathan set the evidence bag with hair and tooth inside on top of the fridge—out of Little Man range—and handed Gill the reports. "You're going to find this interesting."

Gill leafed through the pages.

While Lathan waited for the moment when everything clicked for Gill, he rubbed the pain in his chest.

Gill sat up straight. "The Strategist? Never saw that coming."

"Me either."

"So Janie Carson and the hair-and-tooth victim are both linked to the Strategist." Gill seemed to be speaking the words out loud as if that would make them more believable. He scribbled a note on a pad of paper next to him. "One thing the lab noticed was the slower rate of decomp on the eye comparative to Janie Carson's body. They're running tests to see if a preservative might've been used. We might even be able to find a brand and then get a list of purchasers. The eye could give us the lead we need to find him."

And all because Honey had a dream. "You get me some comparison samples, and I can tell you which preservative was used."

"If the tests are inconclusive, then we'll bring you in." Gill sat back in his chair and pinned Lathan with a sharp look—the kind that would cut a lesser man. But Lathan had a thick skin. "Don't you think this is strange? She claims to be having dreams where she brings stuff back to reality, and that stuff just happens to be things from the Strategist's victims. And you just happen to be the only person who knows the Strategist exists." Gill shook his head. "I don't believe in coincidence."

"I don't either, but I'm telling you, we went to bed and she had nothing with her, but when she woke up, she had the hair and tooth. I can't explain it. I just know it happened."

Gill didn't say anything. There wasn't much to say. He had been there, had seen her reaction, her terror when she opened her hand. And when she passed out, Gill had been the one who thought she needed to go to the ER. It wasn't until she woke ten minutes later, teeth chattering from cold—just like Lathan told him she would—that Gill left the room. That was when the shift happened for Gill, when he started to believe.

"What I do is nearly impossible to explain. That's why we keep it so secret. What if she's got some weird thing like me?" Part of him felt sorry for her having to go through what she did, but part of him felt less alone too. Like he wasn't the only person with a freakish ability.

"I've been thinking the same thing. Have you ever heard of…?" Gill typed the letters in his phone and handed it to him.

ONEIROLOGY. Oh-nay-ruh-ology

"Say it five times in a sentence." Lathan put his hand on Gill's throat to feel the vibrations of the word.

"Oneirology is the scientific study of dreams. Oneirology is the scientific study of dreams…"

Lathan memorized the pattern of Gill's lips moving over the word, the way his mouth opened and closed, the length of the movement, and the vibrations under his fingers.

He put his hand to his throat and tried to form the word, looking to Gill for his accuracy.

"Close enough. Get this. There's an Institute of Oneirology just outside Sundew. Doesn't that seem bizarrely *coincidental*?"

"I wonder if she's been in contact with them." The knot in Lathan's chest clenched. He thumped on it with his fist.

Gill noticed his action but didn't say anything. "I'm wondering that too. While you were doing your thing with the evidence, I checked them out. Eric says they've got serious pull with Homeland Security, but couldn't find anything else."

"Why is a place that studies dreams involved with Homeland Security?"

"That's what I want to know too. I'm thinking we make an appointment for Evanee and ask them all our questions."

"I'll ask her about it when she wakes up."

"She's not here."

"What?" Surely he didn't understand that right.

"She asked me to take her to work."

The lump of pain in Lathan's chest felt like it was going to explode. He grabbed his keys off the counter.

"Junior's out there. The Strategist too. And the simple fact that she is somehow connected to his cases puts her danger. If anything has happened to her—"

He ran out of the house to his bike before he could think how to finish his sentence.

Chapter 8

LATHAN BLASTED THROUGH THE DINER'S DOOR. STOPPED. Scanned the place. No Honey. But he smelled her scent mixing with greasy food and the musky stench of male desire.

The whisper of last night's memories wrapped around his brain and squeezed. *Junior on top of her sucking at her face like a vampiric demon. Her, so small and fragile in the shower.*

His heart fell out of his chest and landed in his boots. He was supposed to keep her safe. That was his compulsion, his duty, his obsession. And he feared he'd failed. Again.

She emerged from underneath the counter, placing a bottle of Tabasco on her tray next to a platter of food.

His heart slingshotted out of his boots and lodged back in his chest. *Seeing* her safe just wasn't enough. Touching her was the only way to wash away the stain of panic that still colored the fringes of his world. Before he was even aware of it, he was halfway to her.

Honey delivered the food to a pumpkin-round man who stared at her chest like he was sitting at pervert's row in a strip club. He wasn't the only one. That musky stink Lathan had noticed when he walked in... All of it was for her.

He fisted his hands, gripping them so tight his knuckles popped. Oh, how satisfying it would be to rampage down the row of booths, systematically plucking out the eyes of every asshole that ogled her.

She turned. Surprise flared in her eyes at seeing him, and then she smiled a smile so radiant, it rivaled a sunrise. And that smile was aimed directly at him. A gift to him alone.

"Are you all right?" He stopped in front of her, looking her over. She looked safe. Whole. Healthy. Even her bruises from the night before had faded to mere shadows.

"I'm fine. I didn't mean to worry you, but I had to be at work at four."

Not knowing her work schedule was a mistake he wouldn't make again.

She grabbed his hand and led him down the row of booths. He should've taken his gloves off. He needed to feel her skin sliding against his.

She stopped at the last booth in the back. He slid in but didn't let go of her hand.

"What would you like?"

What would he like? He hadn't been in a restaurant since he was a small child. He couldn't eat food other people touched. Their scents affected the taste. He could smell every person who had sipped from a coffee mug or used a utensil. Could practically taste their mouths. His stomach rolled end over end.

"If you've got a paper cup, I'll have a coffee." The roasting process usually eliminated all traces of human touch from the beans. Usually.

"Be right back."

He hated to let her go, but he forced his hand open to allow her to walk away. That's when he became mesmerized by her skyscraper legs, by the perfectly rounded globes of her ass, by the sensuous sway of her hips in those hooker sexy shoes. No wonder every man lusted for her. She was sizzle-your-innards hot.

He tore the gloves from his hands. A desperate need rode him. He craved her skin against his like a crack addict craved white rocks.

She returned to his table with a Styrofoam cup, a lid, and the pot of coffee. "Black, right?"

He nodded, his voice buried far beneath the urge to touch her.

His palm found her just above the knee. Her skin was supple satin. She leaned into his touch, shifting closer to the opening of his booth.

The residual echoes of panic and fear evaporated. Only desire remained. His dick grew hot and heavy and uncomfortable in his jeans. The stupid thing sent a message up to his brain—*Kiss her*. His little brain took control, bypassing his big one.

Slowly, to show his intention, he reached up to her neck and drew her down. In her eyes, he saw himself. Saw the blur of the tattoo on his cheek and knew, in the deepest sense of knowing, that they were destined to inhabit the same space. Just as their lips touched, she closed her eyes, but he didn't. He watched her as he felt the softness of her mouth on his.

She licked the seam of his lips. More from a sense of surprise than any knowledge of kissing, he opened his mouth to her. Her tongue swept inside and met his. Warm, sweet honey exploded across his taste buds. She tasted as good as she smelled. He devoured her, felt her hand on his head, pulling him closer, grinding their mouths together in mutual hunger.

All his senses, except for hearing, were dominated by her. He tasted her honey. Smelled the warm sweetness of her desire. Felt her straining into his touch. All the while, he watched her beautiful face as he kissed her. He reveled in the sanctity of her.

He slid his hand up her thigh until his fingertips brushed the edge of her shorts. His dick was going to bust the zipper, but he couldn't stop. He wanted her. More than he'd ever wanted in his life. Her. Only her.

"Order up!"

Holy Jesus. Even *he* heard that.

She jumped away from him, sloshing coffee over the table. She blinked as if just waking from a dream, then winked—*winked*—at him and hurried to the kitchen window.

A giant smile cracked across his face. He probably looked demented, but he couldn't help himself. Not only had he finally had his first kiss, but she'd winked at him without regret or embarrassment at his ill-timed sprint toward first base.

From the kitchen window, Mr. Clean shot hate bullets directly at Lathan's head, but that did nothing to dim the wattage of his smile.

Lathan drank a barrel full of coffee while he waited for her shift to end and focused on his new hobby: watching her—and only her. His hands had begun to tremble from the caffeine overload, and he'd started to notice the SMs. Even though he'd had no problems controlling them since he met her, they now hovered at the periphery of his mind, testing the firmness of his boundaries.

Had to be the caffeine. He'd never drunk so much

coffee and been around people at the same time. Lesson learned. Too much caffeine affected his control.

He needed to leave, get away from the people before the SMs tried to take over, but he couldn't leave her alone, unprotected against Junior and the Strategist.

The vision in his left eye wavered, then disappeared as one of the trucker's memories played.

Her ass swayed, luscious in its movements as she walked away from him. She shouldn't be a waitress. She should be a stripper. He imagined her at a classy joint like Barely There. Topless. Perfect tits. Nipples tilting skyward just how he liked them. On the stage, she melted to her hands and knees and crawled toward him. She bowed low, lifting her ass in the air like a satisfied feline.

Lathan pinched his nose closed and inhaled sharply through his mouth. The SM was some asshole's memory of imagining her in a strip club. He tried to shove the SM out of his mind—focus on the diner—

Her tongue crooked, beckoning him like a finger. She cupped her full breasts, pinched her nipples.

No, those weren't her breasts. They were some asshole's imagination of what her breasts looked like.

Lathan shot to his feet, bumping against the table. *I need to get the fuck out of here before—*

Honey was in front of him. Her lips moved, but he couldn't concentrate on reading her words or even trying to hear them. He closed his arms around her, buried his nose in the skin of her neck, and sucked in her scent. The

SMs retreated as if they couldn't exist in the same space she did. She was a miracle. His miracle.

Her jaw moved against his chest, and he faintly heard her voice. He pulled back to see her words.

"What did you say?"

"Are you okay now?" She touched the space between his eye and his hairline and kept her gaze riveted on his left eye. "What happened?"

Holy Jesus. He had probably looked like he'd been possessed by the Antichrist. "I'm fine now."

He could practically see the questions lining up in her brain, and he didn't want to lie. "It's just something that happens sometimes. Not a big deal. Nothing to worry about." *Please, don't ask*, he pleaded with his eyes.

She must have understood because she changed the subject. "I just clocked out."

A woman emerged from the hallway next to the kitchen with a tray of food.

"That's Brittany. My roommate. Tonight's her first night. She's trying to stay busy by picking up this job. What happened with Junior scared her. Really scared her."

Really scared Honey too. And if Lathan was going to be completely honest, freaked him the fuck out. What had Junior been trying to do? Suck the soul out of her? He'd nearly succeeded.

"Junior is claiming she tried to roofie him but accidentally roofied herself. He's saying that I was trying to rob him and he was defending himself. And of course, the cops believe him."

He wished he could go back in time and wrap his hands around Junior's neck—and feel the delicate hyoid bone break as he crushed Junior's throat and extinguished his life. Instead, he tucked Honey into his side and walked down the row of booths toward the door. He needed some fresh air to calm the murderous impulses.

Outside, he stopped. "You can take your shoes off. Your feet must be killing you."

"You have no idea." She slipped the glossy black heels from her feet, then reached for his hand, tugging him gently. "Come on. I'll show you my new place. It's dilapidated, dirty, and definitely disreputable, but it's home. For now."

Inside her room, the noxious fumes nearly singed his nostrils. Sex. Drugs. Depraved acts that should be illegal. And that wasn't even mentioning the mice feces and cockroach dung. He breathed through his mouth, trying to block the stench.

Lathan stood in the middle of the room. No way could he sit on that ratty bedspread and have those smells stuck to his clothes. She sat on the edge of the mattress. He dragged the wooden chair from the corner and positioned it across from her.

"I know it's gross." The spoiled dairy scent of her embarrassment accompanied a sad smile. "You probably had better things to do than just sit there all evening, but I appreciate it. If I'd missed work today, Ernie would've fired me."

"He wouldn't fire you. He's got a thing for you."

She seemed surprised. "Why would you say that?"

"It's in the way he looks at you." Did she really not see it? "The way he shot hate bullets in my direction all night."

"That's just Ernie's normal face. He always looks like he wants to commit murder."

"Why don't you get a better job?" Even as the words left his mouth, he knew that was exactly the wrong thing to say.

Burning cinnamon filled the air. "Do you seriously think that I'd be working there if any other place in Sundew would hire me?"

Any words he could say were going to land him on dangerous ground. "Give me a moment." He left her sitting on the bed, went into the bathroom, got a faded but semi-clean washrag, soaped it up, and returned to the room with it and a towel. He might look weird still wearing gloves, but no damned way was he taking them off in this place.

He yanked the chair up close to her, sat down, then lifted her feet to balance across his legs, and washed the stench from the pavement and the carpet off her. Starting with her left foot, he massaged the red indentation cutting into her skin. "I hate to see you work so hard. I hate to see what it does to you."

"That wasn't exactly an apology, but you're forgiven." She closed her eyes, her head lolling to the side. "As long as you don't stop."

"Tell me what happened that you ended up at Sweet Buns." He stared at her, waiting for her to answer, but she didn't speak. He shouldn't have asked. Not when he couldn't give her any answers about himself.

"I don't have a lot of work experience." She didn't say anything for a minute. Slowly she began shaking her head—not an act of denial, but one of resignation. "You might as well know the truth. Do you know what a kitten is?"

A kitten? Did he read that right? The word *kitten*

didn't really fit in the conversation they were having. He hated asking people to repeat themselves, but that was the only way to understand. "Did you say *kitten*?"

"Yeah. Kitten. You know what a kitten is?" she repeated.

It seemed like some sort of trick question, but he couldn't find the trick. "A baby cat?" he asked hesitantly.

She smiled, the scarred side of her mouth tilting up while the other side angled down a bit, making her look oddly sad. "No, not like a baby cat. Kitten as in a young woman who is taken care of by a much older man."

Ooohhh. The implications of what she was about to say forced him back in his seat. But he didn't let go of her foot. Nope. He held on and kept the massage going, as much for him as for her. Touching her—even through his gloves—grounded him.

"When I hit eighteen, I was desperate to get out of the house. Away from Junior. Did you know he's my stepbrother?"

Lathan managed to make his head bob up and down on his shoulders. He wasn't sure he could've spoken if he'd needed to.

"I didn't have a job or money or friends—those things were all forbidden to me. But I needed out of there. I don't even remember how I heard about kittens. I just joined this kitten site and started chatting with some guys. I found a guy here in town—someone I knew of, someone who was rich and powerful in the community. I knew Junior would never mess with me if I was with him. We set up a meeting, and we...well... we hit it off, I guess. I became his kitten." She looked up at the stained ceiling tiles. "He took care of me. Got

me a place to live, a car, spending money. In exchange,
I'd be his eye candy at conventions, provide a haven
from his work, go on dates with him, and you know…
whatever he wanted."

Sex. She meant sex. The tangy scent of pine laced with
burning cinnamon—jealousy and anger—practically
seared his nostrils. He wanted to mutilate and murder this
older man who'd taken advantage of a vulnerable girl.

"Basically, I was a whore."

All his bad feelings evaporated. He couldn't hear
the self-loathing in those words, but he could see it on
her face. See that she thought less of herself because
she'd lived through desperate times that called for desperate measures.

"Honey, no." He tore off a glove and settled his bare
hand against the side of her face. Her skin was cool and
soothed him. Did she feel as comforted by mere touch
as he did? "Don't ever say that."

She looked him in the eye, and he could tell she was
determining whether to believe him or not.

"Were you safe from Junior with this guy?"

"Yeah. Junior and my stepdad wouldn't have dared
to mess with me."

"Then it was worth it. Right?"

Her gaze never left his. "I guess. It just makes me
feel—I don't know—not good about myself when I
think about it. Back to your question about how I ended
up working at Sweet Buns. When things ended, I had
nothing of my own. Everything was…"

Lathan couldn't read her last word—the guy's name.
Probably good he didn't know it anyway. He might be
tempted—if he thought too deeply about it—to seek him

out and… Yeah. That wouldn't end well. He slipped his glove back on and started in on her feet again.

"He was nice about it. Gave me a few months to find a job and a place to live. Gave me some cash. But no one wanted to hire me. I had no real job experience. Sweet Buns was it. On the bright side, the tips are great and it's a free commute to work."

She stopped talking, closed her eyes, and leaned back on her elbows while he worked over her feet, massaging her arches with his thumbs.

He focused on working out the deep cleft her shoes had made. When he looked up, she had an odd expression on her face.

He stilled his hands. "Am I hurting you?"

She shook her head, then lifted her hand to cover her mouth. The side of her jaw moved.

He heard the sound of her talking, but couldn't shift the odd pieces into words.

She was testing him—and he'd failed. She fucking knew he had hearing problems. Now would come the sympathy and the exaggerated lip movements and treating him like he'd lost his brain instead of his hearing. He set her feet on the floor and stood, trying to turn away, but she grabbed his arm. "Were you just going to keep it from me forever?"

Forever? She thought they'd have forever together, when he never dared to think beyond the moment? Each second she spent with him was a gift he'd never expected, when his entire existence had been dominated by his genetic anomaly.

"Why didn't you tell me?"

From the moment he'd awakened in the hospital after

the attack, he'd realized that having trouble hearing wasn't the worst thing. Dealing with everyone else was the problem. "I don't want your pity."

Her eyes snapped with anger. She smelled of burning cinnamon, not pity. "Good. Because I don't pity you. I'm pissed at you for not telling me. I feel like everyone was in on the secret except me. I just got done telling you about being a kitten. That wasn't easy for me. And you couldn't share this one thing about yourself?"

"I hate being treated differently."

"I hate being made a fool of."

"That was never my intention."

"What was your intention?"

"For you to know me first. Before my hearing problems. To see that I'm normal." The words rushed directly from his heart and out his mouth. Who the fuck was he kidding? Like the tattoo on his face made him normal. Or the SMs.

"So, you read lips?"

"Mostly. I hear some things but not others; there's no reason to it. The combination of reading speech and what hearing I have left works for the most part. Sometimes I miss a few words, but usually I understand everything from the context."

"Is it hard? Reading speech."

His parents, Gill, none of them had ever asked him that. "It takes a lot of concentration. Lots of words are formed inside the mouth, so I only understand them within the context of the sentence. Some words look exactly the same. The better I know a person, the easier it is for me."

"Have you had trouble reading my words?"

"Only a few times. I didn't know your name for a while. *V*'s and *f*'s look the same, and I'd never seen the name Evanee before." Whoa. He hadn't exactly written a novel on being hearing impaired, but he'd just talked about it more with her than he had with anyone else. It felt kinda…good. To not hide it. To be able to be himself.

"So that's why you called me Honey. Because you didn't know my name." Nothing in her words conveyed disappointment, but her eyes spoke it.

"I call you Honey because you smell sweet, like honey, to me."

"I smell sweet?"

Damn. Damn. Damn. Don't go down that road. Not now. Not yet. "I couldn't read your guy's name either."

"Matthew Stone. Everyone calls him Matt." She wrapped her arms around herself like she got cold just mentioning him.

Lathan wanted to go to her, to hold her, but he wasn't certain yet if he would be welcome. "Got it."

"Were you born with hearing problems?"

How should he answer the question? He couldn't tell her about being in the psych unit. Couldn't tell her about the other patient jumping him from behind and jamming sharpened pencils into his eardrums to kill the demon he believed lived between Lathan's ears. Couldn't tell her that he half believed he *did have* a demon in his head. He hadn't known the visions were SMs until he underwent extensive testing as an adult. "At thirteen I was attacked. My ears were damaged."

"That's why you're jumpy when someone comes up behind you?"

"Yeah." *Change the subject. Quick.* "Come stay with me for awhile. It's nicer than this place."

"Why?"

Why was a lot better than a flat-out *no.* "I don't have any expectations. I'll even sleep on the couch."

She shook her head. She was about to reject him for this nasty motel room.

"I don't have a ride back and forth to work."

"I'll bring you and pick you up." He tried to keep the relief, the excitement out of his voice. "As long as you don't mind riding on the back of the bike." He was gonna need to get a car. Never thought the day would come.

"Why would you do all this for me?"

"Because you and I both know Junior isn't done yet. And I won't let him have an opportunity to hurt you again." He'd wait to mention the Strategist until she was good and moved in.

In her eyes, he saw complete trust. And something more. He couldn't exactly place a name on it, but he recognized it because it exactly mirrored what was inside him.

"You don't have to sleep on the couch."

"You stay with me, you're not sleeping on the couch. You're sleeping in the bed." His barely resisted the urge to say *my bed*.

She stood on her tippy-toes. "You aren't sleeping on the couch." He started to protest, but she put her hand over his mouth. "And neither am I."

Chapter 9

THE SKY WAS THE COLOR OF GLOOM. OR MAYBE DOOM. Definitely doom. Impending doom.

"Eight a.m. is too early for an appointment. Especially since I didn't get off work until midnight and didn't get to bed until after two." Damn if she hadn't fallen asleep the moment her body hit Lathan's mattress. That hadn't been her intention.

Gill didn't answer with words, but he gave her a look in the rearview mirror that said he might be enjoying her misery a teensy bit.

She stuck her tongue out at him. "You sure we actually *have* an appointment? Or are you just trying to torture me?" Snark dominated Evanee's tone. She couldn't help it. She supposed Gill and Lathan thought she wasn't a morning person, but it went way beyond not getting her morning cup of wake-up juice in her rush to get out the door.

At least Lathan was with her. She wasn't going to have to endure entering Matt's domain alone.

The car crested the last hill before their destination. Alongside the road, the bear totem caught her attention. The animal had been there her entire life, but it had been something that lived on the periphery of her vision, never gaining her full attention until now. The carving was exquisitely detailed and so lifelike that she turned in her seat and studied the inanimate wood, half expecting the bear to turn his head and watch them drive down the hill.

When she turned back around, she caught Lathan staring out the back window toward the bear totem too. Maybe he'd never seen it before.

Gill slowed the car at the bottom of the hill, and Lathan turned to face front again. "You realize this is the place you sent me to work a few months back?"

A confused look passed over Gill's face.

"The Isleen Walker case." Lathan said as if Gill should remember.

Lathan had worked the Isleen Walker case? Just what kind of job did he have? Everyone knew Isleen Walker. Her story had been all over the news. She'd spent years being tortured before Matt's nephew, Xander, had saved her. Only for her to be kidnapped again from this property. Shortly after all that went down, Matt had broken it off with Evanee.

Gill shook his head and let out a low whistle, then pulled into the driveway. He turned to Lathan. "I didn't realize the Institute of Oneirology was on the same property." He faced the driveway again, gassing the car to gain enough momentum to carry them up the steep driveway.

The forest on either side of the car was dead, desiccated, despairing. Her rib cage tightened around her heart and lungs—protecting her vitals from the pummeling they were about to endure.

Gravel crunched and popped under the car tires, drilling into Evanee's brain with all the annoyance of a jackhammer to the eardrums. The noise was just convenient to blame for her frazzled feelings. The core of her problem resided at the end of the driveway. Matt's place—the Ohio Institute of Oneirology—a colossal reminder of her shame.

The car pulled around a deep curve in the drive, and the OIO came into sight. Only it didn't look like a research facility. It looked like a log-cabin mansion had married a fairy tale and they'd had a baby—the OIO.

The house seemed to grow out of the forest as if it were part of the landscape instead of man-made. The structure was as tall as the trees surrounding it and nearly as wide as the clearing it rested in. A deep porch wrapped around the building, hugging the angular curves like a ballerina's tutu. Windows of all shapes and sizes ornamented the front and sides in organic symmetry. The place was like nothing else.

A sense of awe tried to steal over her, but shame drowned it.

What was she going to say when she saw Matt? What would he say? Her stomach crawled halfway up her throat. She'd never been carsick before, but today might be good day for it. She'd be sure to spew all over Gill's cushy leather seats and on the carpet, and it'd be awesome if she could aim right at his Ken doll face. What sweet retaliation that would be for forcing her into this interview!

Lathan twisted in the passenger seat, his expression one she'd seen too damned many times since she'd met him—concern. "Explain why you're ashamed to be going here."

His words were an arrow directly through her thoughts. Obviously, she wasn't doing a very good job of pretending to be okay with the forthcoming humiliation. She tried to smile, but her execution was off—it felt more like a grimace. "I'm fine."

"You're lying." The freckles on his face that she always found so endearing seemed to darken, hardening him. The tattoo on his cheek became menacing. Scary. "Don't ever lie to me. I'll know it every time."

"He's right. He's a human lie detector," Gill chimed in from the front seat.

She felt like slapping the back of Gill's head, NCIS style. Could he be serious? Could Lathan really be a human lie detector?

"Stop the car." Lathan spoke like he was in command of a platoon.

Even though they were within sight of the house, Gill jammed on the brakes. Evanee whiplashed forward, then slammed back against the headrest. *Jerk. He did that on purpose*.

"Spill it." Lathan's tone held no room for refusal.

The last bit of her dignity ghosted away. "Remember me telling you about"—Crap. What was she gonna call him with Gill sitting right here?—"my ex?"

"Yeah." Lathan's voice sounded cautious.

"His family owns this facility. He lives here." She hoped Lathan couldn't hear the dread dripping off each of her words. She didn't want to be pathetic, even if that's how she felt.

"Shit."

"Yeah."

"I don't give two shits who owns it. You're still going to the meeting." Gill whispered the words. "So don't try to get him to let you out of it."

The lid on her Can-O-Angry-Woman popped off. She pointed a finger at Gill. "Don't ever talk to me so quietly that Lathan can't hear."

Lathan's attention snapped to Gill. For a split second, she saw the vulnerable little boy Lathan must've once been, but any weakness disappeared behind a shield of menace and a tattoo that threatened blood. She couldn't see it, but she could feel the shadow monster of Lathan's anger grow and grow until it engulfed the interior of the car.

Maybe she shouldn't have said anything. Even as the thought crossed her mind, she knew she couldn't let Gill talk to her behind Lathan's back. That'd be like plucking the feathers off an eagle. It would diminish his beauty, his grace, his strength.

She unlocked her seat belt and scooted forward toward Lathan. His attention turned to her. She couldn't read the exact message his gray eyes sent her, but she could translate enough to know that Gill's action had been a betrayal. The kind that carved to the bone and took a long time to heal.

"Gill didn't say anything important. Just that he wanted me to attend the meeting." She left out any attitude. Didn't want to make the situation worse. "You know how much I don't want to be here, but I am here. Maybe the OIO can give me some answers about what's going on with me, tell me how to make the dreams stop. That would be worth it."

No words came from Lathan, but he reached for her like a parent reaches into the backseat for a kid. Somehow, she found herself in his lap in the front seat, his nose buried against the skin of her neck. She could hear the rapid sounds of his breathing as he tried to calm the fury—hurt—Gill had caused him. She wrapped her arms around him and held him tightly to her. She sensed the anger shadow fracturing into a thousand harmless fragments. His breathing slowed. His lips brushed her in a gentle kiss that zinged all the way from her neck to her toes and then back up to the top of her head.

Gill didn't say a word, just shifted the car back into gear and drove them the fifty remaining feet to the massive arch overhanging the front door.

Evanee didn't let go of Lathan, and he didn't let go of her until Gill parked the car. Lathan helped her out of the vehicle, then exited himself.

All the anxiety, the shame, the embarrassment she'd felt minutes ago had vanished. Now her number one priority was Lathan. She could handle everything else as long as he was all right.

Lathan tucked her body into his massive one. Her hip just below his, the side of her body touching his, his arm a crossbar of safety across her back. Energy and strength galloped through her system, fortifying her to deal with what was in front of her—Matt's brother. Dr. Alex Stone.

He waved a welcoming hand from the porch. She was struck by how different the brothers appeared. Both had wide faces with sharp features and the muscular build of a quarterback. That's where the similarities ended. Matt's brother had gray hair and wrinkles earned by age, while Matt fought aging with Botox and collagen and plastic surgery.

"Evanee. So nice to meet you." Dr. Stone's words sounded friendly. Friendly? Had Matt told his brother about her? She searched the doctor's face for any hint of deception or mockery. Only honesty stared back at her. Weird.

Dr. Stone turned his attention to Lathan. His tattoo to

be exact. "A feather. Usually representing healing. But this one is a blood feather. The most powerful. And it's broken." A smile identical to Matt's, with the left canine tooth slightly overlapping his front tooth, stretched across the doctor's mouth. "Brilliant symbolism. You must be Lathaniel Montgomery. I've heard many things about your exceptional work. You are certainly distinguished in your field. I'm Dr. Stone."

Distinguished in his field? What was his field? Human lie detector? Real-life James Bond? Maybe. Evanee felt kinda stupid. Everyone knew what Lathan did except her.

The doctor extended his hand to Lathan. As they shook, Dr. Stone examined Lathan's gloves. Another thing she'd never asked about. Was he a germophobe? He didn't seem like the type.

"You wear synthetic gloves. Is it by touch that you—?"

"Sir," Gill interrupted, stretching his hand out to the older man—an invitation only rudeness would refuse. "I'm Gill Garrison. We spoke on the phone."

"Ah, yes. Mr. Garrison. Very nice to put a face with the voice." Dr. Stone pumped Gill's hand, then stepped back and gestured toward the front door. "Welcome to the Ohio Institute of Oneirology. And my home. I'll give you the penny tour before we get started."

They followed Dr. Stone through the magnificent arched doorway that she could imagine more on a castle portal than a mansion in Ohio. She expected to see Matt inside but couldn't muster up the nerves to care. Lathan was with her. She could handle anything.

But no one was there. Only a vast and spacious space that reminded her of a cathedral. The vaulted ceiling spanned up, up, up, so far up it could almost classify as part of the sky. The room—but dear God, it was so much larger than the word *room* implied—was decorated with cozy seating areas that made her yearn to curl up with a good book and read away an entire afternoon.

To the left was a wide-open gourmet kitchen that looked straight out of a magazine. Straight ahead on the other side of the room was a spiral staircase leading to a second-floor loft that overlooked the great room. On either side of the loft, two open-to-below hallways ran along a balcony with three doors on either side. Bedrooms, she supposed.

"I designed the place myself. I wanted my home and the Institute to be under the same roof. Makes for a pleasant commute in the mornings."

"If dream research doesn't work out for you, I think you might have a bright future as an architect." Gill's voice was filled with the same wonder Evanee felt.

"Makes my place look the size of a Cracker Jack box," Lathan said. "My whole house could fit in this room. Twice."

"I was simply trying to design a place worthy of the woman I loved." Dr. Stone looked around his home. Love remembered shone in his eyes.

"Xander's mom?" Evanee couldn't help but ask. She'd gone to school with Xander, but they'd run in separate circles. Hell, she'd had no circle.

Dr. Stone's face clouded over with sadness. "No." He spoke the word on a breath. "Follow me." He turned and crossed the expanse of living space.

Gill gave her the why-the-fuck-did-you-ask-him-that look. She stuck her tongue out at him.

They followed Dr. Stone through the house, then down a set of winding stairs to what should've been a basement, but wasn't. At the bottom of the steps was a reception area. Dr. Stone faced their little group.

Did Gill tell him about Lathan's hearing problems? Or did the doctor just prefer to be looking at the people he spoke to?

"We formed the OIO forty-five years ago when no one else was studying dreams because they were believed to simply be a throwaway function of the brain. We were pioneers. Still are. Only now is the scientific community beginning to study what we've devoted nearly a half century to."

The doctor stopped at a doorway. Inside the room, a metal table was positioned under a light, and medical machines lined the walls. "This is our surgical suite. We really don't need one, but to be classified as a *medical research* facility, we had to comply with basic standards."

He showed them a sleep lab that looked exactly like a fancy bedroom, except for the medical apparatuses flanking the bed. And then ushered them into his office.

Half the room looked like every office Evanee had ever been in, with bookshelves and a desk with two chairs in front of it. The other half was an inviting living room with a couch and chairs separated by a coffee table. Natural light flowed into the room from rectangular windows set high in the wall, just above ground level. Even though the day was overcast, the play of light inside the room wasn't cold or harsh, but serene.

She and Lathan sat on the couch. During the entire tour, he'd kept his arm around her, and even now while sitting, he held her tightly against him.

Gill and Dr. Stone took the chairs across from them.

"So Evanee, Mr. Garrison has told me a little about your experience, but I want to hear it from you."

Her face suddenly blazed like she'd been in the sun all day without sunscreen. A bead of sweat formed above her lip. She swiped at it. What she was about to say—to a doctor—would make her sound certifiable. "You're going to think I've cracked up and send me on a winter vacation to a padded cell at the nuthouse."

"Evanee, I assure you that in forty-five years of researching dreams, I've heard it all. There's nothing you can say that will surprise or shock me."

Lathan shifted away from her to see her face when she spoke. She missed his touch, the courage it gave her. Like he'd read her mind, he reached out and took her hand. She pushed her fingers between his and held on tight. It was going to be a crazy ride. While her body was aimed toward Dr. Stone, her face was turned to Lathan. No way would she have a conversation and intentionally leave him out of it.

She told the doctor about the first dream. And then the second one.

Dr. Stone listened. Really listened. His brows were drawn together over his eyes in an expression of intense concentration. He never once interrupted.

When Evanee finished, she drew in a deep breath. She felt like she hadn't inhaled since she started talking.

"I want to make sure I understand," Dr. Stone said. "The objects were given to you in the dream, and you had them with you when you awakened?"

Why didn't he sound disbelieving? He should be telling her she was full of shit. Like Gill had the first time she'd said it. "Yes. But I know that doesn't make logical sense."

"What happened after you woke up and realized what you held?"

"I freaked."

A mild smile twitched the corner of his mouth. "After you freaked."

Lathan answered for her. "She passed out. Both times. Was out about ten minutes each time, and then woke up shivering with cold."

"I passed out? I don't remember that. I remember being cold..." She knew Lathan wasn't lying, but it didn't feel right to have things happening to her body without her being aware of them.

The doctor spoke to Lathan. "Could she have had a seizure?"

"Seizure?" The word exploded from her mouth. "As in epilepsy? No way. Wouldn't I know if I was having seizures? And why would I all of a sudden start having them? That doesn't make sense. None of this makes any sense." Even she could hear the hysterical quality to her tone. "I just want to make it all go away."

"Evanee, your reaction is normal." The doctor's tone was the same one adults used on frightened children. "This is difficult stuff to wrap your mind around. Allow me to explain." He sat back in his seat, looking comfortable.

She sat on the edge of the cushion. Lathan's hand holding hers was the only thing anchoring her to the seat.

"While you are asleep, your brain directs your body through the cycles of sleep. But when you are having one of these *special dreams*, your brain is on double duty. It's directing you through the sleep cycles *and* navigating you through this whole other experience. Your brain is experiencing two realities at once." He repeated the words with extra emphasis. "*Two realities at once*. Upon waking, the brain short-circuits from the overload—usually in some form of seizure. It takes a while for everything to come back online."

"My brain short-circuits?" Maybe she was short-circuiting right now. None of this conversation was on the same page as logic.

"How can something from a dream end up in reality?" Gill asked. "It's against the laws of physics or something, isn't it?"

"Depends on which laws of physics you are following," Dr. Stone answered.

Lathan nodded his head as if he fully understood Dr. Stone's meaning. Evanee didn't understand. Was Dr. Stone saying that more than one set of rules governed the universe and the objects in it? She was starting to feel like she was in an episode of *The Twilight Zone*. Or being punked. Or in an alternate universe where everything looked the same and sounded the same, but somehow wasn't the same.

Gill leaned forward in his chair, his gaze resting on her before turning to the doctor. "I wouldn't be going down this rabbit hole with her if I could find any other logical explanation. The Bureau wants more than my word and Lathan's word."

"I'll do what I can to reassure them once I have more information." Dr. Stone turned his attention back to her. "To confirm what you are telling me, we'll need to conduct some baseline tests, then study your sleep and dream patterns. Maybe we can even record the psychic phenomenon on—"

"Whoa. Stop the insane train." She held up her hand, silencing his speech. "We're having a misunderstanding. I'm not psychic. I think you're misinterpreting what I'm saying."

Dr. Stone gave her a tolerant grin that reminded her too much of how Matt used to look at her sometimes. "You are partly correct. During your waking hours, you are not psychic. But during the dream state, you are connecting to another plane of reality that science has difficulty studying because it only exists inside you. It *is* a form of psychic phenomenon."

She shook her head slowly, taking in both Lathan's and Gill's faces. Both seemed to be buying what Dr. Stone was selling. "Do you guys believe this?"

"It's worth considering," Lathan said. He was serious. *Serious*. How could he think any of this was even possible?

She turned to Gill.

"You better hope there's something to this, or you'll be at Quantico answering tougher questions than I've ever given you."

"Hundreds of people have made compelling claims of having one form of psychic dreams or another, but under the weight of scientific testing, their claims fall apart," Dr. Stone said. "I've met only one individual whose psychic dreams have been documented and their accuracy demonstrated repeatedly. We have so much proof, in fact, that we have a direct line to Homeland Security. They use the information from our dreamer to save lives. In the past four months, thirty-seven lives have been spared."

Four months. Isleen moved here four months ago. Was she the dreamer Dr. Stone referred to?

"If what you say is true, your ability is vastly different than anything ever studied. It's oneirokinesis."

"O—what?" she and Gill said at the same time.

"Oneirokinesis. The ability to move objects from the dream state to reality."

"It has a name?"

"It most certainly has a name." The way Dr. Stone spoke the words sounded like he was offended by her question.

"I'm sorry. I don't mean to be difficult. I just don't believe in all this."

"You can choose not to believe in the law of gravity, but your beliefs don't make it any less true. What's happening in your dreams is not a matter of belief. It's happening. It's real."

"Why me? Why now? How can I get rid of it? I don't want it."

The doctor looked from her to Lathan. "The first time you had one of these special dreams was the night you met Lathan. Correct?"

"How do you know that?" She glanced at Lathan, who obviously wanted to hear the same answer.

"I've got a theory, but I don't have enough information yet. Why don't we start tonight? Come back at eight p.m. We'll conduct the baseline tests. Then you can spend the night and—"

"I need to think. About all of this." She stood and so did Lathan.

"I know this is hard to understand, but it's your new reality. Things will go easier for you if you embrace your power, rather than fighting and fearing it." Dr. Stone's eyes gleamed and widened. She felt like he was trying to tell her something more than what his words conveyed. He handed her a business card. "My numbers are on it. Call me. Anytime."

As Dr. Stone led them back through the house, she replayed the conversation. For all the time they'd spent with him, she felt like none of her questions had been answered—especially not the biggest one—how to get rid of the nightmares.

As they drew near to the front door, muffled conversation sounded from the other side. She recognized one of those voices. Matt.

She froze. Everything from her head down went numb.

Matt entered first. Evanee hadn't seen him in months and soaked up his appearance. Didn't take long. He looked exactly the same.

Matt took in Gill, then Lathan, and then his blue eyes froze on her. The smile on his face shattered like glass thrown against a concrete wall. "What are you doing here?" Shock threaded with embarrassment powered each of his words.

Lathan drew her in closer and tighter against him.

Xander and Isleen entered. The moment Xander saw them, his arm, already around Isleen, tightened, and his other one wrapped around the front of her as if to shield her from the bomb he thought they might throw.

Isleen smiled at them, looking sweet, innocent, and kind, while Matt and Xander looked ready to rumble.

"Lathan Montgomery." Xander's tone wasn't exactly friendly, but definitely familiar. "What are you doing here?" Xander's gaze darted to his father.

"I didn't realize you lived here." Lathan aimed his words at Xander.

The guys knew each other.

"Gill Garrison and Lathaniel Montgomery are here with Evanee to consult about her dreams." Dr. Stone spoke in a weird tone, almost like they should know exactly what that meant. Maybe they did. Maybe Isleen really was the other person he'd mentioned.

"You shouldn't be here." Matt's voice captured her attention. He reached out to grab at her, but instead ended up with two hands—Lathan's hands—on his chest, shoving him away.

"Don't you touch her." Lathan moved in front of her, shielding her from Matt and Xander.

She peeked out from behind Lathan's back. Xander shifted Isleen behind him and moved in next to Matt. Gill stepped up next to Lathan.

Oh crap. Oh damn. Oh shit. A four-man brawl.

"Everyone, stop. Xander. Matt. Stop it. Your manners are atrocious." Isleen's disembodied voice came from behind Xander. She moved out to stand between the two groups of men. Isleen was all of five foot two and probably didn't weigh ninety pounds, but her sweetness was an antidote to everyone's anger.

Xander moved in next to Isleen, tucking her into his body. And when Isleen looked up at him, the expression he gave her was filled with adoration and love. God. They loved each other. Really loved each other. A love like Evanee had never seen.

Longing hummed through the chambers of her heart. All she'd ever wanted was someone to look at her that way. With her history though—never gonna happen.

But even as those words crossed her mind, she recognized she wasn't quite being honest with herself. Lathan looked at her like that. But was it a look of love, or was he simply trying to understand her speech?

"Don't you see it?" Isleen asked Xander.

"Are you sure?" Xander asked her. They talked like no one else existed in the room.

"Isn't it obvious?" Isleen and Xander and everyone else looked at Evanee and Lathan.

Sometime within the last few seconds, she wasn't even aware of when exactly, she'd nestled into Lathan's side with his arm around her. Almost exactly like Xander had his arm around Isleen.

"What are you talking about?" Evanee asked.

"I suspected," Dr. Stone said.

Isleen smiled, her expression full of offered friendship. "You've met your protector."

Chapter 10

LATHAN COULDN'T REMEMBER ONE THING ABOUT THE drive home from the OIO. He completely lost himself in reflecting on Matt's memories. What he saw set his rage on simmer.

He'd witnessed for himself, felt for himself Matt's total indifference to Evanee. The only emotion the man had toward her was anger because she'd shown up at his place.

What really burned was that asshole could've protected her from Junior, but never cared enough to open his eyes and see the truth. Just thinking about it cranked Lathan's rage up to boil.

He snapped out of his thoughts at the same time Gill parked in his driveway. Lathan was out of the car and dragging Evanee behind him up to the house before Gill even had a chance to unlock his seat belt. Maybe the guy would get the hint. Gill wasn't exactly tops on Lathan's friend list at the moment. Trying to talk to Honey without him knowing was a betrayal. Lathan needed to be alone with her to calm all the emotions.

But when they entered the house, Gill was right behind them.

Fucking damn.

This wasn't going to end well.

"What now?" he asked Gill and made sure his tone conveyed the warning of his impending boil-over.

A rush of burning cinnamon emanated from Gill. He was just as pissed. "What's your problem?"

"You." Not all Gill—some was on Matt—but Lathan wasn't going to explain. "Talking to her behind my back. Trying to keep secrets from me." Gill knew—fucking knew—how Lathan's hearing problems isolated him and had used that against him.

"I'm the only one watching out for you. You're acting like some pussy-whipped motherfucker, panting around after her because you finally got fucked. And trust me, the pussy might be new now, but it'll get old. It always does. Then what?"

He didn't bother correcting Gill's mistaken assumption. "Leave. Now." Lathan spoke the words through clenched teeth. The only thing holding him back from going all MMA on Gill was Honey standing next to him. He dropped her hand and moved a few feet away. Just in case.

"Can't you see what's going on here? Her ex was Matthew Stone. The guy's old enough to be her grandpa. Look where she works. Look where she lives."

Lathan wasn't going to enter a debate with Gill about Matt. "You saying my house is trash? 'Cause you didn't seem to mind before." His muscles constricted, on full alert, waiting for the command to strike.

"She's moved in? Are you that fucking desperate? Have you asked yourself what she might want from you? What she has to gain by being with you? At best, she's taking advantage of your generosity. At worst, she's working with the Strategist."

Rage at Matt and at Gill overflowed, pouring straight into Lathan's swinging fist. He connected with Gill's

cheekbone. His knuckles compressed. The impact reverberated up his arm. Now to get ten more shots like that
in, and he'd be feeling just about awesome.

Gill's head snapped to the side. He lurched in that
direction, but regained his footing and tackled Lathan
low in the torso. Lathan stumbled back a few steps
until the counter stopped him. He shoved Gill off and
came at him with an uppercut. Gill blocked and swung
for Lathan's stomach, but Lathan braced. The blow
hurt but didn't give Gill what he wanted—Lathan bent
over sucking air.

Lathan heard Honey, but couldn't make out her
exact words.

"Stay the fuck out of the way," he yelled, then
chanced a glance toward her. She charged Gill.

Pain radiated from the side of Lathan's mouth. Gill
had landed a punch in that brief moment when Lathan's
attention was on Honey. The lights went out. Back on.
Blood gushed onto Lathan's tongue.

Honey tried to tear her way in between them, tried to
shove Gill back.

Inside Lathan's mind, the future played out. He saw
Gill swing for him, but his aim was thrown off by Honey
pushing against him. Gill would miss him and land the
punch squarely on her nose.

Lathan shoved Honey out of the way. "Stay back!"

Gill's fist connected again with the same spot on
the side of Lathan's mouth. Blood flew from between
his lips in fat droplets that would need to be wiped off
the floor later. Lathan slammed his right fist into Gill's
stomach, followed by his left into Gill's nose. A wash of
crimson gushed down Gill's face.

The stench of their mingled blood and anger was thick in the air. Lathan jammed Gill in the chest—his form of a truce—and waited until Gill caught his balance. "Get the fuck out."

Gill stood in the middle of the kitchen, looking like he was contemplating coming back for another round.

"And don't come back."

Something flickered in Gill's expression, but Lathan was too amped to try to interpret it.

Gill raised his fist in the air. For a moment, Lathan thought it was an invitation for the fight to continue, but Gill fixed him with a middle finger. This time, there was no disguised meaning, no humor in the gesture. A fuck-you full of anger. Gill walked out the door.

Lathan turned on Honey. "For fuck's sake, woman. Do I look like I need help?" He spread his arms wide.

"I'm not going to watch someone I love be thumped on. And you're a…if you can't accept help from a girl."

He missed a word, but got the gist.

"I'm plenty big enough to handle Gill on my own. A good ass-stompin' wouldn't have killed either of us. I don't want you getting hurt. Especially on my behalf."

His brain must've been operating in delay mode because her words from a few moments before finally got absorbed. *When someone I love*. She'd said she loved him. Loved him. Fucking loved him.

His heart pumped up two sizes. A smile cracked across his face. He saw her confusion at his abrupt change. No way was he going to tell her why he was really smiling. Didn't want her to clarify or, worse, take those beautiful words away from him. "You're pretty fearless. You know that?"

"I've had to be." She didn't say his name, but Junior hovered, an invisible specter between them.

An instinctual urge, so ingrained that it wasn't even on the level of thought, rose up inside him. "I'll kill Junior if he ever tries to hurt you again."

"Sit down." She pointed at a chair and watched him until he complied. Anything she wanted from him was hers. She wet a clean dishcloth. He opened his mouth to tell her not to mess with the blood, that he'd take care of it, but she walked right past it to stand in front of him.

She moved into the open vee of his legs. Her scent folded around him. He ripped off his gloves, spared a fleeting thought of wonder for the fact that Gill had punched him skin to skin and he'd had no reaction from the contact, then settled his hands on her hips.

She grabbed his chin and tilted it upward to bring his gaze to hers. "Hold still." She wiped the blood off his face and neck with the washcloth. He couldn't breathe, but he didn't need to. He had something more important than oxygen. He had her taking care of him. Something no one else had ever been able to do.

He couldn't *let* anyone take care of him. Touch was a good-bye to reality, something he couldn't tolerate. But this, with her—Holy Jesus—he felt special. Loved.

If he was less of a man, he might've fucking bawled like a baby. But he was no baby and she definitely wasn't his momma.

"This is going to sting."

She pressed the cold cloth against the split in his lip, but he felt no pain. She and pain couldn't coexist. That's why his lip no longer hurt, why her touch had the power to calm him, why the SMs couldn't survive in her presence. She was his miracle.

She bit her bottom lip as she worked on cleaning him up, but the scar at the corner of her mouth still tilted jauntily upward. A beautiful imperfection. He touched the line briefly. The raised ridge felt wrong in a way that went beyond words.

"How'd you get this?" he asked.

The lavender scent of her sadness engulfed them. Without answering, she walked back to the sink.

"I shouldn't have asked." He spoke the words to her back.

She returned to the vee between his legs and applied the newly cold rag to his lip. "I got in trouble for telling a lie."

"Someone hit you? Junior?" Should've known.

She turned the cloth over and pressed the cold side against his lip. "My mom."

"Your mom? How old were you?"

"Five."

Five. Just five years old. What kind of lie could a kid—a little girl—tell that warranted being hit? "What happened?"

"I told her about Junior."

He wished he hadn't read the words right. "You were only five when Junior started..." He trailed off. Couldn't let her know how much he knew. "What kind of fucked-up mother would hit her own daughter for telling the truth? 'Cause that's what it was. The truth."

"Apparently, my mom." He couldn't hear the sadness in her voice, but he could smell it and see it in the clouds over her dazzling eyes. "I used to wish I could jump back to the moment before I told Mom. And not tell her. It was like from that moment on, she hated me. All I ever wanted was for her to love me as much as she loved Junior."

Lathan didn't possess any words of consolation. He just put his hands back on her hips and held on tight.

A blush, fresh and new as bud in spring, dusted her cheeks. "I've never told anyone that before."

"You can tell me anything. Everything. You know that, don't you? Nothing you say to me will ever change..." He gestured between them to indicate their connection and stared into her eyes, willing her to open up, to tell him her pain. He wouldn't feel so bad about already knowing and hiding it from her, if she just out-and-out confided in him.

"Are you hungry? We didn't exactly have time for breakfast this morning."

The abrupt subject change meant she didn't trust him. And why should she? Just because he felt connected to her didn't mean she felt the same way about him. "I'll make us something."

"I'll do it. It'll be fun to cook in a kitchen instead of using a hotplate or a microwave." The smile on her face wavered. "Unless you don't want me messing around in your kitchen."

"Everything I own is yours." He gestured to indicate his entire home. "I want you to feel that way."

Surprise flared in her eyes, diminishing the clouds.

Might as well lay it all out there. He ate the way he ate. Couldn't change it. Couldn't hide it. And if she thought he was a freak... No, he didn't want to go there. "But, I'm particular about my food. Really particular."

"Gill said you didn't do dairy."

"What else did he tell you?" He better not have mentioned the SMs. No, of course he didn't. She was still here.

"He told me to ask you about your hearing and about your childhood."

"Fucker." Anyone who knew how he'd spent his childhood would be as frightened of him as his own parents were. He clenched his hands into fists. He wanted another go-round with Gill. Needed it. Owed it to Gill.

She held up her hand as if to placate him. "I'll make you a deal. You don't ask about my childhood, and I won't ask about yours."

"Deal." He didn't have to ask to know her childhood was shit. He'd seen bits of it in Junior's memory. Those bits were revolting.

"So you're picky about food. Picky how?"

"I don't eat anything bought in a grocery store or from a restaurant."

Her eyes widened. "You don't eat anything from a store? Nothing?"

"Nothing."

"How is that even possible? What do you eat?"

"I eat what I harvest from my garden. I can fruits and vegetables to put back for winter. I buy flour direct from an Amish mill and make my own bread. I buy peanuts and grind them myself to make peanut butter. I eat a lot of peanut butter. For the protein."

"You"—she pointed directly at him—"can your own vegetables and bake your own bread?"

He nodded.

A smile hitched up her cheeks, then morphed into laughter. She was laughing at him. Emotions sliced through him, and yet he couldn't name them. All he knew was that none of them felt good.

He pushed out of the chair and headed for the back door, then stopped but didn't face her. "You have no idea what it's like to struggle for food. To spend the entire spring prepping the ground and planting. Then there is the eternal fight with bugs and fungus and disease. If it's a drought year, I'll be out there watering, nearly running my well dry, to keep the plants alive. And canning the harvest doesn't even exist in the same dictionary with the word *fun*. But I do it all to have some variety in my diet." He opened the door. "I'll take you to the store to get whatever you want to eat when I get back."

A weird heat started in his chest the moment he walked away from her. He rubbed it as he headed away from the house toward the pathway to his office. The cool autumn air, the stark beauty of the world waiting for winter, didn't even register.

She'd laughed at him.

Why wouldn't she? He was a mutant. A genetic anomaly that shouldn't have survived, or found a way to thrive. And yet he had. Reality was that no matter how hard he tried, he was never going to be normal or have anything related to normal in his life.

The burn inside his chest ratcheted up to an inferno. Fucking heartburn.

He stepped up to the retinal scanner, waited for light to flash from red to green, and opened the door. After he secured himself inside, he went to his desk and ripped open the bottom drawer. Only one thing could ease the desolation inside him. He grabbed his machine and took it into the small bathroom. In minutes, he was ready to go.

Shirtless in front of the full-length mirror he reached for the tattoo machine to begin, but his gaze snagged on his chest. On his tattoo.

He'd always referred to the piece as the Dark Seduction of Night.

From his left hip, an immense, gnarled tree ranged up and out over his chest, curling around his sides and toward his neck. Branches twisted and deformed. Trunk tumorous and knotted. Behind the bare limbs, a bloated harvest moon hung low in the sky. It was an eerily alluring picture, made more so by what he now noticed.

The trunk—how had he never seen it before?— wasn't tumorous, knotted wood. It was knees and elbows and shoulders. Bodies. Two of them. Male. Female. Entwined in an eternal embrace so impassioned that he almost felt embarrassed looking at them. And they were on his damned body.

How had he done that—made the trunk from a pair of bodies—and not even been aware of doing it? He never planned his tattoos. He just did them and was always surprised at what he'd wrought when it was completed. That's what tattooing was to him, a place beyond thought, a nirvana where only ink and blood and pain lived.

The lights began to flash to tell him someone was outside. Only two people knew about his office. Gill and Eric. Eric wouldn't be making the trip from Quantico without at least calling first.

Opportunity was standing right outside his door—the opportunity to transform Gill's preppy boy good looks into something only a zombie could love.

He yanked on his shirt in less than two seconds—no

one had ever seen the ink on his chest—and was across the office and nearly ripping the door off its hinges to get it open. "I'm ready for round two, ass—" The rest of whatever he'd planned to say evaporated.

Honey stood there, holding a tray with a platter of peanut butter sandwiches and two glasses of water. "I wasn't being malicious. That's what you thought, isn't it? You turned your back on me and walked away before I could explain. I didn't want to chase you down and startle you."

He neither confirmed nor denied her words.

"I was laughing because you're such a big, muscly guy. You seem like the type to work construction or be a professional wrestler. Not a gardener and baker. I wasn't being mean. I was enjoying how unexpected you are."

He smelled her sincerity.

He stepped back.

She entered, scanning his environment—the walls of bookcases filled with vials of baseline scents he used to distinguish similar specimens from each other. What was he going to tell her if she asked about the vials? Was he going to lie? Didn't want to lie. Didn't want to tell the truth either.

He secured the door, then watched her settle the tray on his desk. Having her in this room was weird. Hell, it was a little weird that she was even in his life after all the years he'd spent alone. No one other than Gill and Eric had been inside these walls, and then only briefly to check the security or provide more baseline scents. With her here though, the room seemed less antiseptic and tons more cozy.

He sat in the chair behind his desk.

"Tell me why you don't eat dairy and don't buy from grocery stores and eat mostly what you grow."

Heat crept up his neck. He didn't want to have this conversation. "I'm extremely picky about where my food comes from. I can't stand it when other people touch my food or its packaging." *Truth. Not the whole truth. So help me God.*

Her eyes darted to the platter of peanut butter sandwiches.

"You're okay though." He grabbed one of the sandwiches, handed it to her, and then got one for himself. He took a bite. Honey exploded across his taste buds. He closed his eyes for a second to savor the flavor. It tasted like a kiss. "You can touch my food anytime."

He thought maybe he heard her giggle before she started eating.

Surprise flared across her face. "Wow. This is good. I can actually taste it."

"Why wouldn't you be able to taste it?"

"I can't taste food. Haven't been able to for years."

He almost asked why but knew it had to do with Junior. Didn't need to know more. "How about your sense of smell?"

"I can smell some things, but not others."

"If your nose doesn't work right, food doesn't taste right." Did that explain why he never got SMs from her? No. She should have some SMs from before she lost the ability to smell. "My sense of smell is extremely sensitive. That's part of why I eat this way." He hadn't told her how acute his nose was, but he'd taken the first step.

"So you wear gloves because you don't like to touch things other people have touched?"

To him, wearing the gloves was akin to wearing clothes. Until she mentioned it, he hadn't thought about an explanation. What she said sounded like a logical leap, so he nodded.

She gestured with her half-eaten sandwich. "What is this place?"

"My office."

"Dr. Stone said you were distinguished in your field, and I felt stupid not knowing what your field was."

"I'm a special skills consultant to the FBI." Other than his parents, he'd never told anyone about his job.

"That sounds important. What's it mean?"

Hmmm…how to explain without explaining. "My job is similar to a profiler, but different."

"As in serial killer profiler?" She leaned forward in her seat.

"Exactly. But I mostly work cold cases. Until recently."

"You got a promotion?"

"Not exactly. A number of my cold cases were all committed by the same killer. The Strategist. And we've"—he gestured between them—"just linked two very recent murders to him."

"We?"

"Hold on to your seat. I'm about to blow your mind. The eye, the hair and tooth—I've confirmed they're all from victims of the Strategist. Because of the lead you gave Gill about Guadalupe Mountains National Park—and after preliminary DNA confirmation—a team was sent there to search for the body of Juanita Valdez. She went missing from her home in Salt Flats, Texas, the night you dreamed about her."

Evanee set her mostly finished sandwich on the platter. Her hand was shaking.

"For all his threats about Quantico, Gill knows you weren't anywhere near Salt Flats, Texas. He was here all night and knows no one gave you the hair or tooth. He's at least trying to understand what's happening. Even if he is acting like the King of Anuses."

Confusion nestled in the wrinkle between her brows. "The Strategist. A serial killer. My dreams were about his victims?"

"Yeah. I've found thirty-eight murders. You've given evidence of two more, and there probably are more out there we haven't discovered yet. The things you've brought back from the dreams have given us leads."

She slouched down in the chair. "Two weeks ago, all I had to worry about was earning enough money to get out of town. Now I've got Junior and the Strategist in my world."

Lathan smelled the faint garlic of anxiety. "You don't have to worry about either of them. You're here so I can keep you safe. Your safety is my priority."

Her face crinkled up all wrong. "I'm here so you can protect me. It's your priority."

Was she asking a question or making a statement? He smelled lavender—sadness. Why was she suddenly feeling sad? "You're providing us with priceless information on the Strategist. But that puts you too close to him. So of course I want you here, where I know I can keep you safe." He thought his words would sooth her, but the scent of sadness only got stronger.

"I appreciate everything you've done for me." She stood. "But I need to be alone for a while." Without a backward glance, she left.

He stared after her. Lavender. Why was she sad? Because Junior and the Strategist were in her life? No, she'd been anxious while talking about them, but then she'd gotten sad when he talked about protecting her. He replayed their conversation in his mind, but couldn't pinpoint an explanation for her sadness.

Something was wrong, and he wasn't going to let her close off and not tell him. He couldn't fix what he didn't understand.

He followed her, but by the time he got the door secured behind him, she was nearly out of sight—running. "Wait!" He knew he yelled the word, but she continued.

He didn't catch up to her until he found her upstairs, curled in on herself on the far side of the bed. Sadness heavy in the air. He sat next to her and stroked her hair.

"Tell me what's wrong."

Her lips moved, but from the angle of her head, he couldn't read the words. "Can you look at me and say that again?"

She faced him, her bottom lip pushed out in an adorable pout. "Nothing." Her eyes shimmered beautifully in the gray afternoon light.

"You're lying." The itchy pepper scent of it tickled his nose. "Try again." He caressed her face. His bare fingers grazed over the skin of her cheek, then down her neck to the delicate skin just behind her ear. Her honeyed scent intensified, mingling with the lavender in one heady, sweet blend.

"I don't know if I can do this." She gestured back and forth between the two of them. "With everything else I've got going on with Junior, with the dreams, with work and money."

Was she trying to tell him the bond growing between them was over? He had trouble breathing. His heart had trouble beating. "What do you mean?"

"Are you going to make me say it?"

"Yeah." If she didn't say it, he wasn't sure twenty guesses would give him an accurate answer.

"I thought there was something special between us. But you were only protecting me."

"You think the only reason you're here is so I can protect you?"

She nodded, her lip pushed out in a deeper pout.

He cupped her face in his hands and then waited for her gaze to find his. "You're here because I need to be near you. You're here because I couldn't leave the diner last night without you. You're here because I need you in my life to feel normal."

I need you.

Fuck. He sounded like a toddler with separation issues, but the words had flowed out of him on a wave of swear-on-a-holy-book truth.

"You need me?" Her gaze searched his face with all the thoroughness of a polygraph machine.

"I do." He couldn't have lied to her—about this. He'd already committed the sin of lie-by-omission too many times with her.

She reached up to him, placing her cool hand against the tattoo on his cheek. Reality shifted. Time got lazy and loitered along. He lost himself in her eyes—in the silver flecks swirling against the midnight-blue irises, like stars forming the mythical constellations aligning to tell their story—hers and his. A story of something eternal that had no name but was vast beyond time and place and reason.

A swell of silky heat effervesced through his veins.

Her hand slid from his tattoo into his hair. The vision, the trance, whatever it was, vanished and all he felt was the gentle tug of her hand on the back of his head, pulling him to her mouth.

The sweet pressure of their lips touching was a beautiful death—the ending of one thing, so another even more magnificent kiss could be birthed by their tongues thrusting wildly against each other.

The taste of her exploded in his mouth, permeated the air around them, surrounding him with the essential essence of her. Desire zinged along his nerve endings, converged, and swelled in his groin.

She wrenched his T-shirt from his jeans and slipped her hands inside, smoothing them up his chest, down his sides. His heart drop-kicked to his groin, back to his chest, down to his groin. He wanted more, more, more.

He tore his mouth from hers and ripped the shirt over his head. Anticipation heated his skin. Only her touch would soothe him.

But her attention wasn't focused on *him*; it was zeroed in on his chest. The tattoo. He stood still, let her stare her fill. The artwork was complicated, not the kind a thing a person could take in on a glance.

"Who are they?" she asked.

"Us. The us that was before." He didn't know why he said that, but the truth of it resonated deeply within. Taking the words back would've been blasphemous.

She sat up, moved to the edge of the bed, and touched the tattooed outline of the male figure. Up the male's calves, over his buttocks, his shoulders to his head. She caressed the male's cheek as if he were in the image of a loved one. Damn, if he didn't almost feel her stroking the skin of his actual cheek.

Goose bumps covered his skin. He was never cold. Never. But now he felt feverish and freezing at the same time. Skin chilled. Insides sweltered. Dick burning with a need for her cooling touch. As if she'd read his mind, she released the button of his jeans and wrangled down the zipper. His erection scraped against the metal—a perverse pleasure.

He stepped back, kicked off his boots, shucked his jeans. In nothing but the raw, he stood in front of her, not moving. He wanted this to be about more than just fucking. He wanted this to be about her. About showing her the depth and breadth of his feelings, so she would know she would never have to be alone again. "You're in charge."

She cocked her head ever so slightly, almost as if she were listening to the words he hadn't spoken.

"Take my clothes off." She stood in front of him. Waiting.

Maybe he should be nervous—he was a thirty-three-year-old virgin. But this felt destined. Written in the fucking stars in her eyes.

His hands were as steady as those of a seasoned brain surgeon. He reached for her leggings and pulled them down her seven-mile legs. Those legs… How would it feel to have them wrapped around him? Rapture. He pulled her sweater over her head. She wore a simple white bra and white panties. Nothing fancy. And yet they were sexier than any fantasy.

"What's next?" He wasn't certain he had a voice when he spoke.

"Bra and panties."

To his ears, her words were disjointed, but his eyes saw her heart reflected in her face, and his nose smelled her honeyed musk. He drew the scent in and savored it.

He didn't remember taking the last of her clothes off, but he must've because she stood in front of him. Naked. Beautiful.

Her breasts were capped with raspberry-colored nipples. Would they taste like raspberry or honey or some erotic flavor uniquely their own?

The sharp ripple of her ribs demarcated the plane of her stomach. The short-trimmed black hair between her legs... Fuck, the ability to think vanished.

With his mind's camera he captured a picture of her and tucked it away, knowing it would be an image he would cherish until the last feeble beat of his heart. Before he'd met her, he'd resigned himself to being alone. To never sharing intimacy with a woman. But here she was—an eccentric combination of fragility, strength, and beauty. His miracle.

"It's been awhile for me. You too?" She stepped closer. Only a foot separated them.

"Forever." Nope. Hadn't lied.

She knelt in front of him. His heart double-kicked in his chest. His throat pinched off his air supply. Instead of choking, she became his oxygen, his breath, his absolute.

Fuck, no. Fuck. She couldn't be going to... Her breath fanned across his skin. Warm, then cool, warm, cool. Her gaze flicked up to him, and she lowered her mouth to him.

He watched her devour his dick. Lost the ability to think. Could only feel. Hot. Wet. Pressure. Sensory overload. Raw sensation licked him from the inside out. He felt flayed open, flaming, and she was the soothing breeze blowing across his burn.

She cupped his balls. The pleasure, yet the pain of trying to control himself—a masochistic mixture. The beginning of his finale surged. Too soon.

"Stop. You've got to stop or…" The words died when she slid her tongue down the base of his dick, then back up in one long, sleek stroke. Ecstasy and torture. She took the head into her mouth and sucked gently. Every ounce of energy in his body—the spark that kept his heart beating, that kept his breath pumping in and out—converged in his dick, then expanded and multiplied until he was energy. He was life. He *was* the orgasm that began to crash over him.

He pushed away from her. Couldn't come in her mouth without her permission—couldn't do that to her. He came in great, heavy spurts, cupping the mess in his hand.

When he finished, he hung his head and stared down at himself. At his fist still wrapped around his dick, at his hand covered in come.

Holy fucking Christ. He'd basically cranked one off in front of her. This was supposed to be about her. About giving to her, instead of taking. About being a better man than any of the assholes she'd ever been with.

She ran her hand over his arm, trying to get his attention, but he couldn't look at her with shame in his eyes.

"I didn't want it to be that way for you." He went into the bathroom, shut the door. He washed the come from his hands and dick. After he dried himself, he stared in the mirror at a face he didn't recognize—his own. It was his face of course, but something had changed, shifted, transformed inside him and he no longer felt like the man in the mirror.

Underneath his feet, he felt the slight pressure of her walking across the hall, stopping. He opened the door to her.

"I wanted it that way. I thought it was hot watching you…"

Her words were a forgiveness and a permission he couldn't resist.

He was on her. His mouth on her neck, kissing, licking, tasting. His arms banded around her back, his hands gripped her buttocks, pulling her up into him, grinding his erection into her stomach. Flesh to flesh. Everywhere.

Somehow, he got them to the bed.

His mouth found hers. Their tongues dancing together the way their bodies would. Male instinct took hold, overwhelming him with a need. One he couldn't control.

He moved over her, covering her body with his. It was so right, the way they fit. He stared into her eyes—saw his own desire mirrored there, but still asked the question, "Are you ready?"

"Yes." She reached between them, her cool hand wrapping around him and guiding him to her.

Timeless pressure built inside him. He pushed into her.

So hot. She was fire. And tight. Deeper he pressed, until she'd taken all of him.

Flesh recognized flesh, reacquainted, melded, and moved to the cadence of their combination as if they'd been together throughout a millennium. Every molecule of him became strangely alive. His skin tingled as if a brisk wind rushed over him. He could feel his hair, each strand magnetized, strangely alive. His fingernails, his toenails... Holy Jesus, it was like he could actually feel them growing. Inside his body, his bones grew harder, stronger. He felt powerful. Invincible. Truly alive.

"Do you feel that?" He heard his own voice. No static. No distortion. He could fucking hear. How? Why? Didn't matter. He could and there was only one thing he wanted to hear—her voice.

"My God. Yes." Her words were a throaty sigh that sang along his nerve endings.

"Say my name. Quick."

"Lathan." His name dawned on her lips, a glorious sunrise to his ears.

He closed his eyes. "Again."

"Lathan. Lathan. Lathan."

"I can *hear* you." His voice caught. Almost sounded like a sob, but it wasn't. No way was he going to cry like a fucking baby.

"Lathan." She gasped his name. It was the sexiest sound he'd ever heard, the sound of her on the edge of pleasure. She grabbed his face between her hands and stared into his eyes as he continued to move inside her. "You hear me? Really hear me."

"Yes." He rocked against her, deepening, lengthening his stroke, giving her all of him. Every piece of him.

They came together with her wrapping her legs around his waist, her body contracting and clenching around his dick. The orgasm slammed into him like a boulder in a still pool of water, radiating out through him in ripples of intense pleasure. He felt reshaped, remolded into something different and new and untested. Something greater.

Chapter 11

ETERNAL WHITENESS EXPANDED OUTWARD IN EVERY DIRECTION. Silence was sovereign, supreme, and sharp as a scalpel. She remembered what had happened last time when she made a sound. This time she'd keep her lips clamped shut. No one could say she wasn't a fast learner.

Knowing she *should* remain quiet made her want to call out to Lathan. Could she yell loud enough for him to hear her, to wake her up? Surely not. Dr. Stone said she was in a different dimension when she had one of these dreams—a dimension reality couldn't find. Even if she could yell across dimensions, Lathan wouldn't be able to hear—unless they were having sex. That was something neither of them knew how to categorize.

Evil was behind her. She felt its malicious energy changing the air, charging it with apprehension, making it heavy and thick and resistant when she tried to suck it into her lungs. Her arms and hands quivered. Her insides fluttered. Muscles twitched in her eyes. Fear settled on her back, riding her like an invisible demon.

Wake up. Wake up. Wake up. She pinched her arm. Nothing. Slapped her cheek. Nothing. No escaping.

"Please. I need your help." A male voice. Volume normal, not excruciating. So everyone else's volume was normal, but hers would be punishing?

She forced herself to face the horror she knew was behind her.

Lying on the ground was a guy. His brown hair boyishly long, feathered over his forehead like a pop star. In his eyes she saw the fading hubris of someone who thought he'd live forever, but made it only to his early twenties. He looked so normal.

Except his torso was severed from his hips and legs.

Organs oozed out of him onto the stark white surface. Blood pooled around him, framing him in crimson. His foot twitched, slapped in a puddle of blood. *Splack. Splack. Splack.*

Vomit gushed from her mouth, slobbering down her chin and neck. She bent and heaved on the floor. Splatters of her foulness pelted the guy's face. He didn't flinch, didn't blink.

"God, I'm sorry. I didn't mean to—" She fastened a hand over her mouth, but then realized her volume was normal. Normal. Not the magnified resonance that threatened to liquefy her brain.

Her legs wobbled, threatened to let her down, but she locked her knees. She might be shaking so badly she looked like she was seizing, but she was going to keep control of her body this time.

The guy's chocolate-colored gaze met hers. "Tell my mom to stop looking for me. I don't want her to find out about this." Water swelled in his eyes, overflowed. His Adam's apple bobbed as he swallowed and cleared his throat. "It would kill her, and she needs to be strong for Kallie."

"Kallie?" She shouldn't have asked, shouldn't encourage communication with him when he felt so, so...evil.

A genuine smile brightened his eyes. "My little sister. She's my heart. She has leukemia. Me being gone will be hard on her, but if something happened to Mom, it would decimate her. She's only twelve. She has an entire lifetime in front of her."

Evanee's eyes burned, but she swallowed back the tears that wanted to form. Crying never solved a problem. "I'll tell your mom. And I'll tell your sister how much you love her and want her to live."

Maybe she could handle these dreams. If all she had to do was relay a message.

"You need to take this." He held his hand out to her. Scarlet covered his fingers, coating the chunky ring he held.

"I'll give her your message. That'll be enough." She felt like a shit for saying that, but she didn't want to touch him or his ring. He might look like a typical guy—except for the severed torso—but there was still an aura of wrongness about him.

The Thing, that invisible force that controlled her, grabbed her arm, yanked her toward what the guy offered.

She clenched her fist. The Thing hadn't taken over her hand yet. And she wasn't going to let it. She concentrated all her energy on clenching her fingers as tight as they would go. Her jagged nails sliced into her palm. A bead of blood welled up, higher and higher until it hit the tipping point and dripped. It hung suspended in midair for an impossible length of time. Then crashed to the floor.

A sonic boom gusted over her, whipping her hair around her face, burning her ears so badly she swore they had to be bleeding, but still she didn't open her hand.

The Thing, invisible to her eyes but very real, tugged at her fingers, harder and harder. Her hand shook with the effort it took to maintain a fist.

The pressure vanished.

Had she won?

She watched her thumb rip backward, felt the crack, the pop of her bone being torn out of its socket, but didn't hear anything. Pain ricocheted from her thumb to her wrist, up her arm to her elbow, and faded as it got closer to her shoulder, then boomeranged back down to her thumb and back up again with each beat of her heart.

Her knees buckled. She fell, landing in her own vomit, but her arm remained bizarrely suspended in air. Her shoulder socket stretched and strained from the suspension of her hand. The warm, wet weight of the ring fell into her palm.

"Honey. Wake up." Lathan's voice penetrated the White Place like the omniscient voice of God.

The white faded away. Underneath was nothing. Nothing she could see, name, hear, or feel. A void.

Her heart, already running a sprint, kicked up the speed as if it recognized a threat her mind couldn't comprehend. "What's going on?" she asked the guy, but he was gone. The blood was gone. She was alone.

And then she fell. Arms flailing. Body twisting. Screaming. Waiting for impact.

———✺———

Impact. Her entire body—arms, legs, torso, head—hit at the same time. But it didn't hurt. And it should've. Was she dead? She held her breath, waiting for someone to answer that question for her. But if she was asking the question, that at least meant the neurons in her brain were still firing, so she had to be alive. Right?

Awareness, *true* awareness dove into her mind with all the grace of a belly flop.

She vaulted upright, but something anchored her left hand, holding it immobile. Panic burned through her stomach. The Thing. Her gaze swung wildly, found Dr. Stone standing at the foot of the bed—*What was he doing here?*—then landed on Lathan. He knelt on the floor next to the bed, cradling her hand against the tattoo on his cheek. Worry wrinkles creased his forehead, and concern colored his eyes in sadness.

"Hey, I'm all right." She reached out to him to massage the wrinkles from his face, but her hand was splinted and wrapped in a thick, brown bandage. "What happened?"

"Your thumb was dislocated," Dr. Stone answered.

"What are you doing here?" she blurted out.

"I called him." Lathan pressed her hand tighter to his cheek. His stubble licked against her skin, eliciting a very specific memory from their afternoon of sex. The memory of him rubbing his cheek against her inner thigh right before he'd tasted her. "You vomited in your sleep. Your thumb was dislocated. You wouldn't wake up. It's been over an hour." Worry rode each syllable he spoke.

His words seeped through her skin, struggled to get through the thick bone of her skull, then finally permeated deep enough to make sense. She looked down. She'd fallen asleep naked—in Lathan's arms—but now she was wearing one of his thick sweatshirts. And the sheets were not the same ones she'd slept on the past few days. "My dream… It was…bad, really bad, and then I heard you." She flexed her fingers against his cheek. "I heard you tell me to wake up, and the White Place disappeared and—"

"We'll talk about your dream in a moment."

Impatience sped Dr. Stone's speech. "Any dizziness? Disorientation? Brain fog?"

"No. I feel fine." If she were being totally honest, she would've said she felt better than fine. She felt good. Energized. Like she was ready to run a 5K forward and backward.

"Doesn't your thumb hurt?" Dr. Stone asked.

"Not at all. Is that weird? I've never dislocated a bone before."

Dr. Stone's gaze locked on her hand pressed to Lathan's cheek. She could see him analyzing and formulating an opinion about them. Yeah, it probably looked odd. So what? Lathan didn't mind and neither did she. It was sweet the way he held her hand so tightly to him like he didn't ever want to let her go. Like she was precious.

"I set your thumb, but you'll need X-rays to be sure there aren't any chips or bone fragments. Come by the house tomorrow, and I'll do that for you."

"How much will I owe you?"

A calculating gleam narrowed his eyes. "A small favor is all."

Warning. Warning. Warning. Lights, sirens, alarms all shrieked through her brain. "What *kind* of favor?"

"I'd simply like for you to take your hand off Mr. Montgomery's cheek."

"That's it?" If that's the only thing he wanted, she was getting a super door-buster deal. She tried to tug her hand away from Lathan, but he held on to her. His eyes seemed to speak the word his mouth never uttered. *Don't.* But then he released her.

A chill sank into her chest, settled into her heart, pumped out into her extremities. She began shaking, her teeth clacked, and her hand pulsated sharp stabs of frigid pain. She hunched in on herself, cradling her injury to her chest.

"You're hurting now, aren't you?" Dr. Stone stated.

Lathan grabbed her hand and slapped it against his cheek.

Heat spread through her, melting away the frigid agony. Dear Mother of Mercy, what was going on?

"Pain is gone, isn't it?" A satisfied-with-himself smile quirked the corners of Dr. Stone's mouth. "I knew it."

"Why? How? What's going on?"

Lathan answered, "I don't know what's happening, but I know you feel better when you're touching me."

"You feel it too?" Dr. Stone spoke to Lathan, but Lathan's attention was on her.

"It's a cool, fluid connection, almost like a magnet drawing us together." Lathan never took his gaze off her.

"It feels warm to me."

"You feel connected because you are. Mr. Montgomery, you are her protector. And she is yours. You possess the power to heal each other."

To heal each other? The words echoed in Evanee's mind. Was that why Lathan could hear when they were intimately connected? "Can you hear right now?"

"Only when your hand is on my cheek." He turned to Dr. Stone. "Why? Why can I hear when her hand is on my cheek, but when she takes it off, I can't?"

"What is the nature of your hearing problem?"

"When I was thirteen, I was attacked. My eardrums were punctured." He spoke the words matter-of-factly.

She gasped. She couldn't help it. She couldn't

imagine Lathan ever being a victim. And yet in some ways he still was. He still reacted with fear whenever someone touched him from behind.

"The doctors repaired as much of the damage as possible, so I do hear some sounds."

"I would speculate that your ears are healed. They just never healed properly, and something about touching her hand to your tattoo bridges the healing gap. It's no coincidence that the tattoo on your cheek is a Native American symbol for healing."

She'd forgotten about that. "I don't understand what's happening." She sounded like a whiny brat.

Lathan moved from kneeling next to the bed to sitting with her. It was awkward trying to keep her hand pressed to his face at the same time he moved. They probably looked like they were playing some odd form of Twister, but she didn't want to let go of him any more than he wanted to let go of her.

"You know the bear, right?" Dr. Stone asked.

"The bear?" She and Lathan spoke at the same time.

"The carved bear at the top of the hill. Near my place."

Just this morning she'd noticed how lifelike the totem appeared, had half expected the bear to turn its head and follow their progress toward Dr. Stone's driveway. "I'm not following what the bear has to do with anything."

"Damn…" Lathan spoke the word as if he'd gained some long-lost recognition.

"Not many people know the story behind the bear. But I do. And you both need to hear it. It will explain so much about you both." Dr. Stone pulled a small leather book from his pocket—the binding worn and frayed from many readings. With care, he opened the book, stared at the page for a moment, then began speaking.

"A man, different than all others, used to roam this land. A man who was more than man. He carried a bit of spirit inside him. But even that bit of spirit was too great to contain within. Some of it showed on his skin..." Dr. Stone's voice spread, completely immersing her in another time.

Evanee saw in her mind the outcast man named Bear and the abused maiden he rescued named Fearless. Witnessed how Bear kept Fearless safe even though the Bad Ones constantly stalked them and tried to steal Fearless from him. But nothing could hurt Fearless and Bear when they were together. They possessed a bond stronger than the hills. They were a shield against harm. Both carrying the power to heal each other.

"As long as the light shines in one of you, the other shall live." Dr. Stone's words resonated through her like someone had plucked a chord of pure truth.

Evanee's mind delved back into the story. Watching Fearless find joy and laughter with Bear. Watching her possess night sight and, with Bear by her side, becoming the wisest woman in the region—sought after for her guidance and counsel. Together she and Bear brought peace and prosperity to the region unlike any seen before.

Dr. Stone's voice became heavy and labored as if he were speaking through great emotion. "As they approached the end of their earthly lives, Bear carved a totem on the crest of the highest hill to remind all in the region; he would protect Fearless into eternity.

"They went to the ancestors together. The tribe built a great funeral pyre in honor of them and anointed their bodies in bear grease before setting the blaze. Every village in the region witnessed the black smoke burning in the sky.

"A week later, after the fire cooled, the tribe gathered the ash and rubbed it over Bear's totem to seal their power together inside the carving for eternity."

Silence broke the story's spell.

Fearless and Bear's world faded from her vision—as if it had been playing out in her memory instead of being just a story. An iron knot lodged itself in Evanee's throat, and unshed tears burned her eyes. She wouldn't let herself grieve for Fearless and Bear—that just seemed silly.

Dr. Stone scrutinized her and Lathan, almost like he saw through them, beyond normal to the realm of possibilities. "I believe you are Fearless and Bear come to life."

She had anticipated those words, and yet they split her into two halves.

Half of her recognized she had felt safe with Lathan from the moment she'd met him. And when they made love, it was... She almost couldn't put words to it. It was fresh, exciting, and new, but comfortable, easy, and familiar. Like lovers reuniting.

The other half of her scoffed. "Everything you want me—us—to believe defies reality. How can any of this exist?"

"It doesn't matter *how* it exists. It does. If you don't believe me, remove your hand from Mr. Montgomery's face. The pain will hit in seconds. That *is* reality."

"She's not moving her hand." Lathan's tone carried his true meaning—*I'll fucking kill anyone who causes her pain.*

"Maybe I have a psychological problem that makes me believe I feel better when I touch him."

"How do you explain Mr. Montgomery's ability to hear?" Dr. Stone shot an arrow straight through her defenses. He'd just hit upon the one thing she couldn't explain away. Lathan could hear. His eyes, always colored in a layer of sadness, now shone bright as silver. For him, she wanted to believe everything the doctor said, but two people blocked her way.

"What about Xander and Isleen? *They* are Fearless and Bear."

Dr. Stone's brows rose—the only indication that her leap of logic was right on. "What makes you certain there can only be one pair?"

"Because there were only Fearless and Bear in the story."

"What if their power is too great to be carried by one couple? What if the power had to be split and divided? What if—"

"It's all a giant *what-if*, isn't it? You're asking me to believe in something I don't understand, accept something I want to reject, and trust in something that could hurt me."

"Honey." The way Lathan spoke her name carried an urgency and a yearning for her to understand. "For months now, I've been drawn to that bear carving. Compelled to stop there, but every damned time I left feeling stupid because it was just an inanimate hunk of wood. This explains it." His phone buzzed. He glanced at the screen. "That's Gill telling me he's arrived."

"Now? Why's he here now? You two just had a fight." She noticed the split in his lip was completely healed. Gone. Like it had never been there.

Lathan must've followed the path of her gaze. With his free hand, he touched his mouth, probing to find the injury that was no longer there. "I texted him to pick up the ring you brought back from dreamland. I have to let him in. I'll hurry—be gone no more than thirty seconds." She could tell he was worried about leaving her in pain.

"I'll be fine." She leaned in and gave him a quick peck on the lips, but he deepened the kiss until she felt boneless and breathless and weightless. Then he was gone, his boots thudding down the stairs.

The pain was low grade, a minor annoyance. "Are Isleen's dreams the same as mine?"

"Hers are very different. She is taken to a place she says looks like heaven—"

"The White Place."

"—but then it changes. She's shown a series of events and how they will play out if someone doesn't intervene. And she has somnambulism—she's a sleep-walker. Xander's up half the night following her around, making certain she doesn't hurt herself. Sometimes she acts out parts of her dreams."

"Why doesn't Xander wake her up? If it were me, I'd want to be woken up."

"As long as her life isn't at risk—that's why Xander follows her to make certain she is safe—she wants to use her dreams to help people."

"My dreams are of murdered people. My dreams aren't helping anyone."

"Are you sure about that? These things you bring back aren't random. They serve a purpose."

What purpose? As soon as she asked herself the

question, Lathan's words played through her mind. *Because of the lead you gave Gill about Guadalupe Mountains National Park—and after a preliminary DNA confirmation—a team was sent there to search for the body of Juanita Valdez. She went missing from her home in Salt Flats, Texas, the night you dreamed about her.*

Lathan hurried back into the room before she could devote some brainpower to puzzling over what that meant. His gaze was immediately on her, assessing her for pain.

"Barely hurts anymore." She raised her splinted hand and mimicked a cheesy dance move, then pointed at him. "You. Come here."

He resumed his spot on the bed next to her. After everything he'd done for her, there was no way she'd deny him the ability to hear, and she couldn't very well get out of bed. She was fairly certain she wasn't wearing anything underneath his sweatshirt.

Gill walked into the room. Stopped. Took in everything. "Dr. Stone, what you doing here?"

"Mr. Montgomery called when Evanee wouldn't wake up."

"Looks like she's awake now." Muttered sarcasm made a wide trail through Gill's words.

"Wow." She matched Gill's sarcasm and raised him one. "Seriously?"

Lathan threw his words at Gill. "You're pissed at me—fine. Be pissed at me. But stop being an ass to everyone else."

Gill faced Lathan, surprise lit his eyes. Guess he hadn't expected Lathan to hear his mutterings.

"When she touches my cheek, I can hear." Unrestrained excitement filled his voice. And she was happy for him. So happy to give him the gift with her touch.

Gill didn't say anything, but disbelief narrowed his eyes.

"I'm not bullshitting. Thought you deserved fair warning. Talking behind my back won't be tolerated."

Gill mock-saluted him with his middle finger.

Instead of inflaming the already tense situation, the disrespectful gesture made Lathan chuckle.

Dr. Stone's cell phone rang. He checked the screen and then answered it. "Matt?" He listened for a moment, then his gaze darted to Evanee. "I'm with her right now." He held the phone out to her. "It's Matt."

Matt? Why the hell did he want to talk to her? She didn't want to talk to him, and she didn't want to take her hand off Lathan's cheek to hold the phone. "Hello?" Her voice came out harsh and laced with attitude.

"Thomas called me. He doesn't have your phone number and thought I'd know how to get hold of you." His tone was an accusation.

"Okay." What was she supposed to say? "I'll call him in a few days."

"Evanee." Matt's voice softened and she heard the echo of past affection, but he didn't say anything else. The seconds ticked by.

This was ridiculous. As if she didn't have enough shit going on in her life. She sure didn't need to be having random phone calls with Matt. "I'm hanging up."

"Thomas said…" The volume of Matt's voice trailed off. "He said your mom's dying."

Only three words—*Your mom's dying*—but they weighed more than any others ever spoken to her. They settled on her shoulders, binding her to the awful moment.

"He said your mom has only a few hours left, and she wants to see you. She's at home."

The line fell silent.

Evanee couldn't think of anything to say. No words seemed to exist. She handed the phone back to the doctor.

Lathan placed her hand on his cheek. "What is it?"

She met his gaze and couldn't look away. "I need to call Ernie. I'm not going to be at work tonight."

"What's going on?" All of Lathan's attention was on her.

"I need to go to my mom's. Right now."

"What's wrong?"

"She's. Dying." She spoke each word separately, yet they still added up to the same meaning as when Matt had uttered them.

"I didn't realize she was sick."

"Neither did I."

Chapter 12

Six hundred ninety-six Dandelion Lane.

A strangeness came over Evanee. Numb, but hyper-sensitive. Dizzy, but steady. Disconnected, but coherent. Anger mixed with fear, desperation, and shame. No words could adequately describe the emotions waxing and waning inside her.

Every time she visited she entered an endurance test for her masochistic side. Long ago, she had discovered her masochistic side was quite small and fragile.

The Victorian mini-mansion was painted lively yellow, trimmed in pristine white, with red, blue, and green striped awnings covering all three of its expansive porches. Its design was distinctive in a town where most of the residents cobbled together their homes room by room.

On either side of the front porch pillars, Rob's traditional autumnal display presented a magazine-perfect picture—bundles of cornstalks, pumpkins, and mums. Behind the decor, ugly memories crouched in the shadows.

"If you don't want to be here, we can leave." Lathan shifted to see her face, his eyes full of understanding he couldn't possibly possess.

"I don't want to be here, but I can't leave." She wasn't making any sense, but Lathan accepted her words.

She forced her feet to move up the sidewalk, flanked

by Lathan and Gill, who insisted on coming to watch his friend's back. Gill might be an asshole, but he was a good friend to Lathan—most of the time.

Lathan knocked on the door. Good thing, since knocking hadn't occurred to her.

An older woman answered. Her thinning gray hair was twirled into a tiny bun and perched on the tippy top of her head like a bird's nest. She wore autumn-themed scrubs and a heavyhearted smile of compassion. "You must be Rosemary's daughter. You look just like her." She motioned for them to come inside. "She has been waiting to see you. I've administered another dose of morphine so she's resting quieter now."

Evanee walked across the threshold and felt diminished—like she was three feet tall, a helpless little girl again. She hated the feeling, but it settled into her, nestling beneath her skin and burrowing into her brain. Nothing ever changed in the house. Maybe that was why she always felt like she'd never grown up whenever she entered it.

Gleaming hardwood floors. Ornate antiques—a Victorian collector's dream. No dust. No dirt. Nothing out of place. She didn't need to look to know the wedding photo was over the mantel. The entire home was designed to produce a picture of family happiness. All of it a lie.

Lathan tucked her tightly to his side, his arm a steel band of strength and protection across her back.

"Why didn't she tell me she was sick?" The words blurted out of her mouth.

The lady drew in a slow, deep breath through her nose, then answered. "I've been encouraging her to reach out to you and your brother, but she was adamant that you not be burdened. It wasn't until today, until she felt the end was close, that she requested to see you both."

Evanee didn't have any words to say in response so she just nodded.

"She's upstairs—" The nurse kept talking, but Evanee wasn't listening as she started up the ornate staircase.

And suddenly she was standing in the doorway, staring at the nightmarish figure reclining in the raised bed.

That *thing* couldn't be Mom.

It was a skeleton covered by a thin layer of blue-tinged flesh. The ridges and contours of its skull were apparent through the skin. Its cheekbones jutted out at sharp, angry angles. Dark, sunken-in hollows where cheeks should be. Its mouth open, gasping for each breath. Tongue thrusting out like it needed to taste the oxygen. Wheezing, slurpy sounds as if it inhaled through water. The sound was a fresh kind of horror.

Evanee's head buzzed. Her stomach soured. She felt terrified and sickened at the same time.

How could *that* be her mom?

Yet it was. Evanee recognized the thick mass of black hair—a legacy that she and Thomas had inherited from their mother.

Lathan hugged Evanee to his chest, a powerful wall insulating her, but she couldn't look away from Mom. He spoke against her hair. "Ahhh. Honey."

Everyone in the room turned toward them. Rob and Junior were on one side of Mom's bed. Thomas—her baby brother—on the other. He was taller and broader than she was, his face more heavily chiseled than hers, but they shared the same color hair and eyes. Only his eyes turned down a bit at the edges, giving him an expression that resided somewhere between kindness and sadness. And his face was a splotchy red, like it always got when he was upset.

An excited pang resonated through her heart at the sight of him. They'd never been close, but she'd missed him.

Her brother glanced up at her. The look he gave her said *Please don't make a scene*.

Rob looked the same as he always did. He must've made a deal with a demon so he'd never age. As usual, his casual clothes were a uniform of their own. Starched khakis and a polo shirt. The perfect combination of casual and professional.

A lumpy raspberry bruise spanned up Junior's cheek and down his neck. Must be from the fight at the motel where Lathan didn't kick his ass but apparently kicked his face.

"Dad. That's Lathaniel Montgomery."

"Aren't you a little old to be a tattletale?" Evanee pulled away from Lathan to stand in front of him, blocking him from Junior and Rob.

Rob puffed up into his sheriff stance and walked leisurely toward them. "Son, you're in a lot of trouble. You need to leave before I call the boys and have you removed."

Anger colored Evanee's tone. "Don't call him *son*. He's nothing like your son. Call your boys. They can witness how fucked-up this family really is without the varnish and shine you layer over the shit. I'm done pretending. If they come, I'll talk. And I've got a lot to say."

Rob stopped halfway across the room as if he'd run into an invisible force field. His eyes widened, his mouth opened, but no words came out.

"I'm not taking any more of your shit." She pointed at Junior. "Yours either."

"Ev, stop it. Now is not the time for your drama." Thomas's big, blue puppy-dog eyes turned on her, but she was immune to their charm.

"My drama?" Evanee's volume was too high, but she couldn't control it. "Are you blind or stupid or in on it?"

Thomas flinched away from her as if she'd just slapped him. The expression on his face was one she couldn't quite read—confusion, sadness, and the hard realization of something he hadn't let himself acknowledge until just now.

"Ev, I need you to tell me what you're talking about." Thomas's tone was equal parts urgent and serious.

"Ehhvv…" The gasp of sound came from Mom.

One moment Evanee was in the doorway, the next she shoved in next to Thomas. Lathan bracketed her safely into his side.

"I'm here." A harsh undertone spiked each word. She forced her voice to go soft. "I'm here, Mom."

"We both are." Thomas sounded huskier than usual.

"Mom, I'm here too," Junior said and grasped Mom's hand.

Mom coughed. Wet and choking and struggling.

Evanee flinched, and Lathan's arm around her tightened. The sound of her mom dying wormed into her brain, latching on to her memory banks.

Mom's eyes were partially open. The blue irises slid over, focusing on her.

The nurse stood at the end of the bed, gently rubbing Mom's leg. "You can talk to her. She can hear you. Her body just can't respond."

What was she supposed to say to her dying mother? *Why did you let Junior hurt me? Why didn't you love me? Why didn't you tell me you were dying?* "Why, Mom? Why?"

Mom's eyes never left her. Evanee bent closer, searching for something like remorse, but saw nothing. She hadn't really expected Mom to pop off with an explanation that made everything all right, but a tiny piece of her had hoped. Obviously, the time for answers had passed.

A good daughter would tell her mom she loved her, would even say she forgave all the bad, but she supposed she had never been a good daughter and couldn't make herself say words she didn't mean. How could she love someone who had condoned Junior hurting her?

"Mom. *I'm* here." Junior's voice cracked with emotion. If he had been anyone else, Evanee might've felt sorry for him. "Mom. Mom. Look at *meeee*."

In this, Mom's last moment, she completely ignored Junior. Evanee couldn't help feeling a bit triumphant.

A tear slipped from Mom's eye, slid down the hollow of her cheek where it trembled on the ridge of her jawbone. She heaved a great undulating breath that seemed impossible for such a frail body.

Life faded from Mom's eyes. And then...

Stillness.

Silence so quiet it ached. A hush so bitter it hurt.

—～—

Death.

Lathan had smelled it the moment he entered the house.

And now he stood with his arm around the woman he cherished at the bedside of a living corpse—a decaying, rotting body whose heart just realized it was pumping blood to dead organs.

He turned his attention to the SMs. One day when he told Honey about his genetic defect, he could share her mother's last memories. Choosing an SM was as easy as selecting a DVD off a shelf. Watching it would only take a few seconds. He inhaled deeply through his nose and allowed her mom's SM to encompass both eyes.

A full moon hung above them, casting silver over the world and illuminating the shadows in shades of midnight. The night sounds—insects and tree frogs—were the perfect accompaniment to Evan's low humming. He held her tightly to him, swaying in a slow dance under the dome of the sky.

She pressed her nose against his bare chest and inhaled the smell of him. There weren't any words she could use to describe his actual scent, but warm *and* smooth *fit best.*

She kissed him right over his heart. Her lips swollen from his kisses, her body aching in that delicious way only a well-fucked woman can feel.

Evan whispered. "A hundred years from now, when we're dead and gone, somewhere in time, in space, maybe in heaven, this moment will continue to exist."

Her heart was full, painfully full of love for him. He was her moon and stars and night sky. He was her sunshine and green grass. He was her entirety. There was no her without him.

———

She could barely eat, she was so nervous. No, she was excited. No, scared. She was all three.

Evan didn't notice her watching him eat. He was always hungry after his shift at the sheriff's office, and today she'd cooked his favorite meal. Fried chicken, mashed potatoes, corn, and homemade rolls.

"Evan." She waited until he looked at her.

A my god, woman, you can cook smile was on his face as he chewed.

"I'm pregnant."

His smile tumbled off his face—she swore she heard it splat in his gravy. He swallowed, then looked at the table she'd set with her fancy dishes, platters of food, candles, and flowers. "That's what this is about." He jabbed his fork toward everything.

Not what she was expecting him to say. Not at all. Disappointment poured tears into her eyes. "Well, yeah."

Evan shoved back his chair and stood.

She wanted to say something, but wasn't sure what to say. He seemed…mad. But why would he be mad? They hadn't exactly talked about having kids, and it wasn't like she'd planned to get pregnant, but it had happened.

"Evan—"

He threw his fork across the room. It clattered and clanked against something.

Her heart slapped against her sternum.

He picked up his plate, threw it with just as much violence. Before she could utter a sound, he flipped the table over. The crashing of dishes and splintering of furniture hurt her ears, and she shrunk back in her chair—the only chair still standing.

Evan stalked from the room out the door. She sat in stunned silence. In less than five seconds, he'd destroyed her meal, their kitchen, and her life.

Part of her wanted to pack her bags and leave. The other part—the part reminding her that she was having his baby—couldn't let go so easily. Maybe she'd said something wrong. Maybe he'd misunderstood her.

She ran after him and caught up with him just as he was about to get in his truck. "Evan. Wait. Talk to me. What's wrong?"

He grabbed her arms, his fingers digging into her muscles painfully and backed her against the driver's door, trapping her with his body. In his eyes, the man she loved was gone, replaced by a rabid beast.

"Whose is it?" he shouted, his breath smelling of mashed potatoes.

Distantly, she heard a car approaching, but she couldn't focus on anything but Evan. Tears washed her cheeks with their salt. She could barely speak around the terrible sobs racking her body. "Yours, baby. Yours."

He was a jealous man. She'd known that from the beginning, but it had never been an issue. He was the sun she revolved around. There was no one else. Never would be.

He grabbed her chin, his fingers no more gentle than they'd been on her arms. She whimpered and tried to pull away, but he forced her to look at him—in his eyes. "What was the meal about?"

"It was supposed to be a celebration." *Messy sobs strangled her words, but she knew he heard them. Her entire world had been ripped apart. Everything she'd envisioned for their future—gone. He let go of her chin. She turned her head to the side, couldn't bear to see the beast inside him.*

"Evan. Let her go. You're scaring her." *Rob, Evan's best friend, stood close beside them with his son, Junior. The kid watched her and Evan with wide, apathetic eyes.*

Stupidly, she felt embarrassed that a kid would see her in such a powerless position.

The rigid length of Evan's body mashing against her relaxed. The anger in his eyes faded until the man she loved returned.

Gently, slowly, he gathered her to him, wrapping his arms around her, holding her close, but it felt different—she felt different. She felt stiff as a two-by-four and couldn't make herself relax into him, couldn't hug him back.

"I'm so sorry. I just love you so much and I thought—I was being crazy—I thought you were telling me someone else got you pregnant. I don't know why I thought that. Maybe because you surprised me." *He whispered the words against her ear, then drew back. His gaze locked on her jaw, on the place he'd grabbed, on the place that still hurt.* "I'm so sorry. I'm sorry." *He knelt in front of her and put his forehead on her stomach.*

The fear, the hurt that had clenched her tight loosened.

"Forgive me. Say you forgive me." *He kissed her belly.* "Both of you."

He won her over with both of you. *"I forgive you."*

"You two are having a baby?" Rob asked.

Evan kept his attention locked on her, but didn't answer the question.

"Yes. We're having a baby." She spoke with an even, unexcited tone, so different from how she'd felt before everything bad had happened.

"Well, then, congratulations."

She pushed a smile onto her lips. "Thanks."

Evan hadn't said anything about being excited to be a dad. But he loved her again, and wasn't that what was most important? As long as they loved each other, they'd figure everything else out.

―――――᠊ᠰᠠᠬ᠊―――――

"Leave him," Dad pleaded. "Be the mom you want to be to Evanee and Thomas instead of just some woman who visits them a few hours a week. They need their mom, not an old man, raising them."

Dad's words hurt but were the truth.

A few hours a week―Evan's rules. Not what she wanted, but what she had agreed to in order to keep him happy. The simple fact that she put Evan's happiness above her kids made her a bad mom. The worst kind of mom.

She rocked her sleeping baby boy gently. Just like Evanee, he'd been born with a thick cap of black hair. And just like when Evanee was born, Evan had insisted she make her father watch him. Evan hadn't seen Thomas since his birth, and that was the last time he'd seen his daughter too. He had absolutely no feelings for either of his kids beyond jealousy for the few hours she spent visiting them at her dad's house.

She'd thought she could change him, make him love the kids, but now she realized how naive she'd been.

"You can move back here. Save your money. I'll be here to help if Evan gets out of control. You won't have to deal with him alone."

Dad wasn't saying anything he hadn't said a hundred times over the past two years, but today it was tempting in a way it hadn't been before. She was tired, worn down mentally from being split between pleasing Evan and knowing she was letting her kids down. Up 'til now, she'd focused on Evan, made changes for him, while he made nothing but demands of her.

"Okay. You're right."

Dad slumped in his chair like he'd gone boneless. "Finally."

"I'll go home tonight, act like everything is all right, then while he's at work tomorrow, pack my stuff and be gone by the time he gets home."

"That's probably wise." Dad had seen Evan in a temper. That was part of the reason he'd agreed to take both Evanee and Thomas. Didn't want Evan to hurt them when he got into one of his moods.

"I've got to go." She handed her sleeping son to her father, then knelt down next to Evanee. "Baby, I'll be back tomorrow and I won't leave ever again."

Evanee never looked up from playing with her doll. Why should she? Rosemary was practically a stranger to her own daughter.

She tousled her child's hair, stood, and walked out the door.

Once she was in her car, the doubts crept out of the dark corners of her mind. She loved Evan. How could *she leave him? The man she fell in love with was still inside him, still knew how to be a romantic, still knew how to twist her heart into a love knot. But lately, the bad days had been outnumbering the good days. Ah, but the good days weren't merely good, they were spectacular.*

She glanced in the rearview mirror. The two empty and rarely used car seats were a glaring reminder of everything wrong with her life. Her resolve returned.

She pulled into their driveway, suddenly aware that she didn't remember one moment of the drive home. She parked next to Evan's cruiser.

A stillness settled in her body, something she hadn't felt in so long that it was foreign. She was doing the right thing. She just had to get through tonight.

Her legs were steady as she headed up the sidewalk.

Inside, the house was too quiet, too neat—not at all how it should be. Cartoons should be blaring on the TV. Thomas should be fussing, and Evanee should be banging her toys together. Toys and bottles and laundry should be all over the place. The house should sound and look like a family lived there.

And suddenly she couldn't stand to be there. But she knew she couldn't leave—not yet. She picked up the phone and dialed Rob's number. He'd intervened a number of times when Evan got out of control. She needed him now.

"Who you calling?"

She startled so violently that she dropped the phone. It clattered to the floor, dangling by its cord.

Evan stood in the kitchen doorway. He still wore his uniform. As he walked into the room, he took off his gun belt and draped it over a chair. "I said, who you calling?"

"I'm moving back to Dad's." *She shouldn't have blurted the words out. She should've kept them secret and hidden until she was safe, but a sick part of her wanted him to beg her to stay, wanted him to promise to change, wanted to give him one last chance.*

"The hell you are." *The beast in his eyes promised to hurt her. Bad.*

She turned to run, but he caught her around the waist and slammed her face down on the kitchen table. Pain dazed her senses, and by the time she could think again, she realized he'd cuffed one of her hands to the table leg. Her wrist ached from the way it was bent over the edge of the table at an unnatural angle. She bucked her hips, tried to move, but Evan pinned her legs against the other end of the table.

"Evan. No! Don't do this." *She screamed against the wood. "I won't leave. I promise. I'm sorry."*

———

She lay underneath his body. His blood gushed over her, scalding her back and pooling underneath her torso. It dripped and poured onto the floor, the sound loud as a faucet in the silent house.

She'd shot him. Killed him. With his own gun. She hadn't meant to, or maybe she had. Why else had her free hand sought his gun belt? Why else would she have aimed the gun over her shoulder at him?

She began crying and knew she was never going to stop. She cried until the blood cooled, then chilled, and she shook as much from her sobs as from the cold.

"Rosemary." *Rob was suddenly there, hauling Evan off her.*

He uncuffed her wrist, but she couldn't move. She was too sore. Too tired. He pulled her off the table but lost his grip on her, and she sank to the floor.

"Rosemary. Tell me what happened." Rob's tone carried the calm authority of a policeman. He knelt next to her, his face expressionless.

"I...shot him. I killed him." The sobs ratcheted up to a new level of miserable.

"Stop." Rob's voice was a sharp crack of sound that startled her into silence. He looked around the room—blood covered the table, the floor, had splattered against the wall and part of the ceiling—then back at her. "You'll go to prison for this. You'll be lucky to be out by the time Evanee and Thomas have graduated."

She wanted to die. She needed to die. Life was over. She reached for the gun.

Rob grabbed it first, ignoring the blood all over it, and tucked it inside his pants. "That's not the answer. I have an idea, but you'll owe me. I'm putting my job and my life on the line for you."

"Anything, Rob. Anything. Just make it go away. All of it."

And he did.

~~~

"Mommy, Junior hurt me between my legs."

Her hand lashed out, cracking against Ev's mouth hard enough that her palm stung. She was horrified at what she'd done, but buried the feeling deep inside. If Ev ever told anyone, Rob would kill her precious daughter.

"Liar. Never say that again. Ever."

Fat tears swarmed in her child's miserable blue eyes.

A red palm print stood out on Ev's pale face, and blood drizzled from the corner of her mouth.

"Go to your room. Don't come out until tomorrow morning."

Ev ran up the stairs, the sound of her sobs trailing behind her.

On wobbly legs, Rosemary crossed the room and sank down on the sofa. She had destroyed Ev's life. All because of her own stupid decisions.

Now she was trapped in a marriage to a pervert and his equally twisted son. Trapped too well to leave. She had no family—Dad's death still haunted her. No money. No job. No car. Where could she and the kids go that Rob wouldn't find her? How had she ever looked at him as her savior?

Once she'd threatened to confess everything, but Rob reminded her of what would happen. She'd end up in the psycho unit with the crazy label. She had no proof of anything. No gun. No body. No evidence. No way of implicating Rob in covering things up. Who would believe her over the deputy sheriff who was the sheriff's chosen one?

Her children would suffer even worse. With no other relatives, Ev and Thomas would remain in Rob's custody, no matter what happened. Once she was out of the picture, it would be a matter of time before not only Junior was messing with her girl, but Rob too.

It came down to degrees of awful. Junior messing with Ev was less awful than Rob. Junior was technically still a kid. He couldn't hurt her as badly as—

The SM ended.

Lathan's vision returned. Honey's hand was on his

cheek, her thumb caressing his skin. He smelled her worry in the air.

"Are you all right?"

Shit. He'd stayed in too long. It only took a few seconds for each SM, but somehow Honey had noticed. His face heated up, a bead of sweat tickled its way down his spine. He felt like he'd just been caught in the middle of an immoral act with his pants down.

"I'm fine. It was nothing." Dealing with his shit was the last thing she needed.

"What happened? It was the same as that night at the diner."

He felt everyone's eyes watching him. Knew exactly what they'd seen. It wasn't natural for anyone's left eye to roll around the socket independent of the other one. Gill called it his poltergeist look. "Later. We'll talk later."

"He's fine." Gill spoke from the foot of the bed. Must've come running when he thought Lathan's ability was about to be exposed.

Honey kept her hand on his face. "There's just one thing I need to do, then I'll be ready to leave." She faced Junior and Senior.

Junior looked and smelled like his entire world had just died. That was odd. Lathan would've thought the asshole incapable of love.

"I'm going to offer you both a deal you don't deserve. When I walk out of this house, I'm never going to think about either of you ever again. You're going to leave Lathan alone, forget you ever met him. And if by chance I see you out in public, you better turn and go the other direction. Because I'm done with the secrets, and I'll start talking to anyone who'll listen."

Chapter 13

BY THE TIME GILL PARKED AT LATHAN'S BACK DOOR, THE gray sky had finally faded into evening. The day was almost over. About time. Honey had soldiered through everything, but every warrior had limits and Lathan didn't want to test hers.

He heard Honey speaking to Gill, but couldn't make out the words.

Gill raised his hand in a semi-friendly acknowledgment. Honey got out of the car. Little Man greeted her with his paw in the air, doing his best impersonation of a good dog.

Lathan paused, hand on the door handle, a chuckle tumbling around in his throat.

Honey fit into his life so seamlessly that he didn't want to remember the pre-Honey days. If Gill would quit staring at his colon and pull his head out of his rectum, he'd see how much better Lathan's life was because of her. Worry about being overwhelmed by SMs—gone. Struggling to understand speech—gone. He could hear. Fucking hear. It wasn't perfect—her having to touch his cheek—but he wasn't going to tread on the miraculous.

Gill touched Lathan's arm, gaining his attention. "I'll be back tomorrow morning. I need Evanee's statement about the ring."

"When you're done, can I get a ride to the car dealership?"

"You're going to buy a car? For her?" Gill jutted his chin toward Honey.

She was scrubbing at Little Man's ears. Anyone who thought dogs weren't capable of facial expression had to be blind. Little Man's jaw hung open, his eyes were partway rolled up in his head, and his normally dangling jowls were pulled back in an intimidatingly toothy grin.

"For us." Lathan said, still watching Little Man and Honey. Gill touched his arm again.

"You don't have experience with women. You don't know what they are like."

Lathan sent him a look full of warning.

Gill held up his hands in a gesture of peace. "You sure about her? This thing with her is speed-of-light quick."

Lathan met his friend's gaze. Held it. "She's the only thing I am sure of." He got out of the car and was only vaguely aware of Gill driving off as he watched Honey and Little Man. Honey darted in one direction, changed course, went another, and Little Man frolicked after her. Fucking frolicked—like he was a twenty-pound puppy, not a two-hundred-pound beast. Joy bubbled out of Lathan in a laugh he didn't hear, but felt in his chest and throat and mouth.

Honey finally ran up to him, laughter on her face, the smell of spring on her skin—happiness. That she could be happy after the bipolar kind of day she'd had was evidence of her strength. "You're feeling good." He couldn't *not* touch her. He put his hand on her neck, his thumb caressing the sharp bone of her jaw.

"...like all the bad has died so something good can take root and grow."

He understood. More than she meant him to.

"But it has been a long day." The scar at the corner of her mouth hitched up into a giant grin. She pretended to yawn. "I'm going to go to bed early. Want to join me?"

He drew her to him and brought his mouth to hers. "Fuck, yeah," he said against her lips. She pressed her mouth to his, sliding her tongue into him. Her flavor exploded across his taste buds, traveled through his body, and converged in his groin.

Tap. Tap. Tap.

Her hands slid into the back of his jeans, over his ass, squeezing and kneading. He almost couldn't think, couldn't continue kissing her from the erotic sensation of her massaging his ass.

Tap. Tap. Tap.

She hooked one leg high on his hip. He lifted her and she straddled him. Her warm feminine center settling over his erection.

Tap. Tap. Tap.

She shimmied against him. The friction—exquisite, excruciating. He wanted their clothes gone. Now. Needed to eliminate all barriers, wanted the slip and slide of flesh against flesh. He carried her into the house.

Tap. Tap. Tap.

Halfway through the living room, Honey pulled away from him. "Is that your phone?"

The sensation that he'd been ignoring crashed into his awareness.

Tap. Tap. Tap. The unique pulsation meant one thing. His parents.

And they never texted for the sheer fun of it.

"Shit. Fuck. Damn."

"What is it?" Her legs tightened, pressing his erection

even harder against her center. He felt the groan in his throat, knew it was full of the sounds of wanting and frustration.

"I have to take care of something. You go on upstairs. I'll be up in a few minutes."

She unlocked her legs from his waist, but he held on to her until he was certain her feet were solid on the ground.

"Go on up." He gave her a quick peck on the lips and a smack on the ass to get her moving. The scent of her desire was heavy in the air around him when he finally pulled his cell from his pocket to find a text from his mom.

Your father and I just pulled in.

Fuck. Fuck. Fuck. He read the next message.

We're at your door.

Getting rid of his parents—priority one.

He untucked his T-shirt to hide his erection and hauled in a giant breath. The air smelled and tasted like Honey's desire. Which didn't help with the erection situation. He walked to the front door—Mom was always one for formality—and opened it.

The rush of scents clogged his airway. He coughed into his fist. Amber. Sandalwood. Orange blossom. Vanilla. Deer piss. Fucking deer piss. In Mom's perfume. He was half tempted to tell her, but didn't want to engage in any unnecessary dialogue.

Underneath the stench of Mom's perfume, Lathan

smelled the truth. Discomfort. Disgust. Annoyance. Anxiety. The same feelings his parents had every visit. The reason every visit was torturous.

Mom wore a black dress better suited for a gala than visiting his home. She was petite with long blond hair—that he was certain wasn't all hers—and never seemed to age. The miracle of modern plastic surgery, he supposed. She reminded him of those women on that *Housewives* show.

Dad was decked out in slacks, a tie, and a jacket. Mom always picked out his clothes.

Mom signed. *Son. Hello.*

He was tempted to answer her in sign, just so Honey wouldn't hear, but he hated signing. It never felt natural to him. Never. He attempted to control his volume as he spoke. "Mom, don't do that. I can still hear some things, and I can read your speech as long as you look at me when you talk."

"I'm just trying to make things easier…"

No, she wasn't. Being the mother of a hearing-impaired child was something his mom had made trendy. Oh, how she had enjoyed the accolades of her friends when she'd taken class after class in American Sign Language. It hadn't mattered to her that he didn't like sign and didn't intend to use it.

"I prefer speech reading. And have ever since I was thirteen." Reading his parents' speech took concentration. He only saw them twice a year for a few minutes each visit. Not enough to firmly learn their patterns. He shifted to block the entire doorway. "Now is not a good time for a visit."

That look of eternal consternation—the look she

always wore around him—pinched his mother's lips. "Gill called... weren't acting right... not having an episode, are...?" Mom always called them his *episodes*. Those times when he'd gotten so lost in an SM that he couldn't find his way back to reality.

He clenched his fists. Knuckles popped. "Gill should mind his own fucking business." Just when he thought shit between them was getting resolved. "I'm a grown-ass man. Don't need you checking up on me. And do I look like I'm having an episode?"

"Lathaniel. The use of foul language makes... sound lowborn," Mom said.

Lowborn—to Mom, that was the worst insult. She used it for anyone not born with a golden spoon up their ass. Or those who generally pissed her off.

"...might not be having an episode but... are not behaving normally... haven't invited us in, and we drove all this way."

"I'm fine, and now is not a good time for a visit." He repeated the words slowly, hoping they would penetrate.

Mom threw her hands in the air in a gesture of unrestrained exasperation. It was always like that with her. They never meshed. Everything he said, everything he did was always the opposite of what she wanted from him. Always.

Honey's scent fluttered to him an instant before she slid in next to him. She wrapped her arms around his waist and gave him a tight squeeze. Tension that he hadn't realized resided in all his muscles eased under her touch. Her hand slid up to his cheek.

The gesture wasn't because she was in pain; it was so he could hear. Her thoughtfulness melted his resistance.

Mom's gaze locked on Honey's hand on his cheek. He covered Honey's hand with his own, feeling like he needed to protect her fingers from the calculating look in Mom's eyes.

"Hi, there. I'm Evanee. You must be Lathan's parents. He's got your build"—she nodded toward his father, who was staring at her with open admiration—"and your eyes." She nodded toward Mom.

"Linda and Nathan." Lathan supplied their names.

"Oh, I get it. *L* from *Linda* and *athan* from *Nathan*. What a cool way to name your child!" Honey's voice was filled with enthusiasm.

Too bad he hadn't had time to warn her about his mom.

"You've got a girl." He hadn't heard his father's voice since he was thirteen, but there was no mistaking the incredulity in his tone. "And a good-looking one at that." He winked at Honey.

She giggled. "You're not so bad yourself. I see where Lathan gets his looks."

"Like father, like son." Dad smiled, and Lathan realized he hadn't actually seen his own father smile in… He couldn't even remember the last time. Was his family that miserable? Yeah, it was.

Mom focused on Honey. "Eevvaneee…" The way Mom spoke her name sounded like they were long-lost friends finally reunited. "So nice to meet you, darling." She reached out her perfectly manicured hand. A hand whose hardest workout came from lifting all the gold and diamonds she insisted on wearing.

Honey reached out with her splinted hand. Her fingernails jagged, her skin red.

Mom hesitated, a look of revulsion crossing her features.

"I keep forgetting about this thing." Honey touched her splint—mistaking the meaning of Mom's look. "It doesn't hurt. I promise." Honey clasped hands with his mom, pumping enthusiastically—completely unaware that she was holding the hand of a snob.

"He's a handsome one, isn't he?" Mom's gaze flipped to him only momentarily, before returning her full attention to Honey. He hadn't heard his mom's voice since he was thirteen, and even he could hear the over-the-top friendly tone.

Honey looked up at him, warm affection naked on her face. "He sure is."

"I so wish he hadn't destroyed his face with that ghastly tattoo. Is that why you're covering it up?" Her tone was all fake innocence. Her face the picture of angelic purity. "You can't stand it either?"

Mom's tongue wasn't sharp. It was a surgical laser. But her words no longer hurt him. He'd long since realized he'd never be his mother's image of a perfect son. Her perpetual anger at him was really a reflection of her own frustration at not being able to present an immaculate family image to all her society friends.

"Evanee. What a unique name." Dad's words rushed out—an attempt at distraction from Mom's nastiness. Which was rare for him. He hardly ever poked his head out of the foxhole when Mom had her sass on. "How very nice to meet you."

Lathan heard Honey's silence. Smelled her anger.

"You come here to Lathan's home—uninvited—then insult him?" Her fingers on his cheek flexed, and her short fingernails dug into his skin, but not enough to be painful. "What's wrong with you?"

Dr. Stone was right. She was as much his protector as he was hers. Damn if he couldn't help smiling like a goof.

Mom raised her hands as if in surrender. "Oh. No. Dear. I mean no harm. No disrespect. It's just with his episodes…"

The smile fell off his face and crashed on the floor.

"Well…he does unpredictable things. Like tattoo his cheek. Or lose control."

Evanee looked up him. "What's she mean by *episode*?"

"Lathaniel Montgomery." Mom clasped her hands to her chest, feigning shock. The woman was theatrical enough to have been an actress. "You haven't told her? She has a right to know. Evanee, my son has—"

"Enough." Lathan roared the word loud enough that everyone jumped. "Leave. Now."

"Evanee." Mom stepped forward, one arm open wide, looking like she wanted to scoop Honey up into a protective hug. "You should come with us. He's upset." Mom sounded so sweet, so sincere, so much like a snake.

Lathan didn't wait for Honey's response. He dragged her back from the doorway, sent an apologetic look toward his father, and then slammed the door in their faces. Locked it.

Honey's anger at Mom faded to the scent of garlic. Fear.

She pulled away from him. Everything inside him urged him not to let her go, but he did.

"What are your episodes?" Evanee moved in front of Lathan to make certain he could see her every word.

The sharp planes of his face hardened with an emotion that lived somewhere between anger, hurt, and sorrow. Touching him would soothe whatever he was feeling. She reached for his hand and held it between both of hers.

His skin was hot and dry. He latched on to her, his grip secure and strong, and yet she felt the uncertainty beneath his flesh and bones.

"Does it have to do with what happened at Mom's earlier? You know, with your eye?"

"I don't want to talk about it right now."

"But I need to know right now."

He shook his head, the cords in his neck tight with tension.

Something was wrong. Very wrong. He had episodes. His bitch mom made them sound scary. And violent. "Are you sick?" Tears congregated in her eyes. She hadn't been able to find one drop of mourning for Mom, but the mere hint of something happening to Lathan was enough to make her cry an ocean.

"No. God, no. I'm fine." His expression softened. He caught a tear as it started its slide down her cheek, brought it to his lips, and tasted it.

Her heart went weightless inside her. She felt like it was falling but recognized what the sensation was—she was falling in love with him.

"Don't cry over me. I never want to be a source of your pain." Sincerity sounded in his voice.

"Then tell me. I need to know or I'm going to think the worst. Especially after seeing Mom…"

He closed his eyes and shook his head in timeless resignation. "I didn't want to do this. Especially not today." He swallowed, his Adam's apple bobbed. "I have a genetic anomaly. The olfactory regions of my brain are twice their normal size. My olfactory sense is off the charts. They literally can't even measure it. I can smell everything." His sad gray eyes opened and bore directly into her soul. "Even memories."

Even memories. Even memories. Even memories. Memories. Her memories. Did she even have any good memories? Not until she'd met him. Her face began to tingle. A muted throbbing began behind her eyes. She wanted to call him a liar, claim that what he said couldn't possibly be the truth. But his honesty was etched in the misery on his face. "How?"

"Every moment of our lives we're breathing. Our brains automatically link whatever scent is in the air to activity in that moment. The action of linking scent and memory leaves energy markers on people. My nose smells those markers, and my brain sees the memory contained inside."

The throbbing intensified. Her throat felt funny, like she couldn't swallow. Could she even speak? "You've seen my memories."

"I can't smell your memories. I think it has something to do with how you said food doesn't taste right. Scent plays an important part in people's appetites."

Thank God and all his tubby little angels. If Lathan ever saw the horrors in her mind, her humiliation would be deeper than a bottomless abyss. "So an episode is when you're having…er…smelling someone's memory?"

"Pretty much."

"And that's what happened at Mom's? You were smelling a memory."

"Yeah."

"Whose memory?"

Something shifted in his eyes, softened into an expression she'd never seen from him before. Recognition slammed into her. Pity. He was giving her a look overflowing with pity.

That day he'd almost hit her in the kitchen, he'd gotten mad at her for pitying him. Back then, she didn't understand his anger. Now she got it. Pity sucked giant elephant balls. His pity made her a *victim*. Pity pissed her off.

"You know." Her brain paused, letting the space between thoughts grow infinite while she waited for confirmation.

"Since the night I met you. From Junior."

He hadn't even questioned what she meant. He didn't need to. He knew. No wonder he never asked her questions about Junior. About her mom. About her life. He already knew the answers.

"How could you not tell me something this important? I trusted you." She tried to pull her hand out of his, but he kept a viselike grip on her.

"And I've never betrayed your trust. Not once. Let me explain." He spoke with a calm his face didn't express.

"Explain!" The word exploded from her mouth loud enough that he had to have heard it. "You just did. From the moment I met you, you've been secretly looking at everyone's memories about me. Not many good ones, are there? Bet you really enjoyed Matt's and—"

"You wanna know why I didn't tell you?" The volume of Lathan's voice overrode her. "Because of the reaction you're having right now. And—" He dragged her toward the stairs.

She tried to pull back, but his strength was far superior to hers. "Let me go." Anger made her resist him the entire way up the stairs, but his grip never slackened.

In the bedroom, he stopped in front of his dresser and dropped her hand. Curiosity kept her rooted to the spot.

He ripped open the bottom drawer and scooped out an armload of files. He dropped them at her feet. "—this. This is why I didn't tell you. Because after you read through just a few pages, you'll prefer Morty's Motor Lodge over staying with me."

His face was red. His eyes bloodshot and shiny and pleading. He turned and left the room.

Anger at his deceit roiled beneath her skin. There was nothing these papers could possibly say that would excuse him for not telling her he knew every rotten detail of her life. She almost followed him to tell him as much, but the file titled *Children's Hospital* caught her attention.

She opened it.

June 12, 1989
Name: Lathaniel Owen Montgomery
DOB: May 28, 1983
Presenting Problem:
Six-year-old boy of below-average weight and above-average height. His parents have brought him in—at the insistence of the boy's pediatrician—for his continual violent outbursts. On several occasions, he has struck both of his parents, but both insist they don't believe his violence is intentional. He becomes unresponsive to them and appears to be responding to internal stimuli—hallucinations—and

acts out according to what he is *seeing*. The boy rarely eats, claiming his food always tastes bad. His pediatrician has mentioned a feeding tube if the weight loss persists.

Observations:

The patient acts in a bizarre manner. He sweeps his hands through the air as if he is blind, yet his eyes are open. His left eye flutters and moves independent of the right one. His parents claim their doctor has said their son's eyes are normal. The boy's behavior is always worse following this kind of episode where his eye is moving.

Mental Status Exam:

The patient is unresponsive to either of his parents, direct questions, or external stimuli in the room. He will obey simple commands if repeated and guided through the motion of them. Affect is labile. One moment he is sitting quietly; the next, he is batting at the air and shouting.

Course of Action:

Patient will be admitted to the Children's Behavioral Unit for further observation and testing. Antipsychotic medications will be administered to combat the hallucinations.

Patient will be tested for seizures.

A consultation appointment will be scheduled with an eye specialist.

Parents will be referred to the Parental Coping Skills Class.

Provisional Diagnosis: Psychotic Disorder Not Otherwise Specified.

Prognosis: Guarded to Poor.

All the anger inside her faded to shocked curiosity.

Her legs folded beneath her, and she sat on the floor in the middle of the papers. Papers about his life. His terrible life.

He'd only been a little boy. A sweet, innocent child.

She rummaged through the documents. Page after page of admissions. All for the same problem. She wasn't educated, but it seemed like the doctors pumped him full of enough drugs to sedate him, then sent him home. At six years old, he'd been medicated and sedated.

A pink carbon-copy page—dated years later— grabbed her attention.

Incident Report

11/3/96, 7:15 p.m. When I heard screaming, I ran into the common room. Lathaniel Montgomery was on the floor. Justin Slider was sitting on his shoulders, jamming pencils into Lathaniel's ears, screaming that he was killing the demon living inside Lathaniel's brain. Justin was restrained, placed in isolation, and administered a sedative. The emergency code was called. Lathaniel was transported to the emergency room.

F. Anderson

Lathan had said he'd been attacked, but she'd never imagined something like this. He was so strong and proud that the thought of him being a victim just didn't fit with what she knew of him.

She flipped through the rest of the papers.

Until he turned eighteen, he'd been admitted to Children's Hospital at least every few months, sometimes for months at a time.

She grabbed the next folder. Two Vallies Mental Health Center. She leafed through the pages. More of the same. Admission after admission. Drug after drug.

Date: 7/16/03
Name: Lathaniel Montgomery
Interventions: Patient has not responded to medications. ECT treatments will be scheduled.
Dr. Despare

Evanee's mind flashed back to high school psychology class, to Mrs. Roman showing them the video clip of Jack Nicholson's character being given shock treatments in *One Flew over the Cuckoo's Nest*.

Date: 7/18/03
Name: Lathaniel Montgomery
Interventions: Patient was returned to his room and is resting after his first treatment. A course of twenty treatments will be administered.
Dr. Despare

Guilt and shame and nausea roiled in Evanee's belly for how she'd treated him.

Date: 7/19/03
Name: Lathaniel Montgomery
Interventions: Gill Garrison, who has Lathaniel's

power of attorney, removed patient from the facility against medical advice.
Dr. Despare

What was your intention? she had asked him when
she discovered he'd been hiding his hearing problem.

For you to know me first. To see that I am normal.

Those words took on a deeper meaning. They were
about a man who'd experienced a shitty childhood,
who'd survived pencils jammed in his ears, who'd
endured shock treatments, and felt that no one would
accept him and his genetic anomaly.

And she'd rejected him—just like he'd expected.
All because he knew her deepest shame and darkest
moments. Moments she wanted to keep hidden away,
because if anyone knew, they'd look at her differently,
treat her differently—the exact reasons Lathan kept his
own secrets.

She was a total and complete hypocrite. She hated
hypocrites. Hated herself for how she'd reacted when
he'd handled her issues with grace and treated her
with dignity.

Evanee left the papers scattered over the bedroom
floor and ran from the room. Not one more moment
could pass without her apologizing, without her telling she loved him—genetically weird abilities
and all.

When she was halfway down the stairs, Little Man
started barking. The sound wasn't the woofing and
chuffing of him playing outside; it was angry and menacing. Fear licked the back of her neck.

Pguull!

A gunshot.

A canine scream of pain.

Silence.

A terrifying rush of certainty iced her skin. She knew, she just knew, Junior was outside—and he wasn't target shooting. He was here to *kill* Lathan.

"Lathan!" She yelled his name with all the force inside her at the same time she hit the bottom step.

He was in the kitchen, hunched over the sink, head down, dragging in ragged breaths of torment.

He looked up. His chiseled features were ravaged with agony that went beyond body and mind, but spoke without words of how she had wounded his spirit. Guilt wanted to gut her, but that would have to wait.

"Lathan! Run!" She screamed so loud her throat burned.

The back door exploded inward. Splintered shards of wood scattered across the kitchen. Gun first, Junior stormed inside.

Evanee ran toward Lathan, but time held her in its elusive grip, slowing her progress, while speeding up everything around her.

She watched, utterly helpless, as Junior aimed the gun at Lathan. Pulled the trigger.

The sound was an earthquake. It shook her knees, rattled her body, and knocked the breath from her lungs.

Lathan jerked, but remained on his feet.

Impossible hope flooded her mind. Maybe Junior had missed. Maybe he'd fired a warning shot, not a kill shot.

Time finally released her. She skidded to a stop in from of Lathan, waving her arms wildly at Junior like he was a basketball champ and she was blocking him from scoring the game-winning point. "Stop. You want me. I'll go with you. Just leave him alone."

Junior's face was a nightmare. The melding of handsome features into the too-harsh lines of evil.

Lathan settled his hand on her shoulder, and reassurance flooded through her body, chasing away the panic. But then his hand slid off, banishing the comfort. She turned. Lathan went to his knees. Blood geysered from his chest. Splattered to the floor. Shock paralyzed her.

Fear, anger, hurt were all absent from his eyes. What she saw was the gentle acceptance of someone who loved her. She wasn't sure she deserved that kind of love—especially after how she'd treated him.

He collapsed.

"Lathan! No. You can't die. Not now. Not now!" Something immense cracked inside her. If it broke open, she'd die. She went down next to him.

As long as the light shines in one of you, the other will live. The story of Fearless and Bear. An absurd calm settled over her. She only had to heal him. *As long as the light shines in one of you, the other will live.* And her light was a fucking beacon.

She reached for him.

Junior grabbed her by the hair and yanked her back, nearly ripping the hair off her head and her head off her shoulders. She scrabbled to get leverage, footing, something to ease the sensation of being scalped, but her feet and legs were slick with Lathan's blood.

"Don't fight me. Don't you fight me." Junior yelled the words.

She forced herself to stillness. The pressure on her head eased, then he let go of her. She rolled to her knees and launched herself at his legs, taking him down. The moment he hit the floor she was on top of him, wrestling him for the gun. He swung his gun hand up over his head, out of her reach, and smacked her with the other. The crack of his palm against her cheek startled her to a stop.

"You hit me." He'd molested her, raped her, restrained her, defended himself from her, but had never hit her. She stared at him and didn't recognize what she saw. The monster inside him was more vast, more evil than she'd ever imagined.

His gun arm swung. A second too late, she realized his intention. The gun in his fist smacked her in the temple.

Pain exploded in her head. Everything blinked to black. It felt like just a moment, but when color returned, she realized too many things all at once.

She was naked. Junior was on top of her. Her breast ached with a deep, throbbing burn that pulsed in time with her heartbeat.

"I've been too lenient. Dad kept telling me, but Mom said you'd come around, that you needed time."

Something wasn't right with her body. Her limbs felt too thick and too heavy and too slow.

"No more. Today you're getting the punishment you deserve. Look what you did." He grabbed her face, forced her head to the side to look at Lathan's body. He was so still. He wasn't breathing. His eyes open, but no light in them. And blood. Blood everywhere.

"You killed him. *You* did. With your actions." Junior's hands squeezed her face.

Pressure built inside her head. She didn't want to give him the satisfaction, but she couldn't control the whimper of pain that escaped her lips.

"You're selfish. You always have been. You act all self-righteously angry with me, but have you ever once thought about how badly you've hurt me?"

"What are you talking about?" Her voice was slurred and tired sounding.

"I had to live with knowing you were fucking Matt Stone. I had to live with knowing you were fucking this guy. Do you know what that does to a man? To know his woman is fucking everyone but him? It eats him up inside. It devours his heart."

"I was never your woman."

"Yes, you are." Junior slammed her head against the floor, the force of it so powerful she couldn't even tell what part of her hit. Her entire head was a writhing mass of pain. Her mouth tasted like hot garbage. Her body stopped working. Her eyes rolled, unable to lock on any one thing.

Something hot and wet misted over her face, but she couldn't see anything in her swinging vision. Couldn't find the strength to reach up and wipe whatever it was off her face.

Gurgling sounds. Choking.

Junior moved off her.

Muffled thumping.

Silence and darkness slid over her.

Chapter 14

NIGHT BROUGHT HARMONY TO THE BARREN WOODS. A breeze wrestled with the dead leaves, filling the air with soft sighs. Naked branches clacked together, the sound hollow and melodic like wind chimes made of human bone.

Even though James had been watching Lathaniel's home for seventeen hours, inquisitiveness vibrated in his bones, keeping him wide-eyed awake. Curiosity had fought a brief but violent battle with his prudence. Curiosity won. Now he was going in. Going to find out what happened after the last gunshot.

He covered every bit of his body with the cleanroom suit, palmed his Ruger—just in case—and moved through the forest toward Lathaniel's house.

The massive dog was still alive. It lay on the ground, heaving great bellowing breaths as its body fought against the bullet lodged in its chest. The animal's black eyes watched James walk up the porch steps, but it could do nothing else to defend the homestead.

The back door stood wide open—a portal to the great unknown. Kitchen lights shone down, displaying the scene before him as if it were on a stage.

James's first impression was of Death's invisible presence.

Death's immensity filled the room. It changed the air, made it empty and hard to fulfill his body's need for oxygen, and transformed sound into muted shadows.

James never feared Death.

Death was his creation, but here in this home, Death became his friend and ally, and blood was the only color that existed.

The crimson stain was everywhere, on everything and everyone. It was inspiring. Beautiful. Would've been an enchanting image to record on film.

Three bodies. Two male—one of which was Lathaniel Montgomery. One female. Lathaniel's woman.

Death sidled up to James, breathed into his ear, telling him exactly what had happened between the two men. He had no reason to question Death's assessment. Death never lied. It was part of their agreement; James fed Death, and Death was loyal to him.

Death didn't speak of the woman. She was alive and of no consequence to Death. But she captivated James.

Her naked torso wore blood like body paint. Despite the coating, James could see a jagged ring of tooth marks marring her left breast. A human animal had masticated her. A prelude to rape—foreplay for the perpetrator. The wound itself wasn't that remarkable. He'd seen that kind of injury on no fewer than a dozen women during his career. He had granted Subject 57 that experience.

He could still remember the tremendous pressure it took to bite through Subject 57's breasts. Human teeth weren't designed for biting and chewing raw flesh.

The reason James had been watching Lathaniel—the entire reason—was to figure out how a lowly special skills consultant obtained hair and a tooth from a victim not yet discovered by the authorities. And the eye. He'd somehow found the eye. There was no conceivable explanation. James's answers had vanished along with Lathaniel's life.

An idea slid out of James's mind, squirming and
wriggling like a freshly birthed babe: Take the woman.
She and Lathaniel were obviously lovers; he could get
answers from her.

A thrill of electric energy raced up the back of
his neck. This was what had been missing from his
kills. Spontaneity. But spontaneity led to mistakes.
Spontaneity was just another word for losing control.
Control was more than his religion; it was his Father,
Son, and Holy Ghost.

So, take control of *this* scene. Wouldn't be hard to
do. With Lathaniel dead, no one would ever suspect
the Strategist.

Another idea—a twin to the first one—birthed: Set
the scene. Arrange the evidence to indicate *she* killed
the two men and then fled. While the local law enforcement officers searched for her, she'd be imprisoned in
his bunker.

She hadn't regained consciousness. That worried
James. And worry wasn't a skill he cultivated. He'd
planned every minute detail of every experiment he'd
ever conducted so he wouldn't have to worry. But with
this situation, nothing had been planned and everything
was impulsive.

He carried her across the bunker to the small bathroom. The space looked more like a studio apartment—
one giant room that housed his computer station, his
living area, the kitchenette, and the bathroom—than an
impenetrable fortress designed to keep him safe in the
worst of worse-case scenarios.

With a gentleness he didn't know he possessed, he settled her in the bathtub and turned on the tap, adjusting the water until it reached the perfect temperature. The blood covering her from root to tip had dried, mottling her in shades of crimson and rust. She looked like the heroine from a B-rated horror flick, and yet, he found the gore and her nakedness resplendent. He wanted to leave her that way, but the biological material was already decomposing. In a few hours, the stench would be unbearable.

Crimson streamers began trailing off her wet skin, coloring the water. He wet a washrag and wiped the blood from her face. With stroke after stroke of wet rag to bloody face, her skin was revealed.

A scar damaged one side of her mouth, pulling it up unnaturally. Without it, her face would've been one of the few examples of perfect symmetry—a biological indicator of beauty. An ugly stain of deepening red radiated out from her temple, engulfing her eye, her cheek, and part of her forehead. In a day or so, the bruise would deepen and darken and deform her face with its swelling. She probably had a concussion.

He removed the splint from her hand and examined her fingers. No swelling, no bruising. Looked normal.

The bathwater had turned shark-attack red, but he continued to use the rag to wipe the blood from her body and rinsed it from her hair. He drained the tub, refilled it, and then repeated the process two more times before the water remained clear. Only then did he soap up another cloth.

He toiled over his cleaning of her. He ran the cloth over her chest, around her breasts—careful of the beautiful bite — over her stomach, down each leg, and between her toes. He watched her face as he slid his cloth-covered hand between her legs and scrubbed her cleft.

His penis engorged.

He'd raped women. Men too. All in the name of research, but he hadn't really enjoyed the process. He'd always needed Viagra during those times. With the level of planning required for each experiment, the act had turned mechanical. But this, cleaning her while she was unaware, was more stimulating than anything he'd felt in years. He let his fingers slip out of the washcloth, let them explore her by touch. He felt like a teenager. He wanted to masturbate with one hand while he caressed her with the other.

So he did.

When he finished, he cleaned himself with the same rag he'd used on her — a perfect symmetry. One he normally would've relished, but his neck cramped and his body felt tense and uncomfortable inside his skin — a sensation he hadn't felt before. He paused to examine the feelings, to put a name to them. The answer that came to him was so unexpected he could barely acknowledge it.

Guilt. He felt guilt for what he'd just done to her. But why? It was trivial. He'd done far worse during his experiments. Maybe that in itself was the answer. He wasn't looking at her the same as he looked at his test subjects. He was looking at her like a human being.

He drained the water from the bathtub — didn't want her accidentally drowning like an unattended baby — and went to the bed, spreading a layer of clean towels on the mattress.

He lifted her from the tub. Her skin was slick and warm, and he knew that one day he wanted to touch her while she was awake and aware and make her enjoy it. He settled her in the bed.

Her muscles twitched, and her eyelids fluttered like dragonfly wings. He watched as her body slowly returned to consciousness. The moment her eyes fully opened, he began speaking. "Everything is all right. You're safe here."

If he wanted to gain her trust, one of the tricks would be to offer information instead of withholding. Her gaze took longer than it should to shift and find him.

"My name is James." Shouldn't have given her his real name. Too late now. "You're injured. I'm fairly certain you have a concussion. And I need to bandage the wound on your—"

"Where's Lathan? Where am I? I need to go to him." Her voice cracked and broke over Lathaniel's name. She tried to get up, her effort too weak and feeble to be effectual. "Where is he? I can heal him. Make him better. Where is he?"

James didn't meet her eyes—counted on his body language to send a message she would recognize. Her hand found his arm. He froze. Her skin was clammy. He imagined he could feel the intricacy of her lifeline melding into his flesh, marking him. No one ever willingly touched him. All his subjects shrank from him. But this—a touch freely given—was something he'd been missing his entire life.

He shooed the bizarre thought out of his mind and allowed his gaze to meet hers, but did not speak, just blinked and blinked, like the movement of his eyelids held back great emotion. The wait would make her feelings more intense. The more emotional he made her, the more vulnerable she would be to his influence. Finally, he looked down at the floor and shook his head once.

"No. No. No." Giant tears welled in her eyes, then spilled over. "Where is he? I need to see him. I need to heal him. I need to…" Her words slurred, and her eyes lost their focus. She would be unconscious again in less than five seconds.

James stroked her damp cheek with the back of his finger. Goose bumps peaked across her skin at his touch. Her reaction could be a fear response. Many of his subjects had that reaction, but it was usually paired with a flinch, a recoil. Could it be a pleasurable sensation? No way to know until she was fully awake, and right now, she could either be deeply unconscious or riding just below the surface of consciousness.

"You're hurt. I'm going to treat your wounds." If she was semiconscious, she would hear him, understand his actions. If she was out, well, at worst he was talking to himself. He spread antibiotic salve over the bite on her breast. The rough ridges of skin were swollen and had to be painful. She needed stitches, but she wasn't going to get them. He fought the urge to bend down and lick the raw wound. "I hope I'm not hurting you."

He placed a large bandage on her breast and taped it in place. "All done. You'll start feeling better soon." He wrangled a button-down shirt onto her limp form and then covered her with a blanket.

"Lathan?" she whispered.

He hadn't realized she was awake.

"Lathan? God, my head hurts. Lathan? Where's Lathan?"

James held a bottle of water to her mouth. "Drink."

"Don't want any." There was no petulance in her tone, just a thin hopelessness.

"You're going to drink two swallows. I'm not letting you die of dehydration."

Without further question, she drank the offered water.

"Lathan." Her voice was full of knowing.

"I'm sorry. He's…he's…gone." James breathed the last word for effect.

Anguish contorted her face. Sobs racked her body. Sorrow poured from her eyes.

He held her hand while she cried. It was too soon to offer any further comfort. Finally, the sobs ebbed to simple tears.

"Where am I?" she asked, closed her eyes, losing the fight to remain conscious.

"Safe. Where no one will hurt you," he answered, not sure if she heard him.

She didn't say anything else.

He sat next to her on the bed, caressing her wet cheeks with the back of his finger. It felt so strange to be touching her—skin to skin—when he'd spent so much of his life not daring to come into contact with anything that could ever be traced back to him.

The wireless in his ear pinged. He moved into the bathroom and shut the door so she couldn't hear.

He had known this call would come, knew exactly how to handle it. He hit the receiver to pick up the call, but didn't say a word. A breathy groan escaped his lips.

"Eric here. Major doings with Lathan Montgomery in

Ohio. Leaving Quantico in forty-five minutes. Briefing on the way."

James remained quiet.

"You hear me?"

Just like Eric not to even notice something was wrong.

"I won't be attending. Stomach flu." He forced weakness into his tone. Stomach flu was always a free pass. No one wanted someone vomiting all over the crime scene. Let alone their fear of him being contagious. "I'll pass the message on."

Click.

James spent the next few moments making the necessary arrangements to free his calendar. He wouldn't go back to work until after the weekend. Until she was on the mend. Until he convinced her that she *wanted* to stay with him.

Chapter 15

AWARENESS RETURNED TO EVANEE, BUT COHERENT thought refused to form. Her entire existence had degenerated into two elements: sensation and pain. She felt horizontal on a soft surface, felt the weight of blankets on her body, and yet her limbs quaked partially from cold, partially from pain. A thick, obtuse throbbing resonated from inside her head. Her chest burned with serrated agony. Heartbreak tormented her.

She floated in misery for eons until fragments of thought and memory finally collided, coalescing, forcing her to remember what she most wanted to forget.

Lathan was dead.

He was dead because of her. *She'd* brought Junior into his life. *She'd* relied on Lathan to protect her like he was ten feet tall and bulletproof.

Guilt pulled her too taut, threatening to tear her apart.

As long as the light shines in one of you, the other will live. Maybe he *was* alive. Even as the thought rose inside her, she recognized it for what it was: denial, hope's best and worst friend. Hope warmed her cold body and inflated her heart until the muscle threatened to burst. Hope forced her eyelids open.

Light pierced her brain, so she peeked out through the fringe of her lashes. A man sat beside the bed watching her. She willed his features to sharpen into the chiseled lines of Lathan's face, his eyes to morph into silver, his skin to darken with thick freckles. No matter how long she stared, he didn't change.

"Oh, you're awake." He placed his hand on her forehead like a mother—not her mother, of course—checking a child's temperature. "It's been almost three days. I was worried." When she couldn't find any words to say, he continued. "I'm not sure how much you remember from before. I'm James." He spoke in a perfectly articulate manner—so different from the slight distortion of Lathan's speech.

"Where's Lathan?" Her words were a frantic whisper. "Where is he? Where am I?"

James patted her hand. "You're safe from whoever hurt you. No one will find you here. But Lathan…" James's voice trailed off, his eyes aimed at a spot on the wall. "I-I don't know his exact location, but I-I…assume a morgue or maybe a funeral home." He winced as if he could see how his words broke her.

He kept talking, but she wasn't capable of listening.

The last fragile thread bearing the full weight of her sanity snapped. Evanee heard the soft snap, felt the pressure release resonating through her body. Hopelessness smothered her, killing the will to live. But her heart continued to pump and her lungs continued to suck. Her stupid body hadn't gotten the message her mind was sending. She was done. Done with life. Done with death. Done with all of it.

She came back to reality when James picked her up and carried her across the room to the bathroom. He settled her on the toilet. She let loose of her bladder. He wiped her like a child. She didn't care. He was a stranger, touching her intimately, and yet she couldn't find the will—a reason—to care. He could torture her, rape her, kill her, but he'd never be able to hurt her as badly as she ached for Lathan.

Without any emotion, she watched as he filled the tub with water. He unbuttoned her shirt, removed it, then picked her up and settled her in the water. She wanted to go back to sleep, and more than anything, she wanted never to wake up, but Mr. Sandman wasn't cooperating with the first of her wishes, so the asshole probably wouldn't comply with the second.

James washed her as tenderly as a child. She didn't care she was naked and he was seeing her body or scrubbing her private places. Her body didn't matter; her mind didn't matter. The only thing worth caring about was gone.

"I can't live without him," she whispered, afraid to say the words too loud.

James paused in his washing and met her gaze. "Hush now. The darkest night always births the most breathtaking dawn."

She sensed his words held a profound meaning, but couldn't see beyond her pain.

After the bath, he dried her off, re-bandaged her chest, dressed her, and tucked her into bed.

"Now go to sleep, Evanee. You'll feel better the next time you wake."

She closed her eyes but knew nothing was ever going to make her feel better.

"Evanee. I need you to wake up. Come on. Open your eyes, Evanee. You can do it. Just for a little while."

James's voice wheedled and droned on and on and on, keeping her just awake enough to know how awful she felt. Finally, she gave in and opened her eyes, just to shut him up.

"Good girl. I knew you could wake up." He held a glass full of a white liquid. A jaunty pink straw poked out the top. "I need you to drink all of this. You haven't eaten anything in four days. Your body needs calories, protein, vitamins, and minerals to heal itself." He held the straw to her lips.

Took too much effort to argue, so she began to slurp it down. The drink was cold and slimy in her mouth, and she suspected it was a blessing that she couldn't taste it. When almost two-thirds of the drink was gone, she paused. "Where's Lathan?" she asked.

James stared into her eyes. "I know you remember. What I don't know is why you keep torturing yourself."

"So I don't ever forget it's my fault he's dead." She sucked down the rest of the drink. After the last swallow, she said, "My fault. All my fault."

Mr. Sandman must've been in a good mood because he granted her sleep the moment she closed her eyes.

Infinite, incessant, infernal whiteness in every direction.

The White Place.

No longer possessing enough energy to hold herself upright, she felt her legs fold beneath her. She didn't brace herself against the fall, but the ground rose up, capturing her body in a cushioned embrace. Even that novel experience wasn't enough to make her care. Nor was the sensation of not being alone anymore.

She *felt* a presence with her. The presence didn't possess the terrible wrongness she normally felt in the White Place, but it sure didn't feel benign. It wanted something from her and was frustrated with her. And then she recognized the presence. It was the Thing that could control her body, The Thing that hurt her. And still she didn't care. Maybe this time it would kill her and she could be reunited with Lathan in whatever form the afterlife took.

Kill me. Kill me. Kill me. The words were a benediction.

A bizarre kind of silence halted all her thoughts—turned them off completely, leaving a fearful void where her mind used to be.

You will overcome. The Thing spoke, but it didn't. The words bypassed her ears and originated from deep within her brain in a soundless voice. *You are the Bearer of Dreams. You are required.*

Her thoughts floated out of the abyss. *I don't care.*

You are needed.

I don't care.

I will force you.

I know.

So why fight?

I'm not fighting. I'm submitting. I give up. But this is the last time. For some moments, she was completely alone in the blank space where her thoughts used to be. Maybe the Thing had left.

No. Its energy charged the air, and she could feel its invasion in her brain—taking her thoughts.

You would end your existence?

Yes.

Because you are absent your protector? The Thing

sounded attitudinal, like she was a recalcitrant kid it had to put up with. *Open your eyes, Dream Bearer.*

When she didn't bother complying, the Thing pried them open for her. No surprise there. She expected to see white, or a body, or something gory and frightening and horrifying.

Her eyes took in the image, but her brain had trouble with the translation.

Lying next to her, mere inches away, and looking so breathtakingly alive was Lathan. He wiped at the tears wetting her cheeks. His touch was electric, jump-starting her dead heart.

She settled her hand over his tattoo. Underneath her fingers, the scratch of his whiskers, the warmth of his skin, the suppleness of his flesh teamed up and tried to convince her that he was real. "Am I dreaming inside this dream?" she whispered around the stone of grief choking her throat.

"I don't know." His hand wandered into her hair and settled over her temple, the source of the constant ache in her head. Warmth and comfort and safety flowed from him into her. The pain eased.

"Are you..."—she struggled to say the word—"dead?"

"Honey, I don't know." Sincerity and sadness shone in his silver eyes. "All I know is I'm here with you right now, in this moment, the only moment that matters."

Her chin trembled, and a fresh flow of tears fell from her eyes. "I don't want to wake up. I want to stay here with you. Forever."

She placed her hand on his heart, over the gunshot wound she refused to look at. She couldn't bear the confirmation that he was as dead as everyone else she'd ever seen in the White Place. "I'm sorry. So sorry. It's all my fault. All of it."

He gathered her tight into him and draped his leg over her hips, encasing her body with his. They didn't speak. Words weren't needed. They fulfilled each other in such a way that they were one united entity, not requiring speech because they were inside each other's thoughts and feelings.

He witnessed her guilt and grief and absolved her of it. He saw inside her soul to the damage Junior had done and healed her with his understanding. He showed her an image of herself, one reflected through his eyes, and what she saw filled her with awe. Her soul was a beautiful tangle of fragility and tenacity and bravery.

She reached into Lathan's mind. Felt his fear. Fear of a world overlaid with images—memories—that weren't his own. Fear of being attacked again. Fear of her rejecting him. She banished his fear and allowed him to see himself as she saw him. As a man of courage, strength, and kindness, with a little bit of superhero tossed in.

Chapter 16

JAMES SAT NEXT TO THE BED, WATCHING HER, VIGILANT for any indication of distress. Sleep for her was continually fitful.

Behind her closed eyelids, her eyes darted. REM sleep. Dreaming. Was she having a nightmare? Could she possibly be dreaming of the person who'd been taking such tender care of her? It was too soon for him to be having such thoughts, yet his mind wandered in sentimental circles around her. He couldn't help it.

The past days of caring for her had endeared her to him in a way he never would have suspected possible. On a fundamental level, she appealed to him because of her total dependence on him for shelter, food, cleanliness. She even needed him for her mental acumen. If he let her, she'd slip off the slope of sanity into suicide. The desperate sadness around her told him as much. But he held her in a firm, unwavering grip, and he didn't intend to let go. He planned to heal her. Put her back together in such a way as to make him her other half.

She flinched and cried out a small animal sound of pain. He grasped her hand and held it tightly in both of his. Instantly, she calmed and tightened her grip on him. Her hand might as well have been wrapped around his heart, the way the muscle contracted from her touch.

Because he couldn't resist, he stroked her cheek with the back of his finger. Instinctively, she turned into his touch until he opened his hand, allowing her to nestle her face against his palm. She received comfort from him, and he gloried in the novel experience. So different from how people flinched and fought him. And why wouldn't they? He specialized in ending life—Death had been his life.

As a naive, traumatized kid, he hadn't seen any other option but to follow Death. Now the adult version of him saw a new path. Taking her pushed him over the finish line and through the starting gates of something new.

To her, he could be whatever he wanted to be. He could be her tormentor or her savior. He could make her need him or want him. He could make her hate him or love him. She changed all his rules.

Even the cold concrete walls of his bunker no longer seemed so drab. The utilitarian furniture not so sparse. The quiet of being underground no longer lonely.

In her sleep, she lurched, a full-body jerk so violent and unexpected that he startled. And he didn't startle easy. This woman was full of surprises.

"Shh…" The left side of her face was a rainbow of painful bruises, and her eyes were puffed and pink. He contented himself with simply stroking her cheek with the back of his finger. "You're here with me. Safe."

Her tortured eyes locked with his. Guilt and sadness lived in the dark-blue irises, but something new had begun to grow—a fragile bud of trust in him. He expected her to ask about Lathaniel again, but she didn't.

Finally, he'd taken the lead in the race against Lathaniel's ghost. It'd only taken five days.

Victory pumped inside his chest, warming him like he'd just downed a shot of whiskey.

Her gaze shifted away from him to where he still held her hand in one of his. "Do you feel it too?" Her voice was scratchy from disuse.

"What do you mean?" The moment he spoke, he felt it. A warm, hard nub between their palms. An object that hadn't existed moments before was suddenly, undeniably, unexplainably there. He yanked away from her. In a fluid motion, she scooped the item out of his palm before he had a chance to see it and clasped it in her fist. "What is it?"

"A bullet." Tears welled in her eyes. "The bullet that killed Lathan." She cradled her fist to her heart, wincing when she touched her injured breast.

James sat back in his seat. The past thirty seconds replayed in his mind. One moment there was nothing between their palms; the next there was something. Something she claimed was the bullet that had killed Lathaniel. Impossible. And yet, James had felt it. He opened his hand. A crimson smear of blood.

"I...vvv...dr..." Her speech slurred, her tone disintegrating into a guttural groan. Her eyes darted sideways, seemed to stick there, trembling inside their sockets, eyelids blinking so hard he could actually hear them clicking.

"Evanee? What's wrong?"

Her head jerked to the side in the same trembling motion as her eyes. Her lips pulled back over her teeth, her entire face contorted in a grimace. Sounds he associated with death came from somewhere inside her—grunts and moans of an agony so great words didn't matter. Every one of her muscles tensed, held tight, and then quivered. Her face went gray, her lips purple.

Death had been James's friend, his coach, his advisor, so he recognized Death when he saw it crouching over her. "You are not taking her. She is mine. Not yours."

He grabbed her shoulders, inserted himself between her and Death. Underneath his hands, he felt unyielding power and instantly recognized what was happening. A seizure. Only a seizure. Death wouldn't claim her today. He released his hold on her.

Not knowing what else to do, he stroked her face, rubbed her arm, tried to hold her hand, but her fingers were curled in tight. "Evanee. I'm here. You're not alone. I'm here. I've got you. I'm here." He kept repeating the words until the tension relaxed out of her. It was ending. Her eyes rolled slow and unseeing around their sockets. Her head lolled loose on her shoulders.

He gulped down mouthfuls of air as if he'd been the one to go through it. His heart charged around inside his chest. He sat next to her and held her limp hand tightly in both of his, waiting. Finally, her gaze found his and locked on. Clarity had returned to her eyes.

"How are you feeling?"

She raised her hand, palm up. Somehow, he translated the gesture to mean she wasn't sure.

"You don't know? Or you're confused?" he said. "You just had a seizure. Are you an epileptic?" She didn't answer, but he could see her taking in his words, processing them, understanding them. "Are you having trouble talking?"

She dipped her chin and squeezed his hand—an acknowledgment.

"Give it a few minutes."

She swallowed and ran her tongue over her teeth.

"Are you thirsty?"

A squeeze.

He held the glass to her lips and let her drink.

"Bllt. Nd bllt." Her words were slurred so badly he didn't understand. She slapped around the bedding awkwardly until she found the bullet. *Bullet. Need bullet.* Finding the metal soothed her. She fell promptly asleep, but he kept a vigil for any further seizure activity.

Twenty minutes later, she stirred, stretched, opened her eyes.

The questions floating in his mind burst out at her. "Can you talk now? You had a seizure. Are you epileptic? Do you need medication? Or was it an effect of the concussion?"

"I'm all right," she said, as if she were soothing him, but her voice lacked comfort, seemed stuck in a flat monotone. "It was the dream. My brain short-circuited—I had a seizure—when I woke up with the bullet. It's this strange thing that sometimes happens to me when I sleep. Dead people give me things."

Dead people give me things. Her hand lay open, revealing the spent bloody round. A bullet she didn't have until she awakened. A bullet that somehow materialized out of thin air to suddenly be between their palms.

He never spoke like this, but these were the only words in his mind. "What the hell?"

"I know. It's hard to wrap your mind around. The look on your face is exactly how I felt the first few times it happened." Her words were the correct ones, but they lacked animation and emotion. They were words spoken by a robot. Someone so far beyond mere sadness and depression that they skimmed the edge of suicide.

"It's happened before?" He couldn't keep the incredulity from his tone. He couldn't stop staring at the bullet. It felt like reality had just shifted a click or two off the norm and he hadn't caught up yet.

"The first time was the worst. I woke up with a girl's eyeball."

Invisible fingers tightened around James's neck, choking off the easy flow of air. He stood, turned away from her so nothing on his face would betray his thoughts. *A girl's eyeball*, she'd said. Janie Carson's? Was Evanee getting the evidence of his kills, not Lathaniel? Was she playing some bizarre game with him? Had all this been a setup? Just to trap him?

He inhaled a deep, slow breath, held it for a few seconds, then blew it out in a steady stream. His gut told him she wasn't playing him, wasn't setting him up, and certainly wasn't trying to trap him.

"What happened the other times?" He spoke while he stared at the wall, unwilling to face her while his deeds were under discussion.

"I woke up with a wad of hair and a tooth one time. Another time a ring. And now this."

He felt upside down, like he was an hourglass and someone had just turned him over. His heart beat inside his brain from the pressure.

"James?" Her voice was small and fragile. It was the first time she'd used his name, and it felt like the sweetest melody to his ears.

He hid his thoughts in the furthest corner of his mind, relaxed the tension in his face, and turned to her.

Her eyes were focused on him, and inside those dark-blue depths, he saw fear. Was she afraid of him rejecting her? Or was it something else, something he couldn't fathom right now. His feet moved his body back to the bedside, and he sat in the same spot where he'd held vigil over her for the past five days. "Tell me everything."

She told him about three dreams and how dead people really did give her things and how she really did wake up with them in her hand and how her brain overloaded when that happened. Each thing she brought back from a dream pointed to the Strategist. Each thing carried a clue—some new lead.

James was fully aware she'd left out the dream that led to her having the bullet that killed Lathaniel. Later, when she fully trusted him, he'd ask. For the moment, he'd grant her this secret.

She said there was a name for what she did. Oneirokinesis. He'd Google it, but he already believed her. Not only did she have no reason to lie, but she didn't have the mental strength and fortitude to formulate such an intricate deception about something so bizarre.

If he boiled everything that had been said down to one base concept, she had been dreaming about *his* kills. His.

Her dreams—the evidence she brought back from those dreams—brought them together. From that first dream of hers, they had been destined. That feeling of fulfillment with her was the recognition that they were fated to meet. Fated to have this time, these moments. The upside-down, one-click-off feeling dissipated, then re-formed into a peculiar bond with her.

She cradled the spent round to her chest.

"I'll get rid of that." He held out his hand to her.

"I want to keep it." She fisted her fingers around it. "It touched his heart," she whispered, emotion strangling her voice, but her eyes remained on him, telling him she wouldn't give it up voluntarily. When he made no move to try to take it from her, she asked, "James, where am I?"

He translated the deeper meaning behind the question. Distraction.

A smile stretched his mouth wide. She was healing, and millions of questions were going to be part of the process. One of the tricks to gaining trust was to *offer* information so it appeared he had nothing to hide. "You're in an underground bomb shelter my grandpa built during the Cold War." The lie slipped out smooth as a strawberry milkshake, but strawberry wasn't his favorite flavor.

He disliked lying to her, playing with her mind, but he'd dislike it more if she fought him, tried to escape, or was frightened of him. The lies he would tell were necessary. Once this brief moment of history was over, once he built the foundation that would sustain them, there'd be no more deceit between them.

"You had a concussion and were pretty out of it so I brought you here, where no one would find you."

She listened, but she was distracted. Her gaze perused the bunker, paused on the kitchen area, then returned to him.

"I tried to take you to the hospital, but you said not to." Another necessary lie. He squished his brows together to convey a look of confusion. "Don't you remember what you said when I found you?" He forced an expectant look on his face, a look that said *You should remember this.*

She looked up and to the left—a classic sign of searching her memory. But she would never find the memory. It didn't exist.

"You were wandering around in the woods naked. Covered in blood. I was going to take you to the hospital, but you said if I did, *he* would find you. Kill you. You looked like he'd already tried. Terror rode you. And I believed you." He searched her bloodshot eyes. "Don't you remember any of this?"

She looked up and to the left again. "None of it. Why would I be in the woods just wandering around? Why would I leave Lathan?"

"I don't know those answers. Maybe the concussion has affected your memory."

She half nodded, a look of pure concentration on her face.

"Right now, it's safest for you here. At least until you feel good enough to begin making decisions about your future." Decisions he would influence, mold, and shape. He waited for her to comment, but witnessed the distraction on her face. It was in the way her gaze perused the bunker, the way it paused at the kitchenette like she was searching for something before moving on.

"Decisions about my future? What do you mean?" she finally asked.

"The police are searching for you. They say you killed Robby Malone and Lathaniel Montgomery."

"They're saying I killed Lathan?" She bolted upright. Gasped. Swayed. Cradled her head between her hands like she expected brain matter to leak out her ears. Her facial muscles tensed—not from grief. From pain. James recognized the victory. Physical pain had finally taken precedence over grief. So many victories today.

"Slowly. You've been horizontal for five days." He placed a pillow behind her back, then guided her shoulder back so she leaned against the headboard.

"Five days? It's been five days since…"

"Yes." He answered when she didn't finish her sentence.

"I didn't kill Lathan. Junior shot Lathan, attacked me, and then… I don't remember what happened. Maybe I did kill Junior. He deserved it."

"You did say it was your fault he was dead. I assumed you meant Lathaniel, but maybe you were talking about Robby Malone." Sprinkling truth around a lie was like fertilizer. It made the lie stronger, heartier, more believable. "I taped some of the news reports. Figured when you were feeling better, you might want to see them. To know what you're up against."

With a few pushes of a button, he had the recording queued up on the flat-screen across from the bed.

Sheriff Robert Malone stood outside the police station flanked by officers. "Evanee Brown murdered my only son. We have conclusive evidence of this." The sheriff held up a family photo of a man. "This is a great tragedy to this community who loved Junior, or Robby, as some knew him. I am personally offering a reward of $20,000 to anyone with information about her whereabouts." What appeared to be a driver's license photo of Evanee floated in front of the screen.

The next recording was a press conference. Eric McCallister, with Gill Garrison standing next to him. "Evanee Brown is five foot nine. Long, black hair.

Slender." The same driver's license photo flashed on the screen. "She is considered dangerous. Do not approach her. Call the task force number at the bottom of the screen with any information."

James paused the action with Gill and Eric on the screen.

"Why haven't you turned me in? There's twenty-thousand dollars waiting for you." Something in her voice still wasn't right. Her eyes darted back to the kitchen, then to him again.

"There's right and there's wrong. It felt right to hide you. I saw your injuries. I know how badly you were hurt. You are safe here. You can heal here. You can decide what you want to do when you leave here. It felt wrong to turn you in. Leave you alone. Unprotected against them." He waved at the image on the screen.

"You're a good man, James. Taking care of me when I'm a stranger and the police are after me. Thank you." For a brief moment, sincerity outweighed the numbness in her tone.

Heat passed over his face. Was he blushing?

"I need to leave for work soon. I'd like to check your wound before I go. Would that be okay?"

"Um. Yeah."

He unbuttoned the shirt and bared her bandaged breast, all the while careful to disguise the hunger in his eyes with a clinical expression. "After everything you've been through, I know this is uncomfortable for you. I'm sorry." He meant it.

He picked at the medical tape on the side of her breast until he found a fingerhold and gently eased the tape back. Two of the deeper tooth marks still seeped and bled. Her breast would bear those reminders forever.

Chapter 17

James had left. A minute ago? An hour ago? A day ago? Evanee couldn't understand time anymore. The only thing she could feel was the dagger in her lungs each time she breathed. The blow to her chest each time her heart beat. The absolute torture of living while Lathan was dead.

Life had never been fair, but she'd always hoped that out there somewhere, something great waited for her. That something great had been Lathan. But he was gone. The promise of love—her happy ending—shot dead in front of her.

She was tired. So tired of living. Of struggling. Of fighting. Of losing.

The bullet—she held the solution in her hand.

She tossed off the covers and got out of bed. Upright, legs trembling and heavy from disuse, she felt the world lazily floating around her like cotton blowing on an early summer breeze. It took a moment for her to realize the world wasn't floating; she was dizzy. She braced herself against the nightstand until her vision stabilized. Nothing, certainly not a little disorientation, was going to deter her from her goal.

In the kitchen, she found a plastic cup and filled it with water.

The bullet blazed hot against her skin. She held it just inches from her eyes and stared at the tiny piece of metal. So small, almost delicate. How could something so innocent looking overpower the strength of Lathan's life force? But it had. The proof was in the dried blood caked in the crevices and on her palm.

She wanted this piece of metal, this piece of him, inside her. She popped the bullet in her mouth. Its weight and size were foreign. She focused on her tongue, on her taste buds, willed them to give her Lathan's flavor, but she tasted nothing. She rolled the piece of metal around in her mouth, exploring the contours, the dips, the valleys, the sharp edges. A primitive part of her brain engaged, and she was a child once more, finding comfort in suckling—but this time it wasn't her thumb.

She lifted the cup of water to her lips and drank deeply, swallowing the bullet. She set the plastic glass on the counter, opened a drawer, and searched for a knife.

The water and bullet sloshed heavily in Evanee's stomach. She ripped open another drawer. A silverware separator, but it only contained spoons. No forks. No knives. Where were the knives?

She pulled open the rest of the drawers and cupboards, pulled out pots and pans and baking sheets, knocked cans of food over in her search. But there was nothing in the kitchen she could use to cleave open her vein.

Weariness settled in her marrow. She sank to the floor, not caring that the concrete was hard and cold or that James would find her and know what she'd half-heartedly intended.

James leaned against the back wall of the packed auditorium. From his position, he had a dominant view of his father. The room was filled with the curious, the impressed, and the depraved.

His father's voice rose, then fell, his cadence quickening, then releasing with that timeless quality all good storytellers possessed. He'd learned to balance entertainment and the macabre in such a way that even the most gruesome of tales transformed into poetry. Into something beautiful.

That beauty had made Death attractive and yet something to be feared. That beauty had grabbed James's attention as a child.

An exit door on the audience level opened. The dim light offered no more description of the person than the outline of a man.

Good luck finding a seat in the dark room.

Purpose drove the man's stride, his gaze never wavering from Dr. Jonah. James followed the man's progress toward the front of the auditorium. Another man entered through the same door. The way this guy carried himself, the outline of his form, was familiar. Gill Garrison. What was he doing here?

"I smell him. Where is he?" The first man spoke in a shout and effortlessly leaped onto the stage. For only a split second, James caught a glimpse of the man's face. Logic revolted against the message his eyes conveyed. Tension grabbed hold of his neck and started strangling.

Lathaniel Montgomery. Couldn't be. And yet it was. Somehow, despite what Death had revealed to him, Lathaniel was alive.

And his story wouldn't match the evidence at the scene—James had seen to that. Lathaniel would know someone else had been there. But he wouldn't know who.

His father's theatrical voice faltered. Stopped. He gaped at Lathaniel, backed away as if afraid. Not one person in the entire auditorium sneezed or coughed or cleared their throat. The silence was impressive.

"Where's the Strategist? You've been in contact with him. I smell him on you." Lathaniel's volume wasn't affected by his proximity to Dr. Jonah. He probably didn't even know he was shouting.

The muscles in James's neck fisted into a knot of certainty. It felt like time had slowed down, but James recognized that his brain was actually speeding up. This situation could play out in at least ten different ways that had nothing to do with fingers being pointed at him. But there was still a chance, and *a* chance was one chance too many.

James slipped out the door nearest him, then walked across the hallway and outside. He knew what he had to do. Escape.

The years of planning and preparing for this moment flooded into his mind, giving him clarity of thought, guiding his actions, and shutting off his emotions.

He strolled to his car, ensuring his gait was slow and smooth and not attracting attention.

If, by chance, no one pointed an accusatory finger at him, he needed to be able to explain his sudden absence. He dialed his father's cell number, knowing the phone was turned off. When voice mail picked up, he forced weakness into his voice. "I had to leave early. Not feeling well." He left the number for a car service, then hung up.

If they were on to him, they could track him via his cell. He pried the SIM card from his phone, snapped it in half, turned his phone off, and dropped them both in the bushes.

The *professionals* used many ways to classify killers, but James had his own system. Killers landed in either of two categories: the ones who thought themselves so invincible that they'd never be captured or the ones who were so chaotic in their kills that they didn't worry about being caught. James had created a new category.

Each of his kills was designed around his escape route. First, he chose a subject by random means. Next, he planned primary and secondary escape routes. Finally, when all the pieces were in place, came the kill.

He approached his silver Toyota Camry. He could afford a better car, but the Camry figured in his escape. It blended in among the nearly three thousand other Camrys in the area. Eyewitnesses notoriously had a hard time distinguishing between gold, silver, and white.

The most important thing was maintaining invisibility. Act stupid, and everyone would notice him. Act innocent, and people looked right through him. He was familiar with invisible. He lived invisible. Odds were, somewhere nearby, someone in a Camry was acting stupid and getting noticed. That person's behavior would buy him extra time.

He knelt next to the dent beside the license plate on the back bumper and ran his hand over and over the blemish. Anyone watching would see that action. With all the skill of a professional magician, he slid the magnetized license plate off and into his jacket. A fresh plate resided underneath. Something else to confound anyone looking for him.

Out on the road, he adapted to the flow of traffic.

He drove past suburbs full of cookie-cutter houses all trying to compete with one another for their worthiness in the neighborhood. He drove past country estates with miles of fencing showing off the prosperity of the owners. He drove until he reached the real country where people lived miles apart and had a silent understanding of enforced privacy.

Out here, the woods became thicker, the farmland sparse. He pulled down a one-lane gravel road bordered on both sides by forest. In the spring, the blooming redbud and dogwood created the sensation of driving through a bouquet. But now the leafless, lifeless woods held no wonder for him.

He followed the lane to the end where he turned into the driveway of a tidy little cottage. Behind the home was a garage.

On paper, Mr. Franks, the owner, was very much alive. His social security checks were deposited every month into his account. He paid all his utilities on time, and he even subscribed to AARP. But no one had actually seen Mr. Franks since the day James killed him years ago.

James parked in the garage. Next to the Camry was a gold Honda Accord. Mr. Franks's car. A year from now, it'd be James's getaway vehicle.

It was unlikely the FBI would ever find this place. Even more unlikely that they would ever link it to him. But he still switched the Camry's vehicle identification number. He'd had the engine replaced so it wouldn't match the VIN. Anyone who cared to examine the car would run into dead end after dead end trying to link it to any one person.

Behind the garage were acres and acres of forest. He forced himself to yawn twice to suck in oxygen, then ran. A full-on sprint.

The path through the barren woods was nearly invisible. Animal trails were more distinct. Branches reached out and slapped at him as he ran, but he didn't duck, didn't dodge, didn't want to affect his running time.

He hated running, always had, but it figured in his plans so he forced himself to train, then maintain. Never in all his years of practice had he experienced that elusive runner's high, until this moment when the pounding of his feet against the dead leaves and the muffled sound of his breathing mixed with the rhythm of the world, connecting him to plane and planet in an elemental way. He knew without even glancing at his watch that he was clocking the best run of his life.

The trail ended abruptly behind his shed. Hide in plain sight, in the bunker underneath the shed. He didn't spare a glance at the house he'd lived in for nearly a decade. It never mattered to him; it had always been just a piece of his plan.

They'd live better when they started over. They—he and Evanee. Right now, he could walk away from it all and be content. Because of her.

He felt around in the thick grass until he found his hold and lifted the heavy panel. The seventy-five-pound door was six inches thick with a soundproof core. With the grass he'd carefully cultivated to grow over the top, the door weighed nearly a hundred pounds. Inside, he secured the steel with a series of heavy metal bars running up and down each side of the door. No one would ever get in without using explosives.

Evanee heard the muffled sound of the hatch being closed and then James's soft gasp.

"Evanee…" James knelt beside her. "I knew you were going to try it." Resignation and acceptance lowered his tone. "Why do you want to die?"

"It hurts too much to live." She sobbed through the total destruction of her soul. James grabbed her shoulders and pulled her up to him, tucking her face between his neck and shoulder.

"Cry, Evanee. Cry right now for everything lost and stolen from you. For the life you were going to lead. For the love you were going to have. Cry it all out. All of it."

If she thought she'd experienced grief before, she was wrong. Grief was a full-body-contact emotion. No padding. No safety gear. No escape. A cage fight. For her life.

A violent, piercing wail burst from her mouth. The sound contained her entire world of pain. Every vicious and vile thing she had ever endured was a blade protruding through her soul. Every wicked or wrong decision she'd ever made shoved the blade deeper, killing that special little spark of energy that had created and animated her, until there was no *her* anymore. She was gone. All that remained was the body. Bones that scraped at the confines of skin. Innards that threatened to hemorrhage. Lungs and heart that cruelly pumped life through the body.

"Evanee. Evanee."

From far off, she heard James calling her name. She tried to ignore him, tried to maintain the numb nothingness, but he invaded the space she hid in.

"Enough." His word commanded her, and suddenly she was staring directly into his eyes, unable to look away. "From this moment on, you are done with the past." James's voice contained a quiet force that bent her will to his. "You will not think about it. You will focus on being here right now—in this moment."

...this moment, the only moment that matters. Those words, Lathan's words, spoken to her in her dream, floated into her consciousness, carrying a heavier meaning than they had when uttered. Maybe, wherever Lathan was, he continued to watch over her. Maybe he'd sent James to her. Could he be speaking through James, trying to teach her how to go on without him? Live. Without him.

James gathered her to him again. "In this moment, you are in my arms. Feel them around you." His arms tightened, pushing her further into him, toward the lifeline his words offered.

"Feel my skin against your face. Smell it. Taste it." His tone was barely a whisper, but it captured her complete attention.

Despite her nose not working, she inhaled, then touched her tongue to his neck. The intimacy of her action registered, but she pushed it out of her mind.

"Feel my clothes against your bare legs." He shifted, scraping the fabric of his pants against her. "Feel it all, Evanee. Feel the power of being right here. Right now. This is the only moment. There is no past—no pain, no sorrow. There is no future—no expectancy, no might-have-beens. There is only right now."

"Right now." She tested the words on her tongue. They felt good. "I'm here. I'm with you, right now." It suddenly occurred to her that she had never really *looked* at James. She'd been too lost to see the path right in front of her. She eased back to see him.

The way his neck cradled his head lent him a dignified, almost regal air. His features weren't sharply chiseled, but neither were they sunken and weak. Tender mahogany colored the irises of his eyes, highlighting his face with warmth and kindness. But there was something elusive underneath the surface of his gaze, something that made her think he was a lot older than he looked. It took her a moment to recognize it.

Pain. The stain of having endured something horrific. She herself carried that wary, scarred look. "Something bad happened to you. I can see it in your eyes. What was it?"

Without warning, the answer to her question shoved into his mind. He moved away from her, stood, stared at the room around them, and tried not to let those bad things from his past—things he'd never dared to think about—overwhelm him.

"I'm sorry. That was too personal." Her voice was small and thin and laced with hurt. Rejection.

He sat down amid the mess she'd made of the kitchen and leaned his back against the cupboards. "This is personal." He motioned back and forth between the two of them. "I've bathed you, wiped you, fed you. If this isn't personal, I don't understand the definition."

A flush worked its way up her neck and spread across her face.

"Evanee. Come here." He shoved a colander out of the way and patted the spot beside him.

Without hesitation, she moved in next to him. If she'd exhibited the slightest hint of reluctance, he'd never have considered telling her. He'd never told anyone.

There would be benefits to divulging his greatest pain—binding her to him even tighter. Would she look at him differently? See him as a weakling? He suspected not. There was a very clear power hierarchy between him and her. He carried her sanity, which was too heavy for her at the moment. That implied strength on his part. What better time to tell her?

The scared little boy inside him feared speaking of it, but he was a powerful adult man now. The past could no longer hurt him. If it tried, he'd kill it.

He stared across the room to the ladder leading up to the hatch. A thickness gathered in his throat. "My dad loved me, but he was a busy man. An important man. As a child, I tried not to bother him. I spent all my summers outside, doing those nonsensical things kids do. Busting open rocks to see what was in the middle. Playing down in the creek. Exploring the woods behind our home."

"Where was your mom?"

"She died shortly after I was born. Brain tumor."

"I'm sorry." Evanee reached for his hand. He had plenty of time to move away from her, but he allowed her to grasp him, to gently squeeze, as if giving him courage. He couldn't help wondering if she chose that gesture because some unconscious part of her brain connected with him holding her hand and it soothing her.

"One day I came across a man camping in the woods. I was scared at first. Dad never allowed hunters or campers on our property. But Stanley was friendly. He offered me a pack of his dehydrated food. I was a kid. I was curious. So I hung around. Stanley was like a new toy to me. I could ask him anything, and he'd give me an adult answer, not the *Wait until you're older* or *You're too young to understand* kind of answers my father always gave me. During the first two weeks, he taught me how to track animals, how to kill and clean them, how cook them over a campfire. I learned more from him than I ever learned from my father.

"I remember the innocent excitement of those first weeks. Stanley gave me my first beer. I was eight. Didn't enjoy the taste, but I felt so grown-up sitting around his campfire sipping that beer. As an adult, I learned there was a name for what he was doing. He was grooming me." He swallowed. "The first time he—" A wad of fear and shame choked off any words he could say to describe what happened. So he skipped that part. "I was so scared I would've told Dad, but Stanley said he'd kill him, then me. He could track and knew how to kill, and I believed him. Stanley made me visit him every day that summer. Then one day he just disappeared. I never told anyone until now."

The pressure of her hand around his tightened to an almost painful grip that was oddly reassuring.

"I know what it's like," she whispered.

He didn't look at her, kept his eyes focused straight ahead. "I know you do. That's why I told you. It was your stepbrother, wasn't it?" His voice was as soft as hers.

"Yes." She spoke the word with a resolve that surprised him.

"It changed us, made us different from everyone else. I couldn't let anyone get close to me. I was afraid they'd hurt me like Stanley did. Or hurt my dad. I started studying my dad's research books in order to distract myself." A partial lie. He did need a distraction from what he'd been through, but the real reason he'd started studying Dad's books was to figure out how to capture, then kill Stanley. Somewhere along the way, his goal had gotten warped.

The lights blinked once, then an alarm sounded. His motion sensors had been activated.

They *had* been after him.

"What's that?" she asked.

"Someone is outside." James stood, pulling her up with him, and pointed toward the dresser. "Get dressed. Warm. Layers. Lots of layers. We're going to be outside most of the night." He was already at his computer desk calling up the video feed from the hidden camera trained on the door.

Chapter 18

Five days earlier

THE MINERAL STENCH OF BLOOD CHOKED UP LATHAN'S nose. He snorted and wheezed through the sadistic smell, but it was inside him propelling him toward consciousness, insisting he remember every brutal second.

Where was Honey?

He worked at forcing his eyelids open. Each one suddenly weighed ten pounds. Face mashed in a pool of blood—his and Junior's. Scarlet. Everywhere. He tried to speak, but the memory of watching Junior bite Honey's breast clogged Lathan's throat.

He concentrated on the scent of blood. No honeyed undertones. Not hers. A small measure of relief. Where was she? He inhaled deeply, searching beyond the obvious odors of blood and death for her. She was there. Faint. Too faint. An echo of where she'd once been, but was no longer.

Another smell mingled with hers. His brain sorted and categorized—the same process as always. Vanilla. He smelled vanilla. That wasn't right. Couldn't be right. He refused to believe the message his nose was relaying to his olfactory region. He sucked in another breath, tamped down on the rush of pain in his chest. Vanilla again.

He'd only encountered that potent smell clinging to

the evidence of forty-one murders. *Please. God. No. Let me be wrong*, he prayed to a god he wasn't sure existed.

The Strategist.

A rigid pole of panic rammed up his spine. He cried out—*Honey*—but didn't feel any vibration in his throat. No vibration, no sound.

The Strategist. Here. How? Didn't matter. Had to find Honey. *Find her. Find her. Find her.* And he could. His goddamned nose was a miracle. A blessing. Given to him for just this moment. He'd track her.

He moved his hands to his sides into push-up position, pressed his palms to the floor, and lifted his torso. Pain feasted on his heart, chewed, and swallowed him into unconsciousness.

———

The scent of sterile commercial cleaner combined with the rot of sickness to burn Lathan's nose. Hospital. He was in a hospital—they all smelled the same. What was he doing in a hospital?

Burning. Aching. Thrumming pain in his chest. Junior shot him. Hurt Honey. The memories flared through his mind, giving him a tail fire of adrenaline. He bolted upright. Something violent and wrong ruptured inside his chest, stealing his ability to suck air. He fell back, clawing at the bandage over his heart. His vision frayed around the edges. Consciousness became a disintegrating string, but one he clung to by sheer resolve.

Motionless on the thin mattress, he forced oxygen into his lungs, then pushed it out. Didn't matter how much pain he was in; he needed to find Honey. The Strategist could be torturing her at this very moment.

He needed to find her. He was the only one who could save her. No one else.

A nurse entered the room and spoke to him, but his brain was on turtle speed and couldn't process the movement of her mouth. She checked the bags of fluids plugged into his body. The moment she turned to check the monitors, he ripped out the tubes tethering his hand—felt no pain. Except for the constant roar in his chest. Blood dripped down his fingers. The scent of it triggered cruel memories of pain, both physical and mental, at having to watch Junior hurt her and being fucking helpless.

His ears picked up frantic sounds from the nurse, and then she was reaching for him. He batted a floppy—not quite cooperating—arm in her direction, then tried to stand. She pressed a button on his bed and started yelling. He wasn't even trying to listen to her.

Honey. Find Honey.

His legs were rubbery underneath him. *You will do this. Honey needs you, and you're not letting her down because your fucking legs feel weak.* He took a lurching step forward, nearly fell, grabbed onto the bed. Pain wrestled him, squeezing, cinching tighter and tighter. Water drenched his face—sweat or tears; he didn't know which.

Whatever he was going through was nothing—fucking nothing—compared to what she was enduring. Or, had the Strategist already killed her? Lathan couldn't breathe past the thought.

People rushed the room, rushed him. Hauled him back into the bed as if he were a wayward toddler.

Exhaustion weighed heavy underneath his skin. He could fight it, but not everyone else too.

"No. No. No. Need to find her." He shouted the words, but wasn't certain they came out coherent or a garbled mess. The first restraint lashed his wrist to the side of the bed. He thrashed. A restraint on his ankle. He lashed out. Someone caught his arm. "Stop. I need to find her. Don't do this."

Suddenly, Gill and his parents stood at the foot of his bed.

Mom's perfume was no less noxious, her attire no less formal. The only thing different was that she no longer disguised the look of disgust on her face behind her snooty rich-woman mask. His parents had been through too much with him to see him as anything more than an aberration, a problem, a disturbed person. And this just reinforced their view.

Dad tried to catch Lathan's remaining free leg. He kicked out, avoiding his father's hands, and focused on the only person who would help him. "Gill. Don't let them do this. Don't. I've got to find her."

Gill's attention was grabbed by the nurse speaking to him and then by Lathan's mom, who kept gesturing at Lathan like it was his fault he'd gotten shot and ended up in the hospital. Gill glanced back at Lathan and said something, but Lathan's brain couldn't translate the words.

"Can't read your speech. The Strategist has her. The Strategist. The Strategist." He kept repeating the name, trying to be articulate, hoping Gill understood. "I've got to get out of here. Find her."

Mom started signing the moment Lathan said he couldn't read Gill's speech, but nothing Mom could say would ever be as important as what Gill had to say right now. He focused on his friend.

Gill switched to their teenage bastardized version of sign. *The Strategist?*

Lathan nodded. Dad caught his leg, held it firm while a nurse tied Lathan's ankle to the bed. Gill began loosening the bonds on Lathan's wrists and barked a nasty something at one of the nurses and finished unleashing his hands.

"Junior shot me. I killed Junior. The Strategist took Honey."

Fuck. Fuck. Fuck. How? Why? Gill signed.

Those were questions that needed to be answered, but not now. "Need to find her."

Everyone's looking for her. Thought she shot you.

"Help me up."

Bullet in your chest.

"Don't care. I can track the Strategist."

Gill gave a quick nod. He unlashed Lathan's legs. Lathan swung them over the side of the bed. Unconsciousness snuck over him. He was out before he hit the floor.

———— ∿ ————

The reflection of a dim orange light pulsated in the dark hospital room. Lathan idled, motionless. The ethereal dream of Honey still wrapped him in its comforting embrace—him, her, tangled together. One entity. Floating in a place not in the vertical plane—no past, no future, only them.

The peace of the dream faded. Reality intruded. Deep internal pain began drilling into his chest, but it wasn't as intense as it'd been before. He felt... *Better* wasn't the right word. Stronger, maybe.

Gill slept in a chair next to the bed, his suit jacket over him like a blanket. All the previous shit between the two of them seemed so paltry and stupid. Gill had always been there in the most hellish moments of Lathan's life. This time was no different. A true friend. Better than the people he was attached to biologically.

Lathan pushed himself upright, a dull resonance thrumming in his heart. Everything inside him screamed to hurry, hurry, hurry, but he couldn't afford to end up unconscious again. Gill awakened, stood, and stretched his arms above his head.

Lathan got out of bed. Tested his weight on his legs. Somewhat steady. Gill handed him a pair of scrubs pants. Lathan half sat, half leaned against the bed and pulled them on. After he situated the pants well enough to cover the necessary parts, he let the hospital smock fall off his body. His chest hurt every time he moved his arms. He'd go without a shirt rather than trying to lift his arms through sleeves. An inch-thick bandage covered his heart.

The room was too dark to see Gill's mouth, but he seemed to know exactly what Lathan was going to do. Lathan ripped out the tubes in his hand. Gill handed him a towel to wrap around the bleeding.

Lathan shuffled across the room toward the door. "I'm ready to go."

Gill draped his jacket over Lathan's shoulders. Lathan gave him the finger—his version of thanks— then opened the door. A nurse power walked in their direction, irritation pinching her face and scenting the air. Gill pointed toward the elevators, and Lathan continued in that direction. Let Gill handle the nurse.

Once he was in the car, exhaustion snuck into Lathan's bones, but every time he closed his eyes, he was back on that kitchen floor watching Junior bite Honey's breast, back there feeling so angry, so helpless, so fucking weak. Sleep was not his friend.

The headlights of Gill's car sliced through the bleak darkness of the highway. Gill pushed the speedometer into the high eighties. Miles and miles of blacktop passed without them seeing another vehicle. Lathan imagined the entire world had simply gone to bed, granting him the small gift of unimpeded progress toward home.

A cuticle of bloodred sky split the horizon, soaking the world in its sinister color. His skin tingled with foreboding.

Gill parked at Lathan's front door, turned on the overhead light, and touched his arm—a request for attention, when he knew Lathan was nearly delirious with worry. "There are some things you need to know. I sent your parents home. Told them not to come back. Your mom was lobbying for you to be shipped to the nutty ward. Between her and her checkbook offering donations to the hospital, she almost succeeded. You weren't even medically stable or mentally unstable. I'm not sure that she's not going to try some legal craziness to get her way. She wasn't happy."

Lathan nodded. Didn't really expect anything less from his mom.

"And Junior shot Little Man too."

"Asshole shot my dog." Lathan's fists clenched tight. "If I hadn't already killed him once, I'd kill him again. And again. And a-fucking-gain."

"Little Man's alive. He's at the veterinary hospital.

The bullet lodged in his shoulder muscle. He's had surgery. The doctor says he should be back to normal in a few months, but because of his size, he'll always have weakness in that leg. Probably a limp."

As fucking sissy as it made him sound, Lathan wanted to run his hands over Little Man's gangly body, wanted to smell dog dander and all the places Little Man visited in a day. He wanted to watch the big oaf flop down on the floor in a fit of canine ecstasy at having his ears scrubbed. He missed his dog. He missed Honey. He missed his fucking life.

"Evanee's prints were on the gun that shot you. And on the knife that killed Junior. She was gone. The evidence pointed to her. Dr. Jonah reinforced the theory. He suggested that her mother's death was the inciting incident.

"If the Strategist was in your home, he staged the scene. And did a flawless job. There's nothing to support what you say happened, and everything points at Evanee."

"She didn't do it."

"I'm only going to ask you this one time, and I'll never ask it again. Are you certain—one hundred percent—that she wasn't working with the Strategist?"

"I'm so far beyond certain that your question is bizarre." Lathan didn't waste time pondering the answer. He got out of the car.

Like in the movies, crime-scene tape was wrapped around his front porch.

Gill used Lathan's house key to slice through the police seal and open the front door.

The stench of decomposing biological material bashed into Lathan like a physical entity. His gag reflex kicked open his throat. He dry heaved over the side of the porch, each spasm of his throat sparking a punch of pain in his chest. How the fuck was he going to go in if the smell was so overwhelming he couldn't stop heaving?

Swallowing hard, he summoned his willpower. Underneath the rot was the smell of people. Strangers. Probably EMTs, police, FBI, crime-scene techs. How many people had been in his home?

Without going in, Gill reached inside and turned on lights.

From the front door, Lathan could see the kitchen. See the horror. Blood. Everywhere. On the walls. Gallons of it on the kitchen floor, some seeping into the living room. A flood of blood. No way that was all Junior's. Some of it, a lot of it, had to be his too. How had he survived? Honey. She was the answer.

Lathan walked in the door, but didn't move any closer to the nightmare in his kitchen.

He closed his eyes and inhaled slow, long, and deep breaths, searching for her scent underneath all the layers. His brain sorted and sifted. A whisper scent, a thin thread in a complicated weave. He strained to lock onto her. Sweat slicked his armpits and trickled down his bare chest. Every time he almost got her, another scent overpowered hers.

"How long have I been in the hospital?"

"Five days."

Lathan's heart liquefied, the last bloody bits of hope evaporating in the reality of time. Five days. He'd been gone five days. *The Strategist never keeps his victims long. She's dead.* The Strategist probably killed her four days ago.

Lathan beat his head with his fists, heard the sounds of anguish escaping his mouth.

Dead. An instant image flashed into his mind, her crying out for him, begging him to find her, save her.

He lurched to the stairs, stumbled. Fell. Half scrambled, half crawled, half ran upstairs to the bedroom—shrugging away from Gill's too-fucking-helpful hands—to the one place where her scent would be strongest. His bed.

He careened into the bedroom. Sheets gone. Pillows missing. Another fucking loss. He sank down, face to the stripped mattress and sucked in a lungful of her honeyed scent.

Tears scalded his eyes. Exhaustion took over his body.

―∿∿―

Lathan woke nose mashed to mattress, a diffuse misery pervading his soul. For a moment, he didn't remember why his body and heart hurt. Then he remembered. He wanted to forget. Wished he had an erase button on his brain. But he didn't. There was only one way to forget, but he couldn't go down death's highway until he finished one last task—find her body.

He struggled to his feet. Guilt and grief threatened to drive him to his knees, to force him into a lump of useless sobbing. He knew how to get beyond the feeling. In the past, he'd tattooed himself until the bliss of physical pain overwhelmed all the mental shit, but he was a thousand miles beyond tattooing.

He found the knife in his dresser drawer—a long-forgotten Christmas gift from Gill when they were in that awkward teenage state where they felt like they had to give meaningless gifts to each other to solidify their friendship.

He carried the knife into the bathroom. The mirror reflected a haunted, hollowed-out man that he didn't recognize visually, but he felt exactly like that asshole looked. Like the breathing dead.

The knife felt clumsy in his hand—a cheap hilt, not balanced for performance. Didn't matter. He pressed the blade into his arm. The first stroke across his skin brought little pain and even less satisfaction. He bore down. *Should've used a jagged, rusted, serrated blade.* Blood welled in his cleaved skin and dripped down his arm. He worked over his flesh, concentrating on lengthening, deepening the strokes, until her name was carved in bold, beautiful letters from the inside of his elbow to his wrist. Warm scarlet streamers chased down his arm, tickling and caressing his skin. Sensation smoldered, ignited into a scorching burn. Finally.

Like an old friend, pain obliged. He held his arm over the sink, closed his eyes, and savored the momentary physical release.

Underneath his feet, he felt the vibration of Gill coming up the stairs, then entering the room. Didn't want to see the condemnation in his friend's face. Didn't want to *talk* about it.

Grabbing Lathan's arm, Gill slapped a towel around the bleeding and applied pressure. More blessed pain. A nirvana of pain.

Gill yanked on Lathan's arm, startling his eyes open.

"You fucking trying to kill yourself?" Gill smelled like anger and wood and blood. Odd combination.

"Not yet." Total truth in those words.

"Listen. It's not over until—"

"We find her body." Saying the words didn't hurt as much as Lathan had thought it would, but that was probably because adrenaline was choking off his emotions.

The tension on Gill's face melted, but he didn't say anything. He lifted the towel. *Honey*—her name in weeping scarlet letters.

"You have company."

"Don't want visitors."

"Dr. Stone says it's important. He's got Xander, Isleen, and Evanee's brother with him. Says it's about Evanee."

Evanee—his magic word. But nothing any of them could say was going to make this situation better.

"Take a shower. Bandage yourself up, then come downstairs." Gill stepped back. "Or do I need to babysit your ass to make sure you don't do anything stupid?"

Lathan flicked his middle finger in the air, a teasing response so Gill would stop riding his ass. The tang of cedar scented the air around Gill—fucking pity. Didn't want to see it expressed on his friend's face, but Lathan felt so goddamned sorry for himself that he didn't have the gumption to be pissed about Gill feeling the same way he did.

Lathan stared off across the bathroom to the shower—the place Honey had sat, water scalding her skin, anguish tearing her soul. So much hurt in her life, and he'd barely had a chance to give her happiness. What might have been if she was still alive? He would've asked her to marry him. Would've made her happy. Would've given her kids—if she wanted them—something that he'd never dared to think about before he'd met her.

Lathan crossed the room and knelt at the spot Honey had occupied. He placed both hands on the slate, yearning to feel some connection with her by simply touching a place she'd once been. But he felt nothing. Nothing. When he looked back, Gill was gone, along with the knife and the shaving razor. *Figures*. Lathan tore off the bandage on his chest, didn't bother examining the scab and bruises blooming outward from the wound. He stripped out of the scrub pants, stepped under the spray.

The water was liquid fire to her name carved in his arm. He held it directly under the spray, absorbing the pain, savoring it. He stayed in the shower until the water ran like ice and his body quaked from the cold. The torment he'd put himself under slowed the exsanguination of his soul to a trickle and gave him enough strength to begin the search for her body.

He dressed and headed downstairs to face life without her in it. Before he even reached the bottom step, he could smell the difference in his home. The overwhelming stench of rotting blood was nearly gone. Gill had transformed his kitchen from slaughterhouse to construction zone. The floor had been stripped to the joists. Bet he was going to catch hell from his superiors for destroying a crime scene. If he kept this nice shit up, Lathan was going to feel guilty for wanting to end it. Maybe that's why Gill was doing it. Fucker knew him too well.

Dr. Stone, Xander, and Isleen stared at him, killing kindness on their faces. Evanee's brother paced around the space like a caged animal ready to attack. Why the hell was he here with them anyway? Was he friends with Xander and Isleen?

Thomas stalked toward him, his face splotchy and red. "I'm with the Bureau of Criminal Investigation—"

So that's how he knew Xander and Isleen. Xander worked with the guy.

"Everyone is looking for her. We're going to find her." Thomas's face went cartoon, blow-your-top red. "She's all the family I've got, and we're going to fucking find her."

At least one other person felt as strongly as he did about getting Honey home. Lathan wanted to believe the guy could find her, but it wasn't that simple or he already would have.

No one else spoke. What was there to say? *Sorry a killer took your woman? Sorry she's probably dead? Let me know if there's anything I can do to help out?* Words would only make it worse. "So why the fuck are you all here?"

Isleen flinched at his tone. Xander pulled her closer to his side at the same time he delivered a look of anger— deserved anger—at Lathan. Isleen was a tiny thing with expansive ocean eyes full of shadows. And Lathan had just scared her.

He felt like a shit. "Sorry. I'm… Fuck… I don't…"

Isleen moved toward him, dragging Xander with her and nudging him in the ribs.

"Back when… were working Isleen's case. When they called… in after she was taken… I'd been shot, right?"

Lathan missed a few words, but knew what the guy was talking about. He felt his head nod on his shoulders. He wasn't sure he could speak beyond the grief for Honey jammed in his throat.

Xander lifted the hair off his forehead. "I caught mine

in the head." A round scar dimpled at his hairline. "It's amazing what our girls can do."

It's amazing what our girls can do. Can do? The guy talked like Honey was alive. Hadn't anyone informed him that she was dead?

"This thing between us and our women, the strange abilities we all have—it kinda makes us a family or something. And family backs up family."

"Too little, too late, man. It's over. She's…" Lathan couldn't force that word—the word that meant the end—from his numb lips.

Isleen tipped her head up, waited until his attention focused on her. "She's alive."

Her words cut him deeper than any knife ever could. He couldn't correct her. He might fucking start sobbing if he opened his mouth. The best he could manage was a jerky shake of his head.

Isleen reached out to him, then dropped her hand like she knew he didn't want to be touched. "I dreamed about her. My dreams are never wrong."

Lathan's joints went melty. He slumped down and sat on the stairs. "You're saying you dreamed that she's alive? I don't mean to be a bastard, but don't do this to me. I don't have the mental space for false hope."

Dr. Stone moved in next to Xander and Isleen, hovering over him.

"Isleen is the other dreamer I told you about." Dr. Stone settled his hand on Isleen's shoulder. "I can vouch for the accuracy of everything she says. She's never been wrong."

Lathan wanted to ask for more information, but couldn't make his mouth work.

"She's in a windowless space," Isleen said. "Reminds me of a basement studio apartment. Her face is badly bruised, but she's alive. There's a guy there… She calls him James. He's taking care of her. Not hurting her. They seem like friends."

Lathan couldn't help it; his gaze darted to Gill. He read Gill's expression—*I told you. She's working with the Strategist.* Lathan shook his head. She couldn't be teamed up with the Strategist. He'd have smelled her deception. He knew, he fucking knew in his DNA, that she loved him. But, if she actually was alive, why hadn't she called? Sought him out? Come home?

Did he really believe she was alive?

Didn't matter. All that mattered was finding her. Dead or alive.

"Something inside me tells me where Isleen is when we're not together." Xander's protective arm around her tightened. "It's like an urge, a tugging that guides me to her. I'm sure you have the same thing. You just have to recognize it and listen to it. For too many years, I ignored that feeling and Isleen suffered because of me."

"There is no urge. No tugging inside me. Only the constant drilling ache from being shot." Despair burned Lathan's eyes and nose. He gulped back the urge to rage on himself, harm himself—fucking carve her name on every square inch of his skin.

Dr. Stone spoke. "As long as the light shines in one of you, the other will live. That's why you aren't dead and neither is she. Wherever she is, she's alive. When you find her—and you will—stay together."

"You have to be touching to be truly safe." Xander

glanced down at Isleen. "When you know that, really understand it, it's hard not to be touching."

"The answer is inside you." Dr. Stone's clear-blue gaze locked with Lathan's as if that simple gesture would make his words true. "You just have to find it."

Lathan wanted to believe. But belief was as solid as a cloud. He smelled the Strategist. Knew the Strategist had taken Honey. But he didn't *know* that she was alive. Didn't *know* how to find her.

Lathan sat stuck to the stairs, unable to utter a word as everyone left the house.

Whether he believed Isleen or not, he needed to find Honey. Gill would help him—if for no other reason than to prove Honey was working for the Strategist.

"Find out Dr. Jonah's location. He's fucking going to help me find the Strategist."

Hope could be a dangerous dream.

Chapter 19

LATHAN STOOD CENTER STAGE AT A PRESENTATION MUCH like the one he'd tried to attend, fists wrapped in the nation's most-respected profiler's shirt, sniffing the guy. He smelled the audience's surprise, apprehension, and fear—a precursor to panic. Felt everyone watching him. What did he expect? With the way he looked, the audience probably thought they were on the cusp of witnessing an actual murder. There'd be pictures of this all over the Internet in seconds.

"I smell him. Where is he?" Lathan didn't wait for Dr. Jonah's answer. He turned to the audience and scented the air. His brain automatically sorted and sifted through all the people, picking up a skinny thread of the one smell that gave him the greatest hope and the greatest fear. "Gill—he's here."

Gill drew his badge and gun and said something to the audience. Must've been some version of *freeze* because no one moved.

"…are…?" The scent of Dr. Jonah's fear grew.

Lathan didn't need to read or hear the words to understand the man's question. "You know who I am."

"I don't."

Lathan waited for the peppery scent of the lie to enter his nostrils, but it didn't. "You know who I am. *You* sent your partner after me at the Minds of Madness and

Murder seminar. *You* have been inside my home. You decided Honey killed Junior and shot me."

The light of recognition sparked in Dr. Jonah's eyes. "Lathaniel Montgomery? But…"

At the mention of Lathan's name, Gill slapped his hand over the microphone. Then fumbled with it a moment, turning it off.

"But what?" Lathan asked Dr. Jonah.

"I didn't know…at the Minds of Madness and Murder seminar." Dr. Jonah spoke so rapidly Lathan couldn't catch it all.

It wasn't important, nothing more than a trivial detail in the greater search for Honey, but for some reason Lathan couldn't let the conversation pass. "Your partner chased me down. Told me *you* wanted *me* to return to the presentation."

"That's strange. Let's ask James."

James. Isleen said Honey was with a man named James.

"Your partner is named James?" Lathan asked, certain he must've read the name wrong.

"Yes."

"James?" This time Gill asked, his gaze colliding with Lathan's.

"Yes." Dr. Jonah confirmed. Again.

Lathan forced himself to let go of his grip on Dr. Jonah. "I don't believe in coincidences. What if…" A memory floated out of the ether of Lathan's mind. That day at the Minds of Madness and Murder seminar, he'd smelled something familiar as he rushed across the grass to his Fat Bob, but he'd plugged his nose before his brain could lock onto it. And then the partner had grabbed his arm. "Holy Jesus. Holy Fuck. The partner. The partner has to be the Strategist."

Gill looked as skeptical as he smelled. "There are a fuckload of people with the name James. Just because—"

Lathan interrupted Gill to ask Dr. Jonah. "The seminar—did you hire an interpreter for me?"

"No. Of course not. I didn't even know you were there." Dr. Jonah's gaze flew back and forth between Lathan and Gill.

"Gill, listen. When I left, Dr. Jonah's partner chased after me, told me the doctor wanted me to return to the presentation, but he"—Lathan flicked his thumb in Dr. Jonah's direction—"never knew I was there. Don't you see?" Lathan waited for Gill to have the spark of understanding, but Gill just looked at him. "*I'm* the only one claiming the Strategist exists.

"What if the Strategist has been watching me, trying to figure out how I do what I do? What if he suspected I had hearing problems and the interpreter was his way of confirming it? What if he was watching five nights ago? That would explain the bizarre timing of him taking Honey. It would explain why the scene was set to look like she'd shot me and killed Junior. Only a professional would've known how to stage it so perfectly."

Dr. Jonah raked a trembling hand through his flyaway hair, his gaze faraway, lost in thought. Lathan could practically see the man shifting puzzle pieces into place—and reaching the same conclusion as Lathan, but for different reasons. Shaking his head, he stepped up to the front of the stage and spoke loud enough that Lathan could hear. "James, come down here." No one moved. "James?"

A guy at the top, in the seat nearest the door, raised his arm and waved it wildly in the air. Gill listened, then turned to Lathan and spoke. "He said a man left through the door right after you came in."

"Why would he leave?" Lathan directed the question to Dr. Jonah. "Does he normally leave?"

"No. Oh my God. I can't believe this. He said he was too sick to attend the crime scene at your home. He's been out the past five days with the stomach flu. I didn't even question him. Why would I?" He swallowed, and sadness lined his face. "He's my son. I should've seen. Should've known. Should've stopped him. I'll take you to him."

His fucking son—one of most prolific killers, and the great Dr. Jonah had been completely oblivious. Compassion for the guy wasn't in Lathan's dictionary at that moment, but neither could he direct any anger at Dr. Jonah. All he wanted was to find Honey.

Lathan inhaled the entire way out of the auditorium, searching for the Strategist's scent. Confirmed for himself the guy really was gone.

Gill drove. Dr. Jonah navigated. Lathan obsessed over their speed. Speed of light wouldn't have been fast enough. He didn't bother trying to follow Gill and Dr. Jonah's conversation. There was nothing either of them had to say that mattered. Only Honey mattered.

Lathan didn't see the roads or the scenery they passed. All he could see was Honey in his mind's eye. Her wiping the blood off his face after his fight with Gill. Her laughing and playing with Little Man. Her as he made love to her. Her. Her. Her.

The drilling ache in his chest eased, faded, stopped

all together. Xander's words came to him. *Something inside me tells me where Isleen is. I'm sure you have it too.* The pain. He'd thought it was from the gunshot, but it wasn't. The pain was a compass. Nothing like pain as a motivator—go in the wrong direction and get hurt. Go in the right direction and feel fine. Terrified excitement bunched Lathan's muscles. Alive or dead, he was going to find her.

Lathan lost track of time until Gill whipped the car into the driveway, the tires fishtailing before finding traction. A neat, nondescript home sat nestled next to a forest. It was painted a shade that perfectly matched the bark on the barren trees surrounding it. The yard was tidy and well kept, not picturesque. Nothing special.

Pent-up energy propelled Lathan out of the vehicle before Gill completed the stop. Lathan slammed into the front door at a full-on run, barely breaking his stride when the door caved and he burst into the house.

He stopped. Scented the air. Nothing. No honeyed undertones. His chest twinged. Wrong direction.

Gill entered the house, gun out, looking like the professional FBI agent he was.

"She's not in the house." Lathan followed the direction in which he felt no pain. It led him outside. The only other structure on the property was a tidy little shed tucked up against the trees. He found her scent— faint, so faint that if he hadn't been hyper-focused on her, he might not have found it. The pain transformed into certainty. He ran. Flat-out sprinted. It was too late to prevent the dangerous dream from infiltrating his mind—her alive. *Please, let her be alive.*

He tore open the shed doors. Stopped. Brain struggling to assimilate the image.

A shiny, green riding lawn mower, hedge clippers, a weed whacker, bags of potting soil, fertilizer. And the scent of the Strategist. What the fuck?

She was here. Lathan fucking smelled her.

"Honey!" He yelled the word. His throat burned from the force of his vocalization. He whipped around to find Gill just reaching the open doorway of the shed. "Do you hear anything?"

Gill paused, cocking his head to the side, genuine concentration on his face. He shook his head.

"She's here. I smell her." Lathan tore the garden tools off the wall and threw them out the double doors. Together they carried the lawn mower out of the shed. Once they'd stripped the room, they searched. Every inch. Bottom to top. Twice. Three times. Nothing. No hint of her.

"You're sure she's here?" Gill asked for the seventh time, his face smudged with grime.

"I smell her. I *know* she's here." Lathan pounded his pain-free chest. The pent-up rage, the frustration of not finding her, vibrated his limbs with unexpressed energy. He slammed his fist into the shed wall, punching clean through the wood.

How could he know she was here if she wasn't? Maybe he didn't have anything that told him where Honey was. Maybe he'd wanted to find her so badly he'd convinced himself he had an ability he didn't. He wanted to stab himself with the hedge clippers.

Lathan pulled his hand back into the shed, scraping his knuckles bloody. He invited the sting. The

Strategist's scent flowed in through the hole. Was he outside?

Lathan paced around the building, testing the air. The Strategist's scent was strongest at the back. He knelt down, nose in the grass and inhaled. The guy had been here. Not long ago. Lathan ran his hands in circles over the ground, stirring up the scent. That's when he noticed it. The grass his right hand touched was as cold as the environment. The grass his left hand touched was warmer. "Something's here."

Gill fell in beside him. Lathan pointed out the temperature differences. He dug his fingers into the earth and ripped out a clump of grass. Another. Another. Until he uncovered the straight line of man-made material. A door.

"She's in there!" The lip of the door was no bigger than an eighth of an inch. Not enough to get his fingers underneath. "I need a crowbar. An ax. A sledgehammer."

Dr. Jonah handed him a crowbar. Lathan had forgotten about the man until that moment. He braced it under the edge, leaned his entire body weight on it, and rocked it, but the fucking door didn't budge.

Lathan grabbed the ax and slammed it down on the metal door with all the force he possessed. The impact reverberated through his hand, up his arm, rattling his bones all the way to his chest. Fucking metal door wouldn't move. He smelled her. She was in there, mere feet away. The Strategist was with her. Every moment Lathan spent trying to get to her was another moment of torment she had to endure.

What was the Strategist doing to her right that moment? Carving out her insides, like he'd done the man in Indiana? Amputating her extremities one by one to see how long she could live? Slicing through her tendons just to immobilize her?

Stop. Lathan pounded his fists against his temples.

The drilling in his chest began again. Something was wrong.

Chapter 20

On the monitor, James watched the two men beat at the door with crowbars. They could beat for twenty years, and the door would not give. Explosives were the only way to get inside. The image was too distorted and grainy to tell exactly who was out there. He suspected Gill Garrison and Lathaniel Montgomery.

How did they find the bunker? No one knew about it. No one. And the entrance was perfectly concealed. He'd have to ponder those questions later. Right now, the priority was escape.

"I'll tell them I kidnapped you. Made you take me here. Forced you to take care of me." Evanee moved to stand beside him and watched the men beat at the grass. One rucked up huge handfuls, clawing and beating at the door.

He'd done a good job with her. She had no idea they were there for him, not her.

"They won't believe you. I left today. Never called law enforcement. And came back here willingly. They'll know that. Will know that I could've turned you in and didn't. They'll charge me with aiding and abetting. As an accessory." He turned to her. "And you won't get a fair shot with these guys. Look at them."

Rage fueled the men's movements. They weren't simply doing their jobs; they were on a mission. A mission to capture him. But she didn't know that.

"Do you trust me?" he asked, and waited for her to look at him.

A small smile teased at the edge of the undamaged side of her mouth. "Obviously."

"I've got a plan. But you have to do everything I tell you to do. Everything. Without question. Can you promise me you'll do that?"

"I promise."

"Good. We're in this together now. I've got your back, and you've got mine. Deal?"

"Deal." She latched onto his words and chose to believe he was right.

She pulled another sweater over her head, then stepped into a pair of long johns. She rummaged through the drawer until she found a pair of pajama pants and slipped those on, tying the waist.

"The only way they'll get the hatch open is with explosives, so that buys us a bit of time." From underneath his desk he grabbed a fat backpack and wrapped a rope around his ankle, securing the pack to his foot. He shoved the desk over to reveal a wooden door two feet in diameter. He unlatched the lock and swung it open.

The tunnel looked too small for a human being to fit inside, but she understood without him speaking that they were going to crawl through there.

She took a step back and ran into the nightstand. "Where's that go?"

"Half a mile into the woods. Everyone will be focused here, not searching the woods. At least not yet. Thank

God, Grandpa was the paranoid sort. He was forever fretting that the Commies were going to invade."

"His paranoia is our escape, I hope." She couldn't take her eyes off the too-tiny tunnel.

James nodded his head. "You can do this." He sounded so sure of himself, so sure of her.

She sucked in a breath, squared her shoulders, and forced herself to move toward the tunnel entrance.

"One more thing, then we're ready." He sat down at his computer and began typing.

On the wall-mounted screen, she watched the men outside. The grainy image distorted and wavered. One man beat the ground violently, rage in his every movement. Was that Gill? If he was doing that to the ground, what would he do to her? He'd kill her. A shiver passed over her shoulders.

The screen went blank. A few keystrokes from James, and a quiet *pffft* sounded. A swirl of smoke whispered up from the computer. James stepped away from the machine and led her to the hole. They knelt, facing each other.

"Do you want to go first, or do you want me to go first?" he asked.

"You."

"Okay. You'll reach forward with your arms and pull yourself." He demonstrated what looked like a chin-up. "Use your toes to help push you. As soon as my feet go in, you follow. We stick together. No matter what."

She nodded, but her head felt heavy with fear.

"Everything is going to be all right. I'll keep you safe." He stroked her cheek with his knuckle. It was a tiny gesture, but it had the same potency as a hug from a dear friend.

He bent down, and his head, his shoulders, his torso, his legs, his feet all disappeared into the tunnel.

Oh God. She reached into the dark hole. The movement strained her sore breast and pressed it to the ground. It felt like a knife to the nipple, but she would endure. For him. For everything he was sacrificing on her behalf.

She shimmied, slithered, and crawled into the tunnel. The earth closed around her. Pressed against her stomach, her sides. She lifted herself and found only an inch or two of clearance above her.

Her toes no longer touched cool, smooth concrete, but instead dug into hard-packed earth. She reached forward, grasped a slight hump in the ground, and pulled with her hands and pushed with her toes.

The space got blacker and blacker. The darkness blinded her. The tunnel tightened around her. Breath squeezed out of her. Loud whooshing gasps escaped her mouth. The air itself wasn't air, but a combination of dirt and roots and oxygen that was a solid, not a gas like her lungs were used to. She choked on something, maybe her own spit, started coughing and coughing and coughing.

James called her name, worry in his voice.

"Imallright," she gasped in the brief space between coughs. "Somethinginmythroat." It'd be a miracle if he understood her. It'd be a miracle if she didn't need the Heimlich.

"In my pack. In the outside zipper pocket is a bottle of water. You have to come to me. I can't go backward."

Disco lights of oxygen deprivation danced in front of her eyes, but she managed to crawl forward while coughing until she ran into the pack. She fumbled around, blindly searching for the zipper, then groping inside for the familiar shape of a bottle of water. She tore the cap off and slugged the liquid down her throat, swallowing what felt like a dry mouthful of dirt. At least the coughing had stopped.

Sweat rained from her pores, rolling down her forehead and burning her eyes. She wasn't going to be able to do this.

"We need to keep moving. Reach."

She heard the movement of fabric from in front of her.

"Pull."

She heard his body scraping against the ground, the sound raw to her ears.

"Reach with me."

She did.

"Pull."

She did.

Everything in the world narrowed down to this moment where all that existed was the cadence of James's voice. *Reach. Pull.* She began speaking the words with him, her body moving in a rhythm. *Reach. Pull.* Almost a melody. An endless melody. One that went on and on and on, until she was certain two eternities had passed.

"Just a few more feet. You're almost there."

It took a few moments for her to understand the meaning behind these new and different words. The oppressive blackness lightened. Relief eased the weight of the earth over the top of her. The end. She'd made it.

"Okay, I'm out. Reach out to me. I'll pull you the

rest of the way." His voice was clear and fresh, not the muffled, muted tones of being in the earth.

She stretched her arms out and waggled her fingers until she felt the solid strength of him, groping in the dark, searching by touch for the magical handgrip of strength that would lock them together.

James pulled. Her shoulders strained in their sockets, the stretch welcome after the eternity of repetitive movements. Head, torso, hips emerged from the tunnel, and she was birthed into a new life with a man she hardly knew.

The tunnel ended—a random hole in the bank of a dry streambed. Starlight shone down on the world, its illumination vast and beautiful to her color-deprived eyes.

James shifted his grip, wrapped both arms around her so her chest pressed to his chest, and backed away from the hole. Finally, her legs fell out of the tunnel, limp, swinging, banging into his shins like they were no longer hers to control.

He settled her weight on her feet, but didn't let her go. A good thing since she wasn't certain about her ability to stand just yet.

"I was so scared. No, beyond scared. So far beyond scared that to be scared would've been a pleasure." A deranged giggle tried to gurgle its way up her throat, but she stopped it.

"You're strong. I knew you could do it." His arms around her squeezed, infusing her with the truth of his words.

She suddenly felt all I-won proud of herself. A bashful blush warmed her cheeks.

Already quiet with the expectancy of winter, the air

around them shifted, almost crackled. Evanee opened
her mouth to ask him if he felt it. A dull, serrated explo-
sion startled the hush. All her muscles clenched, rigid,
then released. He didn't even flinch.

"They exploded the door. They're going to send
someone through the tunnel." He released her from his
embrace and stared into her face. "Are you ready to run
for it?"

She didn't know if she had the strength, the stamina
for running, but for him she'd try. "Yeah."

"Liar." An ornery smile played at the corners of
his mouth.

He was teasing her. Teasing. While they were trying
to escape the police, the FBI, and Ken doll Gill, who
had disliked her from the moment he met her. And yet,
somehow James's lack of worry evaporated her own
doubts and fears. He wasn't devastated at being saddled
with a fugitive. He was enjoying himself.

"I know where there's a car, but it's two miles away.
A gold Honda Accord. I can run to it and get back here in
under fifteen minutes." He pointed out through the trees
to a lonely road she hadn't noticed before. "If anyone
comes, run. But stay on the road." He pointed. "If they
catch you, buy time. Fight. Do whatever it takes to stay
on the road." He gripped her face between his hands and
stared into her eyes. "I won't let them take you."

The intensity in his eyes sealed his words.

Before she could respond, he left her standing alone
while he sprinted through the woods. She stared after
him, not allowing herself to think until she lost sight of
him and lost the sound of his feet pounding against the
dried leaves and twigs.

She walked to the edge of the forest, her knees trembling, and leaned against a tree facing the silver strip of freedom. The wait was going to torture her. One one-thousand, two one-thousand, three one-thousand...

At sixty, she marked the minute with a finger like a kid in grade school.

By minute three, cold infiltrated her. Goose bumps stood on her skin. She shivered, she shuddered, her teeth pattered together, filling the serene silence with their sound. Minute four brought alternating numbness and burning cold to her socked feet. Minute five arrived at the same time as a faint, indiscernible sound. She stopped counting and listened.

The car? She cocked her head toward the road, listening, searching for any sign of James's car, even though the logical part of her knew it was too early. The sound was strongest in the forest. She peered into the dense trees.

Footsteps. Someone ran through the woods. Toward her.

Go away. Go away. Go away. The sound didn't go away. Didn't deviate from a seemingly straight line to her.

If she could hear footsteps, he was close. Too close. Each of his footfalls a damning impact upon the earth. She shoved off from the tree, her limbs stiff and gangly, and reached the road in only a few strides. Once on the pavement, she sprinted. Legs and arms pumped, socked feet barely whispered a sound. Maybe he wouldn't hear her, see her.

"Stop! Evanee! Stop!"

That voice. Lathan's voice changed everything. Stopped everything. Even her body.

She fell. For the tiniest of moments, she was flying, wishing she could just rocket off down the road like Superman. Knees hit the road, rough stones tearing through the layers, splitting her skin. Hands outstretched, wrists and shoulders absorbed most of the violence of her fall. Torso hit. She lay there. Didn't move.

All the pain of losing Lathan that she'd forced out of her mind fought a battle with her sanity, until rationality joined the fray.

Lathan was dead. Dead. Dead. And he never called her Evanee. He was her past, and if she wanted a future, she needed to get back on her feet and run.

He was beside her before she even had a chance.

James's words echoed in her mind. *If they catch you, buy time. Fight.*

Not even looking at the man, she launched herself at him, punching, clawing, biting. Used her knees to land repeated blows to his testicles, his stomach. He grunted from the impact, but the satisfaction of his pain didn't register for her. Nothing registered, other than the primal urge to survive long enough to escape.

She beat him until her arms and legs became too heavy to raise anymore. She collapsed onto the road, limp. Exhaustion overtaking her. It was done. She'd fought the fight, and it wasn't enough.

Chapter 21

LATHAN STARED UP AT A SKY THE SAME COLOR AS HONEY'S eyes. Inside his chest, his heart surged, swelled, snuggled up with his ribs, then shattered. He'd found her. Alive. And yet she'd fought him. Hurt him. Rejected him. He wasn't her savior here. He was the person she'd wanted to escape.

Had Gill been right all along? Had she partnered with the Strategist long before she'd met him?

Lathan tried to force that square thought into the round hole, but he just couldn't make it fit. Her fighting him didn't fit either, and yet she'd done it.

Water leaked from his eyes, from where Honey had tagged him in the nose. He wiped it away and sat up. His balls throbbed so deeply he felt the ache in his chest. Blood flowed into his mouth from his teeth splitting his lip. He spit and then wiped his mouth with the back of his hand.

He shifted to where she'd collapsed, eyes closed, chest heaving up and down. She smelled of dirt and sweat and adrenaline. And the fucking Strategist. Tendrils of hair adhered to her face. Barely touching her, Lathan brushed them back. Dirt crusted her skin, but through the grime, he could see the vulgar color of a bruise reaching out from her temple, swelling around her eye, covering half of her cheek.

"Holy Jesus." He remembered watching her and Junior struggle. Remembered watching Junior bash the gun into the side of her head. Remembered watching her fall, unconscious and completely vulnerable.

"Honey?"

Her face scrunched up. Tears slipped from her closed eyes, cleaning a track to her temples.

"Honey?"

She shook her head, refusing him, denying him. And yet, the pussy-whipped motherfucker in him couldn't tolerate her pain. He took her hand—she didn't resist—and placed it on his tattoo. In the moment of contact, her back arched off the pavement, her face contorted with anguish, then she settled, her features relaxed, tranquil, and content.

Her skin, cold and slick with sweat, warmed beneath his touch. Some ethereal part of him entered her and began to repair all her hurts, while her coolness flowed into him, swirled in his blood, soothing the ache in his balls and the burn of his split lip.

Her eyes opened. Tears shimmered and spilled over. "Lathan?" Her voice broke, and yet it was the most beautiful sound he'd ever heard. Her hand on his cheek flexed. "You're dead." The words didn't sound like a question. Didn't sound like a threat. Didn't sound like a statement either. They just sounded wrong. What the fuck was going on?

Vanilla floated to him on a whispered breeze. From the darkened road, the Strategist emerged phantasmlike. A tiny piece of Lathan had been in denial that the mousy partner could actually be the killer, but his nose didn't lie. Even if he hadn't been able to smell the scent signature, he would've known something wasn't right with the man.

His eyes were a chasm. Shark eyes. Snake eyes. Dead eyes—like Hell's merciless master inhabited James Jonah's body and looked out at the world through the man's eyes. And those cruel orbs were focused on Honey.

Lathan pressed her hand more firmly onto his face, used his other arm to gather her tight to him, and rose to his feet. No way was he confronting death incarnate with his ass cheeks on the ground.

"James?" Honey's voice jumbled with confusion. And a sickening familiarity. She knew him. Was comfortable with him. Not scared of him.

Fuck. Fuck. Fuck.

The Strategist switched on a flashlight and held it backward, illuminating his savage gaze. "Let her go. I don't want to—especially in front of her—but I will kill you." Promise infused his tone.

"James, no! Oh my God. Lathan's alive. He's alive." Honey's voice rose with each syllable. She plastered herself against him, burrowed into him, held him so tight that she was nearly inside his skin. "I thought you were dead. I cried for you. I grieved for you. I almost—" Her words were soaked in sorrow. "If James hadn't been there for me, I wouldn't be here. I would've given up."

"Fucker never should've taken you in the first place." Lathan locked gazes with the asshole. "How long you been watching me?"

"He didn't take me. He found me. In the woods." The unscarred corner of her mouth tipped downward.

Lathan smelled vinegar—the pungency of her doubt. "He's a liar. Look at him. He's got that flashlight aimed at his face. He *knows* I have a hearing problem. That's not something I advertise."

"Let her go." A gun materialized in James's hand, barrel aimed at the ground but rising, rising, rising.

Life narrowed, pinched tighter and tighter, until all that existed were him and Honey and the Strategist with his gun aimed at Lathan's head. Calm certainty hunkered down inside Lathan. If it came down to it, only two of them were going to walk away. One would die.

"James. No. You don't understand. This is Lathan. My Lathan. The man I couldn't stop crying over."

"He knows. He doesn't care."

James's inhuman eyes moved to Honey. He switched off the light, thinking Lathan couldn't hear him. "I found you."

Darkness swallowed James from sight until Lathan's eyes adjusted to the dark. "You stole her."

"I took care of you." The Strategist ignored him and focused on Honey. "I kept you safe."

"James? I don't understand." Confusion melted into her words, infused the air around her.

"I thought we were friends." James voice swooped low on the word *friends*.

Honey flinched, sucked air like the guy had landed an invisible gut punch. "We are." She gasped. "We always will be. Nothing has changed."

"He's fucking with your mind." Lathan didn't hide the disgust from his tone.

"I told you my secret." The words were a shadow of barely audible sound. The Strategist's shoulders sank. He seemed to hunch in on himself, diminishing. In a motion so slow, so deliberate, so fucking appalling, James swung his gun arm up, but the gun passed beyond aiming at Lathan and stopped when it was pressed against James's own temple. "You want to leave me because of my secret."

"No—" Honey launched herself toward James, but Lathan was ready. He'd bet his left nut that had been the Strategist's plan all along.

Lathan lost his grip on her hand touching his cheek, but grabbed her around the waist and hauled her back against his chest. He wrangled her into him, holding her squirming, writhing body, smelling her horror at James's threat. "We're not safe unless we're touching."

As if to affirm his words, James moved the gun away from his head and pointed it directly at Lathan. No question, the asshole was going to shoot to kill.

Lathan is alive. The mantra continued to play inside Evanee's head.

A hush nestled into her limbs. She stilled. Stopped struggling. Allowed Lathan to turn her away from James. Away from his gun aimed at Lathan. No matter what happened, Lathan was alive. Alive. Nothing could hurt them when they were together.

But James—

Pgull.

Her muscles froze, rigid and painful, then released by degrees as the sound of the shot ping-ponged around her skull, finally settling into a constant ear ring.

She pulled back just enough to confirm that Lathan wasn't harmed. He was alive. Just as she'd known he would be.

His gaze was locked on where James had stood. "We're

a shield. He shot at me and it…it backfired." Lathan's somber eyes shifted to her. "Don't look. It's bad."

But she had to.

James lay sprawled on the ground. His feet kicked out. Scraping. Scrambling against the pavement as if death licked his heels. Then he stilled. Quick, shallow breaths popped his chest up and down. Starlight shown too bright, shimmering and shining in the thick syrup gushing from the wound in his neck.

Long moments passed, moments when Evanee couldn't move, could only watch James's desperate struggle against death. Her brain could not translate the scene in front of her into anything more meaningful than a TV show, as if she was a mere observer instead of a participant.

And then guilt cinched around her tighter than a straitjacket, compressing her lungs, forbidding her next breath. He was dying because of her. Because he'd found her. Helped her. Fought for her.

"It's not your fault." Lathan shook her a little.

"I-I need to go to him." In the next breath, she was kneeling next to James, Lathan right there with her.

James's eyes were partially rolled up inside his head, but they retracted and focused on her.

Lathan handed her a wad of material—his shirt. She held it in her hand and stared at it until Lathan guided her hand to James's neck. Oh yeah. That's what she was supposed to do. She pressed it against James's wound. The material soaked through and wet her hands.

"We were destined." Blood gurgled in James's mouth, bubbled and popped like a sadistic gum bubble. "I didn't know it at first, or I would've come for you sooner."

I would've come for you sooner. Evanee stored the words on a shelf in the back of her mind. She'd take them out later, much later, and look at them, turn them over, examine them for all their meanings, but right now James was in front of her, dying, sucking in violent breaths that jerked his entire body.

"Those tears"—a brutal gasp of air—"are for me."

She hadn't even realized she was crying. "All yours," she whispered around the wad of them in her throat. She took his hand, held it up to her face, let him feel the grief leaking from her eyes. Let him stroke her cheek with his finger one last time.

"Death's here." James shuddered in a breath. "For me." His eyes moved to a place beside her.

A weird weightless, dizzy—but not quite—sensation buzzed through Evanee's body. "I don't want you to die." She stroked his cheek with the back of her finger. Just like he'd always done her.

His body jerked. Once. Twice. His mouth slowly fell open. Death had taken him.

"James. I'm sorry. I'm so sorry." The words snagged on her sobs.

Gill burst through the trees on the edge of the road, startling her from her grief. He ran to them, gun aimed at the ground. "What's going on?" His eyes swept over James and her, then stopped on Lathan. "Holy fucking shit. Not now."

She turned to Lathan. His left eye fluttered around the socket, going every direction on the compass. He was doing that thing—getting SMs. From Gill? From James? But she wasn't worried about him. Not like Gill seemed to be. Lathan was alive. Everything else would eventually work itself out. Right?

"Lathan." She placed her hand on his cheek, smearing James's blood on his face. Lathan's eye stabilized and focused directly on her. He grasped her hand, moved it off his face, his expression changing into something she couldn't read and wasn't really in the right frame of mind to try to translate. He gathered her tight to his chest. Like a fortress, his arms closed around her, keeping her safe from everything. So much loss. So much death and blood and misery in the world.

Everything became quiet, silent except for Evanee's soft sobbing. The stillness shattered with the noise of many feet running through the woods. Men, at least half a dozen, burst out upon the road. Bright lights, flashlights suddenly illuminated the four of them as if they were center stage of a grotesque show.

"All clear. He's dead," Gill called.

Everything seemed to still for a beat, but it wasn't a peaceful sound. It was heavy and expectant and impatient. She could feel the men's angry energy, see it in the restless way none of them could stand still and yet all of them were focused on James. She would've thought they'd be more interested in her.

A man walked right up to James's body and knelt down next to him. "Am I the only one befuddled by this? How can he be the Strategist?"

How can he be the Strategist? The words corkscrewed through her mind, drilling through her memories of James, trying to find a way to make that phrase understandable.

"What's he talking about?" she asked Gill.

Gill's eyebrows bounced up his forehead, and she could've sworn he startled a little. His gaze flicked to

Lathan, to her, then back to Lathan. Message clear: *Lathan, take care of this.*

In the spotlights, Lathan's tattoo shone brilliant and detailed like a work of art. She put her hand over it again, smearing more blood on his beautiful face. He wrinkled his nose, but she continued. "How is James's death related to the Strategist?"

Lathan covered her hand on his cheek. "He is the Strategist."

"No. Not James. You've got the wrong guy."

Sadness crinkled the corners of his eyes. "I watched his SMs. He didn't find you. He took you. Came into my house and took you from me. He'd been watching me for weeks. He thought you'd be able to explain how I discovered his kills when no one else could link cases to him. Then he found out about your dreams…"

Lathan wouldn't lie to her about this. He wouldn't. But it went against everything she *knew* about James. "He was kind to me. Took care of me. Wanted to help me."

"Everyone you dreamed about—the little girl, the woman in Texas, the severed man. He killed them all. And so many others that we didn't know about."

We were destined. I didn't know it at first, or I would've come for you sooner. James's words came back to her. She had told him about all the dreams, and yeah, he'd seemed surprised, but not you're-a-crazy-lady shocked like he should have been. "But he was nice to me. Nice. Really nice. He said he found me wandering in the woods, and I begged him to keep me safe."

"You don't remember that. I smell your doubt every time you say it. He lied to you. Fucked with your mind.

Made you think he was one thing, maybe even wanted to be that thing, but that doesn't change who he was."

"He never hurt me." As ridiculous as it was, she couldn't help defending him.

"He did. While you were unconscious. You just don't remember it." The muscles in Lathan's cheek were as hard as bone.

"No." Evanee shook her head. "He didn't. He wouldn't."

Lathan didn't argue. He didn't have to. The look on his face was enough—a combination of pity and rage and helplessness. The truth so awful he didn't want her to ask questions about it.

Her insides shivered. Didn't stop. The trembling radiated outward through her limbs until she could barely stand.

"No. No. No. No…" A man wailed the word nonstop.

She instantly recognized his build, the shape of his face, the color of his eyes. He went to his knees next to James, grabbed his body, and pulled it to his chest, still chanting his one word.

She settled her hand on James's father's arm and waited for him to quiet.

"He loved you." Maybe James hadn't come right out and said the words, but that's what he'd meant. From the little boy who kept a painful secret, always afraid that something would happen to the only parent he had left. To the adult man, always afraid someone would hurt his father. All of that was born out of love. That was the one thing, maybe the only thing, that had been total and complete truth.

No matter how much she hated what the man had done, she couldn't hate the hurt little boy inside him.

Chapter 22

THE CLOUDS OVER THE HIGHWAY ROILED IN NEBULOUS masses of impending gloom. Lathan fumbled with the switches on Gill's car until he found the headlights and flicked them on. He owed Gill for loaning him the car. No telling how long it would've taken for Gill to be done with whatever shit needed to be done to tidy up the mess. It was one fuck of mess. One that would change the Bureau forever. One that would change Evanee forever—no matter how many miles he put between her and the Strategist's corpse.

"Looks like we're in for a drencher." During the drive, he'd found things, made up shit to talk about. She might be asleep, but if he didn't keep talking, she got restless and agitated. His voice soothed her.

The first bloated drop of rain splatted onto the windshield. It clung to the glass overlong, then reluctantly slid toward the roof. The temperature had dropped. Freezing rain was obviously in the forecast. "We're almost home." He choked on the last word.

Home. Where he'd been shot. Where she'd almost been raped. Where the Strategist had found her. Bad memories squatted in Lathan's home now. Where else could he take her?

Gill's bachelor pad that probably smelled of sex and anonymous women? No.

His parents' estate? No way.

Morty's Motor Lodge? No fucking way.

He clenched the wheel, the bones in his knuckles bulging, the skin covering them bleached. He sucked in a slow breath to calm himself and almost gagged— swallowed the urge with a gulp and a mouthful of will-power. She'd been through so much already without him complaining that she smelled.

The sweet vanilla-ish scent of the Strategist's blood clung to her hands—despite her having washed them. His sickening scent adhered to her hair better than hair spray. Lathan had been trying to breathe through his mouth the entire drive, but had forgotten. Now rage and helplessness throbbed underneath his skin, wanting to rip through his flesh and—do what? There was no one to vent his feelings toward unless he wanted to assault a corpse. But that would hold no satisfaction.

He glanced down at her, slumped over, using his shoulder as a pillow. Sleep was best for her. She was injured—he smelled her blood too—but she'd refused all medical treatment. Even when they were finally alone, she hadn't wanted him to place her hand on his tattoo of healing and ease her discomfort.

He understood. She wanted the pain. All he had to do was pull up his borrowed shirtsleeve, peel back the bandage, and see her name carved in his flesh. Pain was holding her together. For the first time, he recognized the abhorrent nature of pain as a coping skill. It wasn't an antidote for agony; it was a diversion. One he would no longer allow her to inflict upon herself.

Lathan slowed, turned into his driveway, and parked near the front door. The sky welcomed them home with a deluge of rain, obscuring the outside world from view.

Honey lifted her head from his shoulder, tried to peer through the downpour.

"Is this okay? Being here? Being home," he asked.

She turned her damaged face to him. His breath hiccupped in his throat. Even though he'd seen it, stared at it, willed it away, he couldn't cover his reaction to the heinous injury done to her. Her eye, part of her cheek, and her temple were stained a vile shade somewhere between burgundy and purple. The entire mass of color was puffy and distorted her features. *She will heal.* He'd make certain of it. Even if the injury changed her features forever, he loved her for so much more than how she looked. He loved her soul. That part of her that no one could see, but that he recognized as the other piece of himself.

Tenderly, oh so tenderly, he cupped her injury. He expected her skin to be inflamed, to feel the anger that had fueled the injury, but her skin was cool and smooth and received his touch like a dry field absorbs rain. It was that sensation of absorption that he recognized. Healing. Some of his strength, his light was flowing into her. Not nearly as strong as when she touched his tattoo, but it was something. As she leaned into his touch, a tear escaped her beautiful bleak eyes, splashed again his thumb, and ruptured his heart.

He had no words. No phrases to make it all better. All he could do was this. Hold her damaged face in his hand and tell her with his eyes how much he loved her. How much he wished for her healing and wholeness and happiness, wished none of the bad stuff had happened.

"There's nowhere else I'd rather be than here. With you." She kissed his palm, then repositioned his hand on her cheek.

For a long, crazy moment, everything in the world fell away except for him and her and the rain slashing the windshield.

Finally, the rain tapered to a drizzle, revealing his house and all the memories hiding inside. He withdrew his hand from her cheek. The bruise was still there, but had faded to a less-intense, less-dense shade of burgundy.

He reached for his door handle at the same time she reached for hers. He got out and walked over to her side before she'd even swung her legs out of the car. Exhaustion weighted down each of her movements. He pulled her up next to him and wrapped his arm around her back, holding her close. Together they would fight the memories.

Just before he opened the front door, he angled his body to block her view of the kitchen and hopefully block her from having any flashbacks. He led her upstairs to the bathroom.

"You're going to get a shower, then I'm going to make you a peanut butter and raspberry sandwich, and then you're going to get good night's sleep." The words gushed out his mouth. "And then, tomorrow, everything will be better."

He hoped. For her sake. She needed a good day. Since he'd known her, there had been too many bad ones. The last five being chart-toppers.

"Your brother will probably want to see you. He stopped by earlier with Dr. Stone, Xander, and Isleen." Lathan watched her face fall, smelled the tinge of garlic in the air. "They were concerned for you. And me." He almost couldn't believe the truth in his own words. "It was Isleen who told me you were alive and gave me hope. She dreamed about you and the Strat—James." To Evanee, the guy had a name, not a killer's moniker. "And Xander told me how to find you." He was babbling.

She was too quiet. Just like that first day out on the road with Junior. Except this was worse. So much worse.

He helped her sit on the closed toilet lid.

She bowed her head, her hair a shroud blocking her from his view. The scent of salted honey found him. Again. More tears.

He knelt in front of her, the rest of his meaningless words dying before they could be born. He parted the veil of her hair, tucked it over her shoulder, and then tipped her chin up, forcing her to look at him.

Tears welled and spilled, sluicing down her cheeks.

She settled her palm against the tattoo. Something electric, magnetic, something more powerful than either of them alone, passed between them and bound them together. Sweet spring coolness rushed into him from her hand and spread through him until it reached his arm—her name carved into his flesh. The skin tingled, itched. He recognized the sensation. Healing.

Part of himself passed into her. The bruise on her face lost its puffiness and lightened.

"I'm sorry." Her voice wobbled, but the sound of it was sweet to his ears. "I know it's stupid. I know I'm stupid for wanting this, but I need…"

"Tell me. Whatever you need, it's yours." He'd figure out how to pluck the damned stars from the sky if that would put the sparkle back in her eyes.

"I need… I need to go to James's funeral."

He heard her, but denial forced him to replay the way
her lips formed the words in his mind. The meaning was
the same either way. *Damn. Shit. Fuck.* That wasn't at
all what he'd expected her to say. His face got hot and
his brain boiled, cooking him from the inside out.

"I know he was bad. He was…" Her tone wavered.
"He was the Strategist. But he treated me with kindness."

"No. He. Didn't." He'd been inside the Strategist's
memories. Seen how the asshole touched her, manipu-
lated her, preyed on her grief, mind-fucked her. "He
stole you from me. Lied to you. Told you I was dead."
Granted the guy hadn't known Lathan survived the gunshot, but that was no excuse for what he'd done. "Tried
to kill me. In front of you. Would've if we weren't special when we're together."

He left out the part about what the Strategist had done
to her in the bathtub. Some things were too appalling to
speak aloud.

"I know." She sounded small and defeated, and
Lathan hated himself for ever speaking. "But he told me
about himself. Told me some things I *know* are true. It's
that part of him—that hurt, desperate boy that needed a
friend—that I need to say good-bye to."

"I'll find out about the arrangements." He tried to
unclench his jaw. Wasn't successful. Maybe the heat in
his head had melted the bones together.

Lathan's phone vibrated, and he yanked it from his
pocket. There was a text from Dr. Stone.

> We've just arrived. Everyone is anxious to
> see Evanee.

He typed in a response without even thinking.

Be there in a minute.

At some point during the long night of questioning, Lathan had texted Dr. Stone to tell him Honey was found. Alive. He'd asked the doctor to relay the message to Thomas.

"Your brother is here. Dr. Stone, Xander, and Isleen, too."

Panic flared in her eyes, dilated her pupils, and infused the already pungent air around her with garlic. "I don't want to see anyone. I can't. Not right now."

"Do you at least want to see your brother? He was worried."

"No."

"I'll get rid of them. Will you be all right for a few minutes?" Translation: *Will you be all right without me?* She was being even clingier than on that first day out on the road.

She drew in a breath, held it for a few seconds, then let it out. "I'll be fine."

The itchy, peppery scent of her deception tickled his nose, but he let her have the dignity of that little lie. "Get in the shower." He squeezed her hand against his face to infuse her with enough healing to last during his absence. "I'll be right back." Breaking the connection took effort, like they were suctioned together.

He shut the door behind him and hurried down the stairs. He didn't want to leave her alone, but he almost looked forward to seeing everyone. An odd thought. He normally would be like her—wanting to hole up and isolate from everyone.

Lathan opened the front door.

Thomas stood front and center, holding a stuffed teddy bear wearing a purple pair of pants. Under another set of circumstances, it would've been comical to see the guy standing around holding a child's toy.

Thomas's forehead wrinkled in concern. "Is she all right?"

"She's"—Lathan could hardly find the words—"rough. Raw right now." He would never speak of what she'd been through to anyone else. It was her decision to share or not share that experience. He looked at everyone standing on his porch, all their faces expectant. All of them concerned about Honey. "Physically, she's cut, bruised, scraped, exhausted. Mentally, she's struggling to hold it together. And doesn't want to see anyone." Lathan was doing his own struggling.

"I hope you killed the fucker who took her." Thomas's face blazed with color, his hands clenched into fists. The burning cinnamon scent of his fury was strong in the air. "If you didn't, I will."

"He's dead. He'll never hurt her again."

"Good." Thomas stared hard at Lathan. A brother sizing up his sister's lover. "'Cause I intend to make sure she's never hurt again."

"You and me both, brother."

"You're good for her, but you ever hurt her and I'll—"

"Won't happen. We're in the same book, on the same page, reading the same fucking sentence." Lathan did something he'd never done before. He held his hand out to Thomas.

Thomas clasped Lathan's hand, and it was like they'd just sealed a deal between them. They were both going to make sure Honey's life was sunshine, rainbows, and puppy-dog kisses from here on out.

Xander stepped forward and caught Lathan's attention. "You know you can heal her." His face was set with a knowledge born of painful experience. "All of her."

Dr. Stone put his hand on Lathan's shoulder, a fatherly gesture full of encouragement. "If you need anything, give me a call."

"Thanks." Lathan looked down at the porch floor and worked to find the right way to say what needed said. "For everything. None of you had to show up, to encourage me to find her when I thought she was dead, but you did, and that meant—still means—a lot. If I'd been only a few minutes later, I might not have gotten her back." He spoke the last bit around the lump of how-things-could've-gone in his throat.

"Keep close to her. Keep touching. Everything will work itself out. I promise. And I always keep my promises." Isleen's smile carried so much self-assurance and absolute truth that Lathan believed her. She linked her arm with Dr. Stone's. "Come on, let's leave them to it."

Dr. Stone, Xander, and Isleen all turned to leave, but Thomas lingered.

"Give her this from me." Thomas held the stuffed bear out to Lathan. "She had one just like it when we were kids. Called him Mr. Purple Pants. He was her favorite thing. Went with her everywhere. Until I cut his head off and stopped up the toilet with it." A smile tipped the corners of his mouth at the memory. Thomas met and held Lathan's gaze. "Have her call me when she's ready."

"Will do." Lathan took the bear. He just couldn't help himself. He liked Thomas more and more each time he talked to the guy.

Lathan watched the carload of people drive off. A menagerie of emotions churned under the confines of his skin.

He sucked in a breath and smelled the crisp bite of winter in the air. Snow would make things better. It softened all the sharp edges, made something beautiful out of the death autumn always demanded. He turned and went inside, setting the stuffed bear on the banister.

Upstairs, steam misted out from the *open* bathroom door. An invitation.

She stood underneath the shower spray, her back to him, rinsing shampoo from her hair. Fluffy white suds slid over the perfect globes of her ass. His dick, unaware of the concept of bad timing, began to swell.

She turned, eyes closed, head thrown back, still rinsing the shampoo from her hair in a carnal pose that drained the blood from his extremities to fill his little head. Water slid over her face and slicked down her chin, her neck, her chest. Holy Jesus. Her breast.

Her entire breast was a vile shade of maroon. Vicious tendrils of purple spanned outward—like the roots of an ancient tree. An almost perfect bloody ring of teeth marks encircled her nipple.

Blood rushed back into his body with a powerful thrust that nearly buckled his knees. His heart pumped more than just blood; each beat pumped water into his eyes.

In the Strategist's memories, he'd seen her breast.

Through that filter, it hadn't seemed all that bad. But here with her standing in front of him, it was appalling.

His vision went sloshy. His chin quivered. He sucked his bottom lip between his teeth and bit down—hard—to shock away the memories. But it was pointless.

He remembered. Remembered the agony in his chest that had imprisoned him, remembered lying helpless on the floor, unable to move, unable to speak, unable to do anything except watch Honey struggle with Junior. Watch Junior bash the gun into her face. Watch her sag, unconscious. And then watch—fucking watch—Junior bite into her with all the coldness of a great white shark taking a bite out of a whale carcass.

In that moment, something unexplainable had happened. Someone had taken over his controls. Someone or something had moved his body, reanimated him. That something had placed the knife in his hand and rammed the blade into Junior's neck. And then vanished, leaving him unconscious until he woke on the floor and Honey was gone.

She stepped from the shower, didn't bother with a towel, water dripping down her skin, over the damage done to her breast. He couldn't look away. She stopped in front of him, lifted his hand, and placed it over her injury. The ridges and hollows the teeth had made in her flesh burned initially, but then he felt the coolness, the passing of his healing into her. The easing of her pain.

She put her hand on his cheek. Sensation expanded, multiplied, intensified, moved across his shoulder blades, down his arm to his hand on her breast, across her body and back to her hand on his cheek. The room around them blurred. God. It was like they were inside a whirlwind. No, they were the whirlwind, spinning away from every bad thing that happened, every bad feeling, until they landed back on solid ground in his bathroom, to a world wiped clean of pain and agony. A world where the only thing that truly mattered was each other.

Xander's words came back to him. *You have to be touching to be truly safe. When you know that, really understand it, it's hard not to be touching.*

"I'm never going to let you go." He stared into her midnight-blue eyes and saw the twinkling of gray in their depths.

"Good."

Chapter 23

THE WHITE PLACE SURROUNDED HER. SHE WAS NO LONGER afraid. She'd been through the worst life could offer and had come out on the other side—with Lathan. Always with Lathan.

The skin on the back of her neck tightened with the familiar feeling of being in the presence of something evil. But maybe it wasn't evil. Maybe it was just a reflex, her body's reaction to being in the presence of something that should not exist, yet did.

She lifted her hands and held them over her ears, prepared for the sonic blast of sound. "I'll do whatever you want." The words remained at normal volume. She moved her hands, spread them open, receptive. "I know you helped Lathan save me. Gave him the strength to kill Junior. I know you brought him here to me so I could heal him." Lathan had told her how after his dream—where she removed the bullet from his chest—he'd finally gotten strong enough to leave the hospital. "I owe you."

Her brain emptied of all thoughts. The soundless voice spoke directly inside her head. *It is the cycle of things. As long as one has light, so too shall the other.*

Are you Fearless? Or are you Bear? The thought fluttered up from somewhere in the abyss of her mind.

There are no divisions, no boundaries, no words to name that which you ask.

Why me? Why do I have to do this?

Why not?

I'm not special.

Oh, but you are. Only those who've had their power stolen can truly understand the supreme importance of ensuring a balance between good and evil. Sacred are the wounded, for they shall balance the earth.

How are these dreams balancing anything?

Balance is maintained by righting the wrongs. By giving you what you need to ensure justice. Now bear this dream that is being given and know that it is your duty to maintain the balance.

Evanee turned to receive the dream.

Her mother. Her mother just stood there.

Not the version of Mom Evanee had watched die, but the version that inhabited some of Evanee's first memories, back when Mom was young and playful and pretended to love her.

"Ev." Her mom held out a hand, expectation lifting her brows and lightening her eyes.

Evanee didn't move. Couldn't move toward the pain Mom represented.

"You know. All of it?" Mom asked.

"Lathan told me. Saw it all in your memories. So don't try to lie to add a shine to the shit."

Mom's features crumpled. "I made a mistake and then tried to fix it, but I made another mistake, and when I tried to fix that one..." A beautiful tear, sparkling with prisms of color, slipped down Mom's cheek. "I trapped myself in my own bad decisions, but you were the one who paid the price. I told myself I had no choice, told myself that I had simply chosen the lesser of two evils for you, but I knew. Deep down, in a place I didn't want to look at, I knew

I should've never chosen anything but happiness for you. I could've done it all differently, could've changed it all. But I didn't see a way out until it was too late. Too late for you to still love me."

"It's been too late since the moment you married Rob." Her tone held no anger, no hurt. "My past no longer has any power over me." *Power.* There was that word again. "And neither do you." Evanee turned her back on Mom and walked away. "That's why I can forgive you." She tossed the words over her shoulder.

In the circle of Lathan's arms, Honey's body jerked, yanking him out of sleep into full-on awareness. She was in the White Place. And he hated it. Hated she had to go there without him. Hated he couldn't be there to protect her against the Thing that had hurt her.

He reached over and flicked on the bedside lamp, then brought her hand to his cheek. Even in her sleep, even as far away as another dimension, her fingers flexed against his face, recognizing her protector.

The power of their connection opened wide, spreading cooling throughout his system, just as he knew she experienced warmth. Carefully, he shifted, never allowing her hand to lose contact with his tattoo, so he could see her face when she awakened.

Just like that, her eyes opened. The light illuminated her features in sharp planes and shadows. He held her hand tighter to his cheek to prevent the seizure from her brain doing double duty. "How are you feeling?"

"Better now that I'm awake." Her voice was strong, carried no fear.

"What happened?" He glanced at her other hand. Empty. This time she hadn't brought anything back.

"My mom. Trying to explain." She inhaled a slow breath and let it out just as slowly. He'd told her everything he'd seen in her mom's SMs, in Junior's SMs, in the Strategist's SMs—except for the one thing he would never speak of. He had held her as she cried out her feelings, and she'd held him as he did the same. Something about their tears had lanced all their wounds, and now they were healing together.

"But I really think the dream was about giving me a chance to use my power. The power to leave the past in the past and truly begin my future with you." She stared into his eyes, then let her gaze slide over his face as if she were memorizing every detail of his features. "Have I ever mentioned how much I love your freckles?"

He felt himself smile and it felt good. "Have I ever mentioned how much I love you?" She shook her head once, her eyes getting glassy and full of water. "You are perfect. Everything about you is perfect. Not in the no-flaws sense, but in the made-for-me-alone sense."

The scent of her happiness made everything all right.

Epilogue

LATHAN STOOD AT THE BOTTOM OF THE STAIRS, EYES LOCKED on the shadowed top step, waiting for his first glimpse of Honey. A dozen candles, held by a dozen friends, cast an intimate warmth throughout his cabin. The scents of flame and festivity filled his nose, and yet, he felt like a goddamned bug on display in some kid's insect collection.

He restrained the urge to tug at his collar or loosen his tie—only Honey had been able to talk him into wearing one. *Come on. Hurry, Honey.*

As if his thoughts conjured her, he smelled her approaching. Her honeyed scent flowed into him, satisfying him in a way mere oxygen never could. She began walking down the stairs, midnight eyes shimmering in the flickering candlelight.

She wore a white strapless gown. No fancy beads or baubles. No extra frills or ruffles. He didn't have a name for the material, but it floated over her skyscraper legs like a wispy piece of cloud. The only ornamentation was a ribbon, the exact color of her eyes, winding around the bodice and secured in a fat, floppy bow beneath her breasts.

Her hair cascaded in dark waves over her bare shoulders, and he could just imagine later, much later, lying beneath her, those dark waves insulating them from the world. She didn't wear heavy makeup, only a bit of color on her cheeks, and her wonderfully wonky smile hitched up higher on one side. He loved that smile.

Her beauty abducted his ability to breathe. Didn't need oxygen anyway. He only needed her. She was his miracle. If he had to go through all the pain, all the suffering, all the hardship again just to be worthy of her, he'd go through it a thousand times—a million times.

He held out his hand. The moment her cool fingers met his, he pulled her against him, fitting them so perfectly together that they could've been carved from the same block of wood.

She cupped his face with both of her hands and gazed at him as if she were memorizing his features, memorizing this moment. The moment right before they were married.

The minister behind them coughed lightly. Someone shifted in their seat and someone sniffled softly—probably Isleen. She had the oddest habit of crying when she was happy.

Over the past month, Isleen and Xander had forged a friendship of shared experience with Lathan and Honey, and Thomas was making up for lost time in being a great brother. Lathan liked that there was another protector for Honey who loved and cared about her in a brotherly way. It was odd, and nice, to have a network of friends beyond just Gill.

"Well, I guess we can begin." The minister waited, probably for them to give him their attention, but Lathan was lost in the flecks of silver in Honey's eyes.

She dropped only one hand from his face, kept the other one on his tattoo, granting him another of her special gifts. He covered her hand with his own, nuzzling her and kissing her palm before settling it back on his tattoo.

As one, they faced the minister and the room full of their friends and his father—each person holding a candle, lighting the wedding with their presence. It was a different setup—them facing the audience and the minister having his back to the audience, but Honey had demanded it. She understood that he wouldn't feel comfortable with people behind him.

Dad sat in the front row, next to Gill, and gave Lathan a thumb's-up and a genuine Montgomery smile. Somehow, it meant something, something bigger than Lathan ever thought it would, that his father was here, looking proud of him and not smelling of anxiety. Mom had elected not to attend. Probably because their wedding wasn't a high-society event.

On the other side of his father, Thomas caught Lathan's eye and smiled a quick upward tilt of the lips. A smile meant to show excitement and happiness. And to everyone else it would. But Lathan could smell the tangle of emotions coming off the guy. Thomas was happy for them, but he was dealing with a world of shit too.

The posthumous letter from Thomas's mother to the local paper outlining every sin Junior and Rob ever committed was bad enough. But the cherry on top: Thomas had requested a voluntary suspension from his job at the Bureau of Criminal Investigation so a full investigation could take place and he could publicly clear his name from any involvement in his stepfather's and stepbrother's corruption.

That was something Thomas had asked Lathan

to keep from Honey until after the wedding. The guy hadn't wanted to ruin his sister's special day. And Lathan respected him for the decision. Later, Lathan intended to discuss the situation with Xander and see if the two of them could do anything to help the guy out.

It wasn't like Lathan to be all Mother Teresa, but he sent Thomas a hang-in-there look. The guy dipped his chin in response and turned his smile up a notch.

Next to Thomas, Ernie—Honey's bald-headed ex-boss—folded his arms over his chest, his body language sullen, but at least he wasn't shooting hate bullets at Lathan anymore. The look he gave was more of a don't-you-dare-fucking-hurt-her look. Which Lathan was cool with—he'd never let anyone or anything hurt her ever again. Him and Ernie were buds in that respect.

The minister cleared his throat and began. "We are gathered here today to unite Lathaniel Montgomery and Evanee—Honey—Brown in matrimony. Lathaniel has requested to skip the fluff and get to the good stuff. So, we're diving right in. The couple has written their own vows. Lathaniel, you may begin."

Lathan sucked in a breath and focused all his attention, all his energy, on Honey. "Do you remember a few weeks ago when I found you crying in the kitchen? You said it was because you'd heard a song that touched you, and I teased you about being like Isleen." From the audience, Isleen sobbed a laugh. "When you weren't looking, I checked your iPod. You'd been listening to *Infinite*. I looked up the lyrics. No words would be as perfect as those on our wedding day."

Honey slapped her free hand over her mouth. "Oh my God."

Lathan spoke slow and clear, as if inking each word onto Honey's soul.

> *I'll be the one you dreamed of,*
> *Your cloudless sky,*
> *Your star-filled night,*
> *Your sun, your moon, your endless June.*
> *I need you until the skies turn dark,*
> *I need you until the days are done,*
> *I need you until everything's gone,*
> *And then I'll still need you.*

And he did need her. Had needed her from the moment he first saw her alongside the road.

Tears swelled in Honey's eyes.

"I'll be the one you reach for…" Emotion weighed his voice down.

"I'll be the one you reach for…" Honey's voice shook and melded with his, reciting the rest of the words to him at the same time he spoke them to her.

> *To stop the world crashing in,*
> *To place my hand in yours.*
> *Your friend, your lover.*
> *Your soul mate.*
> *I need you until the skies turn dark,*
> *I need you until the days are done,*
> *I need you until everything's gone,*
> *And then I'll still need you.*

"I'll still need you." He finished the repeat of the

final verse by himself, but he didn't look away from her. Their gazes were fused together.

"Guess what I was going to use for my vows?" Her voice wobbled with happiness. Tears slipped in silent streamers down her cheeks, but not sad tears. These were happy tears, the kind that smelled like their happily ever after.

Author's Note

In case you were curious about Fearless and Bear, here's their entire story:

A man, different than all others, used to roam this land. A man who was more than man. He carried a bit of spirit inside him. But even that bit of spirit was too great to contain within. Some of it showed on his skin.

The People, suspicious of all things unknown, believed a Bad Spirit had marked him—cursed him— for all to see. For all to avoid. For all to fear. The People believed the Bad Spirit wanted their souls.

So the man lived a solitary, nomadic life, nearly driven mad by isolation. One day a desperate loneliness overtook him. He tried to fight it, but was drawn to a field of women harvesting corn.

The women ran from him screaming.

A maiden stayed behind. Unlike the others, she did not fear him, but walked directly to him. Her face and arms bore the remains of a hundred healing wounds. He held out his hand to her.

She didn't hesitate, but settled her palm in his. A jolt of fire passed between them, but neither withdrew.

The maiden closed her eyes. "Take my life, and you may have my soul."

He stared at her, mesmerized by her fearlessness. Why would she want to die?

When death did not claim her, she opened her eyes and pulled her hand from his.

He saw a pain inside her greater than what her body had endured. "Why do you wish to die?" he asked her.

"I possess dream sight. I've seen my fate and would rather die than submit. Death would be freedom."

"Do you not fear me?"

"I fear this life more than you."

The sounds of many feet running through the forest came to man and maiden.

"Kill me now. I do not wish to survive another sunrise in the village."

"I do not take souls."

The maiden's face twisted as if in great pain.

"Come with me." The man held out his hand.

Men burst through the far side of the field.

The maiden hesitated only a moment before she placed her hand in his. As one, they turned and ran—together somehow swifter than the fastest of warriors. They ran until the dark of night covered the earth and the man no longer sensed anyone following them.

At a stream, they stopped. He lowered himself to the ground and the maiden collapsed atop him, knocking him back against the earth. Fearing his curse had claimed her, he grasped her shoulders and lifted her to see her face.

Her eyes made great pools of water that rained down her cheeks and fell upon his lips.

"Do not fear me." He tried to move away from her. "I will not kill you. I will not take your soul."

She clung to him, pressing her wet face against his neck. "I am not afraid. My eyes wash away the memories of the Bad Ones so I may live in peace."

Her lack of fear, her willing touch, astonished him.

He named her Fearless, and she called him Bear for his great size and ferocity in protecting her. She soothed his loneliness by her presence. And she found joy for the first time. No longer under the control of the Bad Ones, she smiled and laughed when she never had before.

Bear suspected the Bad Ones were trying to reclaim Fearless and moved them constantly. Sometimes his senses tingled, and in those moments, they would do as they had done at the first. Run hand in hand through the forest.

Bear and Fearless grew closer and closer until Bear began to worry over his feelings for her.

His fear came to life when Fearless was struck with a deep affliction. She needed the medicine of a powerful healer to save her. For weeks Bear traveled, carrying her to the wisest medicine woman.

He was not permitted in villages or near dwellings. It was feared the Bad Spirit would claim a soul in each dwelling he passed, unless he himself offered his life. And he would, for he valued Fearless's life above his own.

He carried her to the village center, the location of the tribe's power. The tribe's men surrounded him, brandishing their knives and hatchets, waiting for the wise woman's command.

In the light of the fading sun, the wise woman cried a keening wail that hushed the people. She examined Fearless's wrist, spit on the star-shaped mark, and rubbed her tunic over the spot. Then she raised Fearless's wrist up for the tribe to witness. The people whooped and yelled, welcoming Fearless to the tribe.

The wise woman would care for her now. Bear laid Fearless down gently and tucked the heavy robes around her.

"You." The wise woman pointed her gnarled finger at him.

He stepped back from his only love, his head held high, and waited for death.

"You are the answer to my prayers. My enemies had sought to destroy my power by stealing my babe. Every day I have chanted a spell of protection for her and prayed for her return. You are marked, yet nothing can destroy your bond. You are my prayers come to life. You are her protector."

"She is afflicted and needs strong medicine," Bear said.

"I do not have the power. She is with the ancestors."

Bear dropped to his knees beside Fearless. The light had faded from her, and he witnessed the truth of the woman's words. He lifted his head and howled. The sound roared through the village, startling all who heard.

When he quieted, the medicine woman placed his hand over Fearless's forehead. "I do not possess the power to call her soul back, but you are her destined one. You alone have the power to heal her."

"I do not know the way."

"The Spirit inside will guide you."

Bear stilled, but the Spirit did not speak. The only thing in his mind was Fearless. He closed his eyes and chanted her name, remembered her laugh, her face, the soft sounds of her breathing as he lay with her.

Bear did not stop chanting until Fearless touched

his hand. He opened his eyes. The light had returned to Fearless, the affliction gone.

The wise woman knelt next to them. "Daughter, you are returned to me a woman, but I love you as I loved the babe inside me." She grasped both their hands. "Together you create a shield stronger than the oak. No harm will come to either of you while touching the other. As long as light shines in one of you, the other will live."

At the wise woman's welcome, the tribe accepted Fearless and Bear. The wise woman taught Fearless her healing skills. Fearless's night sight—seeing in her dreams that which she couldn't see during the day— grew until she became the wisest woman of the region.

A time of great peace and prosperity settled over the land. From many moons away, people sought Fearless's healing and counsel.

The Bad Ones tried three times to kill Fearless, but they did not succeed. Nothing ever harmed Fearless and Bear, for they remained always together. Their bond, stronger than the hills, kept them from harm.

As they approached the end of their earthly lives, Bear carved a totem on the crest of the highest hill to remind all in the region that good always triumphed over evil, for he would protect Fearless into eternity.

They went to the ancestors together. The tribe built a great funeral pyre in honor of them and anointed their bodies in bear grease before setting the blaze. Every village in the region witnessed the black smoke burning in the sky.

A week later, after the fire cooled, the tribe gathered the ash and rubbed it over Bear's totem to seal their power together inside the carving for eternity.

Keep reading for an excerpt from

SAVING MERCY

Book 1 in Abbie Roads's new Fatal Truth series

———◦◦◦———

WOOD CRACKLED AND SNAPPED FROM THE SMALL BLAZE IN the fireplace. Shadows and bronze light fought each other for dominance in the small room—the shadows seemed to be winning. Cain didn't mind one bit. The darkness concealed him, smothering the constant worry over her reaction when she finally recognized him.

She'd been conscious, unconscious, and in some crazy in-between state, but from one moment to the next hadn't been able to remember a dang thing—courtesy of the shock treatments. And so far, she'd been too out of it to recognize him, but the time was coming.

He settled his hand on Mercy's forehead—an act that reminded him of Mac—and felt her temperature. For the past two days, she'd run hot with a fever, vacillating between chills and sweats as the drugs metabolized out of her system. But now her skin felt cool and dry. The fever had broken. Finally. They were turning a corner, speeding down a one-way highway that would end either in her acceptance or her total rejection of him.

Her eyes blinked open so suddenly, he yanked his hand off her head as if he'd been caught copping a feel.

"How are you feeling?" He'd asked her the question a dozen times over the past days, but hadn't always gotten an answer.

She turned her head to him, her face scrunching up, most likely from her bruised cheek. "Wow. I feel drunk and hungover at the same time." Spoken with a clarity of tone she hadn't possessed in previous days. "And a little bit like I've got the flu. But, hey, I've been worse." An out-of-place cheerfulness infused her voice.

"Do you remember where you are?"

"Ward B of the Center of Balance and Wellness. The name doesn't fit. It should be called the Center of Indifference. No one here cares—except for Liz. You know Liz?" He opened his mouth to answer, but she bulldozed over him, her words coming out in a rush. "She looks like Nurse Ratchet, but her personality is all Mary Poppins. She always lets me stay up past lights-out since it's the only solitude to be had in the whole place. Once, she snuck a cupcake in on my birthday. Now isn't that sweet? She—" The words were speeding out of her mouth.

Not that he was complaining. He preferred her hyped-up over out of it, but she might backslide if she didn't stay somewhat calm. "Whoa whoa whoa. Slow down. Take a breath. We've got all the time in the world here." Had to be the meds or lack of meds—some strange part of the withdrawals—causing her diarrhea of the mouth.

She grabbed in one good breath, then tossed off again. "You know there aren't many people to talk to in here." She turned her voice down to a whisper. "Everyone's crazy. I mean *really* crazy. Certifiable. It's hard to carry on a rational conversation with someone who keeps talking to the demon that lives in their ankle. You ever have that happen? Where you're talking to someone and all of sudden they lift their foot up in front of their face and start having a conversation with it? It's a bit off-putting, if you know what I mean."

Her expression was full-on seriousness, and he probably shouldn't laugh—definitely he shouldn't—but couldn't help it.

A smile—no, it wasn't quite a smile—tipped the corners of her mouth, giving her a look that said she was thinking about something pleasing.

"We've hit a new phase of your withdrawals. Speed talking."

"Oh my. Your voice. Wow. It reminds me of dark chocolate, a hot bath, and sex, and—"

"Apparently your mental filter is malfunctioning."

"—sweaty, dirty, hard fucking."

Holy Christ. The words had his mind flashing him images of what sweaty, dirty, hard fucking would look like with her. He needed to change the subject, but couldn't remember how to get his mouth to form words. He might've swallowed his damned tongue.

"Why do you suppose your voice sounds like sex on a summer day? It's because I'm horny. I haven't had sex in five years. That's a long time, you know. I have needs."

He finally figured out how to flap his lips, while making sound to form actual words. Maybe he'd had a stroke. "Jesus Christ, woman." The words exploded out of him. "You've got to stop talking about sex." He scrubbed his hand over his eyes, trying to wipe out the

mental images that still played. "You're speaking every
single thought that floats into your mind. No goddamned
censor. It's gotta be the meds or the shock treatments
causing it. Something."

Her bottom lip pushed out in an utterly inappropri-
ate—but adorably kissable—pout. "I don't see anything
wrong with talking about how I feel. Maybe that's why I
can't get out of this place. I won't open up. Won't let Dr.
Payne-in-my-ass into my mind. Maybe if I—"

"You've got to stop for a moment." She opened her
mouth to argue—he cut her off. "I need you to listen for
thirty seconds. A minute, tops. Then you can talk about
sex, Dr. Payne, and your feelings all you want."

"You can't go putting sex, Dr. Payne, and my feelings in the same sentence. Wrong. So wrong."

"Won't argue about that. But I need you to keep your
lips closed."

Pain pinched her features as she lifted her hands,
placing them over her mouth. It should have been a
comical gesture, but all he could see was her hurting. It
had been five days since Dr. Payne had injured her and
the fact that her body still suffered scraped his justice
bone. If he ever got the guy alone, he just might uncage
that part of himself that thirsted for blood.

He cleared his throat and emptied his mind of those
thoughts. "There are some things you need to know right
now. Important things. Like you're *not* at the Center.
You're safe in a cabin in southern Ohio. You've been
withdrawing from the meds for the past two days.
Your short-term memory is shit from the shock treatments. I've been taking care of you the whole time."
He spoke the sentences as if there were a list he'd

memorized—probably because he'd said the same thing
so many times before. "That's why we keep having this
same conversation and you can't remember it."

She lifted her hands off her mouth. "Cool. That works
for me. Never liked that place."

Ooo…kkaayy… She obviously wasn't fully grasping reality. "You're not going to remember any of this,
are you?"

"Probably not. Not when I'm feeling half drunk." She
put her hand back over her mouth, but her eyes sparkled
with laughter.

She might be more coherent, but she definitely wasn't
fully functional. "I just want you to know. You *are* safe
here. I won't let you go back there. And I won't hurt
you. I would *never* hurt you."

She lifted her hands off her mouth again. "I trust you.
I'd know if you were some creepy asshole. I always
know. You're the kind of guy a girl feels dainty and
delicate around."

Yeah. She'd trust him until she actually saw him in
full light, when fully aware. "Um…" He didn't know
what to say. Time for a subject change. "I need you to
drink some water. It'll help flush the drugs out of your
system. I'm going to help you sit up." He slid his hand
underneath her back and helped her upright.

"Man, everything hurts. Feels like a busload of sumo
wrestlers sat on me."

He shoved the pillow behind her back. This was
progress. The first time she'd been upright in days. "Dr.
Payne did a number on you. Looks like he hit you in the
face, the ribs, and on your thigh."

A furrow of thoughtfulness dug into her forehead. "I

don't remember any of that. You'd think I'd remember something like that. Why can't I remember it?"

"The shock treatments."

"Oh yeah. You said that, didn't you? And I forgot it." A thin edge of concern cut through her tone.

"Hey, don't worry about it. The short-term memory problems are temporary. I promise. Drink for me." He held the glass to her lips. She reached up and covered his hand with hers. His heart skipped a few beats, then returned to its regularly scheduled rhythm.

She swallowed down the entire glass of water the same way she talked—full speed and without censorship, gulping and slurping like a child. "That's good. Real good. I'm so thirsty all of a sudden." She didn't take her hands off of his. He tried to move the glass, but she gripped on tight. "No. I want to keep touching you. It feels so good to have my skin on yours."

Holy.

Christ.

He should change the subject, divert her attention in some way, but what came out his mouth had nothing to do with those intentions. "I'm going to be sad to see this side of you go. I like you being affectionate and warm to me."

"Then hold me. Just for a little while. Until I fall asleep again." The words themselves weren't a question, but his heart heard the quiet query behind them.

"Anything you want." He would deny her nothing. She let go of him so he could place the empty glass on the nightstand. Instead of crawling in the bed with her, he picked her up. She nestled her face against his chest and his heart banged extra hard, trying to get her attention. A contented sigh slipped from her lips and he felt more light and carefree in that moment than he had in his entire life. He sat in the chair directly in front of the fireplace.

The fire had burned down to a few low flames, deepening and lengthening the dark, but still putting out a bit of warmth.

"A girl could get used to having a big, strong man carrying her around." Her words were a sigh.

"A guy could get used to having a beautiful lady to carry around."

She laughed, the sound lovely in the same way birdsong enchanted the ear.

"Are *you* flirting with *me*?" One of her hands stroked his chest.

Christ. Was he flirting with her? Was he—Cain Killion, son of the man who'd tried to kill her—flirting with her? Hell yeah he was. Wrong or not. "Are you flirting with me?"

"I don't know. It's been so long since I had anyone to flirt with I'm not sure what it is anymore."

"I think you're a natural." He rubbed his chin on the top of her head. "You're doing better today. I was worried about you."

"You're so sweet. I haven't had someone to worry about me since my family died. Did you know my family died?"

Everything good and warm and happy dissolved. He didn't want to hear her talk about this. Not this. This was too soon. Too close to the bone. Too close to the blood. Too close to his own dark urges.

"They were murdered. By…by…by Killion."

Everything inside of him kicked like a reflex at the name.

"Why am I talking about this?" Her voice hitched. "I never allow myself to think about it. Forgetting is good therapy. But I've never really forgotten how my parents screamed before he slid his blade into their throats." Her voice took on a monotone quality. "The sound of their blood pumping, spritzing, dripping onto the floor—I can't escape it. Or the way Killion stared into my brother's eyes, caressed his cheek, ran his hand through his hair—almost as if he loved him—just before he cut out his throat. And when he turned to me, his blade dripped the blood of my family on my neck. The warmth of it startling and sickening and strangely comforting. I had been scared watching them die, but I wasn't scared anymore. I wanted it. I wanted it over."

His body had turned to stone. His heart a mausoleum of sorrow. His lungs twin pillars of shame and guilt. That she would confess her most horrific moments to him—she obviously didn't know who he was. And now was not the fucking time to tell her.

A pained whine issued from her mouth, growing in volume to wailing, then leveling out at full-body weeping. She shuddered and shook against him, the force of her sobs startling in their power. Her face mashed against his chest, her tears wetting his shirt, his skin.

Life had been perpetually unfair to her. He ached for the pain she'd endured. The pain she still experienced. And the pain she would experience when she recognized him. Because he knew. Knew she'd be afraid of him. And all of this—holding her, flirting with her—would be nothing but a memory.

"Shh... Shh... I'm right here with you." He didn't bother with bullshit words. He stuck with the facts. He was here. With her. Period. He wrapped both arms around her, holding her tightly to him, hoping that by some strange osmosis she'd be able to absorb his strength.

How long she cried against him, he didn't know and didn't really care. He'd sit here holding her for a hundred years if that's how long she needed to grieve. When the last of her sobs subsided, she stilled against him, sniffling and snuffling every once in a while.

"I—wow—sorry about that. I don't normally go all crybaby. Maybe it's the meds." She pulled back to look at him.

His lungs latched down tight, refusing to let in any air.

The last of the firelight caught the wetness on her face and lashes, causing her tears to shimmer like melted gold.

Her gaze roamed over him. He couldn't remember what he should say to soothe her, to reassure her—words seemed inadequate. He tried to tell her with his gaze that he meant no harm. That he wasn't his father. And for a moment she seemed to understand. Then her eyes widened and rolled in their sockets like a frightened foal. She bucked away from him—all the force of fear in her movement. She landed on the ground—nearly in the fireplace—a grunt of pain shooting from her mouth. Mindless in her fear, she scuttled back from him, placing her hand near the glowing coals.

"Careful." He reached for her, to get her away from the fire before she hurt herself.

She screamed—the sound no canned movie scream, but filled to bursting with genuine terror.

He went statue still, arms still outstretched to her.

She pushed herself away from him, further and further until she huddled in the far corner of the cabin, gasping for air like she'd been holding her breath for too long.

He hadn't moved. Hadn't said a word. Had been paralyzed by her reaction. If he was the crying kind—which he wasn't—he'd have felt like having a good old-fashioned water party. That look on her face was something he'd never wanted to see. That was why he'd never sought her out. He'd known what was left of his soul couldn't handle it.

And he'd been right.

His stomach contracted—he grunted from the unexpected pain of it. All the humiliation of lost hope rolled up his throat. He tipped forward in the chair, opened his mouth, and dry heaved. His innards seized and spasmed, refusing to release him as he gagged on self-disgust.

The room went hotter than an incinerator. Sweat dripped off his face and splatted onto the floor. The sounds coming out of him were as wretched as he felt. The phantom barfing lasted a short eternity.

He needed to reassure her that he intended no harm. He turned his head toward her corner, opened his mouth—

She was gone.

Acknowledgments

Dan: You are my first, last, and always thank-you. The thank-you that transcends all thank-yous and goes into the realm of the down-on-my-knees in gratitude that you're my best friend, my favorite human being, and my husband.

Brinda Berry: What would I do without you? I owe you so much! You're always there to read last-minute pages, you always offer the best advice, and I seriously don't know how you put up with all my dumb questions. Thank you so much for everything you do for me. And a super, huge, special THANK-YOU for writing the song "Infinite" that Lathan and Evanee use as their wedding vows. I've said it before and I'll say it a million times— you're a talented song writer, a great author, and an even better friend.

Margie Lawson: At the end of my first Immersion with you, I remember sitting in the Denver airport staring out at the tarmac, debating whether to trash this entire novel. I realized the only way this book would be publishable was if I rewrote the entire thing, when I had already spent a year writing and editing it. The things I learned from you were not quick fixes. They were quality fixes. That's when I adopted the mantra "quality over quantity." I loved the story Lathan and Evanee wanted to tell so much that I decided to rewrite the book. Thank you for that first Immersion. Because of you and what

I learned from you, I got my agent and my editor. A thank-you will never be enough. But thank you anyway!

Michelle Grajkowski: Oh, Michelle! You became my agent after judging this novel in the Four Seasons Contest. Thank you so much for taking me on and always believing in me and my dark writing. You really are a super awesome agent lady!

Sourcebooks: Wow. Thank you to all those people who work behind the scenes to make this book come together. Thanks to Rachel Gilmer, Emily Chiarelli, Laura Costello, Susie Benton, and Diane Dannenfeldt. Beth Sochacki—thanks for all your hard work getting my books out there. I appreciate it! A super special THANK-YOU to my editor, Deb Werksman, for always forcing me to stretch my writing muscles to make my books the best they can be. Another super special THANK-YOU to Dawn Adams and Kris Keller for making a SPECTACULAR cover! You two are magic! I love you both for giving my covers so much awesomeness!

Kimberly Meyer and Celeste Easton: You both suffered through the worst versions of this novel—the make-your-eyeballs-bleed versions—and never complained. Your insights and critiques were invaluable. Thank you both!

Christina Delay, Jen Savalli, Kathleen Groger, and Brinda Berry (yes—she deserves to be mentioned twice): Thanks so much for taking the time to critique this. Your suggestions made this book what it is!

Dreamweavers: Way back in 2014, when we were Golden Heart Finalists, many of you read this book when it was in the Amazon Breakthrough Novel Award contest. Your praise and encouragement back then was invaluable. Thanks so much for always being the best, most talented, most supportive group of writers!

You: When I first started writing, it seemed like an impossible dream that I would ever have a published novel and that anyone would ever read it. Thank you for making my dreams come true. Without you, my books are nothing. Stay tuned for my next novel—*Saving Mercy*—the first book in my Fatal Truth series.

About the Author

Abbie Roads is a mental health counselor known for her blunt, honest style of therapy. By night she writes dark, emotional novels, always giving her characters the happy ending she wishes for all her clients. Her novels have been finalists in many RWA contests, including the Golden Heart. *Hunt the Dawn* is the second book in the Fatal Dreams series of dark, gritty romantic suspense with a psychological twist.

Be sure to visit her website at www.abbieroads.com and sign up for her newsletter to receive exclusive content and special giveaways.